Secret of the Emerald Star

Jason Farrell & Michael de Weever

This is a work of fiction. Names, characters, businesses, places, events, and incidents are either the products of the authors' imagination or used in a fictitious manner. Any resemblance to actual persons, living or dead, or actual events, is purely coincidental.

Published by:
Montauk Beach Press
MARGATE, FLORIDA

Copyright © 2024 by Jason Farrell & Michael de Weever

ISBN: 978-1-7334686-3-3   Hardcover
   978-1-7334686-4-0   Softcover
   978-1-7334686-5-7   Ebook

Editing
Carol Killman Rosenberg ✦ www.carolkillmanrosenberg.com

Cover design and Cartography
Jamie Noble Frier ✦ www.thenobleartist.com

Interior design
Gary A. Rosenberg ✦ www.thebookcouple.com

Book 1 Cartography
Sara Stemle ✦ Instagram: @ loud.color

Printed in the United States of America

The Saga of the Emerald Star began with the award-winning Demon Lord Rising

THE BOOKFEST AWARDS
1st Place, Epic Fantasy,
Spring 2023

READER VIEWS AWARDS
Gold Award, Classics Fantasy,
2023

AMERICAN WRITING AWARDS
Finalist • 2022

"*Demon Lord Rising* is a fantastic fantasy novel and has the makings of a bestseller."
—READER'S FAVORITE AWARDS • 5-Star Review, 2023

"Fans of Terry Brooks, Christopher Paolini and the Dragonlance saga will flock to the newest smash hit in the epic fantasy genre."
—READER VIEWS AWARDS • 5-Star Review, 2023

Available on Amazon.com in print & ebook
www.amazon.com/Demon-Lord-Rising-Jason-Farrell/dp/1733468617

Also available on Allauthor.com
allauthor.com/author/whitewizard1555

"They will live and die for my every whim and pleasure. Their every breath will be in my service, and they will endure pain everlasting for me, fighting one another for the privilege to suffer for my amusement. That will be my testament to life in the ages to come."

ABADON, DEMON LORD

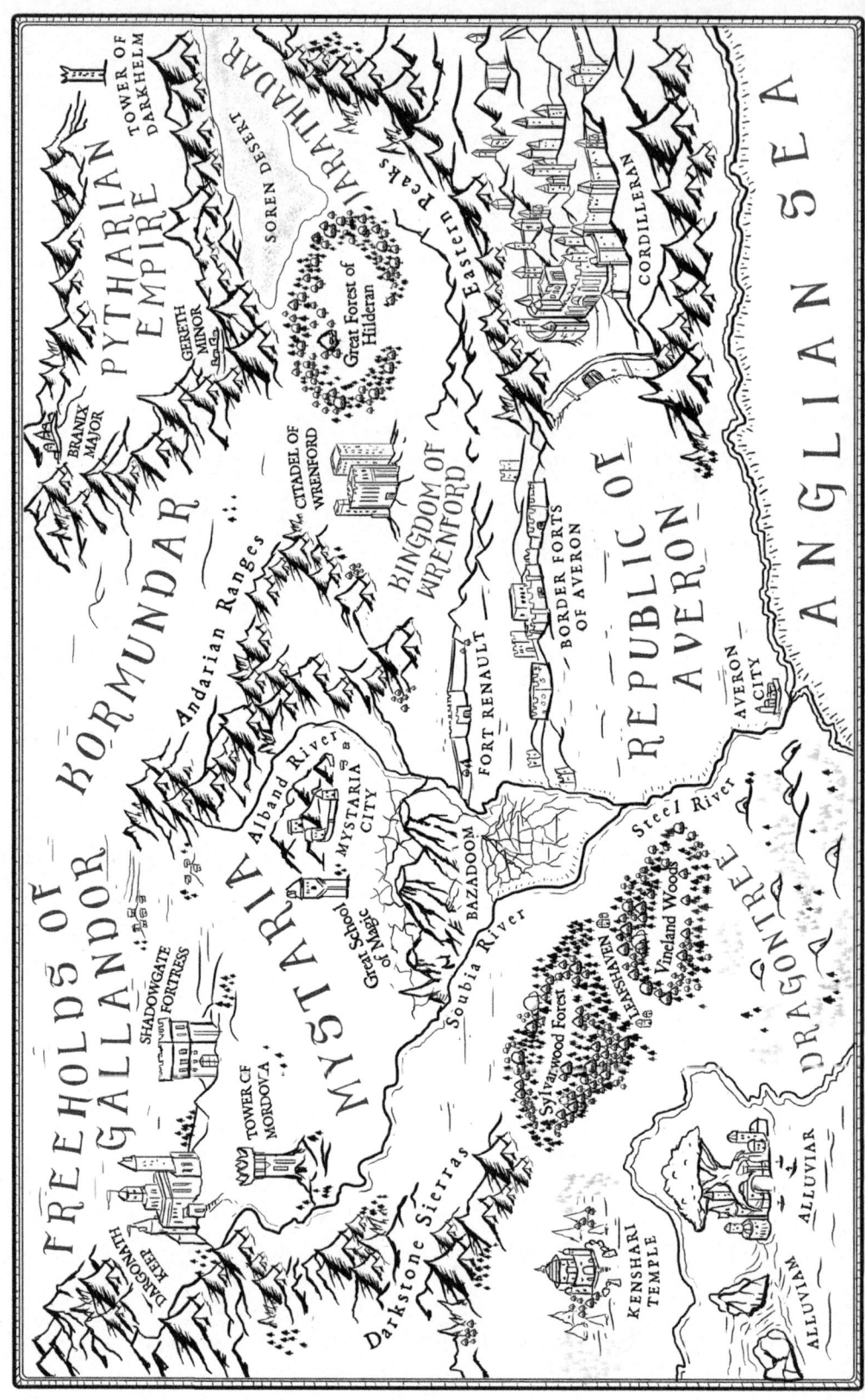

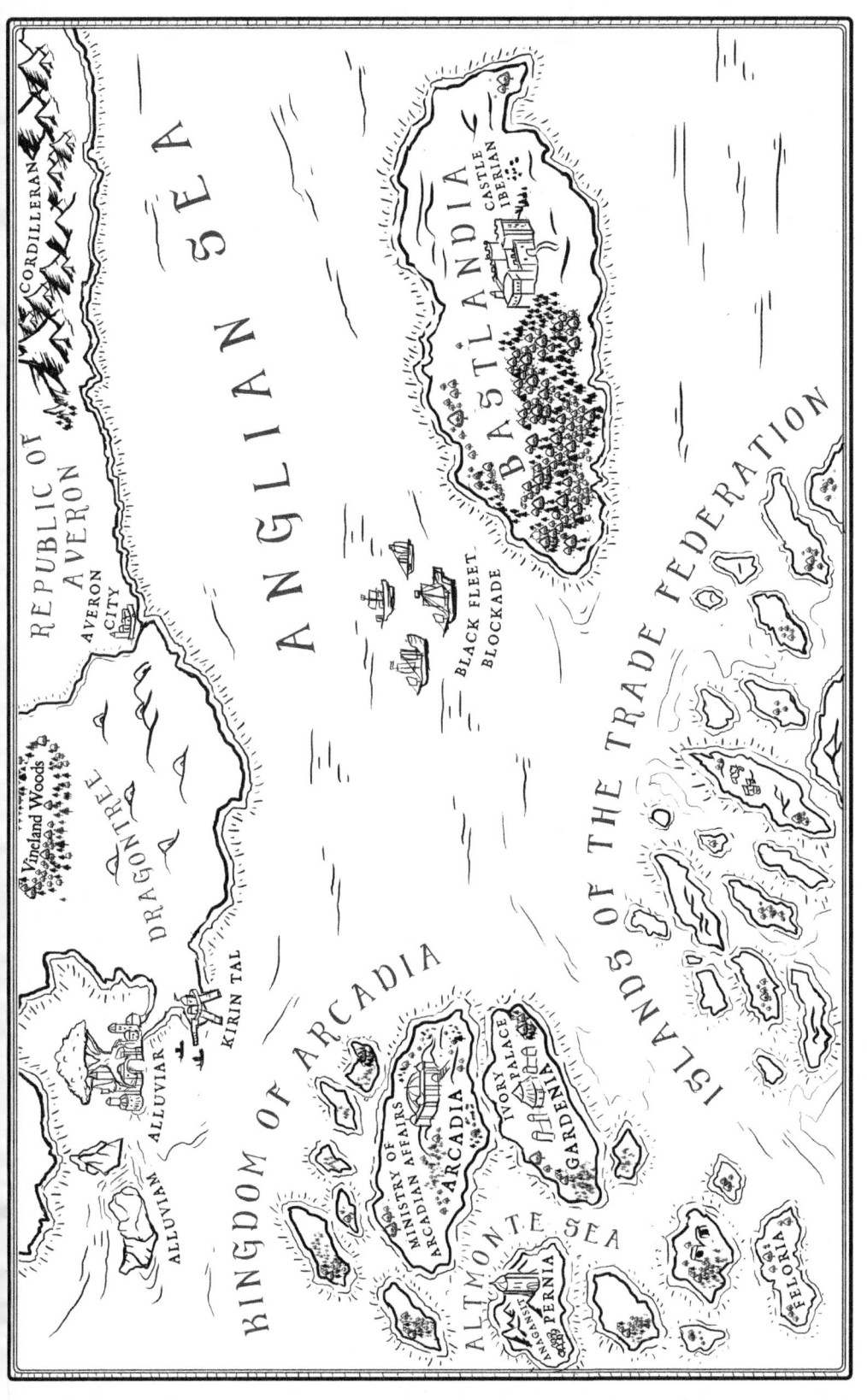

Prologue:
Ages Ago When the World Was Young

Awestruck, the Archmages stood back to behold what they had labored so long to create.

The device was a mingling of science and magic more powerful than anything they could have contemplated individually. Together, they had conceived and formulated a tool far greater than themselves—a testament to the creative spirit, will, and sheer power of the races, such as they were in those times, to achieve the impossible. It had such catastrophic implications that they feared it as much as they dared wonder at it. They called it the Chronos Device, and it was a gateway through the fabric of time itself.

The device was approximately two rods high, the height of two grown men combined, and five rods wide with three sets of stairs at the forefront, which led to a round silvery-metallic platform. Four equidistant cylindrical metal rods with oval-shaped crowns encircled its perimeter. The actual workings of the device—a metallic panel featuring numerous switches and levers—was affixed to the platform from behind. The panel stood in front of a glowing circular glass chamber that contained the swirling mystical energies that gave the great device its awesome power. Many of those present, known as Archmages among their various peoples, had supplied those energies. They were the first, the greatest users of magic—they were the Makers. There were ten of them, a council that had become a brotherhood working to improve their world and the lives of all who depended upon them.

"Now it must be tested," said Archmage Glycas.

The most powerful of the Archmages stepped forward. "Indeed, and I shall be the one to test it," stated Abadon.

"Hold, Brothers, I submit we reconsider what we have done here," said Ranier, wisest and oldest of the Makers. He waved a hand at the device. "This controls forces even we were *never* meant to harness. The inherent dangers of such a creation are beyond our experience."

"Do you propose to do *nothing* with this wonderous gift we have created for the world?" Abadon asked, fighting to disguise his disdain. "We have labored to benefit generations of fools who could never understand our sacrifice. They should worship us as the gods we are for this incomparable contribution. For ages to come, they can learn about the past firsthand, avoid famines and pestilence, prevent wars and deaths, and even assure they will be ruled as they should be."

"We are not gods, Abadon," Ranier replied patiently. "It is only arrogance that allows us to believe we have the right to control godly forces such as time. Forces that are perhaps better left untapped by those who do not understand them."

Abadon lowered his gaze momentarily. When he spoke next, his voice took on a pleading tone, a tone he was unaccustomed to. "Perhaps you are right, Ranier. But, Brothers, I beseech you. We *must* test the device to ensure that it functions, and then we can render it inert, locked away and guarded in secret for all time. If Chaos should ever arise in the world, we would have the means to defeat it without battles or loss of life."

"There is wisdom in Abadon's words," Glycas conceded. "I would see the machine tested. If it works, it will remain here hidden away until a time comes, *if* it comes, when it is needed. Brothers, do you agree?"

All present in the subterranean chamber nodded their agreement.

"Very well," Ranier said with an uncertain sigh. "Abadon, step up to the platform."

But Abadon had already started ascending the stairs. He understood his task: Once Ranier activated the device, he would close his eyes and concentrate on a specific time in the past and the device would carry him there. Conceivably, when he wished to return, he would stand on the exact spot of his arrival, and the time vortex would reopen and transport him back.

Ranier followed him up slowly and approached the panel. "Do you remember what to do?"

"Yes, yes, let us begin," Abadon responded impatiently, closing his eyes.

With certainty in his hands, Ranier pulled levers and flipped switches in an intricate pattern only an Archmage could memorize. Then, he inserted the large gold key into the lock and turned. He removed the key and dropped it into the pocket of his robe.

Abadon concentrated on a specific time in the past, The Before, when he would be the most powerful being in existence. He kept himself from smiling. They were ignorant fools, his brothers, the whole lot of them, but especially Ranier. He had feigned to agree to their lofty reasonings to create the device simply to arrive at this opportunity. For even with his vast power, he could not stand against so many others with powers so near his own. He alone was meant to rule the world—He and no other. Now, at last, was His time.

When Ranier threw the final switch, the energies flowed from the crowns of the cylinders around the platform, creating an explosion of power and light that completely engulfed Abadon in its wake. Science and magic became one in that instant, and the ebb and flow of time folded and became accessible. In the next moment, Abadon was gone.

With pain so unimaginable he couldn't even reason its presence, Abadon felt the matter and energy that comprised his body traveling through time and space faster than his mind could process. The device was not designed to absorb the thoughts of his desired destination, thoughts consumed with greed and domination. With intense panic, he felt as if he were straying from all existence, becoming infinitesimally smaller and smaller until he was just a spark of energy freefalling through a bottomless abyss.

Abruptly, all motion ceased. Something had caught hold of his soul.

Abadon's oblivion had been momentarily stayed. He struggled to connect with whatever it was, to hold on to it, and, when he succeeded, what was left of him shuddered with intense fear. His savior emitted inconceivable power, power that Abadon felt drawn to but also cowered from. The entity oozed with something so dreadfully evil that he felt repulsed by its grip. But despite his fear and repulsion, the soothing whispers seduced him: "Do not fear what you desire. Join with me, and *everything* is yours. Our ecstasy will be unrivaled."

Abadon agreed.

The Archmages anticipated Abadon's return only moments after he had vanished in a great swirl of near-blinding energy.

As Rainer descended the stairs, the ground and walls of the subterranean chamber began trembling, and he lost his footing. He tumbled down the stairs as the platform glowed with an energy that exploded up and outward into a cone of light that quickly carved a hole in the roof of the chamber that reached the surface. The Makers shrank back to the stone walls and watched with disbelieving eyes as thousands of dark forms of varying shapes and sizes passed through the cone of light, heading toward the surface. When the light finally dimmed, a sole figure stood on the platform.

It was Abadon—but not Abadon.

Something was amiss. With eyes closed, the powerful Archmage stood motionless. His hair, normally short and silky, was long, disheveled, and coarse. His smooth bronze skin now looked like worn leather and had taken on an eerie amber hue. Angular clawlike fingers escaped through the arms of his tattered robes.

Fear and uncertainty stunned the Archmages into silence, but when Abadon opened his eyes, they let out a collective gasp. Both iris and pupil were bloodred.

A wicked smile twisted Abadon's once pleasant features. *"I've returned, Brothers,"* he said, speaking in a voice unlike any they had ever heard, as if many voices were meshed to form one. *"Our creation is a success."*

Ranier and the others looked on with horror. As it dawned on the wisest of them what had happened, what they had permitted to happen in their arrogance, a sickly feeling of immense regret enveloped him.

Abadon paced from one end of the platform to the other as he went on, *"You have seen the proof. I, We, stand here again in your presence. And you have seen the army We lead. Though immortal in the Nethertime, my army is subject to the physical laws of your dimension, but that is of little matter. I, We, will breed more. They will do as We say because your world offers a benefit the Nethertime lacks—the opportunity to hunt and devour your kind. They will find that worth the price of mortality."*

Gathering every ounce of magic he could, Ranier charged forward, lifting his hands above his shoulders, and implored, "Brothers, we must destroy this abomination! *Now*, with me!"

Multicolored rays of energy discharged from the Makers' fingertips, striking Abadon in the chest, forcing him backward. He lifted his arms in defense. Their powers drove him back against the panel until he forcefully extended his hands, reversing the rays.

The Archmages stumbled backward, only slightly dazed by their own magic, and quickly prepared to renew their combined attack.

"*You are more powerful than anticipated,*" Abadon said, sounding mildly winded, "*but you lack the power to destroy Me, Us. In time We will acclimate to this world.*" With an oily smile still twisting his face, he walked to the edge of the platform, looking down at the stony faces of his once brethren. His voice had regained its former strength and more. "*IF YOU WANT TO LIVE LONG ENOUGH TO SEE THE HAVOC MY ARMY CREATES, KNEEL BEFORE ME AND BEG TO SERVE ME!*"

The Archmages stood stock-still. They would bow to no one, even if it meant death.

"The device, Brothers, destroy it!" Ranier shouted.

With one mind, the Makers directed the power they had harnessed for a renewed attack against Abadon at the ceiling of the chamber over the device. Within moments, the force of their combined energy brought the earth down upon the great device as well as Abadon. As the walls and ceiling threatened to collapse upon them too, the Archmages joined hands and harnessed the magic of travel, transporting themselves far from the land under which the device had been built.

Shaken and dismayed, the Makers gathered and looked to the sky, half expecting Abadon and his demon army to be in pursuit.

"Did we destroy him, Ranier?" Glycas asked. "What have we done?"

"He lives," responded Ranier with certainty. "We must gather all the forces in the land that will stand with us." He hung his head. "This evil we have unleashed in our foolish attempt to play at being gods will plague us for centuries yet to be counted, I fear. We created the device to avoid this, and yet, we created the opportunity for what we feared to come to pass."

"What kind of evil is this?" one of the other Archmages asked.

"I don't know why I did not see it in him," said Rainer, shaking his head. "This malevolence that our brother has bonded with is the very source of all evil. It whispers to us all, trying to influence our minds from afar. I don't know why I did not see that Abadon had become a magnet for its musings. And now it walks among us . . . *as* one of us."

The other Archmages felt their egos shrink in importance as Ranier went on, "The world will suffer Abadon's curse until a way is found to stop him. Our descendants will be tied to this curse we have so foolishly placed upon the world. No matter what comes, we *must* do all we can to defend the innocents against the price of the immense sin we have committed."

Chapter 1

A lone figure sat weeping upon a grassy knoll on a hill overlooking the once green fields below. The rising sun cast a small shadow past his broad shoulders. It was a shadow wrought with distortions caused by his curly red hair. It was only a blink of his eyes before racing, gray clouds engulfed the sun's rays, dismissing the shadows as fast as they appeared. As he squeezed the pommel of his weapon, his bulging muscles rippled beneath his loose-fitting chain mail, which had been crafted for a taller being.

It seemed like ages ago when last he looked upon these lands, though in truth, it was only a matter of months. It was months ago he was first taken prisoner by the same assassins who had captured Lark and Archangel Royale. The mysterious cult, the Brothers of the Shadow, had been ordered not to kill him but to take him alive.

Closing his eyes, wincing as if in pain, he remembered how easy it had been for them. He had been taken to the land of Mystaria, home of the hated wizards, to be tortured under the careful direction of Viscount Alastair Navarre. He would still be rotting, or dead, behind the walls in the Fortress of Shadowgate if the Sage Algernon and the others had not happened along to free him. At first, he thought it luck that they came to help him, but now he feared it was a curse. If only he had died there, he would have died with the memory of his kingdom as it once was.

The burnt smell of decaying death now saturated the air. The land was stained black with it. It was that odor which transported his mind back to the present. Smoke rose in many places, upward through the sky like a beacon of dread now visible many miles away. Piles of carcasses, rank with the stench of burning flesh, outlined the fields.

Thousands of dark forms now filled the valley that once flourished with life. Like vultures, they picked and clawed at the rocks. The bodies of the dead were still burning and already they had a well-established excavation effort underway. Ogres had wagons and wheelbarrows filled with debris, and Orcs lined up by the hundreds, digging and attempting to move rocks. The men were camped nearby. Hundreds of tents filled the Fields of Aramoor. The barbarians of Koromundar and the nomads of Jarathadar would not dirty their hands when they had creatures to do the work for them.

Never in the deepest, darkest recesses of his nightmares could he have imagined such a sight. As he wiped the tears from his brown eyes, he hoped they would open to see it was naught but a dream of what could be if the powers of evil were victorious. Yet each time he looked, what he saw became more real and more painful. Evil had been victorious.

Dwarven bodies burning. The castle forever buried. The city sealed away. Cordilleran, the Kingdom of the Dwarves, had fallen dead and was lost forever. King Crylar, his friend, was gone. *All* his people were gone. The last defense of the realm had been executed successfully. At least in that he could take some measure of pride and solace. Cordilleran would not be sacked nor overrun with Orc filth nor any other enemy.

"Go on, pig-faces, dig. Dig until your clawed hands bleed for all the good it will do you," he said as he grabbed his weapon, resting the double-bladed edge in the ground and kneeling so that his chin rested on his hands over the pommel of his axe. His long red beard, shot through with patches of gray, was neatly tucked between his chest and the weapon. He closed his eyes for a moment, tears flowing down both cheeks. Then he looked to the heavens. "Forgive me, my people, my king. Only one duty left in this life before I join you . . . if you will still have me."

With that, he grabbed the battle-axe, flexing his muscles so tightly that his arm shook with adrenaline. He walked back toward the horse that bore him; a look of stone etched upon his brow. Usually, he had difficulty mounting a horse due to his diminutive stature, but he did so effortlessly this time. With the reins in one hand and his battle-axe held high in the other, he took a final deep breath and kicked his heels into the animal, driving it forward.

Before it moved even one stride, the horse let out a loud whine and reared up on its hind legs, causing him to lose hold of the reins. He fell backward, tumbling over and landing with his face in the dirt, unmoving except for the muscles in his hand that tightened around his double-bladed axe.

He waited.

He felt a strong arm on his shoulder, and as it turned his body over, he attacked. Striking furiously with his axe, he batted the stranger's weapon away and brought the blunt shaft of his battle-axe across the stranger's face, sending him to the ground. Instantly he felt hands around him from behind. He crashed the back of his head into this new attacker, feeling it strike against his assailant's face. He turned and, with both hands, drove the shaft of his axe up under the second attacker's chin, putting him on his back. He brought the double blade down so that it lay poised at the second attacker's neck, who lay sprawled beside the first.

They were Dwarves.

The one with the axe at his neck was bleeding profusely from his nose. "Don't kill us, General Mekko! Please," he pleaded.

As Mekko looked at them through his shock and disbelief, he realized that he recognized them—Rendek and Toran, advance scouts of the army. Still, he held his axe steady at the level of their necks. "Why in the blazes are you lads here? Our kingdom is a smoldering pile of embers. Are you cowards deserters? Answer me straight and honest, and I'll make your deaths quick and painless. Lie and you'll wish I gave you to the pig-faces before we're done!"

"General, we are scouting for the army. They are camped within the pass in the Eastern Peaks," Rendek replied with a wet cough.

"One more lie, lad, and your head will be sayin' a fond farewell to your neck!" Mekko pressed the blade of his axe into Rendek's ash-colored beard.

"It's true, General. May you take our heads if one word we speak is false," Toran said, licking his cracked lips. "The king ordered the army away with the people of the city and surrounding villages. The king stayed here with a garrison of five thousand men and bought time so the people and the army could escape."

As Mekko looked down at the young Dwarves, he saw fear, but there was no lying evident in their eyes. Hesitating in disbelief, he slowly lowered his axe. "How many men are left in our army?" he asked, his confusion evident in his tone.

"The army is fifteen thousand strong, sir," Toran replied, as he helped Rendek up to a seated position and tended to his nose.

"Who's in command?" Mekko asked.

"General Valin, sir," answered Rendek, sniffling as he wiped the blood from his face and nose.

"Valin! The man couldn't find his arse with both hands if it was under his chin!" Mekko exclaimed as he fell to one knee, resting one hand on the pommel of his axe. "Well, he's a damn good man at any rate, I suppose. He's seen more than his share of campaigns and his loyalty is without question."

"Now what are you lads doin here again?" Mekko asked with a distant look in his eye, almost as if he were speaking to himself.

"We were ordered to keep an eye on the enemy below. Since the kingdom had been taken, many of the enemy have left traveling north, sir. We're not sure where they are heading exactly. When we saw you, General, we thought you might charge down into the valley. We had to stop you. Forgive us, it was our duty." Toran's words were sincere. "When we saw it was you, we thought you were a spirit sent down from the king to avenge us."

With that, the young Dwarves bowed their heads and saluted, fists over hearts.

Something about that simple gesture of respect and affection brought Mekko back to the world of the living. He looked upon them, his face still wet from tears. With both his hands, he raised their chins so their faces met his.

"I *am* a spirit sent by the king. And this day, thanks to you two lads, I am born again to avenge our people." He looked to the skies. "I have been given a second chance, my king, to make you proud. I'll not squander it." He looked back at them with fire and iron in his eyes. "Can our army make it here by sunrise?"

"Yes, Sir!" Toran said with no hesitation. "For you, they would travel any distance in any time!"

"Rendek, stay here with me, Toran, go get our army, all divisions. I want them here by sunrise, ready for battle." Mekko smiled.

As Toran started to stand, Mekko grabbed him by the arm with a viselike grip, a hard countenance upon his face. "Tell the men, lad, that their general lives."

Toran saluted once more and was off like a blur.

Mekko kept Rendek, a highly reliable scout but small even by Dwarven standards, close as they crawled on their bellies as near as they dared, overlooking the blackness of the valley. Rendek was much younger, as was evident by the shortness of his chestnut brown beard; however, he had served in the advance scouts of Cordilleran since he was old enough to lift a sword. Even then the army had been under the command of General Mekko.

Legend among the people and the Dwarven army, Mekko was a master strategist and a great warrior. He was known to never give a command that he himself would not willingly obey. As a result, he had garnered tremendous respect and affection. In that regard, he was not unlike King Crylar. Rendek was as excited as he was honored to be by the general's side. With the news of Mekko's return, hope among the army and people would be restored.

They looked down into the valley and saw the Orcs, the Ogres, and the men trying to excavate the area. They dug in multiple places, and after having removed much of the light debris, they seemed perplexed on how to deal with the monstrous boulders barring the way to the underground city. They continued their efforts, standing together like links in a large chain; handing rubble to one another, clearing away all the small rocks they could find as if they were making progress.

Mekko saw the looks on their faces. They had won, there would be no more resistance, and they had all the time in the world. Still, despite their victory, they would occasionally quarrel among themselves and take to pushing and punching.

Rendek watched Mekko closely. He seemed revitalized, charged with a new energy as he pointed out certain tactical aspects that would be to the Dwarve's advantage when they arrived.

"Listen close today, lad. I'm goin to go over the battle plan with you and when our army arrives, I want you to go and meet them and lay it out to General Valin the way I'm layin' it out to you. You understand, lad?" Mekko asked.

As Rendek nodded, the expression on the general's face changed to one of deep thought.

"You see that great ledge, lad, above where the castle stood? That's where I want the crossbow division. I want them in place and ready by morning. Now, I want the pike division comin' down—" Mekko stopped mid-sentence, his expression now twisted by horror.

Rendek followed his gaze to see what had drawn his attention. Several Orcs were tying a Dwarf body to thin logs by the hands and feet. One had already been placed across two wooden stands over a small fire.

"They are cooking them like dead animals," Mekko bit out, abruptly pushing himself to his hands and knees.

"No, General. No, you can't. Get down, sir," Rendek pleaded in a hushed tone. He used the full strength of his body to force Mekko back on his belly. "Sir, they've been doing this since . . . well, since it ended," the young Dwarf said.

Mekko closed his eyes, grinded his teeth, and dug his hands deep in the earth. His thick fingers closed around the dirt, tearing the grass and weeds.

Rendek watched as his fingernails dug into his palms until they drew blood. "We'll make them pay, sir. We'll make them pay for sure," Rendek said.

Mekko steadied his breathing and looked squarely at his young companion. "Now listen, lad, you focus on the plan and keep your head on where you are and what you're doin'. You follow? I've seen many a battle lost because one side was so concerned with revenge they forgot what they were really fightin' for. We're better than those disgustin' animals down there. Remember, we must never lower ourselves to their level."

"Of course, sir," answered the young scout, wondering if General Mekko's words were intended for him or if they were meant for the general himself.

As the scant rays of sunlight waned and faded, dissolved by clouds, more and more Orcs emerged from their tents. For nearly two hours, the general and scout sat unmoving. Mekko absorbed the scene like a sponge. When he spoke again, it startled his companion.

"Now then, I want the pike division to come down both sides of the smaller mountains and form a line, or gauntlet, if you like, where the Barrick Cropaal stood so as not to let any in the valley escape."

Mekko looked to ensure he had Rendek's full attention. He did.

"Now, for all them camped in tents on the Fields of Aramoor, I figure when the fightin starts, they'll make a charge to attack our pike-men from the rear," Mekko said, stroking his beard. "So, we'll need to deal with them in a hurry before they can do any damage. I think I have just the thing in mind, lad."

Rendek looked behind them as he did every so often to check their flank and did a double take. He saw many weapons pointing at them from the small thicket of trees below their position. "General, sir, we have a problem," Rendek uttered.

Mekko kept his eyes focused on the encampment. "Out with it, lad. Let me guess. With the silence of the still wind, there's a bunch of lads clad in green, like the grass itself, pointin' a whole mess of arrows at our backs or a bunch of armored men pointin' crossbows at us, or preferably both. Which is it, lads?"

Rendek dropped his jaw. "The first one, sir, but how did you?"

Mekko smiled at his bewildered companion. "Relax, lad. My friends promised to bring us help and their promise is better than gold, but you can call it keen intuition if you wish. Relax, boy. Them are Elves. No need to worry, they are friends and allies from the west and just who I've been hopin for."

The morning sun had quickly retreated behind the cover of white clouds. As noon approached, the white clouds gave way to gray ones. The sun's appearance and influence lessened by the day as if it knew its time was running out in this world.

It was a small party, six of the Elven Emerald Watch, which had come ahead of what was now being referred to as the Alliance Army. It had been a long time since Rendek had seen Elves this close before. The Elves' sparkling green vestment had the ability to change color and blend in with any natural surroundings.

The Elves informed them that the army was nearby but did not want to risk an approach until they knew what awaited them. Mekko asked that they be brought to the others at once. Two of the Elves bade them to follow, while the other four remained.

Any trace of warmth that remained of the day had fled with the sunlight. The air was cool, and the wind stirred and bit at them unexpectedly. Even the grass itself had taken on a strange pallor. There had been ample rain the past several days, yet the earth languished as if from a drought.

Mekko's thoughts betrayed his earlier counsel to Rendek. His sole focus was on revenge against the dark forces that had destroyed his beloved Cordilleran and murdered the king. Rather than gnawing at him malignantly, he saw his desire for revenge as a beneficial force that kept him going in some strange way. With a cold and calculating manner that was previously unfamiliar to him, he vowed to be a general and strategist first. He would not idly sacrifice even one of his men to further his own need for vengeance. However, they *would* strike hard and fast, and the one thing he was sure of, the enemy would know fear before the next day's sunset. There would be time for vengeance, and that time was almost at hand.

The Elves led them along for nearly an hour until they reached the clearing where the army composed of Elves and Men had stopped. Though they were out in the open grasslands, there was little to fear; no one would be looking for them or expecting them, save the Shadow Prince, whose retreat had surely put him some distance from this place by now.

At once, Mekko's former companions rushed to greet him. The hard look in the general's eyes was new to them.

Before words of greeting could be spoken, Mekko uttered, "Cordilleran has fallen. King Crylar is dead."

Elenari gasped, then quickly regained herself. "Oh, Mekko, we are so sorry," she said, instinctively coming forward. She leaned down and embraced him tightly.

He could feel the thickness of the chain mail she now wore beneath her earth-colored forest clothes. As her blond hair brushed across his cheek, he felt his chin quiver with an emotion he did not wish to show.

Though part of his heart blamed *them*, his new friends and comrades, for keeping him away when his homeland needed him most, he realized how foolish it was to entertain such anger. As he looked up at them, he saw only the sincerest sympathy, sorrow, and concern for his well-being etched on their familiar faces. He would still be a prisoner, or dead, if not for them.

They were all present, including Kael, the Grand Druid, who had first healed him back in the prison. Though he was tall and foreboding in his dark robes, his hair and beard were grayer than the Dwarf remembered. However, the hard countenance of his brown eyes had not changed nor the sincerity conveyed within them.

Captain Gaston, the tall officer from the Republic of Averon, was there as well. *As good as his word*, Mekko thought, laying his eyes on a long line of the Sentinels of Averon on horseback. It was then he saw the Druid, Galin, and the mere sight of him and his snow-white hair distressed him. Galin had had a full head of brown hair when last they were together. His face also aged more than what was natural. "Laddie, what in the name of . . .?"

"All is well, my friend," Galin assured him. "Evil has marked me so that it will know me in the future and there will be no mistaking one another. Worry not for me, it is you who has my, *our*, gravest sympathy."

Mekko still saw the strength and youth in Galin's crystal blue eyes. He nodded and took the Druid's hand in his. Though he had respect and strong feelings for all of them, he was fondest of Galin.

He then spied King Aeldorath of the Elves and his fair, ebony-haired daughter, Layla, who had led him by the hand through the magic waterfalls of Alluviam. Even the king wore the green vestment of his Emerald Watch, with a flowing green robe to match. A great ash longbow was on his back and a silver scabbard hung loosely at his side, housing a long sword.

The Dwarf was pleased to see another monarch who did not think himself above single combat. Mekko caught a glimpse from Layla as they approached. She looked at Galin. He did not know if the others could see it, but there was a caring in her eyes that spoke louder than words. Mekko watched as father and daughter stopped before him and bowed their heads low.

"Forgive us, my friend, we have arrived too slowly to be of service to you," Aeldorath said.

Mekko bowed his head, came forward, and placed his hand on the king's arm, forcing him to look up. "Not quite yet, your majesty. My king is dead, my land is overrun by our foulest enemies, but the Dwarven people live, and fifteen thousand Dwarves of our army will be here by dawn tomorrow to take back what is ours. I see by the look of things you were victorious in the west."

The king turned and looked off in the distance. "If the loss of so much life can ever be counted as a victory, yes. With the help of our friends from Averon, we defeated the Stygian Knights. And with the help of Kael and all your friends here, it appears we may be reunited with our subterranean cousins, the White Elves. It is an event my heart has deeply longed for." Aeldorath placed his hand on Mekko's arm. "Enough about us, my friend. How is it we can be of service to you and Cordilleran?" he asked.

"How many Elves are here with you?" Mekko asked.

"We are ten thousand strong," Layla, Captain of the Emerald Watch, answered.

"And we have twenty-five hundred cavalry from Averon at your command, General," Captain Gaston added as he approached.

Mekko smiled and fell into a moment of deep thought before leading the king, Layla, and Gaston away to speak privately.

Kael watched them walk away, also lost in thought. He flinched but only slightly when Lark suddenly appeared beside him.

"So, that's General Mekko?" Lark asked.

"It is indeed. We happened upon him by chance. We entered the Fortress of Shadowgate determined to find and free yourself and Archangel. Algernon perceived that you were alive and being held there. I don't think I need to explain to you what it took to convince him to risk the Emerald Star in a rescue attempt. However, we stumbled upon and acquired General Mekko. In that time, he has proven himself a staunch ally and friend many times over. Not your typical Dwarf by any stretch of the imagination, however, in view of recent events, I fear for him," Kael said.

Lark placed the heavy metal glove of his plated armor on the Druid's shoulder. "Fear not, Kael. I know what you risked coming after me. I know what all of you risked, and I know what you lost. I also know what I lost, as does my brother. I wish, more than anything, we had been with you since the beginning. All I can say is we are here now." He paused for a moment to gaze at the Dwarf and then turned back to Kael. "*Now is all that matters.* It is the Shadow Prince's time to fear. It is the Orcs time to fear. It is the time for all our enemies to fear. I am rejoined with my brother and my best friend. The world is right, and life is good. The general's problems can best be solved now on the field of righteous battle. He will be whole again upon our victory, as will we all."

Kael smiled and nodded as Lark drew his huge two-handed sword. He watched Lark approach a nearby tree. There he knelt and prayed as Kael had often seen him do before battle. Kael had dearly missed Lark and his ability to smile in the face of overwhelming adversity. His mere presence comforted him. Still, his thoughts drifted to Mya.

In Lark's absence, Mya had become Kael's strength and courage. He had devoted his life to the service of Mother Nature. He had never thought what it would be like to devote himself to another being. He longed for her. It was not lust he felt. They completed each other in ways physical contact could not hope to approach. They needed each other, and he missed her desperately. Still, her people needed her now, more than ever, to lead them to freedom. With luck, they would be reunited soon.

Archangel Royale sat alone by a tree. His remaining eye was closed in a restful state, not sleep. The Elves of Alluviam had cleaned him up so that he felt more like his old self. His straight hair was pulled back into a ponytail, and he wore a proper eye patch. From a distance, he might appear to be a protruding root of the tree upon which he leaned, as he was outfitted all in brown. A brown robe concealed the leather armor of a ranger. Beside him were a small shortbow, quiver, and the Elven long sword that had been gifted to him.

Sleep did not come easily to him. The realm of dreams plagued Archangel's mind with images of torture, so he simply rested his good eye as often as the opportunity presented itself. Still, something gnawed at him, thoughts he had been unable to dismiss since they left the Vineland Woods. He was humbly thankful to have his brother, Lark, back, but there were details that, try as he might, he could not overlook. His thoughts drifted back in time amidst and between the shades that tormented him to the battle with Lark in the cave.

Elenari walked back through the ranks of the Elven army, searching until she found those she had been seeking nearly at the end of the procession. In a small circle away from the others sat twenty Elves. Though older than most Elves within the larger procession, the Kenshari Masters sat comfortably with their legs crossed and eyes closed. One of them, High Master Quentil Reyblade, sat in the middle of the circle.

The Kenshari were like no other warriors. Each was a practiced master in the weapon or weapons they carried. One was an expert at empty-handed combat. Some wore armor, and some did not. Some had been fighting, learning, and teaching with their weapons for close to a thousand years. High Master Reyblade was the only one Elenari knew for sure was over a thousand years old. She was far and away the youngest and did not feel worthy to even be in their presence. However, despite all their skill and knowledge, they had never fought together in a war or even fought together outside the temple, as far as she knew. She sat down near Master Reyblade and bowed her head.

"Master, why do you not join with the others?" Elenari asked.

"Because, child, we are not part of the others. They are not part of us. We will be here if we are needed—that should suffice," Reyblade stated without opening his eyes. "Have you found a sanctuary for the disciples and students yet?"

"No, master." Elenari replied. "I mixed them in with the ranks of the army until—"

"They should be your first concern, not us," Reyblade interrupted. "*They* are the future of the Kenshari way. *They* must be protected. The teachings must continue. Return to me when you have found a safe haven for them."

Elenari bowed her head. "Yes, master," she said solemnly before departing.

As she walked back through the Elven ranks, Elenari took little notice of their preparations. It was not her responsibility to the Kenshari that occupied her thoughts but her responsibility to Algernon—the venerable Sage who had essentially taken Kael's place as her father many times during much of their quest. All her life she'd had father figures looking after her. Master Reyblade was as much of a father during her youth as Kael, perhaps more. Kael was the only father she ever really wanted but never had for very long. Now he was in love with a good woman, a strong woman, who cared for him just as deeply. She was happy for him but, at the same time, realized the emptiness of her own life. Algernon was gone, Kael had a woman to take care of, and even Master Reyblade barely looked at her. None of it would matter if Hawk were still alive and with her. There were times when she walked and closed her eyes, she could almost feel him there holding her hand. She thought of the tome of Algernon. Perhaps if she began reading the book, it would help her connect with him again.

The sky darkened as evening settled in on the outskirts of Cordilleran. The air itself had chilled, even in the absence of the wind.

Mekko and Rendek reviewed the plan of attack with King Aeldorath, his daughter, and Captain Gaston for several hours.

When they broke, Mekko pulled Rendek aside, putting both hands on the younger Dwarf's shoulders. "Now listen, lad. If there's somethin you don't understand about the plan, now's the time to ask."

"No, sir, I understand everything." Rendek answered affirmatively.

"Good, lad, now go. I want you up in the mountains to meet our army as they arrive. Lay the plan out like I told you. I want all divisions in place by first light. We start when the sun breaks through the clouds. Go, lad, keep your head down and be careful."

Rendek responded by bringing his right fist over his heart in the Dwarven salute, and Mekko returned the gesture of respect. But Rendek did not go. Mekko looked at him expectantly.

"General, it has been cloudy for the past several weeks," Rendek said with some hesitation in his voice. "I doubt we will see sun in the morning."

"Trust me, lad, we start when the sun breaks," Mekko answered with absolute certainty.

As Mekko walked through the trees, back toward the Elves, he observed a fully armored man kneeling on the ground. His hands rested on the golden hilt of a great two-handed sword, which had a frost-white diamond embedded in the pommel. Mekko recognized him to be Lark Royale. He sat beneath a tree and gathered himself before the brisk air of the afternoon. He saw the sincerity in the man's face as he prayed to whatever deity he chose to call god.

"So, you'd be Lark Royale then?" the Dwarf asked in a hushed tone.

His eyes still closed, Lark replied, "I am." He bowed his head, opened his eyes, and stood up. "And you would be General Mekko?"

"Aye, lad, one in the same." The Dwarf reached out and vigorously shook the other's hand. "Not sure that means much anymore, but I suppose that's who I am." He felt the strength in Lark's grip and took a second look at him. "You should know that you have some kind of friends there. They went through a lot to find you, but then, I don't think I need to tell you that. Always speaks highly of a man, the kind of friends he keeps."

"Then I would say both of us are well spoken for, General," replied Lark.

Mekko smiled and nodded. "I understand you and your brother were former guests of the Fortress of Shadowgate. Tell me, have you had occasion to catch up with Viscount Navarre? I owe that cowardly slime a lick or two."

"We did catch up to him," Lark said flatly, eyes to the ground. "I don't think you'll get a chance to pay him back though, General. My brother put a sword in his mouth. His days of inflicting torment are over forever."

Mekko clapped his hands together. "Well, you don't say. That is good news. Best news I've had since comin' home. I'd like to go find that lad and shake his hand."

Once Mekko departed, Lark found Kael sitting not far from where he had left him. Placing his sword down, he allowed himself to collapse to the ground next to his old friend.

"So, Kael, I have heard tales during our journey here from the men of Averon. They speak of Elenari as if she were a living legend. You must be proud. And now, you as well are the Grand Druid of an order you once told me you despised. I must hear how these things took place. Tell me, please, and leave nothing out."

Kael inhaled deeply and proceeded to tell Lark nearly everything that had occurred. From his battle with Talic, to their audience with Thargelion, their adventures within Mystaria, to their battle with the molten creature. He recounted everything he could remember, including the painful memories of the death of Algernon, Thargelion, and what he knew of Hawk's death. Finally, he told him about Mya.

Lark placed a hand on his friend's shoulder. "Ahh. Finally, through the despair comes a bright light. I always wondered when a maiden might catch your fancy. An Elven High Priestess no less, she seemed exquisite when I saw her in Dragontree. It sounds to me like you saved her and her people from themselves. I only wish I could have been with you through it all. So many are dead and so much time has been lost."

"I think we saved each other," Kael said softly and then shifted gears in their conversation. "Lark, do you remember anything of the Shadow Prince's control over you?"

Lark leaned away, clearly taken off guard. "I only remember pain and torture. Beatings, broken bones, humiliation, and degradation. I remember when they took Archangel's eye, and I was powerless to act." His voice trembled, and he inhaled deeply, sniffing. "I remember a voice. A strange voice that tormented me through it all. Even now I cannot recall how it sounded."

Kael said nothing, for what could he say?

"What was Algernon's plan?" Lark asked. "If he were still alive, what would his plan have been for now? What was his plan for the Emerald Star here in Cordilleran? What—"

"Father, may I speak to you in private?" It was Elenari. She had walked up behind them. "Excuse me, Lark."

"Of course, my lady," Lark said, rising to his feet. "I will see if Archangel has met General Mekko yet. We can continue our discussion later this evening, Kael."

When they were alone, Kael asked, "Yes, Nari, what is the matter?"

"Are you sure it is a good idea to tell Lark so much?" she asked, taking a seat beside him.

"What do you mean?" Kael asked, squaring his shoulders.

"What I mean, Father, is that Lark was under the Shadow Prince's direct control and quite frankly we don't know how he came to be out of that control. I do not know if it is wise to trust him with all of our information."

"*You* don't know if it's wise. Well, that's wonderful that *you* don't think it's wise. Let me tell you something, young lady. Lark Royale is my best friend, and he was fighting the evil of the Shadow Prince when you were too young to lift a sword. I thought he was dead—now you are suggesting I not trust a man who saved my life a dozen times over, a man who put his faith in me to watch his back? How dare you suggest such a thing!" Kael exclaimed, standing up and glaring down at her seated form.

Nari put her hands up as if in defense. "All I'm saying is that he was under the Shadow Prince's power and remembers nothing about it. Do you think it is prudent to trust him so absolutely this soon?"

"Prudent? Was it prudence that made you put your sword to Algernon's throat when you thought I was dead?" As Kael let the bitterness of the words escape his lips, he immediately regretted saying them and felt ashamed.

Nari stood up to face him, her mouth agape. Then she turned and stormed away.

"Nari! I didn't mean—" Kael let his head fall in regret. "Damn."

Galin had found a quiet patch of overgrown bushes and a lone chestnut tree to recline against. He watched the sky through the holes in the tree's crown as it became grayer and darker with the evening chill. He looked at his hands and saw that the angular lines and smooth skin, which he had expected, were there. He was unchanged in physical age, though the appearance of his snow-white hair and lines in the corners of his eyes might suggest otherwise. They were the effects of the severe trauma of having been touched by such a potent negative life force as the Lich, Voltan.

"My Lord Calindir?"

The greeting startled him. He did not hear Layla approach. He looked up at her and saw she was alone. For some strange reason, he unconsciously found himself trying to hide his face from her. "I don't recall you referring to me as Lord Calindir in the past, lady. If that appellation is a sign of sympathy for my appearance, I assure you it is unnecessary," Galin said, feeling like a fool as he looked away from her.

In the next moment, he felt something strange and warm on his cheeks.

Her hands. They were soft and gentle, like powder. She turned his head so that his eyes met hers. He had always thought she was lovely, but he never imagined being this close to her. She squatted down in front of him. He allowed himself to stare back into her eyes, which were blue like the sky on a clear spring day. He watched her shoulder-length raven hair blow lightly back in the breeze, and for a moment, he could almost feel her breath upon his face. She looked at his hair, then his face, and squinted her eyes.

"Yes, I think it gives you character and sophistication. I find it most agreeable," Layla smiled, and just as suddenly stood and walked away.

Galin relaxed again and consoled himself that she was just attempting to make him feel better. He knew her well from his history with the Elven court. Until now, he knew her as a soldier who was often outspoken and opinionated. Although she was the Captain of the Emerald Watch, she, like her sister Trinia, was a princess.

However, Layla much preferred being known as a captain and officer among the Elves. The title of princess fit her older sister better. At any rate, whether she felt sorry for him or not, she managed to make him feel better about his appearance and, for that, he was inwardly thankful. It was a kindness she had shown him that he would look for a way to pay back to her.

Mekko came trudging through the bushes, startling Galin to a lesser degree.

"Well, I see, my friend, you're as inconspicuous as ever on your feet," Galin said with humor. But when he saw the Dwarf's face, he quickly stood up.

Mekko's expression was solemn. "I find myself in need of your Druid magic. Come with me and help me find Kael. I have an urgent request that I must ask of you both."

"Of course, General. If it is within our power, you shall have it," Galin replied.

Mekko hinted a smile, grabbed Galin's arm, and together they went to seek out Kael.

Chapter 2

Dwarven horns roared throughout the valley of Cordilleran as if the mountains themselves cried out to the heavens in outrage. It was an uproarious, uplifting orchestra of numerous instruments played together in concert, announcing daybreak like no earthen creature could possibly attempt.

Below, in the dark valley, Orcs wildly fell out of slipshod hammocks and rolled out of their tents. Their heads lifted lethargically, unable to comprehend the unexplained cacophony of noise that had roused them so early. Night's darkness still reigned, so it was unthinkable they were being awoken for the day's work. Next, thundering echoes descended upon them from the surrounding mountains. Many Orcs held their ears, unable to distinguish actual sound from reflected noise. Some frantically awoke, reaching for anything to use as a weapon.

The men were quicker to realize something was amiss but were uncertain what to do or where to go. The jubilant sound came down from all throughout the mountains without any clear point of origin. Now, Elven horns blew, but at a higher pitch and with the same boisterous heartiness of the Dwarven horns. No hint of their location, their melodic tones were exceptionally distasteful to the creatures below.

The Orcs recognized the sound of the Elvish horns. Elaborate ruses perhaps, for they knew the Dwarves were all dead or trapped within their city and that the Elves should have already been destroyed by the Shadow Prince's army. The barbarians of Koromundar and the desert nomads of Jarathadar scrambled for their weapons.

A third wave of horns blew loud and clear, different from the rest, causing even the deep-sleeping Ogres to awake from dormancy. Neither monsters nor men recognized these horns, as this was the seldom-heard signal charge of the Sentinels of Averon.

Finally, all three groups of horns blew simultaneously, long and loud, representing the free races of the known world united in a cry of freedom. This was their harmonious signal to the forces of the Shadow Prince that they were here in defiance of tyranny and for them to beware that the time of their wrath was finally at hand.

Kael and Galin perspired fiercely, their hands outstretched toward the skies. What General Mekko had asked of them had not been done by their kind since centuries past, and even then, only in legend. However, they agreed to use all their powers to achieve what the Dwarf had requested of them. They had begun hours earlier. Under normal conditions, what they were attempting would be extraordinary, but with the poisoning of the lands came darkened gray skies and so their task flirted with futility. Something people of their world could never quite understand was that the weather was a living machination of Mother Nature. When the earth and land suffered, so the skies and oceans suffered. Even the tides of the deep oceans to the south, which drove the winds through the air, were affected and weakened.

The magic they were attempting to summon lay almost beyond their reach in no certain or fixed location. They drew it from deep within the earth, far out in the seas, and beyond the furthest skies. It was elusive, evading their every effort to piece the different segments of it together, like the ingredients of an exceptional recipe. Each was as invaluable as the next and failure was the price for leaving even a pinch of one out.

Their concentration was so acute that even the sound of the horns could not penetrate it. It was then in that moment of stillness to the outside world that they felt it. Their patience had rewarded them with the power they sought. Their feet became rooted to the ground as the magic coursed through their bodies, using them as the earth's natural conduits for its energies. The magic surged up the length of their frames, igniting the adrenaline within them. For a brief moment, nothing came between them and true-life energy. The poisoning of the land did not exist. Evil did not exist. There was only the spark of the world's life force and their connection to it.

Finally, the magic exploded. Unseen, invisible, out through their fingertips toward the heavens of the dark early morning. The omnipotent power they felt from the magic was so addicting, they did not want it to end, but together they retained enough presence of mind to realize it must.

It was the sun. It was that bright star essential to so many life processes on their world. They had summoned it before its proper time through all the gray clouds and weather that sought to hinder it, that it suddenly shone over Cordilleran like a blazing white beacon of hope.

One moment the sky was black, in the next moment, the sun appeared out of nowhere in all its magnitude and glory. Its rays shone down upon Orcs and Ogres, blinding them, exposing them to the scrutiny of its all-encompassing light. The beasts hated direct sunlight as their eyes were especially sensitive to bright lights, and this was like no light they had ever felt. There was nowhere to hide. They began scurrying about, attempting to find shade, bumping and tripping over one another.

The barbarians and nomads, though not as blinded, were so shocked by the contrast from dark to bright, white light that they too were covering their eyes in panic, unable to adjust enough to see clearly. They fumbled about in every direction, shouting unclear orders.

"Now!" said Mekko as he blew his signal horn, overlooking the valley from above.

With that lone signal arose hundreds upon hundreds of Dwarves from the crossbow division located upon the mountainous ledge above the valley. They formed in three rows directly behind one another, hundreds long. Each row fired down into the valley, ducked to reload, and let the row behind them fire. Then they repeated the process.

Before the Orcs and Ogres in the valley even knew what was hitting them, General Mekko signaled the second wave of the attack with another short burst from his horn. "Now Elves!" the Dwarf shouted with excitement, watching his plan unfold.

After having spoken to King Aeldorath and Layla for several hours in private, Mekko had broken the Elven force in half. Throughout the night, half the Elves carefully made their way into the mountains on both sides of the valley. Nearly five thousand split up between both sides of the valley, nestled within protection of the mountains.

Upon hearing the second signal, the Elves fired a hail of arrows, filling the skies above Cordilleran with thousands of wooden shafts, arching down upon the killing field provided for them below. Mekko had created a three-way crossfire into the valley between the Dwarves and Elves. Their arrows and bolts arrived, delivering death by the thousands to the unsuspecting Orcs and Ogres.

As the tormented creatures attempted to look up at their attackers, the glare of the sun beat down upon their eyes, hiding the Dwarves and Elves like a curtain of pure light. They fell upon one another like the dominoes of a child's game.

The Orcs and Ogres frantically pushed their way to exit the valley toward where the Barrick Cropaal once stood, out and beyond to the Fields of Aramoor where the men of the enemy camped. Upon seeing what was happened, the men, in turn, started forming close ranks.

Again, Mekko blew his horn, signaling the next wave. The Dwarven pikemen, who had weathered the passing of the night behind the cover of the mountains, came running down and out either side of the mouth of the valley. Side by side they formed up, the deadly blades of their great spears facing toward the valley and the oncoming rush of Orcs and Ogres trying to escape.

Mekko watched and waited for the barbarians and nomads. He watched them realize the backs of the Dwarven pikemen were facing them and would be an easy target. There was only fifty yards between their blades and the backs of the Dwarves. Just before they charged, Mekko blew his horn yet again.

This time, Dwarven infantry came running out from behind the mountains on either side of the mouth of the valley. They ran out and formed a line several hundred men across, back-to-back, man for man, with the line of Dwarven pikemen in perfect position to guard their backs. The Dwarves of the infantry drew their swords, clenched their shields, and waited.

A heavy crunching impact followed as the Orcs threw themselves into the deadly line of pikes barring their way to freedom from the barrage of missile fire, which plagued them unmercifully. The Orcs impaled and skewered themselves, sometimes three bodies deep per pike, trying to rip and claw their way out. The Ogres hit with terrible force. Even impaled on the pikes, they were strong and dangerous, able to force the Dwarves back so they knocked into the infantry line guarding them. Cries of, "Hold the line!" could be heard among the pikemen throughout their ranks, echoed by their infantry counterparts.

The Elves now concentrated their fire on the Ogres, aiming for their heads, trying to put them down with one shot. They were well out of the range of the Dwarven crossbows, but they would not escape the Elven longbows so quickly. The valley had become a graveyard of dark corpses, in some places two or three layers thick. Thousands fell dead, victims of the incessant missile fire.

As the men of Koromundar and Jarathadar gathered on the Fields of Aramoor, they came to realize that they outnumbered the Dwarves by many thousand. The sunlight had already begun to fade and was no longer a factor. The sun had distanced itself rapidly, being replaced by fast moving-gray clouds. However, for the next phase, it no longer mattered. They charged the Dwarves, as Mekko knew they eventually would.

He blew two short bursts to signal the other half of the Elven forces. They had spent the night creeping up through the fields of Aramoor, lying upon their stomachs camouflaged with grass and their natural ability to blend into the environment. Upon hearing the horn, they came up to one knee and began firing into the camp, which they had surrounded along its perimeter.

Hundreds fell just short of the Dwarven line, arrows buried in their backs. The second force of Elves also comprised five thousand strong along the perimeter of the camp. They fired into targets that never saw the origin of the weapons that caused their deaths.

Once the men realized they were the victims of an ambush, they frantically ordered the remaining forces away from the valley to run north beyond the Fields of Aramoor, away from the Elven attack. There was a hole in the Elven perimeter several yards wide, which the men pushed each other toward and through with all their speed. Many fell as they ran, taking those in front and behind down with them. Those who still lived scrambled to their feet with all haste toward escape. They dropped weapons, helmets, anything that would impede their ability to run faster to safety.

Like lambs to the slaughter, the Elves shot them down. They had herded them like cattle toward the gap in the perimeter north of the camp. Fear seized them. Those who attempted to attack the Elves fell, their bodies had become like pin cushions embedded with multiple arrows. The arrows flew so swiftly, and in such enormous quantities, that resistance was futile. Their only hope was escape on foot.

Mekko blew the horn twice, signaling the Elves to stop firing. Then, he blew his horn for one long note, which he held, signaling the final wave of the attack.

During the previous night, the Sentinels of Averon had ridden north of the encampment, hiding in the hill's northeast and northwest of the Fields of Aramoor. There they hid and waited for the long note. In response, they blew their horns once again. This time the fleeing men of the enemy camp stopped dead in their tracks. The horns came from ahead to the northeast and west. They discerned the origin of the horns easily now, as there were no other ancillary noises to distract them. Just when they thought escape was within their grasp, they quickly sensed their situation had progressed rapidly from bad to much worse—they could do nothing but stand and wait. The rumbling vibrations of the pounding ground came first.

The cavalry of Averon charged from two directions toward them. Captain Gaston led the mounted attack, and as he blew his horn, his men unsheathed their swords and galloped to a charge, releasing a multitude of furious battle cries. The horsemen charged into the enemy like waves crashing on the rocks of the shore. Swinging their swords from side to side, they hacked and slashed the foreigners who vainly tried to evade them. Blood sprayed through the air. The horses slammed into many of the enemies, trampling bones in their wake.

Soon it became difficult to see a clear piece of land throughout the Fields of Aramoor. It was a sea of bodies trod upon by twenty-five hundred horses of the Sentinels of Averon. The horsemen hacked them to pieces, down to the very last man.

Lark and Archangel Royale had joined the mounted charge with Averon's men, their blades were as crimson stained as those around them. When the charge ended, and movement had all but stopped, only the enemy's death throes could be heard.

Not one had escaped.

Back at the ruins of the Barrick Cropaal, the missile fire had ceased, and the fighting became intense as the few surviving creatures attempted to break through the Dwarven line. The pikemen held the Orcs and Ogres back at weapon's length as the infantry came forward through the line to engage the survivors. The Dwarves made short work of the creatures after several minutes of hacking and slashing away at them. All were dead, save one. A massive Ogre remained, his body pierced by arrows and even impaled through the stomach by a pike. As the Dwarves surrounded him, he grabbed the shaft of the pike still sticking out of his body and swung three of the Dwarves to the ground.

The creature stood nearly eleven feet. Its body was a grotesque mass of gray-green warts and bumps. However, its frame was outlined with bulging muscles at the arms and shoulders. Blood leaked from his torso, arms, and legs from over a dozen arrow wounds. The blood spilling from the pike wound appeared blacker and darker than from his smaller wounds. The Ogre backed up, snarling, with blood dripping alongside its mouth. It had one hand on the embedded weapon and held the other out as a warning toward the Dwarves who cautiously surrounded it.

The Dwarves were wary of how dangerous the creature was, even now with so many wounds. Its strength was not to be underestimated. It was at that moment that the Dwarves closest, who numbered in the hundreds, stopped approaching the Ogre and lowered their weapons. The creature looked behind it, unsure why they did not move in to finish him. There, fewer than ten feet behind him, stood a lone Dwarf, taller and more massively built than the rest. It was General Mekko.

Slowly, Mekko pulled the chain mail hood down from his head, revealing his tangled reddish hair that had flattened to the back of his head. His lengthy beard appeared like flame. The blotches of gray, which ran the length of it, were difficult to see.

Measuring his steps, Mekko grabbed his battle-axe with one hand, and while looking at the creature, he pulled a short sword from the pile of dead Orcs at his feet.

The Ogre realized he was being given a chance to fight the larger Dwarf in single combat. He grabbed the shaft of the pike with both hands, let out a terrible shriek, and pulled the weapon out through his torso, tearing a large chunk of skin from its stomach. Blood flowed freely from the wound, but the creature did not flinch. The pain had injected him with a raging hatred that needed to be released on this puny being. He could feel the strength of his arms return as he released a ferocious battle cry, showing his bloody fangs beneath his red eyes. The mighty Ogre foamed at the mouth, pink in color as the saliva mixed with its blood.

Mekko did not move. He waited, knowing the creature was working itself up into such a rage that a charge was imminent. His kept his own fury conspicuously masked. This creature represented the hated enemies that had destroyed his homeland, his king, and thousands of his brethren. He tightened his grip around his two weapons, his knuckles cracking in response.

With an inhuman howl, the creature lunged forward and attacked with a downward two-hand stabbing motion, trying to run the Dwarf through. Mekko stood completely still and, at the last possible moment, stepped back with his left foot, anchoring his weight as he brought both weapons in front of him in an X block.

The pike was blocked, and the creature's momentum forced the pike to slide upward above Mekko's head, exposing nearly the Ogre's entire body to the Dwarf. With his right hand, Mekko furiously struck at the pike, snapping it in half with his battle-axe. Without stopping, the Dwarf spun around to his left with a sweeping sword blow right across the towering Ogre's waistline. It was a slicing gash, which took the creature by surprise, forcing it to take two steps back.

Still attacking with forward momentum, Mekko brought his battle-axe downward, striking the Ogre's left thigh where it connected to the knee, forcing the creature down. With a look that well exceeded pure rage, Mekko stepped forward, bringing both weapons together in a wide sweeping arc so that they met at the Ogre's neck, severing it cleanly.

The expression on the creature's face was one of astonishment as its head flew upward and then dropped to the ground, bouncing twice. Blood spurted from its neck for a moment before the shoulders contorted and the lower half fell forward.

Silence fell upon Cordilleran as Mekko, his face decorated with blood splatter, faced the Dwarves near him on the ground and then let his gaze drift upward to the Dwarves and Elves in the mountains. He looked out to the Fields of Aramoor and watched as the Elves and Men of Averon approached. In one motion, he dropped the sword and lifted his battle-axe high above his head and let out a cry of victory such that the mountains themselves shook.

In the next moment, cheers erupted from all directions.

The Dwarves feverishly began to shout Mekko's name, as some could scarcely believe he was still alive. Even the Elves and Men soon joined in praise of the Dwarf whose cunning plan of attack had led them to their second great victory over the forces of the Shadow Prince. Though Cordilleran may have been lost and the mountain city sealed away beneath tons of rubble, none of the races assembled could deny the merit of such a one-sided victory. They had killed thousands of the enemy with minimal losses of their own.

As Mekko stood and heard his name being chanted, he found himself looking around at dead bodies as far as the eye could see. His land had become a graveyard that reeked of smoke and death. It was a victory, but there was an enormous amount of work to be done. He remembered from what Toran and Rendek had told him, the original enemy force had been nearly three times as great in number as the one they had just defeated and that many of the enemy had gone north perhaps to join an even larger force. They were by no means safe.

The land was theirs for the moment, but what they could accomplish in the next few days would determine how long they would keep it. With that, he raised his hands in an attempt to quiet the cheers. This proved to be a more difficult task than he thought. The Dwarven army was wild, running down from the mountains by the hundreds and thousands to greet their "back from the dead" commander.

As they gathered in a circle about him, Mekko kept trying to settle them down until he felt a firm grasp on his shoulder from behind and heard a whisper in his ear. It was the Elven king, Aeldorath. He had somehow made his way behind him through the crowd of Dwarves.

"Allow them this moment, General. I expect it's the first moment of hope they've had in some time. I think King Crylar would have wanted *you* to have such a moment, too. He looks down upon you and your people with pride in this hour."

Mekko turned, saw the wisdom in Aeldorath's eyes, smiled, nodded, and threw his arms around the Elven monarch. He was touched that the old Elf still remembered King Crylar fondly. Their embrace was a display that earned more cheers from the Elves.

The Dwarves came to him in droves, both saluting and embracing him. He had become their savior in this dark time when they were without a leader. It was then he saw a large gray-haired Dwarf approaching him with tears of joy in his bright gray eyes.

"Make way, lads, for General Valin. Ahh, Valin my dear friend. You've done a wonderful job in my absence. I couldn't have done any better myself, truly." With that, Mekko embraced the old Dwarf.

"General Mekko, my dear friend, my commander. We had given up all hope that you still lived. The king— the king appointed me army commander with great reluctance and only out of necessity. I've always known I could never take your place." Valin swatted at his tears.

"Nonsense, man," Mekko replied. "The bulk of the army is intact, and our people are safe. You're the senior officer, it's only right for you to have had command and I'd say you did a damn fine job of it."

"Well, then let me say it is my privilege and honor to surrender command of the Dwarven army to its rightful commander. Do you accept command?" Valin asked reverently.

A sudden hush fell over the crowd that had gathered around Mekko.

Mekko spent a moment appreciating the expressions of renewed hope and energy on all the faces around him. He smiled and took the old officer's hands in his. "I accept command."

Again, cheers rose from the Dwarves and even the Elves and Men joined in the celebration.

Finally, Captain Gaston of Averon made his way to Mekko. Upon seeing the tall officer, Mekko ran forward, embraced the taller man, and lifted him off the ground for a moment. The two laughed together in celebration. Mekko embraced Captain Layla of the Elves as well. The three joined hands—Dwarf, Man, and Elf—signifying the union of the three races.

At that moment, Mekko saw Galin and Kael in the distance, leaning on each other as they walked. With dismay, Mekko quickly ran over to the two Druids. They had now been joined by Elenari, who helped support Kael on one side with Galin on the other. She had been with the archers on the Fields of Aramoor.

"Are you lads all right?" Mekko asked.

"Nothing a long sleep couldn't cure," replied Galin, his face drained of color.

Perspiration beaded all over Kael's face. "We'll be fine," he said, releasing himself from Galin's arm of support. "Congratulations on your victory, General. Clearly well fought and well planned."

"I—we all owe you Druids a debt we'll not soon forget. Thank you. I still don't know how you did it. How in the name of Crylar did you move the sun, lads?" Mekko asked.

Galin looked at Kael before he responded. "Well, we didn't *move* the sun precisely. We used the natural forces of our world, tides, winds, and a deep power seated in the earth to influence the sun to amplify her powers, making it appear as if it had come closer to our world, if only for a brief time."

"Well, however you did it, Cordilleran thanks you. With Crylar's blessing, go and get what rest you need, lads."

Mekko climbed upon a large round rock so that he stood above all those around him, and with a humble patience, he was able to settle them all down and draw them in close around. "My soldiers, my friends, my companions, both old and new. It is true that we have won our second great victory over the evil forces that threaten us all. And it is our first victory as Dwarves, Elves, and Men united as one."

With that, cheers went up from all around but respectfully died down just as quickly.

"We have taken the field from the enemy only for the moment, and there is much work to do before we can start celebratin'. They'll come back, and no doubt in much greater numbers. We must be ready for them or it is all for naught. Are you ready to go to work?"

Again, cheers of enthusiasm rose up from all those gathered.

And, again, Mekko raised his hands attempting to quiet them. "Very well. General Valin, organize a battalion of men to go to our sanctuary caves in the Eastern Peaks. We need them to bring back fifty percent of all food and supplies we have there, as well as all the siege artillery that was saved. With your permission, Captain Layla, I'd like an equal number of Elven scouts to work with our Dwarven scouts and deploy immediately as far to the north and west and possible. I want them to report into the ranger, Archangel Royale."

He looked to the Dwarves and Men. "I need five companies of a hundred men each to get started on removing all the bodies from the field and knockin down what's left of the enemy camp. Take the bodies to the south near the sea and bury them in large holes, don't burn them. I don't want no smoke signals for a while yet. I need the engineering corps to get started on a wooden perimeter fence separating us from the Fields of Aramoor. Gather all the wood from the surrounding trees that you can, lads. I want two watchtowers put up as tall and wide as possible.

"I want five more companies of a hundred men each deployed as skirmish parties. Lads, I want every weapon or arrow that can be salvaged from the field. I want you to set up an armory, and a place for the wounded. Meanwhile, the rest of us need to set up tents for a base camp.

"Captain Gaston, Captain Layla, if I could impose upon you to set up a perimeter rovin' patrol for the time bein'. All right, lads, let's hop to it."

Mekko clapped his hands and jumped down off the rock. Instantly, everyone turned their focus on the various tasks assigned to them.

Rendek and Toran chose that moment to approach him. As the general turned to see him, he grabbed the young Dwarves by the arms and gave them each a hearty slap on the back. "Excellent work, lads. Fine display, I couldn't be prouder. You got everything right. I'll have to see about promotin' you two. You lads watch those Elves of the Emerald Watch while you're scoutin' now. You can learn a thing or two about stealth from them you hear?"

They nodded, then Rendek said, "General, we were wonderin', sir, we wanted to ask you how you could have possibly known the sun would be out this morning and to our advantage?"

"Ahh, now come with me my boys," Mekko said, as he put his arms around them. "When I was just a wee lad, I had the uncanny ability, mind you, to look at the evening sky and be able to predict, without fail, whether the sun would shine the next morning. It's always been kind of like, well, kind of like magic for lack of a better word. That's not to say other people couldn't predict such things—it's just most don't seem to have the same finely tuned skill that I do. Mind you, that's not ego talkin lads, merely a statement of fact."

For the remainder of the day, Dwarves, Elves, and Men pitched in, helping one another begin the arduous task of establishing a base camp in what was left of the land of Cordilleran. This would be where they would make their stand against whatever forces darkness had left to assail them. The removal of the dead bodies proved to be the most daunting of the labors but the most necessary. A person could hardly walk without stepping on or tripping over a body. Beneath the gray cold sky, it was a situation that lent to a maudlin atmosphere hours after their celebration.

The Elves said a prayer in homage to all those that had died, good or evil, before they began. It was distasteful to be around so much death, although they still found reason to rejoice at the alliance with their new friends. They made use of much of the equipment left behind by their enemies. Wagons and horse-drawn carts were used to load and move the bodies. Dwarven skirmish parties stripped the bodies of any armor, shields, or weapons that were still useable before loading them up for removal from the field. It was unpleasant work, but they managed to stay motivated by throwing themselves into the task with the zeal of necessity.

The first tent set up for the new camp was the largest. Set at the far south of the camp, meant for General Mekko, it would serve more as a command center than living quarters. He had always preferred to be out among his men and would even sleep with them. He could not abide officers who set themselves up as separate from their men. He believed in a chain of command, but it was the soldiers who won battles more often than officers, lords, or kings. To properly lead them, it was necessary to be among them. He stood alone inside his large tent now, waiting as night came to watch over them.

"Sir, may we enter?" General Vain asked from outside the tent.

"Yes, yes, of course, General. By all means," Mekko replied.

General Valin entered with a smaller Dwarf in tow. This Dwarf had a full head of coal-black hair down throughout his coarse beard. Despite his youth, his forearms were exceptionally well developed. The golden hammer insignia upon his tunic was explanation enough.

"General Mekko, this is Lieutenant Bainor, ranking officer among the engineering corps," General Valin said as he saluted and left the tent.

Bainor brought his fist over his heart in salute and bowed his head.

"Come in, lad, come in," Mekko said extending his hand to the younger Dwarf.

Bainor hesitated for a moment and then felt the iron grip of Mekko's firm handshake. "I am honored, General," Bainor said.

"Lad, you've had a great responsibility thrust upon your shoulders. It's a responsibility I'm bettin' you were not quite prepared for. We live in desperate times under the dark clouds of war. It is such times as these, my lad, that have come to define the greatest of those among us, those Dwarves who rose to the challenges before them and found a way to overcome them despite all the odds against them. Don't try to measure up to them or put pressure on yourself. Be your own man, make your own decisions, and stand by them." Mekko walked behind the large, round table and began scratching something down on curled parchment. He looked up. "I'm promotin' you to Commander of the engineering corps."

"Thank you, General. I am, I don't know what . . ." the young Dwarf stammered.

"Throughout our history, lad, the engineering corps has always had a special relationship with the king and the people. The Commander of the Corps answers directly to the king. Until such time as the High Council declares a king, you will answer directly to me. Is that understood?" Mekko asked, as he rolled the parchment in his hands and walked back around the table to stand before the smaller Dwarf.

He put his hands on Bainor's shoulders as if to steady him while handing him his orders. "You know the history of the Corps. I need everything they've got now, Commander. I need everything you've got." Mekko's voice now lowered to a whisper. "We need special weapons to survive this war, weapons to compensate for our smaller numbers. These weapons are to remain a secret from all, save you and I, lad. General Valin will assign guards to you, but no one is to know of them but you and me. Now, go and take command and do whatever you think will be necessary to save our people."

"Yes, General." Bainor brought his right fist over his heart and again bowed his head before leaving the tent.

General Valin reentered the tent. "What do you think about Bainor?" he asked.

"He'll do well, I think. He's a young lad, but he wears an honest face, which usually means there's a responsible mind behind it. Now make sure the perimeter is heavily guarded. We're especially vulnerable tonight. I want long-range scouts out by morning. Where are we on the supplies from the sanctuary caves

At that moment, horns of alert sounded. The two Dwarves exited the tent to the torch-lit camp outside where men were frantically running toward the west.

"Sir, an unknown force has arrived at the western checkpoint!" shouted one of the guards as he ran forward to stand with Mekko and Galin.

A moment later a dozen more Dwarves of the guard arrived around Mekko's tent. Captain Gaston and twenty mounted Sentinels arrived as well.

"General, I don't need to tell you the camp is unprepared for an attack. If they are enemies, we are not prepared to repel invaders. We may have to consider withdrawing to the mountains," the captain warned.

"Aye, Etienne, I don't much fancy fightin' nor retreatin' in this darkness. All we can do is hope for the best," Mekko replied.

A few uneasy moments passed until a lone Elven rider approached. He wore the vestment of the Emerald Watch. Mekko saw Gaston's nod, signifying he recognized the Elf as having been assigned to patrol the camp.

"General, a force of White Elves has arrived. Their leader wishes to speak to you. They are on foot and do not appear hostile," the Elf said.

"Very good, lad. I wonder if you'd give General Valin a ride on your horse there. Etienne, would you be good enough," said Mekko, as he reached his hand up toward the officer of Averon, who quickly hoisted him up on the back of his mount.

"Stand at ease, we'll be back shortly." Mekko told the Dwarves assigned as his personal guard. They watched uneasily as the men of Averon rode in escort toward the western checkpoint of their still-tattered camp. Another horse joined them from behind as they galloped west. Mekko looked back to see Elenari in a dark cloak, armed with her longbow. He smiled to himself.

It was a strange fortune that brought him such friends as Captain Gaston and Elenari. They were outlanders by Dwarven standards, yet both were as interested in keeping him safe as his own people. He knew both would fight to the death to protect him. Their bond was stronger than any spoken word could define. It was the same bond he felt with all the others. The world was a strange place, he thought, for he would gladly risk his life to keep them safe as well. It took these dark times, with the threat of war looming, to forge such bonds. Why, he wondered, was it always so difficult to forge them in times of peace?

As they approached the checkpoint, several hundred Elves formed a firing line with their bows aimed and ready. Behind and above them, an equal number of mounted sentinels stood by with bolts notched in their crossbows. Mekko saw their pale-white faces in the moonlight, though most were hooded and cloaked. He and Valin dismounted and met them at the center on his side of the line. He watched as one hooded figure approached. Mekko's keen instincts detected the subtle movement of General Valin's hand as his fingers slid gingerly around the hilt of his sword. The next moment, the figure lowered its hood, revealing a strikingly beautiful face with shoulder-length white hair, which shone silver in the half-light.

"Mya!" Elenari cried as she quickly dismounted and approached her. As she drew closer, she bowed her head. "My lady, I am pleased to see you again. I'm sure my father will be very glad you have arrived. This is General Mekko, the Alliance Commander."

"General Mekko, I am Mya Almentir. I bring twenty-five hundred White Elves who wish to join the Alliance. We are at your service." She bowed her head.

Mekko looked sharply at Valin.

"At ease! Lower your weapons!" Valin ordered.

Mekko moved forward, taking Mya's hands in his. "You are most welcome, my lady." He turned to face the White Elves standing against the night. "I am General Mekko. Here in this camp, you will find Dwarves, Men, and Elves working and fighting as one against the evil that threatens us all. On their behalf, I welcome you to our Alliance. May it endure long after the evil is vanquished."

The White Elves bowed their heads almost in unison. Smiles could be seen upon their faces far into the night.

"General Valin will see that you are quartered. After you've rested, we've great need for scouts and additional patrols within the camp. General Valin will coordinate with your officers. In the meantime, welcome to Cordilleran—such as it is."

Elenari gave Mya a firm embrace. "Ride with me. I'll take you to my father."

Mya nodded, returning the smile and mounted Elenari's horse.

As the White Elves moved through the checkpoint, Elenari leaned down to whisper in Mekko's ear, "You're really quite an eloquent speaker when you wish to be, General."

"Ahh, nothing to it, lassie," Mekko said with a smile. "Merely one of the many hats a military man must wear, always came natural to me."

Captain Gaston reached down for Mekko, but a stern look from the Dwarf caused the captain to quickly retract his hand. Gaston understood that Mekko wished to climb up into the saddle unaided in the presence of the women. Mekko tried pulling himself up once, twice, and the third time gave a huge tug on the saddle, startling Gaston's horse, which caused it to rear back and move forward, leaving Mekko flat on his face in the dirt.

Mekko popped up. "Damn that confounded dung-for-brains mule. I swear each one's dumber than the next." When he saw Elenari and Mya looking at him, he added, "Ahh yes, what I meant to say is a keen animal such as this can be easily startled. They have razor-sharp instincts, you know."

Gaston pretended to rub his shoulder and quickly opened the hand of his extended arm so that Mekko could jump up in the saddle in seemingly one motion.

"Goodnight to you, ladies," Mekko said.

"Goodnight, General," they replied.

As they rode away, traces of laughter trailed behind them.

"A nice recovery, General," Gaston said.

"Women love me, lad. It's a gift."

Wearily, Kael opened his eyes and found himself staring into Mya's beautiful, smiling face, his head resting comfortably on her chest. "Am I dreaming? If so, I hope to never awaken."

"No, you are not dreaming, my love, but go back to sleep now. I will meet you in your dreams and then I will be here when you awake from them," Mya said stroking his hair.

"Sounds like I can't go wrong," Kael said, drifting back to sleep.

Mya put his arm around her and held his head close to her bosom. She closed her eyes and felt safe. For the first time in too long, they both enjoyed a long, restful sleep.

Chapter 3

The tumultuous white-capped waves roared as the ocean drove them in a rhythmic pattern, heaving up and down as if it were taking deep breaths. An ambient sound emanated from somewhere in the distance. The flap of a few seagulls' wings came through, but the thick fog that surrounded them blocked out any sight of them. The gulls had obviously been blown off course by the previous day's storm. Nevertheless, their presence gave the sailors comfort that another form of life was also held captive within the fog.

The heavy humid air was typical for a summer's day in the Anglian Sea off the coast of the island kingdom of Bastlandia. Bastlandia was the largest single land mass of all the island kingdoms. But summer was long over. The weather had been noticeably erratic. Salty ocean waves crashed against each other, leaving a fine mist hovering in the air as if it were drizzling.

The ocean was deep in this part of the world, although no one really knew *how* deep. Very few ever ventured beneath the tips of the white caps within the Anglian Sea to find out, lest they were its unfortunate victims. Unlike the calm, crystal blue waters off the coast of Arcadia, the waters here were notoriously treacherous. Folklore held that a large sea creature known as the Brindle Squire lived deep beneath these parts of the sea. In this region, tales of its huge, dragon-like form navigating the ocean floor were plentiful.

Stories often told to the children of Bastlandia say that when the creature grows hungry, having not found food for days, it circles near the ocean top, causing the waters to swirl and become violent. The waves would smash against each other with the force of thunder. Only when the Brindle Squire found food in the whirlpool it created would the sea calm and the creature resubmerge deep to the ocean depths. Stories of the Brindle Squire were not told just among children. They became part of the Bastlandian history and culture, as an uncommon number of vessels had mysteriously disappeared or suffered unexplained accidents in this region of the sea. There were never any survivors.

Many of the ships had disappeared within the major trade route between Bastlandia and Arcadia—the two powerhouse merchants of the Southern Trade Federation. There was no other established route to various ports in the south. Many on both sides scoffed at the legends. Bastlandians claimed that the Arcadians, not the Brindle Squire, were destroying the Bastlandian trade ships. The Arcadians, on the other hand, claimed that the Bastlandians had built ships to look like the Brindle Squire. Such rhetoric had continued between the two kingdoms for nearly a thousand years. Within that time, numerous wars had been fought over trade routes. Ships and lives were lost to protect the priceless trade routes of the island kingdoms that could not survive without them. In fact, peace had only been established a century earlier when the Southern Trade Federation was formed among Bastlandia, Arcadia, and some of the smaller islands within the southern waters.

Although it was an uneasy peace, it was still the quietest time in the history of the island kingdoms. Recent rumors of establishing a Great Southern Trade Route with the Merchant Guild of the Republic of Averon on the mainland would mean new goods, new routes, and new security concerns. Whatever the case, it would seal peace agreements between all involved.

This ship cut through the waters with ease, navigating through waves and foam as if the ocean were not there to distract it. The waves broke against the hull of the ship in vain as it plowed through tons of seawater on its way to Arcadia. A constant stream of mist shot up over the bow of the ship as it dipped and lunged through the changing ocean current. The massive sails caught the wind effortlessly, reigning in the sea air and using its strength to propel the vessel through the water.

She was perhaps the largest ship ever to sail the known seas. Her massive form rested upon the ocean as if she owned it. Her sails alone, made of the finest silks, were twice the size of the largest ships. Where most large ships had two or three major masts, she had four. It took nearly two hundred men to run her. The engineers had designed a new pulley system to hoist or release the sails faster than any ship in their fleet. The hull, crafted from the finest and oldest wood from the Forest of Sandbuento, was at least five times thicker than any other ship. Metal strips reinforced the ship from top to bottom on both sides. The wood itself was treated with a glossy paste to make it non-flammable. She was truly a floating fortress.

She was the *Emerald Sea*, the flagship of Bastlandia. This was her maiden voyage, having set sail only two days earlier from port off the northwest coast of Bastlandia. She was heading to Arcadia to celebrate the hundredth anniversary of the creation of the Southern Trade Federation, and it was widely rumored that during the celebration, the treaties to establish the Great Southern Trade Route would be signed as well. The ship's crew had been hand-picked by King Zarian himself. From deck hand to the captain, each man was proud and honored to represent Bastlandia in this way.

As a warship, the *Emerald Sea* knew no equal. She was over three hundred feet in length. She had four enormous ballistae, two fore and two aft. Each fired a bolt projectile nearly ten feet in length. She had twenty catapults with ten starboard and ten port, each capable of supporting hundred-pound rocks in addition to flaming pitch. Perhaps her most devastating weapon, however, was concealed on the lowest deck near the water level. It was a huge retractable metal blade that required twenty men to hand crank to release it. It was capable of cutting through the hull of any enemy vessel ship, causing enough damage to quickly sink it.

The *Emerald Sea* was not only the flagship of Bastlandia and its most powerful warship but also a merchant vessel. It had a cargo hold enabling it to carry more than five times the payload of Bastlandia's average cargo vessel. Despite the fact that it doubled as a battleship, it was escorted by a convoy of five smaller vessels, three war galleys, and two frigates with more than enough firepower to ward off any pirates or greedy kingdoms.

A portly man in a red satin robe looked over the port bow of the *Emerald Sea* into the thick fog. "Truly a work of magnificent craftsmanship," he said to the striking woman beside him who stood nearly a foot taller than he. She wore a white gown with a pearl-lined low-cut neck.

As Helena wiped the sea mist from her brow, she was thankful for the brief respite from the bald spot on her husband's head when he looked up at her. She contemplated the effect that the humidity had on her own, normally well-coifed hair. Frizzy wisps escaped from her tightly knotted bun in an unflattering way. She'd been perspiring and felt perpetually dirty since boarding the *Emerald Sea*.

Though she lived a life of privilege as the wife of the ambassador, Helena often wondered if it was worth the tradeoff of happiness. "Mmmhmm," she murmured in response to her husband's comment, but her thoughts had wandered to the young sailor she'd secreted away with the night before.

As the ship lurched forward, Ambassador Bartholomew Piedmont pulled her close. His large belly cushioned them as they leaned against the rail. "Five years in the making, the most powerful ship ever built is completely at *my* disposal."

Helena pulled herself away from him, quickly bringing her hands up to her hair. "The only reason it's completely at your disposal is because the king is too ill to make the trip," she said.

Ignoring her comment, Piedmont looked over his shoulder to see almost all the men on deck busily carrying out their duties. "Can you picture their faces, my dear? They will be bowled over by the site of this remarkable ship and her convoy when we pull into port. Yes, I'd say the Arcadians will be quite jealous. Wouldn't you say, my dear?"

Helena rolled her eyes, but he was not looking. It didn't matter if she agreed or not.

Piedmont went on, "They are not capable of crafting a ship such as this. Heavens no! This just may be enough to sway the Southern Trade Federation to hand over the security of the Great Southern Trade Route exclusively to Bastlandia. I think they will have no choice but to realize their shipments will be safest aboard the *Emerald Sea*." He laughed at an attempt to brush the hair from his combover out of his face.

"All will see your triumphant arrival in Arcadia," Helena said, feeling the color drain from her face from an uptick in the waves. *No one will miss this monstrosity*, she thought.

"The king should be a little more aggressive with the trade agreements now that we have such a marvelous ship. Not that I'm criticizing his highness. No, never that, however"—he looked about the deck as the men moved about—"I just feel that the Arcadians should be a little more willing to let us take some of the more profitable trade routes. If that means we must flex our muscles some, then by all means let us flex them." He pounded his hand on the rail.

Helena nearly lost her balance. She thought again about the sailor to distract herself as the ship increased its speed, while her husband's voice droned on.

"The king worries too much about upsetting the status quo, about being perceived as threatening in a time of peace. No, no, no, now is the time, I say, to show the Federation just what we are made of." Again, Piedmont struck the rail.

Several deck hands saluted as they hurried past the regal couple. The ambassador returned their salute and lowered his voice. "You know there are many others who feel this way as well, Helena. Yes, some are just fed up with the lack of growth in the Bastlandian economy. Some would even say that Arcadia is gaining the upper hand in the disputed trade routes. Imagine that. Well, not for much longer, I'd dare say, not after this amazing feat." He made a sweeping gestured toward the deck. "Now, I'm not saying the king is wrong, you know I'd never say that, but we must seize the momentum and take that which we rightly deserve."

This time when he struck the rail, he hit bone and let out a curse. Piedmont massaged his injury with the palm of his other hand. Helena did not bother to pretend she cared.

The enormous sails above were now completely taut, catching all the power the wind had to offer. The fog traveled with them, not dispersing with the increased wind as they had hoped. The sailor had whispered to Helena the night before that fog was a bad omen, especially in these waters, though no sailor would voice that aloud to another. With fog came the unknown and the unseen.

"Excuse me, Ambassador," said a young sailor with a prompt salute.

"Captain sent word he would like to see you in his cabin, at your convenience. I would be honored to escort you."

"Certainly, my boy. We shouldn't keep the captain waiting. He's a very busy man." Ambassador Piedmont turned back toward his wife, only now taking note of the pallor of her face and the strained fashion in which she held herself against the rail. "Why, my dear, you look a trifle rumbled. Haven't got your sea legs yet? Why don't you tidy up a bit? Yes, yes, tidy up. When I'm finished with the captain, we can have a nice lunch together." He stood on his tiptoes to give her a slight peck on the cheek and then scurried away.

Helena leaned over the railing and vomited.

The ambassador and deckhand moved briskly across the massive deck, weaving in and out of sailors and between the enormous masts rooted into the deck's floor. For a moment, the ambassador stopped to look around, waiting for the young man to point him in the right direction. They continued heading toward the bow of the ship, then into a doorway and down a dark flight of stairs to a landing. The ambassador had grown slightly out of breath by the time they reached the bottom.

The young man pointed down a narrow corridor to their right. "This way, Ambassador."

"I think I can find my way, young man. I studied the blueprints of this vessel quite closely during its construction," Piedmont replied with a bit of a pompous air and turned down the left corridor.

Knowing full well that passage ended in a dead end, the young man waited patiently as the ambassador disappeared around a corner.

A moment later, Piedmont reappeared. "Just testing you, boy. Now then, to the captain's cabin. Lead on, that's a good lad."

"Of course, sir."

They weaved through the passageway to the right and back up a small set of stairs that stopped at a large oak door with an anchor-shaped knocker. A single word was etched into the plaque on the door: "Captain."

Piedmont waved the young deckhand away. "I'll take it from here, back to work now."

The young man turned on his heels, mumbling under his breath, and disappeared into the dark hallways. The ambassador straightened his robe and cleared his throat before striking the metal knocker against the door.

After a moment, a deep voice from within called, "Enter."

Piedmont opened the door, filling the passageway with light. The door creaked as it shut behind him.

Though a captain's cabin was always the largest and most comfortable aboard any vessel, this chamber felt more like the lavish accommodations of a palace. Large candelabras lit the center of the room; they supported by oil lamps on the walls that flickered with the breeze, which came from the far side of the room. Fine paintings adorned most of the four walls, mostly depicting naval heroes of Bastlandia's past as well as a portrait of King Zarian, the current sovereign, above a large chair behind a mahogany desk. Bowls of fresh fruit decorated the large wooden table, which took up nearly half the available space. The tables and chairs were bolted to the floor along with the accompanying leather ottomans. Portholes, which lined the two far walls, were open, allowing the smell and sound of the salty ocean to diffuse through the room.

As Piedmont moved slowly forward, taking it all in, his eyes fell on a built-in cabinet housing fine china. Some china and silver flatware had already been set upon the table in three places, backed with leather-winged chairs.

Near the back of the chamber, beneath an open porthole, sat Captain Benjamin Montague, smoking a pipe, and holding a rolled-up parchment. He promptly stood up to greet his guest. "Ambassador Piedmont, welcome. Please come in."

The captain's voice was deep and gruff, always seeming to trail off at the end of his sentences, which made it difficult to understand his last words. Though his jacket covered the mark, it was well known that Captain Montague had a large battle scar across his throat, which impeded his speech on occasion.

The ambassador approached with an extended hand. "Captain Montague, wonderful to finally meet you informally without all the ceremony of our glorious departure. I'm very proud to meet a true hero of the Bastlandian way. Yes, very proud to meet you indeed."

The captain returned his handshake. "Thank you, sir, most gracious of you." The gray-haired, bearded officer pulled his hand away, took the pipe out of his mouth, and blew smoke from the corner of his lips.

Piedmont noticed the crispness of his blue uniform with perfect creases in both jacket and pants. The standard tri-bar gold tassels of a captain hung from his shoulders while various medals and ribbons adorned his navy-blue military jacket. Montague was, after all, their most combat-decorated naval officer and quite probably their most experienced commander.

"Please, Ambassador, sit. May I pour you . . ." His question trailed off.

"Sorry, Captain, didn't catch that."

"Wine, sir, let me pour you some wine," the captain said louder, with the same groggy voice. "I was hoping you and your wife could join me for lunch. I can send someone for her, or is she already on her way?"

Piedmont took one of the winged-back seats at the table and eagerly unfolded a napkin in his lap. "I am delighted to join you, Captain, but, unfortunately, Helena will be unable to. She looked a frightful mess a little while ago."

Montague winced. He could not bear the thought of lunch with the ambassador without at least Helena's beauty to distract him from Piedmont's incessant rambling. He had been putting it off for two days now, but it seemed there would truly be no escape from it this day. He filled the ambassador's goblet.

"Yes, wine, wonderful. Wet the palate a little if you will," Piedmont chuckled. "Warm you up from the biting salt wind. Even helps clear the min—"

"I have here the nautical maps and the route we shall be taking to Arcadia," Montague interrupted. "Should be about four days until we hit Arcadian shipping lanes; then another five days until we hit land." He put his pipe back in his mouth.

"Ah yes, very good, Captain," said Piedmont, holding the edge of the table to keep steady as the ship swayed to one side. The chandeliers overhead swayed menacingly and the thought of their crashing down on his head struck him. He shook it off and said, "Captain, now that we have this time alone, there is something I'd like to discuss with you.

Something I think may be of interest to us both. There are some people in the aristocracy who feel, well, they feel the kingdom is not going in the right direction." He took a sip of wine and nodded his approval.

After generously buttering a large piece of bread and taking a hardy bite, the ambassador rose and walked along the edges of the cabin, observing the many paintings and swords decorating the walls.

"They feel the king is . . . soft, weak." He turned to the captain.

With that, Montague quickly removed the pipe from his mouth and threw his napkin on his plate.

"They feel he is unable to gain the respect of certain classes within our society, mainly the military. Yes, he has his elite guard, the High Riders, but they've become almost a decadent symbol of a time long since passed. Let's face it, Captain, the navy should be our primary focus in these times. Times in which the fleets of Arcadia are thought to be superior to our own. I must admit, not to blow my own horn, but if it had not been for my presence on the Homeland Security Committee, this magnificent vessel would never have been built."

Montague stood up slowly and paid careful attention to the ambassador now.

"Some believe our country needs a stronger figure at the helm, so to speak." The ambassador smiled widely. "Someone who will truly fight for what is rightfully ours and who would never back down to Arcadia and the Trade Federation. Of course, this person would need someone with military experience to back him, be his right hand as it were. Someone who could help lead the country into a new era of power and prestige as our forefathers once envisioned."

"Tell me, Ambassador, who would this pompous, self-important, traitorous fool be?" Montague questioned, putting his pipe forcefully back into his mouth.

"Well now, Captain, we—"

A sudden boom from outside rocked the cabin; even the bolted down furniture shuddered.

"What the devil!" the Captain shouted, racing into the narrow corridor.

The ambassador followed. As they headed up the ladder and emerged on the main deck, a second explosion shook the ship. Panic shouts came from everywhere as the crew rushed about. Piedmont stumbled into the captain from behind.

"What the hell is going on?" Montague yelled, side-stepping Piedmont's weight.

"The convoy is under attack, sir!" one young deckhand cried.

"Battle stations!" the captain shouted. "All hands on deck. Secure the masts, standby catapults. Stay focused on your jobs!" With that, he raced up a small ladder to the bridge. "Master of the vessel, raise the ship's colors if you please," he said more calmly, as he extended his eyeglass to survey for a sign of the enemy.

He was a man who was no stranger to combat, and the men under his command knew it. With that, men on both sides of the main deck beat large bells signaling the vessel to battle readiness. The decks of the flagship buzzed like an anthill. Every sailor moved fast as he could. Men climbed the masts to secure the sails and take lookout positions, and archers took their places from high aloft on small battle towers constructed from intricate woodwork far above the deck. Gun crews quickly moved the catapults into place.

"Who would dare to attack us?" yelled Piedmont, astonished as he peered over the bow to see one of the frigates in the convoy. It was the *Royal Meridian*, and she was burning out of control and dead in the water.

Montague quickly ran up to the steering deck and told the sailor at the wheel, "Come about twenty-five degrees. Stand by port catapults."

The men immediately sprang to work. Though the fog obscured their attackers, the steadiness of the captain's orders snapped them to attention. The sails were quickly secured, and the catapults were pushed into place in moments.

"Captain, I demand to know what is happening!" the ambassador said nervously, finally having reached him.

The captain looked at the ambassador and pulled out his pipe. "We're under attack, you dolt!"

The captain ordered his men to signal the convoy to tighten its formation and prepare for battle. The fog was still thick and the smell of smoke and burning wood permeated the air as the crew watched in horror as the *Royal Meridian* was swallowed up by the waves. The remaining four ships of the convoy moved into a defensive ring, closely surrounding the *Emerald Sea* and prepared their catapults to fire.

"Captain, I suggest you deal with this situation immediately!" yelled Piedmont.

"Ambassador, you will be good enough to confine yourself to your quarters, sir, until this is over, if you please. And go back, please, and make sure your wife is attended to." He turned his back on Piedmont. "Gun crews, stand by starboard catapults," Montague said formally.

"May I remind you, Captain, I have final authority here, not you," the ambassador said.

A huge boom followed by a whistling sound overhead snapped Piedmont's jaw shut. The *King's Majesty*, a frigate off the port bow, had been hit mid-ship with a force none had seen before. Planks of wood shot into the air like matchsticks as their main mast crashed to the deck. The ship was instantly aflame. Men scurried around the deck in such a panic that it was total chaos. The *King's Majesty* began listing to her port side.

"Listen to him, that man's in charge!" Piedmont yelled, pointing at Montague. He threw his hands over his head and ran for the ladder.

"Master-at-arms, secure the ambassador in his quarters. I don't want to see his fat head near my bridge again until this is over!" Montague yelled, as his pipe fell from his mouth.

"Aye, Captain."

The fog was still making it impossible to see where their enemy was. How was it possible, Montague thought, that the *Royal Meridian* could be sunk so quickly and without warning? How could one shot have crippled the *King's Majesty* so? What sort of weapon could do that kind of damage? He peered through the fog for their mysterious attacker. It was eerie how suddenly quiet it was, save for the tide splashing against the ship. It was time for action.

"Hard to port! Fire all starboard catapults!" Montague yelled.

Ten catapults launched huge blocks of stone into the obscure haze of the fog. Moments later, large splashes could be heard in the distance. Such a barrage would tear apart even a war galley. However, there were no sounds of hits. How was this unseen enemy able to strike their ships unerringly? They too should be safe, obscured in the blanket of the fog, but it seemed they were sitting ducks.

Again, as if in answer to their blind attack, another boom shattered the silence. A whistling sound pierced the air, forcing some of the men to cover their ears. Whatever was fired exploded in the lower decks of the *King's Majesty*. Within moments, flames engulfed the vessel.

The remaining ships in the convoy began to shoot their catapults starboard, in vain, at the heavy fog. Though smaller than the catapults aboard the *Emerald Sea*, the convoy's weapons were still formidable. The heavy stones flung into the foggy depths splashed into the ocean, hitting nothing. Occasionally, a seaman would think he saw something black moving in the distance, but the lookouts could neither confirm nor deny it. All ships continued to fire their catapults due starboard to no avail.

"All ships hold their fire!" yelled Montague, as he continued scanning the cloudy banks in all directions. He had three war galleys left all in tight formation around him. He didn't like it. With this new weapon fired into the heart of them, they would have no problem hitting something. "Master's mate, signal the *Pride*, tell her to make sail due west. Then, signal the *Queens Grace*, have her make sail due east. Signal the *Conquest*, have her make sail off our bow steady as she goes. Smartly if you please, Mr. Ashkin," the captain ordered. "Master of the ship, prepare to make sail on my mark," Montague said.

"All hands prepare to make sail," said Commander Jonathan Finch, Montague's second in command. Finch waited as the order was repeated down the length of the ship so all the men could hear. He watched with satisfaction as the men scurried up the four masts in place to release the sails. He used the moment to join the captain on the bridge near the wheel. "Sir, what do you think?"

"I think, Jonathan, we need to give our enemy more targets to shoot at while we try to flank her," Montague said through the side of his mouth, handing his spyglass to Finch.

Montague moved beside the wheel and placed his arm on the shoulder of the able seaman manning it, then he waited. He gazed outward as the three war galleys opened their sails and began to slowly distance themselves from his vessel.

"Just a little further now," Montague said as he looked upward, feeling a slight gust of wind. "All hands make sail! Course one hundred eighty degrees hard over!" Montague pressed the young sailor's shoulder as he turned the wheel with all his might to bring the vessel around. Almost as one, sails rolled down throughout the four masts; however, it was a slow turn, and the wind was not in their favor. In the time it would take for the ship to completely around, they would be vulnerable.

"Mr. Finch, put us in that thick patch of fog astern, if you please," Montague said.

"Very good, sir," Finch replied.

The war galleys were nearly out of sight in the surrounding fog when the consistent sound of six separate explosions were heard, followed by the deafening whistling noise they'd come to know and fear. Before they could react, they saw six flaming balls hit the *Pride* in succession on what would be her port side. The ship burst into flames as charred wood flew several feet in the air, splashing down in many places. Body parts, as well as screams of sheer terror cut wickedly short, filled the air. The *Pride* was gone. Though they could not see for sure, they knew she had been destroyed instantly.

Hopelessness overtook the crew of the *Emerald Sea*, and men began to yell, "We surrender!" Some of the younger boys were crying. Captain Montague watched as his crew became so demoralized that there was some standing on the railings, considering jumping.

"Shut up! Shut up, all of you!" screamed Montague as he pulled his sword from its scabbard and held it above his head. "Remember who you are and what country you call home." He pulled the pipe from his mouth and yelled so hard that his face burned red and sweat poured down his brow. "We are Bastlandians! We are the heroes of this sea. Like your fathers and their fathers before them, we will not run from the enemy. We will not throw down our swords in defeat. I say to you today, if this ship is to be our burial ground, then by the gods of Bastlandia, I die a proud and happy man! By the king's honor, we will not go down without a fight! We will fight like Bastlandians, to the death!"

The crew roared back, "To the death! To the death!"

"Let's hear it for the captain, lads!" said Finch.

The crew roared again, renewed with faith in the courageous officer who led them.

"Now back to your stations, and let's give them hell!" Montague screamed as the men ran back to their posts. "We'll do the hunting now!"

The other ships were out of view now but four loud blasts reverberated in the distance. "Eyes open!" the captain yelled to his lookouts. "Eyes open for anything that moves!"

The *Emerald Sea's* sails began catching the wind and moved the ship into the thick fog bank. It was so thick the men had difficulty seeing each other on deck.

"Very good, Mr. Finch. Ninety degrees hard to port. I mean to come around behind them whoever they are," Montague said.

There would be foul magic at work indeed if they were hit in this smoke screen. As they turned again, another boom sounded in the distance, louder and closer than before. It seemed to be whistling toward them from above.

"Incoming fire, all hands get down!" yelled the young sailors from the lookout's roost.

It smashed into the forward bow of the ship's hull with a crash, shaking the vessel and the men aboard her. A moment later, all the men on the main deck rose to their feet. A few pieces of decking crumpled and splintered along the bow but that was it.

"You see, boys, this ain't no matchstick model," the captain said as he got to his feet.

The crewmen cheered in answer.

"Prepare forward ballistae, all catapults at the ready!" Montague yelled as he watched them push two enormous ballistae to the edge of the forward bow. "Ballistae crews go for the main sails of the largest ship you can target. Catapult crews aim toward the masts." Montague looked forward through his spyglass, still seeing no sign of the enemy.

"Ship sighting, sir! Forty-five degrees off the port quarter. It's the *Queen's Grace*, sir. She appears intact," the lookouts reported.

"Very good, we'll be hitting them from two sides," Montague whispered.

Boom, boom, boom, boom, four bursts shot through the fog somewhere in the distance.

"Forward men, steady as she goes," Montague snapped.

For several moments there was silence, save for the splashing against the hull. No attacks, no flaming metal balls flying through the sky. As Montague looked through his spyglass, he saw that the fog was finally letting up ahead. The *Queen's Grace* and the *Emerald Sea* were converging on the enemy.

"Silence on deck," the captain said as he heard the order repeated down through the length of the deck.

"Ships sighted ahead, sir! Multiple ships sighted dead ahead, sir!" the lookouts roared from high atop the main mast.

The whole crew came forward, straining to see through the fog.

Montague pulled the pipe from his mouth and watched intently through his spyglass. "Eyes open, my boys! Weapons ready, on my mark!" he yelled.

As the *Emerald Sea* pushed through the breaking fog, her crew and captain stared dumfounded at the sight before them. Five black vessels, smaller than frigates, stood atop the waves before them. They were the strangest vessels any of them had ever seen on water. They were ships of some kind, but much of the vessels appeared to be floating below the water while the top stuck out above the water's surface. The top sections were like a great shell composed of a thick, black, painted metal. Several round turrets jutted out from the tops of the ships in all directions. There were no sails or even oars that could be seen. They just floated there.

"Fire!" screamed Montague. The great bolts from the twin ballistae fired, each striking the top of an enemy vessel and just as quickly bouncing off the metal that covered their hulls, harmlessly falling to the ocean. "Hard over!" yelled Montague, pointing to the starboard side. He and the crew held fast as the giant wheel quickly turned them to the right, exposing their port side. "Fire all catapults! Again!" he screamed.

The ten catapults fired one after the other, sending huge chunks of stone into the air, nearly all of which struck several of the enemy vessels. With each hit, the crew let out cheers that died away as the stones bounced off, leaving little more than a dent in the metal.

All five of the enemy had at least some of their turrets pointed at them: They fired together. There was a flash, and then a small explosion came from the black turrets. They fired a circular projectile, which appeared to be flaming pitch, but they struck like thunderbolts, tearing through the ships. They had to be metal of some sort, thought Montague, but how were they firing them with such velocity and power? This explained the greater range from which the enemy was able to attack, but it did not explain how they were able to target them in the fog.

At any rate, the fog *was* dissipating, and the *Emerald Sea* was a large slow-moving target, easy prey for such vessels. They took several hits below decks that rocked the battleship, sometimes carving through the wood like hot knives through butter, sending planks flying and men to the floor, but still the *Emerald Sea* kept her bearing. The non-flammable pastes coating the wood kept the ship from setting aflame, which also prolonged their lives.

As the fog cleared further, they could see the *Conquest* now in the distance beyond the *Queen's Grace*. The *Conquest's* hull crackled, little more than burning wreckage afloat.

Captain Montague had had the wind knocked out of him. He looked around for the Master's mate to signal the *Queen's Grace*, only to see him sprawled behind the wheel with a jagged piece of wood buried through half his neck. His eyes glazed upward. A young boy was brushing himself off near the body. Montague took the wheel himself and called to the boy.

"Come here, boy. You know the flag signs to signal the other ships? Come on, boy, out with it!" Montague said impatiently, though he quickly regretted it when he took a moment to look the boy in the eye. He was maybe sixteen and had never seen death up close before. Montague looked about the deck, some bodies lay unmoving, but most of the men were still functioning, keeping their fear in check awaiting orders. He saw Finch running toward the bridge and turned back to the young seaman at his side. "Signal the *Queen's Grace* for me, boy, one last time."

Montague adjusted his hat and lit his pipe once again.

The boy picked up the signal flags and looked at the captain questioningly. "What shall I signal them, sir?" the boy asked softly.

"Tell them," Montague turned his gaze upon the boy, "tell them prepare for ramming."

The boy's face went pale, and he turned away to look at the enemy ships. "Sir?"

"There is no life I would rather live than that of an old man on the sea," Montague spoke softly and then turned back to his young flagman. "There is no place I would rather rest than beneath the waves of the ocean's crest." He placed his right hand on the boy's arm and patted him like a father would to his son. "Signal them, boy, signal them one last time."

The boy obeyed, waving his flags with vigor and determination, fear gripping his soul. It took a moment for the *Queen's Grace* to reply.

"They, they are ready sir," the young man said.

"Very well. Mr. Finch, put her into the wind and aim her at that cluster of enemy ships. All hands prepare for ramming!"

It took most of them a few moments to digest the order, but they knew. They knew it was over. They knew this would be their end. Though they would surely die here today, with the rest of the convoy, they would go down fighting.

Finch knew immediately what the captain meant to do. He made eye contact with him for a moment and smiled bitterly at the man who had been his mentor and, in some ways, father. Montague returned his look with a nod and a smile. No more orders were necessary. Without hesitation, Finch grabbed three seamen and headed below deck.

Montague had the wheel and turned his vessel toward the grouping of five enemy ships, hoping to pick up enough speed to destroy or damage most of them. He looked to the port side and saw the *Queen's Grace* was now in position, about fifty yards off the port bow. He looked back down the front of the main deck below, where his remaining men awaited any final orders. They stared back at him, some of the younger men with faces stricken by fear, the older men with stern, determined looks. The captain blew a puff of smoke from his nose.

"Let me say to you all," he yelled so everyone could hear him, "let me say what an honor it has been to serve with you and to serve aboard this ship." He stepped forward, leaned on the railing of the bridge, and looked down at them. "What an honor it has been." His voice trailed off.

The men screamed back that the honor had been theirs.

Captain Benjamin Montague smiled and took the wheel steady as she goes toward the enemy. "*Great Bastlandian land of mine...*" he started to sing, "*Born from start of time. Serving King or Queen to death. Ruling oceans both east and west.*"

The rest of the men joined him in singing their country's anthem loud and strong as the captain held and steered the wheel fast and true. The enemy lay straight ahead. The *Emerald Sea* was tremendous compared to the smaller metal-topped enemies. Luck was with her as the wind filled her sails, helping her gain the momentum she might need to seriously damage them.

Finch and his crew moved rapidly down through the damaged lower decks over and around bodies of their comrades until they realized they had crossed below sea line when they saw evidence of minor flooding. They moved both down and forward. There might be a chance, if the lower hull of the enemy ships were wooden, they could still win the day, but if they were the strong metal that they had seen thus far, this would be for naught. Still, it would not be the first time he saw the captain turn certain death into victory. Suddenly, they heard three explosions from the distance.

"Incoming fire!" yelled the lookouts from the forecastle.

The balls of flame slammed into the forward main deck, sending wood and metal shards everywhere. Men screamed as their cloths caught on fire. Others lay on the deck screaming and dying limbs severed from the explosion. Amazingly, the hull of the *Emerald Sea* was barely damaged.

She was closing fast now on the five enemy ships. It was then five more explosive balls shot forth from the enemy's turrets. The flaming metal balls smashed into the bow, sending shards of wood as far aft as the bridge. Montague ducked, covering his face from the flames and debris. Though the shots had penetrated the bow, still it was not enough to cause a hull breach.

Montague pulled himself up by the wheel and looked ahead, horrified to see more enemy vessels than they first thought. Five more ships broke off from the main body and began moving slowly toward the *Queen's Grace*.

"Steady!" screamed Montague as he watched the five ships split up in a wide formation. "They will try to encircle us. "Hard to Port!" The order was redundant as he was the man at the wheel, but the ship responded by lurching port and moved head on with two of the enemy ships.

"Prepare to deploy Hull Razor," said Mr. Finch to the men around the crank wheel. He looked out a small glass portal and could see the distance to the enemy ship. The monstrous metal retractable ram, known as the Hull Razor, was referred to by the men as the *Hell Razor*, which is precisely what it would do to any normal ship' however, even he could see underwater that the enemy appeared to be covered with metal, even below the water's surface. "Engage Hull Razor." Finch watched as the men pushed the circular crank with all their might releasing the secret weapon of the *Emerald Sea*.

Montague felt the *Emerald Sea* vibrate. He knew the underwater ram had been deployed. Two flaming balls rocketed into the two forward masts, breaking them in two, collapsing them onto the deck with a thunderous impact. killing at least a dozen men. They still had the main mast, and the mizzenmast, and they were still lined up for a head-on collision.

"Steady," he whispered to himself.

The enemy had expected them to be halted, but they were not. He watched from the corner of his eyes as three enemy ships had broken away from the *Queen's Grace* and altered course toward the *Emerald Sea*. Suddenly, the enemy fired three balls of fire into the starboard side, sending fragments of wood all through the air. Dozens of men fell as the middle sail caught fire and spread up the mast. Men shouted for help as the fire spread to the sails of the mizzenmast. Still, the *Emerald Sea* did not falter in her course.

Montague wiped the sweat and blood from his brow and kept the ship on target. "Hang on!" he screamed as the *Emerald Sea* closed to just a few yards of the enemy. The ship directly ahead tried to veer off so as not to be hit, but it was too late. The Hull Razor hit metal and a terrible wrenching sound, shrouded and masked by the ocean, could still be heard and felt as the *Emerald Sea* slammed into the port side of the enemy ship with such force that all aboard were thrown forward into a heap. Some were even catapulted over the bow into the water.

Montague himself had been thrown off the bridge to the middle of the main deck. With all his strength, he crawled to the forward bow to see that the Hull Razor had been torn off, taking a good portion of the lower bow with it. The hull had been compromised and the lower decks were rapidly flooding. He looked to the enemy vessel, which had smoke billowing from its starboard turrets. It was listing heavily to its port. They had dealt it a critical blow. He turned and raced back toward the bridge.

He covered his head as the sails were engulfed in flames. The men on the deck either lay dead or dying. He could see the aft quarter of the ship rising out of the water, listing toward the forward bow. *Emerald Sea* was in her death throes.

He reached the bridge in time to see the enemy vessel capsize. He had done it. They destroyed one. They were not invincible. He tried madly, in vain, to turn the ship to the port toward the next enemy vessel, but the rudder had been damaged, and Montague realized that the *Emerald Sea* was dead in the water. With all his might, he continued turning the wheel as if he might be able to steer the ship. Water was rushing on to the foredeck as the ship continued its slow descent into the ocean, bow first. Finally, both the center and mizzenmasts collapsed under the strain on the port side of the ship.

Holding fast to the wheel, Montague stood up. Wiping blood from his eyes just to see a last vision of the *Queen's Grace* engulfed in flames and sinking fast. The fog had cleared completely now, replaced with the smoke of burning ships. As he looked down the listing deck, he could see *none* of his men still alive. They laid scattered on the deck. Perhaps, Montague thought, the enemy would try to board her and take him prisoner.

"Over my dead body!" he yelled in protest to the idea. The captain pulled his sword from his side and waited. Smoke from the fires had made it difficult to see. The winds blew up and through the smoke, as the *Emerald Sea* leaned heavily on the port side and began its descent to the ocean floor.

Montague looked ahead, holding fast to the wheel so he would not slip forward. "Gods be merciful," he said as his pipe fell from his lips. His final sight was that of an enemy armada of some forty to fifty black, metal-plated ships bearing down on his position.

The horizon line appeared bloodred, spread across the ocean as the sun set over the Anglian Sea. It was calm, with small waves splashing against one another. Seagulls rested in the water, tired from their long sojourn from land. In the distance, the sound of thunder echoed. Another storm was brewing.

Chapter 4

It took the Alliance army three days to remove the thousands of corpses and assorted weapons from the Fields of Aramoor. The previous day, the battalion that had been dispatched to the sanctuary caves of the Eastern Peaks arrived with much-needed supplies for their new base camp.

A drizzling rain greeted Cordilleran that morning as General Mekko pulled his cloak close about him to fight off the chill of yet another gray morning. He stood atop the small mountains, which flanked the once pristine courtyard that the *Barrick Cropaal* had formerly protected from the outside world. Now, the courtyard was little more than scorched earth, both burnt and blackened.

Two Dwarves stood behind him, Toran and Rendek, whom he had promoted to his personal guards. He instructed them to follow him everywhere and keep their eyes open. To them, it was a duty of the greatest honor, which they obeyed solemnly and with pride.

Mekko turned from the courtyard and looked down to the Fields of Aramoor, trying to remember how bright the green grasslands had been on a spring day before they had degenerated to a field of mud.

"I sometimes think, lads, that if it would just rain and keep on raining enough, all the filth of this world would wash away. It never does though." His voice was a whisper. "It always stops. Then all the filth comes out to dry, and the world remains as dirty as it had been before the rain began."

"Sir?" asked Toran.

"Things always look just a wee bit different from higher up, though, don't they?" Mekko said as if thinking aloud.

Work had begun on the perimeter fence and watchtowers; the rain did not hinder the engineering corps. The special weapons he had requested were under construction as well. Roving patrols of Elves, Dwarves, and Men guarded them in all directions. They also had long-range scouts deployed to the north and west, looking for signs of the enemy.

Mekko knew everything that could be done to prepare was being done, yet something about their efforts felt woefully inadequate. He wished the king were there with him. Crylar had a way of inspiring those around him to overcome adversity and succeed. Now, the Dwarven people were his responsibility, at least until the council appointed a new king. He was host to the Alliance forces, but there was little to offer them. Cordilleran was in no condition to show them true Dwarven hospitality. There would be no feasting, no songs, no expertly brewed beers save what they could scavenge form the sanctuary caves. These things and more weighed heavily upon his mind.

Elenari sat within her tent, legs crossed, palms up and open. Her eyes were gently closed as the rhythm of the rain against the tent eased her into a meditative state of semiconsciousness. Meditation was as vital to the warrior as development of the physical body. She focused on the teachings of High Master Reyblade.

The body is the sword, the mind is that which wields the blade.

She listened for the quiet voice within her but often heard and saw other events through her efforts. Now, she saw Algernon—he was speaking to her, but she could not make out what he was saying. His face and form were clouded, and vague static drowned out the words. She saw a modest cottage in the hills, not unlike her own home with Kael, in Wrenford.

She opened her eyes abruptly. She had heard Algernon's voice with crystal clarity. Just three words had broken through as the vision faded: *Seek the knowledge.*

Often her meditations resulted in strange or unusual visions; however, this was the first time someone who had died seemed to speak to her directly. She decided it was more than just a curious omen. The more her thoughts cleared, the more the vision took on a singular meaning to her.

The tome of Algernon contained knowledge—unknown secrets observed firsthand by one who lived through them.

Beneath the jeweled scabbard of *Eros-Arthas,* her sacred blade, was a tightly bound burlap bag. She reached in and produced the leather-bound tome entrusted to her by the late Sage, Algernon. It had been placed in her keeping for its protection, but now she knew she must read it. It was a huge book. She was tempted to skim the pages but resisted. Instead, she lit a candle and started at the beginning.

"My lady," Galin said in Elvish as he stood outside Layla's tent.

"Come in," came her feminine reply.

"My Lord Calindir." Layla bowed her head and bade him to enter.

"Food has arrived from the Dwarven sanctuary. I thought you might be hungry so I brought you something to eat." Galin handed her a full plate and then turned as if to leave.

"Will you not stay and dine with me?" Layla asked.

"If it pleases you, my lady," he said, smiling.

He looked around, amazed at how she had transformed the drab tent. She had over a dozen candles lit. He recognized the aroma immediately. They were *iniri,* candles that gave off the fragrances of flowers. With her vestment and forest clothes removed, she wore only a white gown, which seemed to brighten the tent even more than the light from the candles.

He watched as she sat perfectly, making no noise. She wore her hair tied back, revealing more of her face and her pointed ears. Here, in this light, she appeared more as the princess and daughter of a king than soldier. She wore no jewelry, makeup, or feminine trappings. She was breathtaking.

She looked at him with a short smile before she began eating. The blue of her eyes was strangely radiant, a characteristic he found inherent in the Elven people. A bond had formed between them, and they had become increasingly closer the past few days.

"Would you like to know why I never referred to you as Lord Calindir in the past?" Layla asked, her lips curving into a sly smile.

"Yes, now that you mention it, I believe I would," Galin replied with curiosity.

"It's because we never spoke before." Layla said.

"That's not—" Galin hesitated, looking down and away as if trying to remember correctly.

Layla faced him with wide eyes. "You were saying?"

"Well, I, I regret if that is so," Galin conceded.

"I regret it as well, considering my father treated you like a son. Did you choose the name Calindir for yourself when you were appointed Druid of Alluvium?"

"You are most perceptive." Galin bowed his head.

"Not really, you are not of Elven blood. It would have been strange if your human parents gave you an Elven name, I think. What is the translation in your tongue, 'He who is for all seasons'?" Layla smiled as she asked the question.

"He who is *at one* with all seasons, my lady," Galin responded. He smiled back, knowing full well she knew the translation.

"Lord Calindir, I wonder if the time will come where you would be kind enough to address me as Layla." She put down her plate and stared deeply into his eyes.

Captivated by her beauty, it took him a moment to respond. "By rights, my lady, I should address you as Princess Layla, though I know you would find that distasteful."

"Not distasteful, merely unnecessary. I am more a soldier than a princess, wouldn't you agree?" Her eyes did not waver from his.

As he stared back, he found himself thinking about his friend Hawk. Hawk had hidden his feelings from Elenari, nearly until the end of his life. He wondered how much it had cost him and what it had cost her. He had always thought it was foolish of Hawk to deny his feelings, but now he understood. He rose and walked to the flap of her tent and turned back to face her. His expression was thoughtful, serious, but then summoned a slight smile and said, "Good morning, Layla."

"Good morning, Galin," she whispered to the space he had vacated.

A few moments later, an Elven soldier pulled back the flap of her tent. His silver helmet glistened, even in the half-light of day, as he leaned in. "Captain, Lorin Faldor to see you."

"Thank you. Send him in," she said.

She watched as a young copper-haired Elf, clad in green and brown forest clothes, entered the tent and, just as quickly, fell to his knees and bowed his head. She walked to stand before him and gently placed her fingers beneath his chin, lifting his head to face her. "Why do you kneel before me, Lorin Faldor?"

"You are a princess of Alluviam. Are you not, my lady?" he asked sincerely, but still unable to conceal a certain pride.

"Here, on the field, I am your Captain. Soldiers and warriors do not kneel to one another, even those of higher rank. Do you understand, Lorin?"

With that, he rose and stood before her, staring straight but avoiding her gaze. "Very well, my lady," he replied.

She nodded and then moved to the back of her tent, where she reached down for something covered in thick dark garments. "You joined us as a scout. I am told your skills are excellent and your talent as an archer rival even some of our best men and women."

"Your people have taken me in and welcomed me as one of their own. I am in theirs and your debt, my lady, as well as your father, the king's. I will give all that I am to serve my kin. And it has given me a chance to—" He hesitated.

"To? Do you wish to take revenge against those who destroyed your people?" she asked.

For a moment, the question hung in the air like leaves fallen from a great height dancing in the wind, then he said, "Respectfully, my lady, I watched them"—his voice cracked—"butcher my people down to the last child."

Layla looked down, holding a long object covered with silk. "I know, and I will not insult you by saying I know how you feel, though I may understand it and even empathize. However, what you must know, Lorin, is that had my people, those of Averon, and those of the White Elves followed our need for revenge, of which there was enough to go around on all sides, I assure you, we would not be here now talking like this. There would be no Alliance, and there would be no hope of victory against those who destroyed your home and your people. It is only because wise men and women found it within themselves to see past their hatred that we have dealt our enemy two significant defeats, in a row, and still our battles, and even the war, are long from ended with the final victory little more than a fanciful dream. Our greatest power comes from hope, not hate. Promise me you will consider this in days to come."

He bowed his head. "I swear it, my lady."

"Good. Then I'd like you to accept this gift on behalf of my father and myself." She removed the covering to reveal a great wooden longbow. He examined it at first, without reaching for it. The craftsmanship was exquisite. It was beautiful, but he noticed there were small glowing shimmers of golden light that seemed to course through it like veins likely not visible to a human eye, but not beyond the notice of Elven vision.

"I asked my father to send our bowyers to fetch some wood from the mighty oak trees at the Shrine of Haloreth, in the Great Forest of Hilderan. May it serve the skill of the last of our woodland kin honorably in the days to come."

At last, he reached for it. "I, do not know what to say, my lady." He started to kneel.

"Lorin!" she blurted out impatiently.

"Forgive me, my lady—Captain, forgive me. I humbly thank you and your father for this remarkable gift. I shall endeavor to be worthy of it in the coming days."

"Much better. You're dismissed." She smiled as she watched him go.

Kael and Mya lay face to face, gazing into each other's eyes.

"Two days alone and free with you. It seems like a dream," Kael said.

Mya placed her hand on his cheek. "Perhaps I did something wrong the last two nights if you are not convinced of our reality together."

Together they laughed.

"Oh, no. I can assure you I was not referring to that," Kael said, kissing her hand.

Mya traced the line of his lips, her finger trailing down the center of his chin. "You have been my dream, freeing me from a nightmare I once thought inescapable. The world is a new place for me, for my people, for us."

"There is still so much to do and so much evil to contend with," Kael responded. "But because of you, for the first time in a long time, I can face it without fear."

"Then let us make a pact," Mya said, leaning up on her elbow. "Let each of us vow to the other that we stay alive until all the work is done, the evil is defeated, and we may find such happiness . . ."

"As two people dream of but never know," Kael said, completing her sentence, and he pulled her closer.

Lark and Archangel spent the morning helping the Dwarves position the siege artillery that had been saved from the castle and brought down from the sanctuary caves. It was comprised of five heavy ballistae and ten heavy catapults, but it would take a few more days to transport the ammunition.

Though a holy warrior very rarely removed his armor, Lark enjoyed rolling up his sleeves and digging ditches side by side with the Dwarves. It was good to be among other warriors, especially as hearty a people as the Dwarves. This was the perfect place for him. A Paladin needed a righteous cause of good against evil, of the strong attempting to oppress the weak or downtrodden, to truly feel alive and useful. He was among people who had a just cause against great evil. He felt it was his duty to keep their spirits high and bolster their confidence.

He and Archangel had made fast friends among them, and in no time at all, Lark had them joining in prayer during their breaks. It did not matter their religion or deity, merely that they joined in fellowship, praying for good deeds and blessings. At times, the Elves, who were already a highly spiritual people, would join in as well.

Together they dug ditches and mounds to properly brace the heavy siege artillery. Then, at the behest of General Mekko, they dug long trenches three feet deep, three rows across, in front of each artillery device. The general had said they would be useful later should the perimeter walls ever be breached. Before long, Lark had the whole lot of them singing while they worked.

Archangel reclined against a mound and smiled as he watched Lark make their burdensome work into a pleasure. There was cheer and laughter among the workers and a growing camaraderie among all. Still, doubt gnawed at Archangel's mind. For the briefest of moments, sometimes when he looked at Lark, he perceived the gray haze over Lark's eyes that had been present when the Shadow Prince had been in control of his mind. Archangel shook his head as if to shake away the worrisome thought. It *had* to be his imagination. He was being ridiculous.

After they had been parted for the first time in days for more than a few hours, Mya found herself wanting to be near Kael again. She found him sitting alone in a small patch of trees just to the southwest of the camp perimeter. She placed her hand on his shoulder, startling him. "Forgive me, I did not mean to disturb you, I will see you later if you wish," she said.

Kael took her hand in his and kissed it gently. "No, my love, please stay. Sit with me."

"You seem distraught. Is something wrong?" Mya asked, settling down beside him.

"I've just been thinking. I'm worried about Elenari," he responded, his eyes on the distance.

"Why? She seems fine."

He turned to her. "She has been through so much. She is not fine. The loss of Hawk, her first love, the loss of Algernon, a man who was more a father to her than I in some ways." His eyes fell to the ground.

"Why do you say these things?" Mya asked, taking his hand in hers and holding it tightly.

"I have never been there for her as a father or barely as a friend. Instead, I've looked to my own affairs and needs. We quarreled a few days ago, and I could do nothing but say hurtful things to her."

Mya nodded empathetically and brushed her free hand along his back. "She will fall in love again, in time, and the loss of Algernon has affected all of us, yourself included. She is strong, she will find her way."

"She is young, so very young and wields ability and responsibility beyond what any woman her age should," Kael replied.

"She is a skilled fighter and highly accomplished ranger, but women in the world of today need such skills. I'm sure you would agree," Mya offered.

"She is more than a skilled fighter," Kael confided. "She is a Kenshari Master and youngest of the Kenshari." He registered Mya's shock.

"A Kenshari—how is that even possible?" Mya sat back a bit, holding her own hands now.

"I found her alone, helpless and starving as a small child. She was the right age and High Master Reyblade was an old friend of mine. It was a time in my life when I traveled, seeking to right the wrongs of the world. I was an adventurer, and I could not bring a child with me to the places I was going. Leaving her with Master Reyblade seemed the perfect solution. I knew she would be cared for and taught to defend herself, certainly better than I could ever teach her. From what Master Reyblade told me, her physical skills and reflexes were beyond anything he had ever seen before in one so young, especially for a half-elf. In only nineteen years, she earned the rank and privilege of a Kenshari Master, having passed all the trials. A feat most others do not achieve in even a single lifetime. Master Reyblade urged her to continue her studies at the temple, saying that she was not mentally prepared for the responsibility that came with such skills, but she did not listen. She contacted me and asked to live with me in Wrenford. That's when I gave up my adventurer's life to take her home and be the father she deserved. It was on the way home from the temple when I was confronted by Talic and forced by combat to become Grand Druid. I believe you know the rest of the story, except to say very few are aware that Elenari is one of the Kenshari. Algernon knew, and I think some of the others suspect, but—"

"I shall keep your confidence," she said reassuringly. "The deep love and bond between the two of you will heal your emotional wounds and make all things possible for you both. You are each other's family. You always will be."

Kael caressed Mya's cheek with the back of his hand. "Now you are also part of our family. I am ashamed to say I have felt guilt over the happiness I have found with you while my daughter has had so much taken from her. But I am renewed in your presence, and I feel guilt no more. I shall endeavor to be there for both you and my daughter from this moment on."

Mya's smile lit up her eyes. "You honor me by taking me into your family. I shall do all I can to help you and Elenari, always."

They got up and walked hand in hand back to the camp.

The Anglian Sea carried a floating piece of debris into the fog, away from the eyes of the enemy. The splintered wood held two survivors. The woman's white clothing clung to her curves as she lay atop the length of the wood. There was no room for the man holding on to the edge of the debris to keep his chin above the water line.

"Swim, Bartholomew! We must get as far away as possible while we're in this fog!" Helena yelled, using her free hand to paddle.

"Of course, my dear, I shall spring into action . . . with the dexterity of a sea horse . . . and have us home in time for evening tea! I can barely . . . keep from drowning myself, woman, what elsw . . . do you want from me?" Piedmont responded, struggling to keep his head above water.

"If you weren't so fat," she spat, "we could move faster than a snail's pace! Our only hope of surviving is getting picked up by a merchant ship or one of our deep-fishing ships. But we're more than two days from home by ship! Please do pick up the pace!"

"I'm well aware of the situation, thank you. I think perhaps . . . you missed your calling, my dear. How is the navy . . . getting on without you, I wonder?" Piedmont answered, spitting water from his mouth.

They moved in silence, carried by the gentle tide of a calm sea. It was a monotonous cycle of paddling, resting, and paddling, unsure if they were even moving in the right direction. All they knew for sure was that the enemy vessels had not seen them escape. After several hours, they were too tired to paddle any longer and just let the tide take them where it may.

Suddenly, without any variation in the waves, the debris tipped slightly, unnaturally. Piedmont's hands released their death grip, as if something had pulled him under.

Helena sat up. "Bartholomew! Bartholomew?"

A moment later, Piedmont's hands found the edge of the wood. He pulled his head above water spit out saltwater and gasped. "Seaweed . . . wrapped . . . around my legs. Help . . . can't hold on . . ."

It occurred to her that she needed Bartholomew's efforts to eventually reach help. She would not survive on her own. She quickly tore off the bottom of her dress to free her legs for swimming. Even in her haste, she realized that part of her dress could be used later to wave like a rescue flag.

"Hold on!" she cried, easing her body into the water. She took a deep breath and went under. She was confused to see her husband's legs dangling, free and unobstructed. To her shock, he grabbed a handful of her hair and pushed down. She writhed and twisted her body, but she couldn't free herself. She tried to grab his crotch and squeeze, but her hand kept catching the fat around his stomach. Finally, she had no fight left in her.

When Piedmont was confidant she was dead, he kicked her body away from him. He then pulled himself onto the piece of wood and collapsed. It felt good to rest.

Though this had been his first murder, he felt surprisingly at ease. Helena had never liked him. He had rescued her from a life of poverty and complacency and never received even a word of gratitude. It was a marriage of convenience, true enough, but while she gained in wealth and status, he gained only the appearance of a loving, beautiful wife at court. And how had she repaid his generosity? With frequent indiscretions, often to his embarrassment. Her constant insults infuriated him just as equally. Now, as a surviving widower, he would make a much more sympathetic hero upon his rescue. Without Helena to downplay his role in their escape and survival, he would surely be promoted. Now, all he needed was a little luck.

Prince Ceceran roamed the stone passages of Castle Iberian, which he had known since childhood, passing the guards without a glance as he approached the throne room of his father, King Zarian. As requested, his father awaited him. However, to the chair at his father's left sat his elder sister, Princess Angelique, heir to the throne. In Bastlandia, regardless of gender, the ruler's eldest child was next in line.

Ceceran knelt. When he looked to his sister's place, he hid his disdain and nodded. "Father, I thought we agreed to meet in private on this matter," he said as he rose.

Recovering from a feverish draft, King Zarian pulled his fur robe closer about him and coughed. "Your sister will one day rule this kingdom. You do not presume that pressing matters of state would be private from her, would you, my son?"

"Of course, not my Lord," Ceceran replied.

Long chestnut hair falling to her bosom, Angelique sat with the statuesque grace of a queen. Even beneath her full-length crimson dress, her feminine features, though voluptuous, had a muscular contour, indicating her excellent physic.

Ceceran detested her for being everything he was not. The prince himself was pale and thin. However, his knowledge of politics or his ambition for power could not be overestimated. He was extremely intelligent with an unbounded capacity for treachery. Treachery, however, had been fiercely frowned upon throughout the history of Bastlandia. Even the *appearance* of impropriety could sometimes be considered worse than a heinous act in the people's eyes. The Bastlandians were historically, and by nature, a gallant and noble people. It was fear and fear alone of his father's elite guard, the High Riders, especially their captain, that kept the prince's more unscrupulous motives in check.

Many times, Ceceran had attempted to ingratiate himself to the people, but it was Angelique they loved. In many ways, she was her father. She was virtuous, righteous, compassionate, and forgiving. She also possessed one other thing he did not—a guardian angel. Krin, the captain of the High Riders, had been her lover and protector for years.

The High Riders were, in the prince's opinion, a decadent and obsolete unit of the military. They were named so largely because of the tall horses, the Meridians, upon which they rode. Something in the grass or soil of Bastlandia caused the horses to grow far larger than anywhere else in the world. Many averaged nine feet tall at the shoulder, some were even larger. The High Riders had also designed a longbow that was seven feet in length and had far greater ranges than bows from the mainland, even greater than an Elven longbow. In ancient times, they served as the main cavalry of the army, but in peacetime, they had become the guards of the castle and royal family. However, his father and the people had their traditions, and they were one of them.

The Royal Council as well, Ceceran thought, a superficial body of bloated, self-important men whose titles were redundant at best. The council consisted of the prime minister, second in power only to the king, the minister of foreign affairs, the minister of naval affairs, the minister of homeland defense, the minister of the treasury, and the list went on. Thinking about it only made his head hurt. However, there was one saving grace to having so many men on the Royal Council: Some of them could be bought. Additionally, not all of them agreed with the king's policies. Ceceran used his adult years to get as close to them as possible.

The branches of the military had an even more complex and multi-layered hierarchy. Again, within certain circles of the military, there was discontentment with the king's handling of foreign affairs.

However, Bastlandia differed from any country in the Southern Trade Federation in many ways. True power rested neither with the military nor the government but with the people. Public opinion ultimately ruled. The people of Bastlandia despised plots, assassinations, secret alliances, or anything they deemed contrary to the common good. They had demonstrated many times throughout history they would not tolerate such things.

Ceceran looked at his father, a man well into his late sixties. He sat cold and shivering on the throne. weak and stupid. An unremarkable crown of gold, void of jewels, rested upon his thinning gray hair. He had the wrinkled forehead and eyes of a man who had let worry age him. He was a cautious man, well-liked by the people, but always made decisions based on whatever would keep the peace, no matter the cost or gain to his country.

Times are changing, the prince thought. *It is a time for boldness and to reap the rewards of such action.* He looked at his sister one last time before he opened his mouth. His plot would have to be perfect. "Father, I have requested that the Royal Scribe be present to record this audience, as I wish my plea to be recorded for the good of the people." The prince pointed to a deathly pale old man in the corner, adorned in a rich purple robe, who sat below and to the left of the throne, meticulously scratching down his words with a long-feathered writing quill. Ceceran's request was more formality than anything else. The Royal Scribe was present recording all throne audiences, those official and unofficial. The documents of the scribe were public and available upon request to the people. Only by the king's decree alone would something happen in the throne room that was not recorded.

"Father, I have asked to see you without the council members so they cannot unduly influence your thoughts. The creation the Great Southern Trade Route that will for the first time link the Southern Trade Federation of nations with the northern countries of the world is a staggering event. It will be the richest trade route in the history of the known world and, as such, the most tempting target for attack from pirates or a foreign power. It is we"—Ceceran shook his upraised fist—"the largest of the Trade Federation countries, who should take the sole responsibility for security of this precious resource. It is we who should take the lion's share of the profits father."

"You asked for this audience to tell me these things as if I did not already know them," the king began. "We have had this discussion, both in and out of council. I did not come here to have it again. There has been one hundred years of peace since the establishment of the Trade Federation. The equal sharing of security for the Southern Trade Route between Arcadia and Bastlandia, with support from the smaller islands will guarantee the peace for centuries to come. You said you wished to discuss a *threat* to the state. Unless you have something else to discuss, this audience is over." Clearly agitated, the king coughed violently.

The prince held his hands out imploringly. "Father, Arcadia is the threat, don't you see? What's to stop them from destroying our fleet and taking over trade in the southern hemisphere? Now that we have the *Emerald Sea*, it's time to press the advantage and strike before they do."

"Enough! I will hear no more talk of this again! This audience is *over*." The king pulled the fur closer still and stood up. He marched angrily behind the throne toward his private chamber.

Both Ceceran and Angelique knelt, standing only when the king was gone.

"I see, as usual, you make no effort to aid me sister, even when you know I speak the truth," said Ceceran.

Angelique retook her seat. "Brother, they are celebrating one hundred years of peace right now in Arcadia. Do you truly believe they are conspiring to break it? I did not help you because I agree with Father."

"Of course. How sweet. Papa's little angel. Far be it from her to have a breath of courage to say what needs to be said. Perhaps you are afraid he might disinherit you. Mark my words sister, you and Father will come to regret this day. You will come to regret that you did not heed my warning." Ceceran bowed his head and retreated.

He thundered through the passageways lost in thought. He needed to speak to his one true confidant, the Royal Tailor, Marko. Marko was perhaps the most well-read and intelligent man within the kingdom. He had a singular, no-nonsense understanding of politics. He often knew the pulse of the court and the people on most major issues before they became public. The prince never made a move without his advice. Ceceran burst into his chamber and found him at his sewing wheel.

"My Prince, can I be of service?"

A young man adorned in the standard crimson tunic of the Royal Court, his long dark hair and rugged features would not suggest he was a talented man of fabrics and clothing. However, there was much evidence to the contrary. He alone was responsible for the elegant tailoring of the many nobles and military men within Bastlandia. He had two servants who were nearly as skilled as he, two boys not more than sixteen years old, who he had trained and entrusted with important tasks.

"Walk with me," the prince commanded.

Together they walked in silence to Ceceran's chamber. As they entered, Marko kindled the fireplace, which had been burning low.

"They are fools, Marko," Ceceran spat. "My father and his cow of a daughter are both too weak to rule. Their shortsightedness will be their undoing. Our time is coming. Soon all will change, and the people will be none the wiser."

"And Captain Krin, my lord, he is ever watchful over the king and Angelique. He is not to be underestimated. I have seen him training his men. His prowess as a warrior is without question. He must be dealt with first before any move can be made against the king and your whore of a sister," Marko said, looking at Ceceran strangely for a moment, and then walked over to him. Marko fell to his knees before Ceceran and began adjusting his belt.

"Your sash, my prince, it has fallen, allow me to fix it."

Ceceran placed his hand on Marko's head and ran his fingers through his hair. "My dear Marko, ever loyal. You will be richly rewarded when the time comes. You will be my prime minister."

Marko raised his eyes. "My Prince, you know I worship you. That would be too great an honor. Perhaps it would be best to give such a title to one not so close to you."

"Nonsense, you'll checkmate the lot of them, my sweet Marko." Ceceran offered him his other hand, which Marko took and passionately kissed.

"Not yet you won't." A voice from the dark corner near the fireplace said.

With that, a dark figure stepped forward into the half-light. He was a shroud clothed all in black and gray with a dark hood about his head, obscuring his face. He stood just less than six feet, but the volume of his robes did not lend to judging his true size. The only thing that could be seen for sure was the dark hilt of a long sword in a scabbard strapped to his back.

"Leave us, Marko!" Ceceran ordered.

"My Prince?" Marko questioned as he rose slowly to his feet.

"Fear not, tailor, I am not your competition for his affections. Now get out!" the dark stranger commanded.

Marko bowed to Ceceran and left the chamber.

The stranger's voice was fluid, a smooth, even tone. "Well, Prince Ceceran, have you made any progress?"

"I met with the king today. He will not listen to reason," Ceceran replied.

"Perhaps I should be dealing with your sister. Perhaps she possesses the necessary influence." The stranger walked slowly across the room and looking detached and disinterested at the decorations about the walls.

"The only thing my pig of a sister possesses is the ability to enthrall men and people to her idiotic ways of thinking. And, in the future," he said, his tone growing angrier, "I would appreciate if you do not invade the privacy of my chambers. We were never to meet within the walls of the castle. That was the arrangement!"

Faster than the prince's eyes could follow, the dark stranger moved to the other side of the chamber. His blade was suddenly unsheathed and at the prince's throat, backing him up into the oak door to his stone chamber. The dark warrior's tone remained steady, calm, and unwavering as he spoke. "My master grows impatient, Prince. As do I. He has therefore taken the first step to create the political unrest you have thus far failed miserably at achieving."

The prince was on his toes as he felt the razor-sharp blade against his throat. He choked out, "There is little I can do without power. Without the ability to rule, I have no say in policy."

"And if you had the ability to rule?" the warrior asked slowly, mockingly.

"Then Bastlandia would owe fealty to your master, and I would forever be in his and your debt," Ceceran said, his breath rapid.

The dark warrior removed the blade, sheathing it in one smooth action. "We will help you in eliminating your father, sister, and the captain of the High Riders. The rest will be for you to accomplish, and then the throne will be yours. However, you must pass a test to prove your loyalty. Be in your father's chamber tonight at midnight." With that, the warrior slipped out of the room like a shadow.

Midnight could not come soon enough for Ceceran. Though he tried to calm himself, anxiety wreaked havoc on his insides. Being king had been so unattainable for him for so many years that even he, with his boundless ambition, had nearly given up on it. Even the hated Captain Krin's offspring with Angelique, if she were to bare children, would rule before him. But that was of no concern now; all these obstacles would soon be gone.

Just before midnight, Ceceran moved through the torch-lit passages of the castle toward the throne room. As he approached, he noticed the two High Riders who normally guarded the way were nowhere to be found. As he moved through the dark, cold throne room, he found that he could not resist. He walked up the four short stairs to the golden throne. The back and seat were softened with lavish cushions built into the chairs. He sat upon the throne, remembering how he played on it as a child. It was not designed for comfort but rather status as the highest chair in the kingdom from which the king looked down at all those in his presence.

It would soon be his.

As he made his way to the royal bedchamber, again the two familiar guards were not at their post. Beyond, he saw that his father's bedchamber was fully illuminated. Slowly he made his way through the short corridor and entered to find five men in black armor around his father's bed. The king, whose mouth was tied with a rag, lay struggling. His hands were tied to the quarter posts of his bed. The dark warrior appeared from the shadows of the chamber, as if from nowhere, and approached him.

"Are you prepared to show your loyalty to the Shadow Prince?" he asked.

"I am prepared," Ceceran answered with a racing heart and sweaty palms.

"Kill him." The warrior handed him a pillow.

Ceceran took it and approached the bed slowly. His father struggled even more violently, shock and disbelief watering his eyes.

This was no test, he thought before looking his father right in the eye. "I bet you wished you listened to me now, eh, Father? I gave you more chances than you deserved." With that, he lowered the pillow across his father's face and pressed down with all his might.

King Zarian made several loud noises despite his gag. His body contorted fiercely as it attempted to cling to life. Several moments passed until his legs and hands stopped quivering. Finally, Ceceran removed the pillow to see the placid death stare of his father. He faced the dark warrior. "I thought the test of loyalty would be something difficult."

Ceceran looked down at his father and spat in his face.

The doors to Princess Angelique's chamber burst open as dark armored men with crossbows filtered in.

Captain Krin, lying beside her, did not hesitate. He sprang up and quickly reached for the night table near his side of the bed. In that moment, a crossbow fired, striking him in the back of his left shoulder. Undaunted, his hand found the dagger he sought. In a backhanded motion, he threw the dagger, burying it in the neck of one of the crossbowmen.

"No! Krin!" Angelique cried when she saw the first bolt strike the back of his shoulder. Two more crossbows fired, putting a bolt in Krin's stomach and right shoulder. Then another crossbow fired. striking Angelique in her right shoulder near her neck.

"No!" Krin cried with renewed strength, as he took her from the bed and in one motion threw her over his shoulder and dove headfirst through the window's wooden shutters. Immediately, the dark warrior was at the window, looking down along the side of the castle to a river below.

"That fall is nearly two hundred feet, sir. There's no way they could survive it," one of the crossbowmen said.

"Get down there and find me the bodies. Use dogs, wolves, whatever it takes. I want the bodies brought to the throne room. Go!" The dark stranger clapped his hands, and the men sprang into action. A moment later, the dark warrior pulled Krin's sword from its sheath.

"Bring him in," Ceceran said appearing in the room.

Two of the dark warrior's men dragged in a badly beaten man and held him on his knees before the prince.

"Sergeant Mulcahy, isn't it true you coveted my sister for years. Now, you finally grown bold enough to take her for yourself, only your plan seems to have gone astray."

The dazed man looked up, only just gaining consciousness. "I-I don't understand." he mumbled.

The dark warrior struck a killing blow across the man's chest with Krin's sword. As he convulsed, Prince Ceceran grabbed a handful of his hair while the man was still in his death throes.

"For my sister," Ceceran said as he slit the man's throat with his dagger. Waiting until his body went limp, he threw him to the floor. He watched and smiled as the dark man placed Mulcahy's sword and bow by his hands and Krin's blade on the floor by the bed.

"One of the High Riders, one of our most trusted guards, Krin's own sergeant. The people will be as outraged as they are shocked."

Ceceran could hear the castle was stirring with life. He looked to the dark warrior.

"I suggest you convene your Royal Council, King Ceceran," the warrior said.

"I need those bodies. You will ensure they are dead, yes?" the newly appointed king asked.

The dark warrior bowed his head, and he and his men were gone with the shadows of the night. It was done.

Chapter 5

Deep in the Black Chasms of Bazadoom, the Orc Chieftain, Red Fang, looked out over his army with pride. Years in the making, they had been building their ranks in secret. Many years earlier, his people had almost been annihilated, a result of border wars on every front as well as civil war among the various clans. Now, with the coming of the Shadow Prince, the clans had united under one banner. They were powerful again, a force to be feared. Here, in the dark mountains amidst deep pools of lava, they had forged fearsome siege weapons of war.

The first attack upon Cordilleran was nothing compared to what was to come. It did, however, mark the first time Orcs and men had ever united against a common foe. Now, with the Shadow Prince's guidance, they would unite with creatures from the Morval Mountains and launch an assault capable of destroying Dwarves and Elves from the land, finally and forever.

Legions of Orcs stared back at him, a sea of yellow eyes and white fangs filled with the same prideful hatred he possessed. Tens of thousands of them stood, armor clad and armed with swords and spears. This was a battle-hardened army forged through centuries of wars. These were the finest soldiers among them, saved for now at the behest of the Shadow Prince.

The Orcs loved war and death the way Dwarves and Elves loved peace and life. Those peace-mongering Dwarves and Elves did not have the same commitment to the sword as they. Though their bloodlust was like a fever that overtook them, this force was more disciplined than the first sent against Cordilleran and would not so easily succumb to its temptations.

The great Orc warlord turned and walked through a stone archway guarded on either side by dark-armored Stygian Knights, each wielding large two-handed swords. The only thing that identified them as other than shadows were the crests of the red Hydra upon their chests.

The heat became increasingly difficult to bear as he continued. They were, after all, essentially in the heart of an ancient volcano that rested within the base of the mountain. Lakes of lava flowed throughout the caverns, but he was approaching the core where the lava still swirled, and the heat was nearly unbearable. A large circular chamber of rock surrounded the slow-churning lava. A throne had been carved into the rock where a lone figure in black sat and looked deep into the liquid fire.

Red Fang approached the throne and knelt with his head bowed low, only inches from the black boots of the dark figure. "The army is prepared for war, my lord," the Orc chieftain began, his tone guttural. "We await your command."

"Excellent. You may rise. It is not quite time yet. We will let them think they have had their victories. The time is near though, so very close. Go, my friend. Wait with your army. Be prepared to march when I summon you. Now, leave me and see that I am not disturbed." Emanating from within a golden helmet, the voice was strained, the result of scarred vocal cords. The voice belonged to none other than Prince Wolfgar Stranexx, the Shadow Prince.

"Yes, master," The Orc growled as he rose and left.

There he sat, staring deep into the lava. Its orange color filled the chamber, like the air itself, with a molten hue. It was then that he felt it. He was being contacted by the dark entity that had saved him from oblivion; the entity that had guided all his actions and strategies with a wisdom not his own. Until now, he had received images that he in turn was able to translate to thought. Now, he could hear the thoughts in his mind. They were loud, almost deafening. The thoughts had a voice, with no particular sound to it, yet the words were definite and clear. Communication between them had become increasingly stronger. His coming would be soon now.

"*They prepare. Do not underestimate them. March the army of Bazadoom east to join with the northern army. Have all forces join. They must fight as one. They will march together on the enemy. You will lead them. You will entrench at Cordilleran. You will attack until they are all destroyed.*"

He sensed something then that he'd never felt before during one of their communications. He felt surprise coupled with uncertainty. It was a sensation the entity had never before conveyed. Always, without hesitation, it knew when and how to proceed . . . but this was different.

"*Listen very carefully and understand fully. There is one who has waited, one who has evaded all prying eyes. For centuries, he has waited for me. He possesses the sorcery of the ancients. He alone could upset the balance of power beyond all planning. He must be killed before the attack can be made, before he joins with them. I will give you the power. The strain will be great on us both. A demon, a demon of the ancient world must kill him for us, a demon that now only exists within my realm.*"

The sound of bending leather accompanied the Shadow Prince as he fell to his hands and knees, abject and subservient. His cape of armor fell over his thick leather vestment. Never had he sensed such urgency or the slightest inkling of doubt, which now permeated through into his mind despite all efforts to the contrary from his master. His show of loyalty must be absolute.

"*I am yours. Command me.*"

With that, he felt both power and knowledge surging through his being, filling the void in his mind and body. He sensed the tremendous strain such an auspicious display of power cost his master. How the entity's power could transcend his current bonds was remarkable. His coming would be soon indeed. When the transfer of power and knowledge was complete, the Shadow Prince sensed all ties to the entity were abruptly cut. His master would be temporarily weakened. The communication had ended. Within the transference, he received not only the means to vanquish this foe but also his location, his description, and his name.

A small opaque crystal swung back and forth evenly like a pendulum, falling ever closer to the land map it dangled over. Arcane whispers accompanied the soundless movement. The old man had been meditating for hours. Through his power and that of the crystal, he had sight beyond sight. The time had finally come when he knew he must make a dangerous gamble to know that which would otherwise remain unknown. He must exert a powerful magic of divination that had not been used since ancient times. It was magic that could reveal his presence and could possibly be sensed even through the protective magic of his mountain sanctuary. No price, however, would be too costly.

He must know. For the sake of all those who had died, all those who had sacrificed, and for those whose fates had yet to be written, he must know. The crystal guided his hand subtly over the features of the map. His wrinkled eyes held tightly shut as wind shot through his cave. Through his eyelids, he could see the light of his many candles burn less bright. Then, suddenly it was ended. He lifted his head back and opened his eyes wide. The light returned to its former strength as he focused on the roof of his cave a moment. His deep inhalations echoed through the chamber as he attempted to slow his breathing to calm the beating of his heart against his chest. He knew it was over. The crystal had landed, but he waited another moment before looking. Finally, he brought his eyes down to bear upon the map.

"Cordilleran, the besieged Kingdom of the Dwarves. Of course! I should have guessed."

He felt a queer relief with the knowledge, though he had expected to feel something else. He expected to feel fear and dread, yet he did not. Perhaps centuries earlier, he would have, but the endless waiting had numbed it out of him. Instead, he felt a degree of intrepidity. This was his chance to redeem himself and the others. Because of them, the evil that was never meant to coexist with them on the physical plane would once more walk the face of their world.

Too long he lived with the sins of the past. For too long he wallowed in self-pity and gave in to despair. Now was his time. Somehow, he would find a way to make it right. He was responsible for the greatest mistake the world had ever known. For a hundred lifetimes, he bore the guilt of the world's sorrow upon his shoulders. Now there would be an end to it, one way or another. He would find the strength, or he would die.

It would be a long and perilous journey, and he would find no allies or solace along the way, only danger. He quickly put together three large bags, which he packed with various provisions. Among them were a host of colored vials containing different liquids, all the potions he could carry.

He packed food and water as well as several small containers that carried various powders and ingredients. Finally, he packed several scrolls and parchments.

He quickly put on a hooded black traveling cloak and grabbed his walking stick. As he neared the exit, he paused. He looked down a moment, then turned to look back at the dwelling that had been his home and sanctuary for longer than he could remember. This place had served him well. The ward of protection he placed upon it allowed the power he possessed to remain concealed throughout the centuries. This was home, and it deserved a final look of fond remembrance. It was here he had assumed the identity of a cantankerous old hermit to those very few he encountered. It was here that he was known as Rex Abernackle.

Hundreds of miles away, within the Tower of Darkhelm, a circular crimson flash ignited the darkness of the vacant throne room. The Shadow Prince had translocated here to the safety of his capital and seat of his former glory. The summoning he was about to undertake would leave him severely weakened, and although the Orcs feared him greatly, there would be no concealing his frailty. He would be vulnerable enough that they could destroy him. They were no rabble of creatures by any means. Most were the elite of the Blood Rock Clan. They did not know weakness or fear. They knew only the art of war and were not to be trifled with. In any event, he would be much safer here in the vacant hall of his tower. A garrison of a dozen Stygian Knights throughout the lower levels would maintain the tower; their fear of him would serve as protection enough.

He sat upon his silver throne in the shadows of his dark audience chamber. The cushions were stiff, atrophied from nonuse. Here, from this seat, he recalled the height of the Pytharian Empire when his rule was absolute in the Northern land. Now his rule extended far beyond the old empire's boundaries and would soon extend to the corners of the world. He would rule the entire world in his master's name.

The master's wisdom was without question. In a short period, nearly all his enemies had been destroyed. Soon his revenge would be complete, and he would place what was left of the world he had conquered at his master's feet. Yet, he found himself perplexed for the first time since his return from oblivion. This old man the master spoke of surprised and concerned him. These feelings had become unfamiliar territory for them both. They bred uncertainty, which was worse than even the petty victories their enemies had achieved thus far. The situation would now be dealt with decisively.

He sat and contemplated the magic and knowledge that had been passed to him. It would not be an easy summoning, and he needed to understand the nature of what he was about to do. As his master had communicated to him, the fabric of time and space had been breached ages earlier and demons from his dimension had entered this world. In the ages that followed, the breach closed or healed, but would forever be slightly weakened. The weakness would be almost inconsequential, but an individual summoning could still be possible. He was to attempt to summon a specific demon for their purpose—a creature designed to hunt and kill its prey. To succeed, it would be necessary to bridge time and space between the two dimensions, creating a vortex that would carry the demon they sought here to this world.

Slowly he rose and moved to the center of the chamber, where he stopped. He removed his armored gloves. He looked at both sides of his hand for a moment, observing the diseased malady that had affected his rotting flesh long before he could recall its former appearance. With the nail of his right forefinger, he sliced across his left wrist, causing his dark blood to flow freely from his veins. He walked in a wide circle, leaving a circular pattern of his blood upon the stone floor. With the circle complete, he stepped back from it, knelt, and raised his hands above to the unseen heavens. He began to chant a necromantic verse totally unfamiliar to him. He was merely doing as he had been instructed with no clear understanding of the powers he was invoking.

From without, the night sky vanished, and swirling storm clouds blotted out the moon and stars as they took shape over the remnants of the Pytharian Empire. Great funnel clouds formed, connecting the sky and the ground in many places. Soon dozens had formed, comprised of raging winds. They seemed to form a perimeter around the Tower of Darkhelm. Above the tower, the sky opened and took on the color of blood. Forked streaks of lightning came through the aperture as if a serpent's tongue was testing the air.

The Shadow Prince felt power coursing through him, pulling on his very essence. Never had he felt such a draining effect upon his strength. He surrendered to it, attempting to stabilize it with his own powers. It was then he felt his astral body leave the physical shell and travel up out of the tower and into the vortex. Through space and time, his spirit body traveled within the conduit he had created. It was a bridge independent of time from his dimension to another.

Upon his arrival, he focused solely upon the object of his search, disregarding all other forms. Even through his intense concentration, he could not ignore the thousands of misshapen creatures, all of them immortal, forever roaming the desolate plains of the Nethertime. At last, the object of his search revealed itself to him. This was the moment that would drain the last of his power and possibly his very life. He used his astral form to transport the physical form of the demon back through the interdimensional conduit.

With a power not his own, he had made it back. With a harrowing scream, he arrived inside his body. He collapsed to the ground and saw, not ten feet from him, the living demon he had successfully brought back with him. He could do naught but lay, unmoving, in awe of the creature. A more lethal killer had never been spawned.

Somewhere in the Andarian Ranges

Suddenly he sensed it, stinging him like venom. Quickly, he turned his head to the northeast, pulling back the cowl of his black cloak. There he saw the distant storm clouds and crimson sky above the lands of the Pytharian Empire.

"Something uninvited has arrived," he mused.

He had revealed himself to the darkness. They would be coming for him. He looked around. Though he knew these mountains better than any being alive, he had no desire to fight a battle in such a confining space. He must make for the grasslands of the Mystarian border. Even a few trees would be useful, but not the mountain trails. He looked up to the black skies, a fierce countenance upon his face.

"*Hear me powers of darkness. I say unto you, come for me if you dare!*"

With that he pulled his hood around his head. Leaning heavily upon his walking stick, he increased his speed through the mountainous trails.

Faster than thought, the demonic creature was on top of him. It stood menacingly over him, jaws snapping, claws raking downward toward him. The Shadow Prince did not have the strength to move, closing his eyes he waited for the violent death. After a moment, he opened one eye.

Still the creature stood over him, but something prevented it from striking him. The creature could barely contain its need to tear him to shreds. Then he remembered. The circle of his blood. The creature could not harm one whose blood surrounded the spot of his arrival.

He could see it clearly now. In ways, it was not unlike the great apes that roamed the jungles of Arcadia, yet this creature was far larger and exceptionally broad in the chest and shoulders. Its entire frame, over nine feet high, bulged with exaggerated muscles. The demon even sat like an ape on its hind legs, steadying itself with its disproportionately long arms. Places where the light yellow-blue fur parted revealed a layer of scales.

The creature's chest was coated with long interlocking quills but extended outward like those of a porcupine. Covering the whole of its back as well, the quills were both defensive and offensive. Like darts, the creature could shoot them from its body and another would grow in its place. The Shadow prince understood that the tips of the quills contained a toxin that attacked the nervous system and cause death in under six seconds.

Though still too weak to move, he found the creature's gaze. It had a pair of oblong yellow slits that wrapped around the sides of its head, giving it excellent peripheral vision. Despite its ferocity, he could sense a cunningness about the creature. It was a predator who hunted not for food, like the animals of his world, but for the sheer pleasure of killing. All the skills and instincts it possessed were groomed for this one purpose. He conveyed a latent telepathic message planted by his master to the demon that contained its instructions.

The Shadow Prince looked up again, and the creature was gone without even a sound. His master had conveyed to him that the demon had limited translocation magic. It could blink in and out but only for short distances. As he lay on the stone floor trying to regain his strength, he felt confident about one thing. Wherever the demon had vanished to, the man known as Ranier would not live long enough to be a hindrance.

The old man made his way through hidden paths only he knew, down the mountains, beneath the curtain of the night stars. Whatever the powers of evil had summoned would be coming now. Though he could not sense it yet, he knew whatever it was would be fast and powerful. Though he could lose anything in these mountains, he did not have time to waste. He could use magic but that could pinpoint his position just as accurately to the enemy.

Centuries of living in a cave did not prepare him physically for the forced pace he now had to endure. Though he knew the maps well enough, he needed to remember that the world would not look the same as it did the last time he walked the face of the lands. Once he got out of the mountains, he would not be as confident of the way ahead. Even with his passages and trails, it would be another day before he would be out of the mountains and within the borders of Mystaria. If nothing else, he would have time to think of the task at hand.

First, he needed to find the key. He hoped the landscape had not changed so much that he would no longer recognize its hiding place. Then he needed to make it to Cordilleran. Once there, the most difficult part of his task would be in the telling of the story. It would be the time for all to be revealed. There would be no more secrets, half-truths, or attempts to protect them from the truth. However, in this case, he knew the truth would create fear, doubt, regret, and despair. If they could battle past their emotional failings and accept what must be, they might have a chance. Regardless of what they believed or accepted; he would give them whatever aid he could. He was the last. There was no other. He felt for them. They had already accomplished so much, risked so much, and lost even more. The knowledge he had to share with them would be of no comfort.

Despite the circumstances, it felt good to be out in the open air again. He could breathe the fresh air deeply, and it was, in a strange way, comforting to be out of breath again. It was a feeling he had not sensed since beyond memory. He had become accustomed to the cave's dank stale air. *This* was night mountain air. If only he could reach the city of Mystaria, he would be able to disappear in the streets of the wizards. *Wizards*— they did not even understand the word. Still, all things must change, he thought. They must evolve, for good or ill. He, of all people, was certainly no one to dare judge others as lesser beings.

Yes, if he could reach the city before whatever evil behind him caught up, it would be difficult to find him indeed. He could get a horse and perhaps tag along with a caravan out of the city. His mind began working again as it did long ago. He used to think of life as a perpetual never-ending game of strategy. The world was the playing field, a great chessboard. The cosmic forces of good and evil were the players, and all the beings that existed throughout the lands were the pieces. Every encounter was a tactical maneuver, giving leverage to one side or the other. However, the rules of his thinking were about to change for he knew the game might conceivably come to an end in his lifetime, with one side finally emerging victorious. This was the only way he could keep things in perspective.

Still, he was often troubled by those thousands of innocents who merely lived their lives day to day as best they could, unaware of the game. What was to become of them? Perhaps their version of reality was truer than his. They lived their lives blissfully ignorant of the greater forces at work, just doing the best they could for their families to survive with a modicum of happiness. One thing was for sure: Their version was wholeheartedly better than his, and in his dreams, he often longed for it.

The trails he followed were descending on a sharp gradient along the mountainside. He braced himself on his walking stick to counter his weight. The trails were seldom used, treacherous and slippery, comprised of small, round rocks. More than once he nearly lost his footing, but nonetheless the downhill trek was a fast one. Night was waning fast. He had to hurry if he were to escape the mountains by daybreak.

It was then he felt it. The feeling was sharp, definite, and painful. Instinctively, he threw himself back against the mountainside. He sensed it. It was an evil of raw and vibrant power. He could feel it now, a demon not of his world. Demons gave off a unique energy signature, which made sensing their presence easy for those who knew how. This demon was powerful, far more powerful than he expected. He knew he must try to avoid it, if possible. It was then he saw it. Instantly, he stood still and chanted a spell to make himself invisible. He looked down the mountainside and saw the creature as it moved near a tree. Its bulk was considerable, but its lean movements suggested an unexpected agility. He caught sight of it maybe a hundred yards below along the mountain base. It moved near a tree, and the last thing he saw were the yellow oblong eyes before the creature joined with the tree and seemed to become part of it. It was a Rasilisk.

Ravager was the common-tongue translation. It was a lethal killing machine, as powerful as it was stealthy. It knew exactly where to position itself and exactly where he would be. The creature would already have his scent and could see in almost any direction where he might emerge from the mountains. His invisibility would be no protection. The creature could see into the infrared and thermal spectrums, but not at the same time. If he remained motionless, the creature may not see him for a few moments. He felt his heart beating rapidly. He never expected to be found out so soon. The enemy indeed went to great expense to employ such a piece in the game. He could not escape or evade the creature, at least not for long. For the moment, the initiative was his, he knew where the creature was, an advantage that may not come again. It was time.

First, he allowed himself to take a deep breath. Then, as if he had not a care in the world, he walked slowly down the slope of the mountain base, leaning heavily on his staff. He maintained his invisibility, though he knew the creature could surely see him now. He caught only a glimpse without looking directly toward it. With its chameleon-like abilities, the demon blended in perfectly with the oak tree. For all its bulk, it had become nearly invisible but had not moved. It was nearly fifty yards away.

His plan was simple, though the slightest miscalculation would mean instant death. He continued along slowly, using his staff until he reached more level ground at the mountain base. He stopped a moment as if to get his bearings, looking around and deciding on a direction. A few moments later, he began his slow walk toward the tree, positioning himself so that the tree would be between him and the demon. As he closed the distance, all he could concentrate on was steadying his breathing and heartbeat. The Rasilisk's senses were so acute that if it detected increased respiration, it would anticipate something was amiss.

His breaths were calm, marked, steady, and evenly distributed. All the ambient sounds of night, the insects and wind rustling, soon became lost to him as he focused solely on remaining calm. He was twenty feet away now, walking on grass toward the massive oak, which had larger, heavy branches jutting out from its midpoint just over ten feet above the demon's location. His strides were slow and narrow, those of an old man—ten feet. He subtly switched his staff to his left hand, closest to the tree side. At the last possible moment, he thrust his staff left just as the Ravager emerged from around the tree.

The crown of his staff burst into a pyrotechnic flash of bright lights that blinded the demon's multispectrum vision. Taking a step back, his right hand shot forth and a bolt of lightning exploded from his fingers, striking the thick huge branch above the Ravager. With a wicked snap, the branch crashed down upon the creature's neck, forcing it to the ground.

The old man took his staff in both hands, stepped forward, and raised it high above his head. He brought it down in a killing stroke, plunging through the creature's left eye. The Ravager released a howl of pain-racked ferocity. He wrenched the staff loose, trying to cause as much damage as possible. The next moment, the old man was off and running, quickly mumbling some arcane words that caused a thick black smoke to pour from the end of his staff.

The demon pushed itself up, the huge branch still on the back of its neck. It brought its massive arms up over the branch and exhaled and roared, snapping the branch like a twig. A stream of blood squirted from its left eye, slowing to a pour down the front of its body. Even its thermal vision could not penetrate the black cloud forming before him, but he could smell the old man; he was still close. The deadly quills on his chest became erect and the beast fired a volley of them straight into the black cloud.

The old man anticipated the ranged attack and lay flat on his stomach and could hear the lethal darts zooming over his head. If one of them merely scratched him, death would be virtually instantaneous. He could hear snarling roars. He had seriously wounded the creature, yes, but in doing so, he had made it many times more dangerous. Demons did not sense pain like humans did. Their existence upon his world made them creatures of flesh and blood; however, when they felt physical injuries, their brains released a hormone that augmented their strength. So, though they did sense pain, it was not a hindrance but an asset.

The Ravager saw the old man emerging from the cloud, coming directly at him about to attack with his staff, but something was strange about his image. It was not emitting the same heat signature as before. The demon's rage distracted it, causing it to hesitate. It was an illusion. The old man had emerged from the side of the cloud on the creature's blind side. As he quickly turned to face the real enemy, the old man appeared to be holding a huge ball of flame.

Before the Ravager could shift its weight, the old man hurled the fireball, which increased in size and scope as it flew through the air. Upon impact, it enveloped the demon, striking with unbelievable concussive force, hurtling the huge form back and slamming it into the oak tree. The creature's back struck the tree like a thunderbolt. An explosion of snapping roots toppled the tree and brought it crashing home to the earth that had spawned it, landing in a bed of flame. The old man raised his arms above his head, and an amber bubble of energy formed around him. In the next instant, he was gone.

The Ravager rose to its feet, hacking and slashing with its claws through the flames that tore at its body. It emerged, its scaled skin singed about the chest and shoulders but otherwise unscathed. Furious it had not detected the deception sooner, it surveyed the area with its remaining eye. The old man was gone, but the stench of magic hung in the air. The man had translocated. He would go toward the nearest city. The demon disappeared in a cloud of smoke.

General Mekko came awake suddenly. He found Toran and Rendek at his bed, urging him to wake.

"All right, all right, lads, I'm up. It's still dark out. Are we under attack, lads?" Mekko asked and splashed water on his face from a basin at the base of his bed.

"No, General, a force of men has arrived at the west gate," Toran responded.

Mekko looked at the two young Dwarves, his face dripping. "In the name of Crylar, must I be awakened for every little thing? General Valin has the watch, does he not? If they are not here to attack us, then what could be the problem?!" Mekko roared.

"He does, sir; however, he asked that we awaken you," Rendek answered.

"Damn that old war horse, will he never make any decisions on his own," Mekko said, drying his face.

"Sir, it is Prince Gideon Crichton of Mystaria, seeking sanctuary. General Valin has denied him and informed him he must leave at once. The prince will not leave and has demanded to speak to you," Toran said.

"Prince Crichton?" Mekko hesitated, stroking his beard, unfurling the knots left from sleep, and slowly standing up. He placed his hands on the shoulders of his two young bodyguards. "Forgive me, lads. You were right to wake me. In the future, never be afraid to wake me again. Gettin' a little grouchy in my old age is all. Now then, help me with my armor and let's go see this Mystarian Prince."

"This is the last time I'm telling you. Wizard, warrior, prince, whatever it is you call yourself, to lead this rabble out of here. You and your men are not welcome here. If you don't leave, we will remove you by force."

General Valin's voice carried some distance at the west gate, and the exchange grew more heated as the general approached the gate with Rendek and Toran. He could see, by torchlight, ranks of Dwarves and Elves growing along both sides of the gate and, behind the Elves, the cavalry of Averon starting to form a line.

At the gate he saw a magnificent white stallion and sitting atop the animal was a man armored in a full suit of golden plate mail. He wore a matching golden helmet with an open face and a crimson robe adorned his back. A huge black crossbow was fastened to the right side of his saddle, while an oversized two-handed sword hung on the left side.

"Have a care with your tone and threats, Dwarf. My patience has limits," the prince responded to Valin.

As Mekko approached, he suddenly, and strangely, remembered the voice of Algernon in his head. He recalled the words he heard at the time of the Sage's death. *"You must ally with your enemy."*

Kael and Elenari were also by the gate. Mekko had heard from them the story of their encounter with the prince at his Tower of Mordovia and of his great hunt, which Mekko was previously familiar with.

"Your patience has limits, does it, Prince Crichton?" Mekko asked as he came into the view of all assembled.

The prince pulled the reins of his horse to the side to face him. He then removed his helmet and placed a circular eyepiece in his left eye. Noticing Kael and Elenari, he bowed his head to them and then faced Mekko. "General Mekko, I have studied your campaigns. Your reputation as a soldier precedes you. I have come here with fifteen hundred Royal Soldiers of Mystaria. We formally request sanctuary, in return for which we will join your Alliance army."

Unable to restrain himself, Kael pushed forward. "How magnanimous of the great Prince of Mystaria. You had your chance to join the Alliance before, Prince Crichton, and you summarily voted against it. Why on earth would you want to join it now, and what makes you think we would ever accept you?"

Crichton kept his gaze fixed on Mekko. "Does the heretic priest function as your tongue, General?"

"When the answers to his questions interest me, he does," Mekko said with a hard countenance.

"Very well." Crichton turned toward Kael. "The council voted not to join your alliance. I however, voted in favor of your proposal."

"How very convenient. I suppose we should take just take your word on that?" Kael responded.

The prince's eyepiece dropped, and he nudged his horse forward two steps so that he was only inches from Kael. His face took on a look of stone, devoid of all feeling. With ice in his voice, he said, "My word is my honor. It is the one thing left in this sick, sad world that can never be taken from me. I have killed men for lesser insults. Were you not this woman's father, you would die where you stand."

Suddenly, all crossbows and bows were poised and aimed at Prince Crichton. The soldiers of Mystaria just as rapidly unsheathed their swords.

"Hold!" Mekko thundered. "There's been enough needless bloodshed. Wouldn't you agree, Prince Crichton?"

The prince suddenly lost the cold look of death as he turned back to Mekko. "Three days ago, without warning, an army of creatures invaded the city of Mystaria. Prior to the invasion, some of the greatest of our wizards were butchered in their sleep. The attack was fast and furious. Even the Great School of Magic was set afire and was burning when we left."

Mekko saw a look of loss cross Crichton's face that he had seen in the eyes of other men. Though it lasted only a moment, such a look could not be faked or rehearsed.

"Those of the ruling council who were not killed fled to their castles in the provinces. Only the Shadow Prince could have ordered such an attack. Only he could have penetrated the magical wards and guards which protect our country. So rather than leading my men to a slaughter, I chose to take them here," Crichton concluded, his expression now flat.

Mekko exhaled deeply. "Your reputation precedes you as well Prince Crichton. You are known to be one of the only members of the ruling council never to have dissected one of my people in your country's many experiments to learn why Dwarves are so resistant to magic. However, I do believe some of my people have participated in your, shall we say, unique, hunt in the past, never to be heard from again."

"I did not come here to apologize for the past, General," the prince said matter-of-factly.

"Aye. The past should stay in the past. I therefore grant sanctuary to you and your men and welcome you to the Alliance army. General Valin will see that your men are properly quartered," Mekko said, bidding them to enter the gate.

With that, all weapons were lowered and sheathed.

"Most gracious of you, General. We thank you for your hospitality." Prince Crichton bowed his head and began to ride in with his men who had already started inside the gate.

"Ah, Prince Crichton I wonder if you'd accompany me over here for a moment," Mekko said, pointing some feet away from the gate.

When they had reached a spot out of earshot of the others, Mekko grabbed his horse by the bridle and looked up at him. "Now you listen here, Gideon. Here, you're prince of *nothin'*. You're the commander of your men and that's all. No one will be *bowin'* and *fetchin'* for you. You and your men will work side by side with the others, same as the rest. You'll be watched every minute. At the first sign of treachery, those involved will be killed; the rest will have their arms and armor stripped and will be banished from this place. That goes for you as well. Do we understand one another now?" Mekko asked.

For the first time, a broad, almost wicked, smile crossed Crichton's lips. "Yes, General. I would say we understand one another quite well." He bowed one last time and rode along with the rest of his men.

As the Mystarian soldiers entered the camp, Mekko rejoined the group. Valin approached with anger etched upon his brow. He was clearly restraining himself with fists clenched and proverbial smoke coming out of his ears. "General, respectfully, I cannot protest this strongly enough. How can you let our enemies within these walls? At the very least, let me confiscate their weapons."

"What *walls*, my old friend? Look around—a bunch of half-built walls, towers, and gates. I don't like him or his men any more than you, but we're not in much of a position to turn away any help. Take a look though." Mekko turned Valin so that he faced the Mystarians. "Every one of those lads, armored in plate mail, probably enchanted with matchin' weapons, all on horseback. Professional soldiers, and our cavalry will be nearly doubled. And Crichton is said to be a powerful wizard and warrior. He may be a better ally than we expect."

"I hope you are right about this, sir," Valin responded and turned on his heels.

"So do I," Kael said without emotion. "You're taking a dangerous gamble, General." He placed his hand around Elenari's shoulder and the pair walked away before Mekko could respond.

The general sighed and said under his breath, "Me too, lad."

Chapter 6

The old man moved through the streets, horrified at the carnage before him. Daybreak no longer announced itself with sunrise, instead the darkness of night merely became less and less until it faded into the gray of morning. Bodies littered the streets of the city of Mystaria. Smoke still rose from the burnt embers of several shops and buildings throughout the city center. As his eyes took in the destruction, he could tell the attack came fast and in overwhelming numbers. The shops, though left in ruin, had not been pillaged. Thievery was not the object of this attack, only the death of the living. He looked at them, the proud wizards of Mystaria, face down, bleeding in the streets, their robes torn and soaked with blood, now fodder for the crows and vultures.

He had translocated there, hoping to vanish within the crowded avenues, but now it seemed he was the only person in the city who still lived. The powers of darkness were as ruthless as they were cunning. They were systematically eliminating all threats. With the Lich, Voltan, destroyed, there was no reason not to destroy Mystaria. Even now, he sensed the enemy would gather his forces for the final battle. There was no need to rush. He had been so very patient and come too far to make any foolish mistakes now. He knew he must reach Cordilleran; he must prepare them. Still, one thing remained, the Ravager.

He knew the demon did not possess the power to translocate such a great distance, but it was coming for him. He could not leave the creature to the enemy forces; it was too powerful. It must be stopped here. This ruined city would be their battlefield. He looked toward the center of the city. The two largest buildings still stood, for the most part, intact, the *Calthredzar* and the Great School of Magic, though they had been blackened with ash and soot.

A tear formed in the corner of his eye as he saw evidence of smoke from within the Great School. There, he thought, was the last bastion of hope for magic in the world. It was the last place where magic might have been properly taught to help and nurture the world. As long as it existed as a place of learning and ideas, a glimmer of hope remained. It could perhaps be such a place again, perhaps, this very day. It was then that the idea struck him. With that, he made his way toward the Great School with haste.

Elenari spent every free moment she had reading Algernon's tome. It was fascinating. Reading it stimulated her thoughts on many levels and made her start to think of possibilities she had never dreamed of. Her mind thirsted for knowledge like a blank canvas thirsted for paint. She had difficulty conceiving how he could have come across such knowledge, which seemed so far beyond her reach. She recalled him once telling Galin that the book was a history of the world, as he knew it, left behind for the generations of the future to learn what they could from it, for better or ill.

As she read through the first few chapters, she became enthralled with the description of a place where life on their world began, which Algernon referred to in his own verse as the Cradle of Life. He went on to say that each race had a different name for it, but that was essentially the common-tongue translation. The description of its location was vague, lacking in detail. Algernon's belief was a cataclysm of some sort occurred that buried the area, driving the early races away from that region to the east. Theory placed it in a subterranean location, somewhere below the Darkstone Sierras. The area was referred to as a natural spring whose life energies were so strong that it spawned the earliest vegetation and animal life, which in turn sustained the first forms of intelligent life.

Then there was an entry of a more cryptic nature, which referred to a guardian. *The place where life began and will always be strongest will forever be watched over by the Guardian.* There was no further reference.

She closed the book and sat in silence for a while within the confines of her tent. She began to think about the poisoning of the lands. It was getting worse, stronger every day. Even the weather had been affected.

Perhaps if they could find the Cradle of Life, something could be done to reverse the process. There was only one spot she could think of that may possess any further clue as to its location, the home of Algernon within the Hills of Renarn—back in the outskirts of Wrenford. She picked up the tome and was off to find Kael and Mekko.

Mekko had called a meeting of his closest advisors within his tent to begin making plans for their next steps.

Archangel pointed to a map. "We have scouts out for miles to the north and west, including the lands between. So far, there has been no sign of the enemy."

"By now we must assume the Shadow Prince knows we have gathered here, in Cordilleran, with our allies and all those who oppose him," Kael added.

"Aye, he'll not venture here, though, until he's gathered his full strength. I don't think he can risk another defeat," said Mekko.

"I don't think he's worried about the possibility of defeat, General. If his armies have just destroyed Mystaria, we're all that stands between him and total victory." It was Lark's voice that had entered the discussion.

"Not all, Lark, you forget the nations of the Trade Federation to the south, in particular Arcadia and Bastlandia. If we can enlist their aid, we may build a force large enough to defeat him," Galin interjected.

"None of you even know how far the Shadow Prince's reach extends. What if his forces have already overrun the islands to the south?" Elenari asked.

"That's precisely the point, Nari, we don't know about the south, but we need to find out," said Galin. "If it is true, and he has taken the nations to the south, we will be attacked on land and sea from several directions."

Silence ensued as none of them wanted to contemplate what that meant, though they all knew.

"That is why Galin and I will be going to Arcadia," Kael said. "First, we will talk to their government, and then we will seek out the Druid Council and see what progress, if any, they have made with the poisoning of the lands. It is a duty I have too long neglected. I will order the members of the council back here to aid you with their magic. Then we will travel to Bast—"

"That's just wonderful!" Elenari shot in. "You and Galin are going to travel overseas to strange lands that we know nothing about, and you don't want me traveling a few days north of here to Algernon's home. You knew you were going to be making this trip all along, nice of you to inform me. Have you at least had the decency to tell Mya yet?"

Kael tried to keep the anger and annoyance from his voice. "Nari, Algernon's home is more than *a few days* from here, even on horseback, even the way you ride. We do not have scouts that far north yet."

Elenari stepped closer to Kael. "I'm sorry, Father, but I believe Algernon's tome holds many secrets that could help us. I believe this *Cradle of Life* could be the key to stopping the poison infecting the lands." She looked at all the eyes on them and pulled Kael away from the others. "I hear Algernon's voice when I meditate. Call it intuition, call it whatever you like, but there could be more information at his home—maps, books, something . . . anything."

Kael held her arms tightly. "I believe you, Nari. I do not doubt you; I just think now is not the time. Algernon knew these things that you read and never mentioned them before. The Druids as well have heard of the Cradle of Life. For us it is a sacred place, but our teachings say it is a place of legend. At least give the Druids a chance, perhaps they know more than we do. I know you can take care of yourself, of that I have no doubt. That's not it. If there were to be an attack while we are away, they will need you here. I would take you with me on this journey if it was at all possible, but in our animal forms, we could not carry you that distance for that amount of time."

"I know, Father," she replied impatiently. "But—"

"There is one other matter." Kael hesitated, his eyes dropping to the ground. When he looked up, his voice had taken on an imploring tone. "I need you to watch over Mya for me while we're gone. I trust her safety to no one else."

Elanari's impatience faded. She felt only concern. Gently, she placed her hand on the side of Kael's face. "Of course, Father. No harm shall come to her."

As they rejoined the group, General Valin entered and asked to talk privately with Mekko for a few moments. The group broke up.

Outside, Kael caught up with Lark. He had intended to give the Emerald Star encased in the metal box within his robes to the only man left who could use it, his best friend. He simply could not risk bringing it on his travels. But just as he would have removed it from his robes, he found himself hesitating. He could not be sure if it was Elenari's admonishments or his own inner misgivings, but at the last moment, he changed his mind.

"What's on your mind my friend?" Lark asked, placing his arm around Kael's shoulders.

"I see you are enjoying your work around the camp," Kael replied, taking notice of the dirt on Lark's pants and shirt.

Lark flashed a brilliant smile. "Indeed, I'm enjoying being useful again. I enjoy hard work amongst the camaraderie of good friends. Seemingly simple pleasures that I always took for granted are now much dearer to me."

"To me as well, Lark," Kael said. "In any event, I would like to ask a favor of you."

"Of course, anything, you know that," Lark responded with the utmost sincerity.

Kael felt ashamed, despite himself. "I was hoping while I was away you would keep an eye on Elenari and Mya for me. Not that they need looking after, mind you, but just every now and then perhaps you could—"

Lark slapped his friend on the shoulder. "I believe I could, Kael, and you're right. They don't need looking after, but for you, I will anyway."

"Thank you," Kael said as the two men exchanged a quick embrace.

"I agree with Elenari, though. I don't like the idea of you and Galin traveling alone such a great distance across the sea."

Kael waved away his concerns with a strong hand. "I am the Grand Druid now. I have a responsibility to the Druid Council, and they have a responsibility to the lands. I have not even met many of the members of the council yet. I don't know who they are or what they are doing, if anything, to help us. If anyone can help us with the poisoning of the land, I feel it is they. This is an obligation I have put off for too long. Additionally, we must try to find whatever aid we can in the nations to the south. It is a crucial trip, and our time grows short I fear.

"I understand, but that doesn't mean I have to like it," the Paladin said with a crooked smiled.

"Until our next meeting." Kael returned the smile, nodded, and walked away.

"Until then," Lark whispered. Kael had risked so much for him and the idea that he may be traveling headfirst into danger without him turned his stomach.

Rendek and Toran trailed behind Mekko as he made his way to the grassy knoll he had found himself sitting upon a week earlier upon his return to Cordilleran. There, seated comfortably in the grass beneath the cool sky of gray clouds, was Galin looking down on their camp and the remnants of the Dwarven kingdom.

Mekko turned to his personal guards. "Lads, I wonder if you'd give us a few minutes alone."

His young kinsman obeyed as Mekko moved forward.

"Have you ever seen Cordilleran, lad. I mean, before the fall?" Mekko asked as he took a seat next to Galin. He held a distant gaze, full of memory of a fonder time. "Have you ever seen the splendor of the great gates of the Barrick Cropaal from miles away? Then as they opened, smooth as silk, to reveal the deep green of the valley beyond which served as only a foyer before a castle of gold. Did you ever see it, Galin?"

Galin looked at him. From the euphoric smile on the Dwarf's face, he knew the general was seeing Cordilleran as it had been.

"No, I was never blessed enough to see your homeland . . . before," Galin finally replied.

"Aye, of course. I know you had the beauty of your Elven Kingdom and havin' been there myself, I'm sure few things can compare to it. But I think you'd have found Cordilleran as magnificent as I did. Yes, I think so," the general mused.

"I've no doubt that I would have found it to be breathtaking indeed," Galin confirmed.

"Well, lad, I come to see you off. I don't mind tellin you, I won't be sleepin' well until you're back again. You've come through for me more than once. I'll not forget it either." Mekko looked to see Galin smiling at him. He could tell the Druid was surprised and touched.

With that, Mekko sprang to his feet. "Well, who the hell's goin watch yer back if I'm not there to do it? I know Kael's a formidable man and you Druids have powerful magic, but if I wasn't with you in Bazadoom, you'd be Orc meat by now."

Galin stood up quickly. "If you weren't with me—"

"Tut, tut, none of your feeble excuses, Druid. It ought to be enough that I let you tag along with me, and then saved you from those Ogres to boot," Mekko joked.

Galin burst out with laughter from deep in his stomach. "General, you and your pig-headed stubbornness nearly got us killed a dozen times over. And who could forget your *strategic* use of song in the middle of the wasteland. The subtle way you used it to alert every Orc in Bazadoom to our presence! Oh yes, how did it go? *And I'll have one more round for the big-bosomed maiden. She'll have you laughin and dancin as she keeps you awaiten.*"

"Now you're singin', laddie," Mekko laughed as he put his arm under the Druid's shoulder, and they joined together in a chorus.

Rendek and Toran looked at each other nervously, unable to comprehend what had come over the two men as they walked toward them singing arm in arm.

"Will you have a glass of ale with me before you leave, lad?" Mekko asked.

"I thought you'd never ask, General," Galin replied.

Kael entered the tent, surprised to see Mya waiting for him near the entrance. She wore her white hair down and long, lying loosely about her shoulders. Her skin seemed silver in the half-light of the dancing flames of a torch. She wore only a thin black satin robe. He stood spellbound by the sight of her.

"I saw your bag packed next to your staff. Are we to be parted so soon?" she asked, deeply as if from her soul.

"I was just coming to tell you," Kael said with an apology in his voice. "I must go to the Druid Council in Arcadia. We need their help and I—they have responsibilities I must see to. Galin will be coming with me. We will try to enlist what aid we can against the Shadow Prince from the nations south of the sea."

Mya stepped forward and gently rested her hands on his chest. "When will you be leaving?" she asked.

He looked into her eyes and found himself lost in her delicacy and grace. It took him several moments to answer. It was her smile that cued him to speak. He could see she enjoyed the effect that she had upon him, almost as much as he. "In the morning. We leave in the morning."

She moved her hands from his chest up to his shoulders and then traced their contour down the length of his arms and rested her hands in his. Her touch was nothing less than magical.

"Then may this night stay with you for the days and nights ahead and remind you to come back to me swiftly and safely."

With that, Kael slowly dropped to his knees and untied the satin belt of her robe. Closing his eyes, he gently kissed her stomach. The feel and taste of her ivory skin consumed him. She smelled like flowers. He wrapped his arms around her hips and held her tightly, feeling her supple hands running through his hair. At this moment, he could not imagine leaving her.

The next morning brought a strange uncertainty. While most of the camp slept, there was scattered movement among those who would bid farewell to the Druids. Their mission, though necessary, was wrought with unknown peril. Since only they could take the form of swift birds, only they could make the journey across the sea within an acceptable time frame.

General Mekko had just finished getting dressed. He spun around quickly to grab the documents he had been working on the night before when suddenly a tall, dark figure stood before him. Instinctively, he grabbed for his axe.

"General, please! It is me, Kael," the Druid said as he lowered his hood. "Forgive this intrusion. I pleaded with Rendek and Toran to let me enter unannounced for I have a favor to beg of you."

Mekko took a deep breath and put his axe down. "Of course, you have but to ask. I am in your debt."

Kael removed the small bronze box containing the Emerald Star from his robes. "General, I give this to you for safekeeping. I have thought long upon it, and for now, I can think of no better guardian."

Mekko looked at him quizzically. He made no effort to reach for the box. "I appreciate your confidence, but perhaps Nari would be a better guardian, or perhaps—"

"I thought about that, General. You may indeed be right; however, she has enough responsibilities troubling her at the moment. I'm not sure how much more she can take. I choose to give it to you, to keep on your person always, until my return," Kael replied. Slowly, Mekko reached out and took the metal box from him and concealed it in his deep pocket.

"Thank you, General," Kael said. "We will do all we can to bring you aid here."

"The Alliance has a little over thirty thousand men and women here, not counting non-combatants, but I fear the army that will come for us may be many times that. We cannot stand, even united, against what's comin'. Give these documents to the leaders of Arcadia and Bastlandia for me. They are official requests from Cordilleran for aid. The language is of a somewhat humble nature for Dwarves. Perhaps that will help sway them," Mekko said, handing him the documents.

Kael held out his hand to the Dwarf. Mekko took it and pulled him into an embrace. "Good luck, and safe journey to you both," Mekko said.

"Farewell, my friend. May Mother Nature watch over and protect you," Kael replied and quickly exited the tent.

Outside, they all waited to say their farewells: King Aeldorath, Captain Layla, Captain Gaston, Lark, Archangel, Elenari, and Mya. In the background, out of their view, Prince Crichton looked on curiously, unseen behind the trees.

One at a time, Kael and Galin went to them, starting with the king.

"May the blessings of all races go with you," said Aeldorath. As the king faced Galin, he looked upon him warmly. "Though I never had a son, I would have wished him to have your spirit and courage if I had. Farewell."

"May Mother Nature guide and protect you, my lord," Galin replied, bowing his head.

As Galin faced Layla, he looked hard at her features. The raven hair and deep blue eyes would stay with him for some time.

She stepped forward and handed him a jade-colored flask. "Within is water from the Fountain of Life from Alluviam. May it strengthen you should you become weak."

As she stepped back, Galin grabbed her hand and held it fast. "Thank you, my lady."

She tilted her head with the sarcastic smile he had come to know well in the last few days.

"Forgive me—thank you, *Layla*," Galin said, good humor curving his lips.

Elenari leapt in Kael's arms and whispered into his ear, "I will always love you, Father. Remember that. Come back to us soon."

"I will, my beautiful little Moonraven." Kael could feel her smile as the side of her face touched his.

Next, Elenari hugged Galin and whispered into his ear, "Bring him back to me."

"I will." Galin whispered in reply.

As Galin shook hands with Captain Gaston, Lark placed his hand on Kael's shoulder as the old Druid returned the gesture. Having said their farewells the previous day, their bonds ran deeper than spoken words.

"I am honored to be counted among your friends. Good luck to you both," said Captain Gaston.

"The honor is equally ours, Captain. Thank you," Kael said.

As Kael shook Archangel's hand, the young ranger said, "I never got a chance to thank you for getting me out of that foul prison."

"Why, Archangel, you speak as though you may never see me again. Surely your brother has told you I am not that easily dispatched," Kael said with a smile.

"Indeed, he has. Good luck, my friend." Archangel said, returning the smile.

As Kael moved to embrace Mya, Galin nodded to Mekko, who watched from the front of his tent. The Dwarf returned the gesture, keeping himself a pace back from the rest.

"One day, my love," Kael whispered.

"One day," Mya replied.

The Druids moved a few steps back from their friends and loved ones and increased the distance between them. With deep breaths, they closed their eyes and spread their arms to their sides. A green light flashed with fire as the forms of the Druids shimmered and shifted. A pair of eagles with white crowns and dark brown feathers took flight from the space the two men had occupied. The eagles' enormous wingspans were magnificent to behold. They swiftly flew to the south, disappearing in the gray of another sunless morning.

Elenari, Mya, and Layla found themselves holding hands as they walked away, long after the eagles were out of sight. The men slowly took their own paths to face yet another dreary day.

Archangel had watched Lark throughout the morning and into midday, as they finished moving the ammunition into place for the siege artillery. Kael's sudden departure clearly weighed heavily on his mind as the light-hearted attitude he had displayed for days before seemed all but gone. An idea came to mind to help the situation. He walked over to one of the catapults where Lark was stacking rocks with six Dwarves.

"Hey, brother, we're just about finished here. I have an idea. Why don't you come with me on a little scouting trip? We could leave now and be back in two days. Maybe you and I can spot something our scouts haven't picked up on. It's been a while since we traveled together, just you and me. What do you say?" Archangel asked.

Lark slapped his hands together and then brushed the dirt off his pants. "I don't know. Kael asked me to keep an eye on Elenari and Mya."

"Come now, Lark. We both know Elenari needs no looking after. Besides, this is the safest place they could be. We'll only go for a day then;

we could be back tomorrow night. Perhaps it's enough just to spend some time away from here."

"What do you think Mekko would say?" Lark asked, contemplating the idea.

"I'll go talk to him right now," Archangel said, patting him on the arm. "Why don't you clean up, get your gear and horse, and I'll meet you by the north gate in one hour." Archangel said, patting him on the arm.

Ranier stood before the majesty of the Great School of Magic. A scattering of robed bodies, as well as the heavily armored bodies of the Royal Soldiers of Mystaria, filled the courtyard, which led to the stairs of the main entrance. He had been busy throughout the day, feverishly spreading different-colored powders from his bags in large, sweeping circular patterns and designs. He began in the streets and then spread them out on the ground so that they encircled the Great School. They were arcane runes, mystical symbols, all of them the same, save the one he was working on now.

It was a slow process that had to be exacting in every detail. If he rushed the design or the powder was not the right consistency, it may not work. Nothing about the demon that pursued him was to be underestimated or taken for granted, especially its intelligence. If his estimations were correct, the Rasilisk would be in the city by nightfall. He hoped he was right, but more, he hoped he would be ready.

As Archangel guided his horse toward the north gate, he watched the construction in progress. There were two high towers on either side of the gate, and then the fences ran east and west, with additional towers on the corners. They were in effect constructing a citadel, or huge fort, for the Alliance. Housing more than thirty thousand people, they had a population larger than some cities. They were walling in an area that started on the southern tip of the Fields of Aramoor and extended south passed the borders of Cordilleran and beyond to the plains, extending to the sea.

It was a massive undertaking. Just inside the north gate was a battery of siege artillery. Another battery of catapults and ballistae faced toward the west gate, and still the largest siege engines took up a line toward the back of the camp.

There was a fenced-off, heavily guarded section in the eastern part of the camp where the Dwarven engineering corps worked on special weapons. Only General Mekko and General Valin had access to that area. Work was proceeding rapidly now. Everyone was pitching in, even the Royal Soldiers of Mystaria and Prince Crichton. The men of Averon, who had extensive experience building forts, were helpful in constructing the walls. Soon they might even be able to withstand a massive assault. All was proceeding, except for *his* area of responsibility; none of the scouts had reported any information on the enemy's movements.

Archangel smiled as he saw Lark waiting for him, already on a horse, fully armored in his shining plate mail, his trusted two-handed sword sheathed in his saddle. He expected nothing less, a Paladin never traveled without his armor, no matter how inconvenient it may prove on a scouting mission.

Archangel mounted his horse. "I see the concept of stealth remains somewhat foreign to you," he said once they were eye to eye.

"A Paladin, little brother, announces his presence when riding into battle. We do not sneak," Lark said with a grin.

"So you've told me," Archangel replied dryly. "Perhaps you will allow me to ride ahead and be your herald, should we encounter the enemy. That way your boldness and bravery will not be wasted, and you'll not have to demean yourself by sneaking."

Lark pulled back on his reins and his horse reared up off the ground but only slightly. "Perhaps I could refrain from announcing my presence in the interest of our mission, of course."

"Most gracious, shall we be off?" Archangel asked as he watched Lark nod. "You see? I knew a little time away would bring your lighter side back."

"What did Mekko say?" Lark asked as they trotted through the open gates toward the Fields of Aramoor.

"He said, he *insisted*, we take some Elven hunters with us," Archangel replied.

Lark looked at him seriously for a moment, "And?"

Archangel flashed a sheepish smile. "And I *told* him we would."

"You lied," Lark admonished in jest.

"Race?" With that, Archangel took off at full speed.

Lark took a deep breath and looked back once toward the camp. He did not wish to be complicit in lying to Mekko, but he knew his brother and had accepted his ways long ago. He hesitated another moment and then dug his heels into his horse, letting out a yell to urge the animal on.

The brothers rode together throughout the afternoon, heading north, past the Fields of Aramoor, beyond the deserted Dwarf villages along the northern borders of Cordilleran. King Crylar had evacuated all the villagers to the Eastern Peaks before the first attack on Cordilleran, and they had been deserted ever since.

Despite the gray haziness of the day, they raced across the empty plains with the wind in their faces. Strangely enough, there was something refreshing about the open emptiness of the lands. Still, everywhere they went, they were plagued by constant reminders of the deterioration around them. Green and blue hues had all but disappeared from the face of the earth. The surface of lakes and rivers no longer mirrored the skies and instead appeared murky and brown. The grass had dried to straw and wilted leaves barely clung to bushes and trees. Birds were scantly seen, and other animals had made themselves unusually scarce as well.

Archangel thought about the Alliance. If this continued, it would be a challenge to find food. If the lands continued to atrophy, the enemy could easily starve them into submission. Such unpleasant thoughts crossed the brothers' minds as late afternoon took hold of the sky and daylight wavered.

They agreed to camp for the evening on the outskirts of one of the villages. The enemy would already know the village had been deserted and would not be expecting anyone nearby. They identified a large tree to shelter beneath, but first rode through the small village and the surrounding territory.

Sturdy rock dwellings served as the Dwarves' homes. While the roofs appeared to be thatched, the men knew that the roofs were made of rock with a straw and wood covering. Each home had a chimney, as Dwarves loved a good smoke as they relaxed by the fire. Even in as small a village as this, a well-defined stone road wound through the center. Houses were well spaced from each other and evenly sized, save for two buildings near the end of town. One was a tavern, and the other likely belonged to the village Alderman.

Though the brothers did not speak as they rode, they knew what the other was thinking: The tyranny of evil had forced a peace-loving people to flee for their lives, forsaking their homes and freedom. Few things stirred more anger in them than the thought of it.

By the time the darkness of night had crept in upon them, they were satisfied with their inspection of the area that it would be safe to camp there for the night beneath the tree they had chosen. Archangel built a small fire. In his pack, he had brought two small kabobs of meat, which they could cook over the open flame. He watched as Lark knelt in prayer before they ate, as was his custom. They sat with the meat, and Archangel waited patiently for the comment he knew would be coming.

"A tankard of ale would go well with this don't you think?" Lark asked, as held the small metal skewer over the flames.

With that, Archangel got up, went to his horse, and came back carrying a satchel. I have something just as good, if not better." He handed Lark a small goblet and poured from a large wineskin.

"Wine, excellent"—Lark swirled the wine in the goblet and put it to his nose to inhale the bouquet—"ah, and a fine vintage by the smell of it. The Dwarves certainly do have a skill with such things."

Archangel lay down on the opposite side of the fire and quietly they cooked the meat and drank wine. Each man looked at the other through the dancing flames. There was much unspoken between them. They had been through more together, in some ways, than any of the others, and until this moment, they had never uttered a word about it.

"Archangel, I am so terribly sorry," Lark said. "You will never know the extent of my grief, my frustration, my failure." His words ended in a whisper.

"It is carved no deeper into you than it is into me," Archangel replied as he stroked his black eye patch. "There is nothing for you *to* apologize for. There was nothing you could have done."

"Let me see it." Lark's voice wavered. It was not a command, more like a weak plea.

Lark had never asked to see his wound before. Exhaling deeply, Archangel removed the eye patch, revealing the deep empty socket outlined by reddish-black scar tissue.

Lark kept his face blank but cringed inwardly, his mind flashing back to the dungeons of Shadowgate when Viscount Navarre's blade dug deep into his brother's eye. All he could do was watch, crawling on his hands and knees, unable to lift a finger to help him. Then he flashed back to their lives as children in Osprey Falls and the first time his father had sat them down and talked to them about their responsibilities to each other. Lark closed his eyes and heard his father's strong voice: *Lark, you are the oldest, you are responsible. It is your duty to protect your little brother. Archangel, it is your duty to listen and respect your older brother.*

"It does not hurt," Archangel said as he readjusted the patch. "I do not let it affect me. I merely have to move my head a little swifter during battle. It wasn't your fault—"

"It was my duty!" Lark exclaimed, tossing the remnants of his wine into the fire, making it flare up momentarily with newfound strength and height. Tears formed in his eyes as if the fire had caused them to burn, but the fire was not to blame.

Archangel sat up to a kneeling position and faced Lark. "Do you not think that every moment I was held prisoner that all I could think of was if you were still alive and how I could get to you? Do you know they did not ask me one single question? Every moment I thought of what they were doing to you, what choices they might be giving you, or how they might use me against you. Do you think the grief is yours alone? Do you think the rage is yours alone? Do you think the death of that assassin has quenched my need for revenge? Oh no, brother, I assure you it has not!" Archangel sat back against the tree and removed one of the knives he kept hidden in the gauntlets on his wrists and twirled it in his hand.

Lark looked at his younger brother and admittedly had not considered what it must have been like from his point of view. He had not contemplated the emotional strain that his concern for his older brother would have upon him. He knew there would be repercussions from the physical torture, just as he felt, but never thought about anything beyond that. However, his shortsightedness and Archangel's anger made his failure seem all the more complete. "Perhaps if I had feigned cooperation earlier with them or given in to their—"

Archangel jumped up. "I'd see myself dead first than have you give in to the enemy. Your Paladin's code would never have allowed it. I know who you are. I knew you would never willingly break, and I expected nothing less. Lark, I admire you more than any other man I've ever known. You've dedicated yourself to a life following a nearly extinct code of chivalry that I could never live up to. I would never see you become anything less than you are, even to save me. We were taken against our will, and tortured, but we are here now together. The very powers of good that you pray to, and have unswerving faith in, have given us a second chance. A second life! We should not misuse it by living in the past."

The two men faced each other for several long moments in silence.

"Who is the Paladin now, little brother, you or I?" Lark asked smiling.

"Come! You drank so little, I thought you ill. Let us toast together, brother," Archangel said as he poured himself more wine.

Lark picked up his goblet and held it out to him. "To what are we drinking?"

Archangel raised his goblet. "First to Kael and Galin. May they have a safe journey and speedy return."

"To Kael and Galin," Lark replied and drank.

"To the Alliance, long may it last," Archangel toasted.

"The Alliance." Lark drank and then held out for another refill.

"To us, family reunited," Archangel added.

Lark paused and this time touched his goblet to Archangel's. "To us, my brother."

They had several more toasts as the night went on, until the wineskin had emptied. Lark drifted off to sleep soon after, while Archangel remained awake on watch. Despite the wine, he knew sleep would still be difficult for him. He removed a whetstone from his pack and began sharpening one of his many throwing knives.

Archangel was as accomplished with the sword and bow as any man, but his true expertise was with smaller edged weapons, in particular, hunting and throwing knives. The Elves had been kind enough to give him all the weapons and equipment he had requested, and even though Elven blades needed no sharpening, it was more a contrived task for something to do. He carried many small knives hidden on his person in addition to two larger knives concealed in his gauntlets.

Lark, on the other hand, fought with one weapon—a great two-handed sword with a frost-white diamond etched in the hilt. It was a magical blade that glowed in darkness. He had acquired many years earlier on his adventures with Kael along with his thick metal skin of shinning plate mail.

It had been nearly three hours, near the end of his watch, when Archangel first sensed it. "Lark . . . Lark, wake up," Archangel whispered urgently.

Slowly, Lark turned over; his eyes were open, his blanket still covering him. "What is it?"

"Trouble. Close, all around us."

Lark saw the two large knives in Archangel's hands held in a reverse fighting grip. He remained lying and eased his hands around the hilt of his sword concealed beneath the blanket. Branches snapped, and, in an instant, several dark forms descended upon them.

Elenari found sleep especially difficult this first night of Kael's absence from the camp. She attempted to read more of Algernon's tome but found she could not keep her distracted mind fixed on the words. She gave up trying and decided to take a walk to the southern end of the camp. While the fences were still incomplete, at the most southern point within the camp, the sea was visible at night and, above, the stars. White specks that pierced the ebony sky were still visible, though she had to look harder to find them.

An eerily familiar voice greeted her. "Beautiful, is it not?"

Startled, she drew her short sword and spun around, leaving the tip at the throat of the tall, dark figure who had come up behind her.

She quickly recognized Prince Crichton by the curls of his darting black mustache and the expressionless countenance upon his face.

She narrowed her eyes. "I did not hear you approach. I would have heard any *human* long before they got this close." She held the blade near his throat a moment longer, observing him carefully.

"Indeed. I am often told I have a light footstep. In any event, I was already here. You seemed distracted and did not seem to notice me," Crichton said with an amused tone.

Elenari looked at him strangely for a moment, considering what he had said and quickly sheathed her sword.

"May I join you?" the prince asked.

"If you must, the land here *is* still free," she replied and turned away from him to gaze at the night sky.

"I wonder if I could inquire as to the whereabouts of young Lord Hawk?" Prince Crichton asked. "I have not seen him."

Elenari looked down, closing her eyes. Her first instinct was rage, but she calmed herself. It pained her to have to explain to *this* man who had tried to kill them, but something was odd about the way he had asked. He seemed to genuinely want to see him.

"He . . . died," she replied, frustrated by the crack in her voice.

"Died! How?!" the prince demanded.

She cocked her head at the confusion drawn on his face. "He was killed by a creature of the Shadow Prince. The creature has since been destroyed." She bit her bottom lip to hold back the tears that were still so close to the surface.

Crichton's expression contorted with fury, and he paced angrily in a small circle, as Elenari watched him curiously. After a moment, he stopped and met her gaze. She saw something on his face she had never seen—remorse.

Slowly, calmly, he walked toward her. He reached down and gently took her hand in his, raising it up only as far as her waist. He bent far over to kiss her hand. "I grieve with you. The world is a far less interesting place without him in it." As he stood upright, he looked into her eyes and realized that Hawk had been more than a friend and companion to her. "Please forgive me if I have offended you." He turned and walked a few steps away and suddenly stopped.

Elenari kept her eyes on him. As she watched his back, she could feel his inward struggle but could not figure out just what he was struggling with.

When he turned back to her, he wore an expression of pure empathy.

She had never seen such a gentle, authentic expression on his face, as he normally wore his emotions like a dark stoic mask.

"I also lost someone close to me once," he said. "The wise say that time heals all wounds . . ." His countenance grew stoney. "You will find it *not* to be true."

Elenari watched him storm away into the night.

Chapter 7

The lush green grass blew in the wake of a warm breeze as the flowers danced about in their earthen beds of rich soil. The *Incarnatious ferinious*, otherwise known as the Flaming Flowers to the local populace of Arcadia, were in full bloom and dotted the main island by the thousands.

Minister of Agriculture Ellis Freefire strode across the flat-green sod that led to the Ministry of Arcadian Affairs with Underminister Misty Treehill. Their elegant blue and green silken robes seemed to float behind them as they quickly moved through the natural gardens that were the lifeblood of Arcadia. They stopped for a moment to enjoy a patch of the famed orange and yellow flowers. Freefire was the senior member of the Chamber of Representatives and his vote carried others with it in council meetings. The fifteen islands that made up the nation of Arcadia were the largest exporters of produce as well as roots, herbs, and medicines in the entire Southern Trade Federation.

Nearly a century earlier, at the time of the Trade Federation's formation, the royal family had taken on the role of beloved figureheads and true power went to the Chamber of Representatives. The king and queen, along with their children, lived on the remote and tranquil island of Gardenia, where they were worshipped and their every need was attended to. They would often be seen in attendance at formal occasions or when entertaining foreign heads of state. Still, they had come to accept their role within their nation long ago.

The Ministry of Arcadian Affairs was a wondrous building, made from green marble and blue sapphire-like stone blocks that had been dug up from the mines on Etheros, a small island north of the mainland. The Ministry housed the Chamber of Representatives, the ruling body of elected officials that formed the government of Arcadia. Most of the buildings and infrastructure on the main island of Arcadia were built from these beautiful materials that sparkled when the sun shone upon them. The Ministry was built between the Green Cap Hills, the highest points on the main island, and integrated into the natural environment so as not to take away from its true pristine beauty.

As Freefire and Treehill made their way up the marble steps, their sandals sliding across the smooth stone, Freefire pulled a stack of parchments from his leather bag and handed them to his Underminister. "I need you to bring these to Madame Floran in the Department of Endangered Species immediately."

As Treehill took the documents, they passed a green marble statue of a woman in flowing robes with doves perched on both arms.

They reached the last stair in front of another breathtaking marble statue, this one white and of a man pointing toward the sky and sitting atop a large bird with an enormous wingspan spread out, his robes blowing behind him.

"If all goes well, Misty, the Representatives of the Chamber will give us permission to go to Pernia and call on the Druid Council for direction."

Freefire hesitated, staring at his Underminister for a moment. She was a pretty, young woman who had just come of age. Her deep blue eyes matched the brilliance of the sapphires that dotted the buildings and statues around them. Her thick blond hair blew wildly in the rising breeze. Having grown up on the southern island of Pernia, she was by no means the typical Arcadian girl. She came from a family of farmers, and it was quite a surprise when the Seekers came to her during the annual *Lestarian Portious*, or Youth Choosing, when all nine-year-olds were joined with a Seeker to determine their destinies according to the teachings of Arcadian religion.

She was the first Treehill to take a role with government officials, and it was a great honor for her family. Since all Arcadian children were taken from their families at the age of nine and trained in their trade for nine years, Misty had not seen her family during that period, as it was forbidden. However, her eighteenth birthday was fast approaching, and he knew she longed to see them again during the *Sathious Prada*, or Rejoining Ceremony.

Minister Freefire had been with her since the beginning, preparing her for her future role in government. He had been her mentor and essentially her father for the past nine years. Soon, she would be ready to be his equal in government.

"You know, Misty, there is no greater satisfaction for a teacher than when the student is ready to surpass him. Though you are young and at times lack a certain . . . restraint, I foresee you will be a great Minister and servant of the people."

"Thank you, Minister," said Misty, bowing to her teacher. "Minister"—Misty bowed again—"as you are aware, the Druid Council has refused our attempts at contact for the last six months. They have barred all visitors to their chambers on Pernia."

Freefire laid a hand on Misty's shoulder. He was not all that much older than she was, but he had an air about him that made him seem wise. "It is true, Misty, that the Druids have refused our company. It is also true that the islands in the north, from Cavrious to Gardenia, are plagued by a disease that is spreading quickly. If we do not act with the help of the Druids, this disease will spread to the main island. That is why today I shall meet with the Chamber of Representatives to explain our findings and to have them send a special envoy to the Druids, begging for assistance." Freefire dropped his hand and gazed into her blue eyes. "Now, do as I say and deliver these parchments and have my Averic made ready for flight. I intend to leave soon after this meeting."

Misty bowed once again. "As you wish, Minister." She walked off toward the east hill.

Freefire made his way toward the Chamber of Representatives, knowing they were anxiously awaiting his report.

The white marble doors stood fifteen feet high and opened slowly and soundlessly as Minister Freefire passed through them. A magnificent entry hall greeted him with ceilings more than fifty-feet high and made from smooth sapphire slabs. The glistening floors were soft white. The chandeliers hanging from on high illuminating the great foyer were carved from a unique wood possessed of an off-white luster. Numerous alcoves, built into the walls on each side, housed statues of men and women in various dramatic poses.

Freefire continued briskly through the entry hall until he came to another set of doors made of thick opaque-colored stone. Two soldiers with white-plated metal armor stood on either side.

One of the soldiers opened the doors and bellowed toward a large round table surrounded by fifteen seats, "Minister of Agriculture, Ellis Freefire, presenting himself to the Chamber of Representatives, before the eyes of Arcadia!"

Freefire strode inside, assured and confident.

The chamber was decorated similarly to the foyer. It was a credit to the highly skilled stoneworkers and architects predominately from the island of Etheros who had designed the marble walls and arched ceilings. Throughout the circumference of the circular chamber, dozens of glorious statues graced the room. An equal amount of praise was to be given to the seamless staff of men and women who tirelessly worked on keeping every inch of the administrative buildings immaculately dust-free. This was a task of no small effort or importance as Freefire observed the ever-present mirror finish of the great council table.

Dressed in white linen robes, outlined in bright green and blue, the men and women stood as Freefire made his way to the one empty chair of green marble. He bowed low to the floor and rose slowly. The men and women nodded to their colleague before returning to their seats.

As he scanned the table, Freefire saw all were present. He knew all of them quite well, having been in the same classes as many during their education, or "life training."

A middle-aged woman with short black hair rose from her seat again and nodded to Freefire. "It is with honor and great admiration that I, Sky Longwood, Representative of Gardenia, welcome Mr. Ellis Freefire, Minister of Agriculture, for the great nation of Arcadia, to the hall of the Chamber of Representatives."

The others clapped lightly.

"The honor is all mine," said Freefire, bowing again.

Another woman, younger, with long flaming-red hair, rose and spoke. "The Chamber of Representatives, chosen by the people of Arcadia, give the floor to the honorable Mr. Freefire to discuss the findings of his report that was requested by this council two months ago and passed by a ten to five margin."

Freefire bowed again. "My fellow Representatives," he began, "I wish I could give you better news of the health of our lands; however, my concerns have been substantiated in my final report to the Chamber. After an exhaustive two months of visiting our fifteen islands, after painfully scouring our mountains, studying our trees and flowers, I have concluded that there is truly a dark disease that is gripping our lands."

Concern and dread overtook the attendees' expressions. They exchanged uneasy glances and desperate whispers.

Freefire continued, "No potions have been able to cure it. No prayers have been able to remove this stain from our pristine lands—"

"As a Chamber Representative of the island of Feloria," a man interrupted, "I ask for proof. I have seen no such poison in the glorious land of Feloria. The island is as beautiful as ever. The birds continue to sing of the glories of our country." He moved his gaze around the table and smiled.

"Honorable Representative of Feloria, your island lays far to the south of our homeland, it does not appear to have spread that far south as yet, but make no mistake, it is coming." Freefire looked to his right. "The gracious Representatives of Gardenia, Thadious, Borona, and Estalious are well aware of this disease which has killed numerous species of plants, trees, and other vegetation throughout their region."

The men and women from those islands readily agreed. One stood and looked toward the Representative of Feloria. "I have seen it firsthand, honorable Representatives of Arcadia. Our fruit trade has been cut in half!"

Another stood. "And our vegetable fields have yielded half of what they were only a year ago!"

Yet another stood, this time a tall woman. "The warm springs of Thadious have dropped nearly five degrees in the last six months. That's more than in the last century!"

One of the older men stood now. "Perhaps there is a logical explanation for this, my dear friends. When most at this table were children, there was a terrible heat wave that lasted six months, you all remember." He nodded to them as if helping them to remember. "We lost quite a bit of trade during those months."

"Honorable gentleman from Vineridious," spoke a woman with a deep voice, "I remember it well; however, our losses were minimal, and this darkness seems to be rooted within the land itself. If unattended, it could be the greatest threat we have ever faced."

"My dear Representatives," spoke Freefire, regaining control of the chamber, "I can assure you there has never been such a poison before. I have reviewed the tomes of Arcadia, back to the time of Alimus Rainbrook and the first Chamber. There has never been an issue where potions have not been useful. Ever." Freefire rung his hands tightly as he walked around the table. He wore his concern impassioned on his face. Deep anguish came through in his speech as he searched for words to convince the Representatives of the dangers they were facing. "Representatives—" He let out a smile. "*Friends*, you have known me our whole lives; I am not an alarmist. The people of Arcadia appointed me to my role of Minister of Agriculture because of my love of our natural resources and my deep will to protect our lands and keep them pure. Listen to me when I tell you that a nameless, sourceless blight has affected our lands. It is only a matter of time before it spreads further south. Great plagues announce themselves as small infections. We *must* act now." Freefire had a raised tone, hinting of desperation, and watched as the Chamber went quiet for several moments.

"Ellis," the woman who granted him the floor spoke, "what do you request of the Chamber?"

Freefire walked toward her and smiled. "I need your permission to meet with the Druid Council on Pernia to ask the protectors of the lands for help."

"Minister, you know as well as everyone here that the Druids have been in isolation for months. They have refused our previous requests for a meeting. They turn away all visitors to their tower. Rumor has it there is an internal struggle among them for control of their council. What makes you think they will meet with you now?" she asked.

"Because, Jarilia, they must. Because if they don't, there will be no land to protect and no need for Druids. They *must* meet with us. I will not leave Pernia without an audience with the Grand Druid."

Freefire stood patiently waiting as they mumbled under their breaths to one another.

"Minister," spoke Jarilia, "as grave a matter as this is, there are international affairs going on that must take precedence. We have received a communiqué from Bastlandia, through the Trade Federation, blaming us for an attack on a convoy of Bastlandian ships a few days ago. The anniversary celebration has been canceled, and Bastlandia has threatened to withdraw from the Trade Federation. They may at this very moment be preparing for war. If we cannot figure out who attacked them, I fear the entire Southern Trade Federation will be thrown into a war that may destroy us." Jarilia closed the distance between herself and Freefire and looked him straight in the eye. "The Chamber *cannot* be dispatched to the Druids at this time. I'm sure you understand."

"Then send me alone—" Freefire's words drew gasps of dismay. "Allow me to take Misty Treehill, my Underminister, with me. We will go, just the two of us."

"Minister, you are well aware of Arcadian protocol. It must be the Chamber as a whole who calls upon the Druids. It is the Chamber that the Druids must speak to. It has been so since the first Druid Council was established on Pernia."

Again, the men and women spoke to one another in hushed tones.

"Honorable Chamber of Representatives, I understand your situation. It seems we have pressing issues on many fronts. I understand protocol, however . . . " He moved his gaze from one to the next. "I don't give a damn about protocol!"

None hid their shock at his outburst.

"As Minister of Agriculture, I call upon the Chamber to cast a vote on my request."

The Chamber members stood and argued loudly with Freefire and one another until Jarilia brought them back to order.

"Minister Freefire, as you requested, by our laws and mandates, your request will be honored." She rang a bell on the round table and the large black doors opened to admit fifteen small children. They entered with quills and parchment, taking their place with each representative.

"Minister, please retire to the foyer to await the vote," Jarilia requested.

Freefire politely bowed low to the floor and went out into the foyer where he recognized a man in silver-plated armor impatiently pacing back and forth.

"Ah, Minister Freefire, so you are the one holding me up," the man said as they exchanged bows.

Freefire returned a dim smile. "Commandant Oseana, it would seem we both have urgent business with the Chamber."

"Indeed. It seems the Bastlandians have unjustly accused us of ambush, yet again. All propaganda, I tell you, they've wanted to go to war over the trade routes for years. They were just trying to invent the best excuse," Oseana said.

"Commandant, a war with Bastlandia can only serve to break up the Federation and hurt their profits as well as ours. I see no benefit to either side," Freefire said.

"Well, Minister, with respect, I believe those issues should be left to the Chamber and the military to decide." The Commandant bowed politely.

"So be it," Freefire replied, returning the bow and allowing the conversation to end with both men saving face.

That moment the Chamber doors swung open and a young boy no older than thirteen, clad in white robes, emerged holding a piece of parchment. He approached Freefire, bowed low, and read from the paper: "The Chamber of Representatives has voted ten to four in favor of your request to meet with the Druid Council on Pernia."

Freefire showed no emotion as the boy continued, "The Chamber asks you to inform the Grand Druid of the reasons for the Chamber's absence. The Chamber hopes the Druid Council will respond favorably and aid us with the issues concerned." The boy bowed low.

Freefire turned and was off, confident he would be as successful with the Druids.

A deathly stillness filled the air in Mystaria. Night had finally come and with it the inevitability of confrontation. Ranier stood high atop the Great School of Magic on the northern edge of the building, looking down into the streets. He held fast his wooden staff with both hands. Strangely enough, he felt more alone at this moment than all the centuries he had spent in solitude within his cave. If he fell here in battle, there would be none alive to know he ever existed at all. None save the enemy, who would soon be revealed.

He could see nearly the entire city from atop the Great School, but he knew full well he would not see the demon. Its powers of camouflage were too keen. He could sense the demon's presence now. It was powerful, moving silently in the shadows somewhere in the city. There could be no reasoning with it, no chance to barter or talk to it. It was a negative life force. Its hatred made it incredibly dangerous, a creature with absolutely no fear.

Ranier found himself experiencing fear of a different sort. He did not fear the Ravager; instead, he feared the price of failure, a price much too high to pay. He concentrated, muttering ancient arcane words of power. Now he could only wait. With luck, the demon would approach the northern face of the building.

After an hour past nightfall, there was still no sign. What made a demon like the Ravager that much more dangerous was its intelligence and ability to control its rage. Perhaps it had not located him yet. After all, it was a large city, but even if it had, no doubt it expected a trap and would study the situation before charging into battle.

It grew very dark as the waiting progressed. None of the streetlights were lit; no candles or fires burned. Ranier had to be cautious, as the creature could end up next to him before he knew it. The waiting continued as they played their dangerous game, neither fully knowing whether they were the hunter or the hunted.

The Rasilisk crept through the streets. Despite its massive bulk, it moved silently and deadly. It surveyed everything with its surviving eye, using its thermal vision to check for signs of life. Bodies decorated the streets, but they were all black, cold, and void of the red glow of energy living beings radiated. He caught the old man's scent some time earlier and had slowly maneuvered toward it, staying close. Its scaled body pressed against the buildings as it moved, becoming one with the colors and textures it touched, disappearing almost entirely from view.

It found itself moving closer and closer toward the center of the city.

The old man proved to be challenging prey. He had managed to not only deceive him but also draw first blood. The center of the city was strategically the best place for him to confront an attacker and see him coming.

He longed to pull the old man's beating heart from his chest with such speed that he would look down victoriously upon his prey and know that the man's last vision would be of him biting into his heart, spilling the old man's lifeblood down upon his face and into his mouth. The demon's satisfaction would come in the old man's bitter taste of his own blood mixed with fear, hopelessness, and finally death.

The more time that elapsed, the more Ranier felt the advantage slipping to the Rasilisk. He no longer felt the precipitation of their encounter could be left to luck. He decided to take the initiative.

Raising his staff in one arm, his free hand above him, a red light began growing as if originating from his back. The light grew, pulsing brightly and expanding in a spherical shape ever brighter until soon it could be seen from anywhere within the city. When he was confident there would be no mistaking his location, he lowered his arms and the light diminished and faded back to the darkness. He had put forth a challenge, knowing the demon would surely be expecting a trap now.

The Ravager saw the old man atop the large building. He was standing close to the edge of the roof of the building, facing to the north. He glanced around the street level surrounding the building. He did not detect the presence of any other life forms. He needed to move cautiously around the building to come up behind his prey from the south. He moved until he was directly under where the old man stood, with only a single street between him and the building. He could see the old man looking down in his general direction, but he was confident that his form was not visible to the human eye. With a final visual examination of the area, he proceeded. One step at a time would soon bring him to his prey. The next step, however, was the first trigger.

An explosion of fire took place on the street beneath him. Finally, thought Ranier as his left hand shot forth from his black robes. A searing, burning bolt of white fire burst from his fingertips, striking in the vicinity of the explosion. He could not see, but he heard the creature's shriek more out of surprise than pain from his first trap.

The white fire struck, singing the creature's leg, burning deep in the flesh as he dove and rolled quickly to his left. The fire trap did not damage the creature; it had only startled him and created a flame that the old man could use to discern his approximate location. As the demon came up on all fours, a second explosion of fire occurred in its face. A flash of orange flame coupled with smoke again appeared upon the street.

Upon seeing the second trap sprung, Ranier pointed his staff and white fire exploded from its head, down toward the second burst of flame.

The demon threw itself forward to avoid the white flames, setting off yet another fire trap. Quickly it focused its vision to the infrared spectrum and saw powdered symbols every few feet upon the street. They were magic traps laid down by the old man. Now his attacks of white fire were herding him toward the center of the street. It was there he saw one circle of magic powder that was different from the rest. That was the old man's trap.

The Ravager salivated; the old man was already dead and did not know it. The demon stood still for a moment, bracing itself. The white flames struck him, burning like fire mixed with cold, exposing his scaled body, singing the deadly quills that covered its chest. He shrieked in pain, an inhuman roar climbing to an increasingly high pitch.

Ranier could see it, mainly the creature's outline, large and menacing. The lone yellow eye glowed in the dark; its blue fur and scales were concealed within the blackness of night, but it had stopped moving and allowed itself to be hit by the fire, and then the next moment, it simply vanished.

Ranier smelled something not unlike sulfur in the air. He quickly turned around to the find the demon beside him, it had translocated to the roof of the Great School not two feet away from him.

Raising its bulging arms, the claws of its hands fully extended, it towered over its smaller prey. With its arms extended, it appeared nearly twelve feet tall. Its deadly quills became erect.

Ranier faced it, not moving. A wizened old man with stringy white hair grasping his wooden staff with both hands looking up at the giant hulk before him, a rock-hard countenance upon his brow as if his black robes and thin little staff would somehow shield him from the imminent deathblow.

As the demon brought its massive arms down for the kill, crimson flames ignited all around the Ravager, encircling it and engulfing its arms. The creature cried out in unexpected pain, coupled with rage and pulled its arms back. Instantly, it looked down about its feet where his infrared vision revealed he was standing on another circle of powder like the one in the center of the street. The old man knew it would translocate to that exact spot for the kill. It watched, enraged beyond earthly concept, as the old man raised his arms above his head.

Imprisoned with the flames, the demon roared, this time with the might and fury of a Firedrake. The deafening sound shook the entire building. Enraged beyond concern for itself or its mission, the demon threw itself into the crimson fires. With a sweeping lunge of its right arm, it penetrated through them, raking the old man, clawing through his robes and into the flesh of his upper left arm. The force of the blow and sheer strength of the Ravager knocked the old man back off the ledge, forcing him to grab for it with his fingertips.

The price of pain the demon incurred was harrowing as the flames nearly burnt through its arm. It fell to its knees momentarily, but within moments was up, roaring, its muscles contorted and flexed to the hilt about its neck and shoulders. Possessed of rage and hatred, it threw the weight of its body into the fires, bouncing off them, hitting them harder each time. Its strength started to increase almost exponentially as it hurled itself from side to side.

Ranier struggled, pulling with all his strength, trying to keep from falling. The runes of imprisonment that held the Ravager would not hold the creature long; he could hear its unbridled fury. If he did not pull himself up now, he would die anyway. He arched his head back and with a great push was able to get his elbows up on the ledge. He saw the demon smashing itself into the fires, letting the momentum of its fierceness drive it. It would be mere moments before it broke through.

Ranier pulled one leg up, then the other, and somehow managed to scramble to his feet. His robes flew open in the night as he raised his arms high above him, a chiseled rage of his own etched into his face. "Rasilisk, Demon, I cast you out of this world! I destroy you and consign you to eternal oblivion!" Ranier bellowed, his voice rising even over the creature's deafening roars.

With that, Ranier's entire form seemed to glow, a bright light emanating from him as the white fire exploded from his fingertips. The fire emerged with a much greater volume, tearing through the red flames of imprisonment, stopping the demon's movement, fully covering its body. Its roar became incessant as it fought to survive.

Ranier closed his eyes and glowed brighter and brighter as the intensity of the white fires became more and more powerful, soon raging with a roar of their own, drowning even the demon's cry in the silence of the night overlooking a dead city. Soon the creature's form could barely be seen within the blazing white flames assaulting it. A moment later, the Ravager shrunk, collapsing in upon itself and then finally blasting apart, leaving nothing but black ashes in its wake. The bright light immediately subsided as Ranier collapsed to his knees.

It was not the fatigue of battle that caused his weakness, though he never wished to exert such power before arriving at Cordilleran. It was the blow inflicted by the demon. His hands shook as he felt the poison of the deadly claws coursing through his body. It was not the poison of the quills but still deadly. He searched through one of his bags, madly sifting through vials within until he found the one he sought. Removing the cork, he quickly ingested the entire potion. It would be enough to keep him alive, but it was not a cure. He removed his black robes and pulled down his tunic to see the four large gashes in his left bicep. For now, all he could do was apply fresh bandages and keep them as clean as possible. He knew they would never heal. He looked the south. Still, he had the key to find and a long journey ahead.

He hoped some of the wizards of Mystaria still lived in the provinces. If they did, they would have observed his battle with the demon. Perhaps it would be enough to give them hope. He picked up his staff and contemplated the next leg of his journey.

Chapter 8

Lark rose, sword in hand, throwing his blanket over the head of their nearest attacker. He grabbed the man's sword arm, twisted his wrist, and slammed the blunt end of the sword into the attacker's covered head. He kicked the man in the backside, sending him reeling to the ground. He looked over at Archangel who had also overpowered one of the assailants.

"Ha! It's been far too long since we fought together, brother, even against backstabbing filth like this," Lark said, his breath labored.

The attackers were garbed in black from head to toe and armored mostly with curved swords. Archangel saw one on the other side of a tree, aiming a shortbow at Lark. He crouched and sprang up with an underhand throw, burying one of his knives in the hooded attacker's throat. He quickly filled his empty hand with another knife from his boot.

There seemed to be seven of them in all, with three on the ground now.

A twig snapped as one of them dashed north.

"Archangel!" Lark called, pointing.

Archangel took off in a mad run on the escaping form's heels. Though he didn't like leaving Lark outnumbered, he knew the odds were quite probably in Lark's favor.

Lark faced his three mysterious black-clad attackers as they spaced themselves out in a wide circle: one in front of him and the other two to his left and right.

They saw the thick plate armor he wore, down to his steel gloved hands and the great sword he bore, which seemed to glow in the night. They hesitated.

Lark smiled. "Ahh, I see. My sword is larger than yours. You feel outclassed. Let me make this easy for you," Lark said as he got down on his knees. "Is this more what you are accustomed to? Perhaps this is the only way your kind wins fights."

With that, the one on his right charged him, his sword reaching behind his back and coming down in a two-handed stroke as if to split Lark in two.

In two quick moves, Lark parried the blow with a horizontal block and then swung the great sword around so swiftly, it cut effortlessly through the attacker's legs, separating them at the knees. His attacker fell flat on his back, screaming in agony, which quickly diminished to a few moans and then nothing. Lark spun a quarter turn on his knees and faced his other two assailants, who remained unmoving, clearly reconsidering their intentions.

"Have you lost your courage so soon?" Lark mocked. "How careless of me, you need more of an advantage, very well." Lark tossed his great sword several feet in front of him on the ground, leaving him weaponless. The two remaining attackers looked at each other, seemingly unsure whether to attack.

"Come on, spineless scum!" Lark exclaimed.

The attacker to his left charged; the one on the right only a step behind. Lark focused on the one that would get to him first. Little more than a shadow, the first took a wide, one-hand slicing attack with his sword. Lark sprang up, and spinning around, he grabbed his attacker's wrist with both hands and leaned heavily into a backhanded elbow strike to the jaw with a shattering crunch. The man relinquished his sword, dropping to his knees. Lark took the sword from his fingers just in time to block the other attacker's thrust and come down across his chest with a killing blow.

Lark quickly turned to the man on his knees. He could see in the light of the fire that blood flowed from both sides of his mouth as he pulled a curved dagger from his belt. As he looked up, he saw Lark already holding his own sword at his throat. He hesitated, the dagger in his hand. He feigned submission for a moment and then lashed out at Lark, attempting to strike between his legs in the weak part of his armor. Lark easily evaded the attack and, with an upward swing, slit the man's throat.

Lark looked around and saw only one still moving, the first man to attack him who had been knocked unconscious. Shaking his head, the man looked to see that he was the last man standing. He saw Lark holding one of their own curved swords. In an instant, he sped off, running in the opposite direction. He quickly picked up the shortbow and arrow of one of his fallen comrades and turned to fire.

Lark did not hesitate and hurled the curved sword in an overhand throw, causing it to fly end over end until it embedded itself in the man's chest, dropping him like a stone. They were all dead, save the one Archangel had chased after. Lark quickly retrieved his sword and mounted his horse.

Archangel pursued one of their lean attackers through the open grasslands north of the Dwarven village. Night was fading and the darkness that might have aided his veiled form was slipping away as dawn approached. Archangel paced himself, staying only a few feet behind. There was nowhere to hide. They were already some distance from the village. Archangel decided to slow his attacker. Coming to a sudden halt, he put out his left hand as a targeting guide and threw the knife in his right hand, burying it in his quarry's upper left calf. The blow caused the man in black to tumble to the ground with a yelp.

Archangel cautiously approached him, with his other knife in his left hand. His dark-clothed opponent drew a short sword from his belt. He was down on his right knee, dragging his left leg behind him, holding the sword out defensively in front of him.

"Who sent you? What was your mission? Speak quickly!" Archangel demanded.

The dark form could see over Archangel's shoulder a rider approaching in silver armor.

With only his eyes visible between his black garbs, he looked up at Archangel. *"When the Shadow Prince comes to this place, know then the hour of your death is at hand."* The masked form turned his sword in toward his stomach and hurled himself upon it before falling to the ground.

Archangel kicked the body over and saw the glassy-eyed death stare as he removed the face and head covering. Even in the surfacing dawn, he could see the tan skin and etched lines of wind and weather about his eyes and face. "Desert nomads," Archangel said, looking up as Lark rode up to him. "A scouting party, what about the rest?"

"They are all dead. Whatever they learned will remain with them," Lark responded. "Such is the measure of their resolve or the fear of their master."

Lark reached down and pulled Archangel up on the horse with him. They rode back to their campsite, where Archangel quickly took to his own horse and scouted around the area. Lark inspected the bodies. After several minutes Archangel returned with the clouds of morning and dismounted quickly.

"Their horses are about a hundred yards to the south of the village; they came from there as I found no tracks from the north. They may have already seen the camp at Cordilleran," Archangel reported.

"Then we were fortunate none survived to report their findings," Lark replied.

"For the moment, but there will be others whence these came. We need to get back and report to Mekko," Archangel said.

Lark nodded. "Let us bury these fellows first. Though they may not have afforded us the same courtesy, we will remain men of honor."

Archangel grinned crookedly. He couldn't disagree more, but there would be no winning this argument. He would never openly admit, but he knew Lark was right. This was part of what separated them from their enemy.

The doors to the Chamber of Representatives were forced open, even as the Chamber was in session. All eyes turned toward the guard, who bowed over low.

"What is the meaning of this intrusion?" Sky Longwood asked.

"Forgive me, Minister. Two Druids have arrived, and one claims to be the Grand Druid himself. He demands to address the council minister."

Commandant Oseana stood up. "Minister, forgive me, but this is outrageous. We are discussing matters of war here. Whoever is outside, Grand Druid or no, must wait."

Suddenly Kael and Galin stormed past the guard and entered the chamber without warning. Some of the ministers stood wearing looks of outrage. Even the guard was unsure how to react.

"Ministers of Arcadia, we beg your forgiveness, but none of us has time to wait, and war is precisely what we have come to discuss and hopefully prevent!" Kael stated boldly.

"Guard, don't just stand there. Call for help and arrest these men! How dare you invade this sacred Chamber without leave or invitation!" Oseana raged.

Ellis Freefire entered behind the Druids. "Oh, but they were invited. They have been invited multiple times, Commandant. Dare we turn them away in our hour of need?"

"Honorable Representatives of Arcadia, please hear us out and then I give you my most solemn word we will surrender without resistance to your mercy," Kael pleaded.

"Please, hear us," Galin added.

"I vote to hear the Druids. What say you fellow representatives?" Freefire asked.

With that, they all took their seats, and after some private whispering and several affirmative nods, Sky Longwood spoke. "Know that this is most unusual and a violation of tradition and protocol; however, the Chamber of Representatives have voted to hear you out. Speak."

Kael relayed all that had befallen them from the beginning. As he spoke, Galin handed him Mekko's formal diplomatic request for aid for their review.

"We believe the Shadow Prince is the principal force behind the tensions between yourselves and Bastlandia. A war between the two largest island kingdoms disrupts trade to the mainland as well as the other islands of the Trade Federation and prevents the military aid of which we are in desperate need."

"They accuse us of destroying their ships, and we in turn have lost ships. It is they, Bastlandia, who has broken the peace. We must respond in kind!" Oseana slammed his fist on the table.

"Ministers, even in our remote island of Feloria we have heard rumors of a black fleet. Ships made of metal, not wood, attacking and sinking vessels of the Trade Federation indiscriminately."

"Commandant, have you heard such rumors?" Sky Longwood asked.

Oseana hesitated a moment. "Just stories. The ramblings of drunken fishermen and merchant captains too long at sea."

"Then you have heard of them?" Kael asked. "You and Bastlandia were about to commemorate one hundred years of peace. You built a trading conglomerate without equal in which everyone profits. Why would either of you risk destroying all you have built now of all times?" Kael moved forward, placing both his hands on the table around which they sat. "What I propose is very simple. We are on our way to Anagansit to meet with the Druids. I have important business with the council, which is very much to your purpose. We will take Minister Freefire with us and, from there, travel to Bastlandia where we will do all we can to settle this dispute, expose those behind it, and reforge the peace between you. If we do this, will you consider rendering military aid to Cordilleran?"

"In the meantime, we lie in wait to be invaded," Oseana retorted. "If the Druid is wrong, and we do nothing, we lose any advantage we may have had and become vulnerable to attack."

There was a long silence, as well several hushed whispers. Kael waited for their reply.

Finally, Sky Longwood spoke. "We ask that you leave this chamber so we may consider your proposal in private."

The doors had barely closed behind them before they were informed of the unprecedented unanimous vote in favor of Kael's proposal. The Chamber of Representatives bid them farewell, dispatching Minister Freefire and Underminister Treehill to Pernia with them to speak to the Druids and as ambassadors of peace on behalf of Arcadia. Commandant Oseana would make defensive preparations as a precaution.

They flew there astride two Averics. Ellis had explained to them that on a nation of fifteen islands, it had become necessary to find alternate modes of travel. They discovered the Averics in the mountains of the northern islands long ago and quickly learned to train and breed them as trusted mounts. Though the military had tried to train them for attack purposes, the birds rejected any and all such activities, having a fierce predisposition against violence. With that aside, many strong bonds had been formed between riders and their birds.

Soaring above the clouds on the Averics provided a unique view of the sky for Kael and Galin in their human form. Much to their surprise, it was equally as breathtaking as in their animal forms. What seemed like only minutes to them was, in fact, a two-hour journey until they descended below the clouds above the green island of Pernia. It was a small island, heavily covered over with thick forested areas. They landed within a small clearing nearly a quarter mile inward from the coast.

As they dismounted and entered the forest, Galin announced they were only a short walk from the Druid tower of Anagansit. He led the way through the thick brush with Kael following close behind. Ellis and Misty walked nervously behind the two Druids. As with many of the islands of Arcadia, Pernia was lush with thick, tropical vegetation, but Ellis noticed an occasional patch of dead grass or decaying fruit. Surely, he thought to himself, the Druid Council would notice such signs of decay on their own island. Perhaps they had closed themselves off in isolation because they were already hard at work on a cure. He hoped that was the case as he pulled an edge of his green and blue silk robe off a prickly flower bush.

Misty walked a pace behind her teacher, attempting to conceal the rush of excitement racing through her veins at the thought of meeting the Druid Council. It was all she could do to contain her euphoria at meeting Kael Dracksmere, the Grand Druid, and famed adventurer of the known world.

While older than she expected, she found him attractive and mysterious. She was not drawn to him physically so much as to his character and subtly of will. She hoped to have more time to talk with him of Druid powers and their connection with the plants and animals of the natural world. That, and the thought of visiting Anagansit, the Druid tower where the Council met, was almost too much excitement for her. One the other hand, she found Galin, with white hair contrasting his youthful face, to be quite handsome, not to mention that his unerring demeanor of confidence sent chills up her spine.

She knew from long years of training to control her emotions on the outside. Her teacher was always in control of his emotions. He would tell her, *One should never govern with the heart but with the head. Emotions lead to distractions of the mind.* She found it a hard philosophy to follow. As a pupil of Minister Freefire, she knew she was always a little difficult to handle. She did, in fact, let her emotions rule many of her decisions. Despite her attempts to hide it, she wondered if her teacher knew.

As the small group made their way toward the tower of Anagansit, they came to a clearing free of brush around a mountainside. As they turned into the clearing, they saw the tower in all its glory. It appeared higher than the highest mountains on the island, rising hundreds of feet in the air, nearly into the low-lying clouds. The base was pyramidical, rising in a long neck and ending at the top with a sphere. The structure's reflective silver tiles sparkled brilliantly with the sun's bouncing rays. Huge stained-glass windows encircled the tower on every level.

They walked further into the clearing and onto an ash-colored brick walkway that led to the entrance. Kael looked at the building with mixed emotions. He felt both deep resentment and strange anticipation. It had been forty years and on a special occasion since he had last seen it.

Every Druid, at some point in their life, was required to make a pilgrimage to Pernia to see Yardrasil, the Tree of Primordial Unity. As the Druid prayed at the large roots of the Great Tree, Yardrasil would bestow a handful of acorns to the visitor without fail. It would then be the Druid's responsibility to go out in the world and plant the acorns. Many legends surrounded Yardrasil, the most prominent of which was that the first Druid, Arkahn, had sacrificed himself, allowing Mother Nature to shape him in the form of the majestic tree to forever symbolize the commitment of the Druid to nature's world. Kael remembered his encounter with Yardrasil fondly.

Now, Kael was back, and head of the Council and Order of Druids. Even those rogue Druids around the world, not of the Order, owed him a degree of fealty. Forced upon him, not of his choosing, he defended himself against Talic months ago to become the Grand Druid. There was no more pushing it aside, pretending he was no different than he had been; he was there, and it was *his* stronghold that lie in wait before him.

Galin watched the changing expressions on Kael's face and could guess his thoughts. *You may not have wanted this, but your destiny awaits you.* Galin grinned from the side of his mouth at Kael and then turned back to the building.

Kael didn't have to guess to know what his friend was thinking. Galin was right. Kael had always thought that he and he alone was in control of his own destiny. Lark, too, would tell him otherwise: *Only the one god or gods know what lies in store for men, and sometimes despite our most sincere desires, it is the will of the gods that wins out.* Here he was, Grand Druid, and now, a political figure. This was the furthest things from what he could have wanted from life. *The gods have a strange sense of humor,* Kael mused.

They continued to follow the path toward Anagansit, the sun still gleaming. Unlike Kael, Galin was happy to be back. He had always considered his role as a Druid essential to the world. His connection to the earth had been established early on in his youth. He heard the call and answered it proudly. Although there had always been a political spin on the Council, Galin could not understand Kael's total disdain for the Druids of Pernia. The Druid Council was the first and last bastion of protection for the earth. He was proud to be one of them and gladly accepted his place in the Order. He was, of course, concerned with Talic's hold over certain Druids on the Council. In truth, he did not like Talic or his policies, but his deterioration had occurred slowly and went unnoticed by all of them for far too long.

They were only a few feet away from the tall arched wooden door that served as the tower entrance. Ellis and Misty looked around in awe. It was not the first time Ellis had been there, yet each time he saw it, he was inspired by its beauty. It was a masterpiece of architecture-built hundreds of years earlier. It was stone, coated with an outer layer of silver panels that reflected the sun in such a way it seemed a spire of white light in the middle of the clearing, a ray of hope in the gathering darkness.

"After you, Grand Druid," said Galin with no hint of sarcasm.

Kael began his walk toward the door with his staff in his hand and took slow controlled steps forward. Suddenly, he spun around, startling his companions. They all turned as well.

Two long-haired feline-like beasts had emerged from the surrounding forest and swiftly approached. Their claws dug deep into the ground as the muscles in their legs rippled. A mane of black hair blew outward, revealing narrow heads that concealed rows of razor-sharp teeth. They each had two whiplike tails, trailing behind them. Shoulder to shoulder with man, the cats circled their prey.

"Trolocs," said Galin as he stood between the beasts and the Arcadians.

"They guard the forests around the tower to alert the Druids of any uninvited visitors. Do not fear, they will not harm us."

Kael looked at the beasts, speaking to them with his mind in their language, reaching out to them in friendship. Strangely, they did not answer. He sensed they had no desire to accept his friendship. Kael eyed them both, waiting, as they began digging their front claws into the dirt as if to charge.

"Something's not right here," Kael remarked.

Galin unsheathed his scimitar, backing Ellis and Misty up against the tower. Instantly, one the Trolocs jumped in the air, claws extended, slamming into Kael and taking him to the ground. The other beast dove at Galin's legs, but Galin was too quick. He slammed the hilt of his scimitar across its head and the beast rolled to the side, quickly ending up on all fours. Kael was back on his feet, using his staff to throw the huge cat off him. He threw off his robe and held his staff with both hands horizontally in front of him.

"Stay back!" Kael yelled to Ellis and Misty.

With a running leap, one of the Trolocs shot into air and wrapped its huge jaws around Kael's staff. This time Kael fell backward, with the Troloc sitting on top of him. Its hind claws were digging into Kael's legs while its forward claws rested on the staff, pushing it closer to Kael's face. They were eye to eye now, Druid and Troloc. Kael felt the hind claws penetrating his skin. With all his strength, he pushed the staff forward and kicked the beast off him, throwing it head over feet behind him.

The other Troloc reared up on its hind legs and unexpectedly struck the side of Galin's face with its claws, leaving three gashes on his cheek. Galin threw his white hair to one side and stood ready. His face bleeding, he thought of summoning fire, but Trolocs were immune to most magic, which made them extremely effective guardians.

The beast rushed Galin, leaping in the air, claws stretched wide. Galin swung his sword at its underbelly, connecting with the fleshy part above the beast's hip. The blow tossed the animal on its back. Galin quickly stepped forward and kicked the beast with all his might. The huge cat let out a whimper and limped away from Galin.

Kael charged the other Troloc. The beast caught Kael's staff in its mouth, locking its jaws down on the end of the staff; it pulled ferociously, yanking its head left to right. A moment later, it pulled the staff from Kael's fingertips and threw it aside.

Misty attempted to move forward as if to help Kael but was quickly held back by her teacher. He could not believe she wanted to get involved in such a dangerous battle, having never been trained in the art of combat. He held her arm tightly.

Sweating profusely from his brow and blood dripping from both legs, Kael stood slightly crouched, his eyes following the Troloc as it paced back and forth, eyeing him, its mouth foaming with white drool. Kael was tiring and could feel his strength waning. He needed to end this battle. He could not concentrate long enough to summon his magic as a defense against the beast, so another strategy was necessary.

Adrenaline surging within him, he summoned the last of his strength and began running toward the beast. The Troloc, taken off guard by Kael's unexpected charge, dug its feet into the earth and pushed forward, running toward the Druid, kicking up dirt in its wake.

Kael ran, concentrating as hard as he could, feeling his heart pound. His arms swinging freely at his sides, his vision locked on the Troloc, all else became a blur. The only noise he was aware of was his own heavy breathing. Closer and closer they came, barreling toward each other like two jousters dueling. Taking his final step, Kael pushed off the ground and launched himself into the air. The Troloc did the same. They were both airborne, gliding toward one another.

They collided with such force that their bodies slammed together, throttling both man and beast. They fell back to the unforgiving earth hard, momentarily knocking the wind from them both. Kael had luck with him as he fell atop the Troloc, giving him the upper hand. He reached into his belt and pulled forth a small silver knife and slashed at the beast's face, cutting deep into its fur and mouth. The cat released a guttural growl as blood shot from its head. Kael quickly rolled off the injured animal. He could barely push himself to his knees to see the Troloc limp away, disappearing into the forest.

As Kael looked to find Galin, he saw him on the ground, a Troloc standing over him with its jaws opened wide, going for Galin's neck. The younger Druid was holding the cat's neck with both of his hands, squeezing tight as its teeth came closer to his throat.

Kael tried to summon his magic, but the collision had taken the breath out of him. He suddenly saw his staff several feet away from him in the grass. Frantically, he crawled toward it.

His strength dissipating, Galin wrapped his hands around the animal's drooling mouth. He closed his eyes, attempting to concentrate on his magic, but it was impossible. His left arm gave out and bent, letting the Troloc's mouth come only inches from his throat. His right arm weakened, and he could feel the beast's snout up against his neck. He could feel its razor-sharp teeth begin to wrap around his skin. It would be over in a moment.

"Galin!" Kael screamed, shuffling across the earth with what strength was left in his aged body. Swinging with all the momentum and anguish he had left, the head of his wooden staff cracked square against the head of the Troloc, rolling it several feet away near a distant oak tree. It lay there twitching in a bed of twigs beneath falling leaves.

Kael collapsed at Galin's side. He could see where the creature's teeth broke the skin on Galin's neck as blood dripped to the earth, but the wounds were superficial. Galin attempted to catch his breath as Kael helped him push himself up to a sitting position. Ellis and Misty ran over to both Druids in alarmed amazement.

"Are you all right, Grand Druid?" Ellis asked, looking Kael up and down watching blood trickle down his legs.

Kael took a deep breath to steady himself. "I am fine."

Misty patted Galin's neck with a cloth that quickly soaked up the blood.

Galin smiled slightly and gently took Misty's hand from his neck. "I will be fine, child. Thank you for your kindness."

Kael helped him rise. Misty looked at them, admiring their fortitude and courage but also with concern. She placed a hand on Galin's shoulder steadying him, "Druid, you have been hurt, perhaps you should sit for a while. You are bleeding—" She stopped in mid-sentence as she looked again to notice that Galin was no longer bleeding. In fact, to her amazement, his wounds were already healing.

"Underminister," said Galin with a smile, "Druids have the ability to heal quicker than most others if the wounds are not too severe."

His tall frame dwarfing the others, Kael looked sternly toward the tower. "I suppose I should have expected no less of a welcome," Kael said.

"This is unheard of," Galin said in frustration. "Never before have the Trolocs attacked without warning, and they would *never* attack Druids."

"If they thought this would deter me, they are sadly mistaken." Kael walked to retrieve his robe, which he cast off during the battle. As he bent down, he felt the aches and pains from the Troloc's claws. Although the bleeding had stopped, it would be a few days before the scars would disappear as well as the pain from their wounds. Brushing his robe off, he walked toward the front door of the tower with the others following. Ellis and Misty walked slowly behind.

Pulling Misty close to him, Ellis whispered, "Stay close to me, young one. Something is amiss here with the Druids."

Misty nodded and moved even closer to her teacher.

Kael opened the tall oak door with surprisingly little resistance. They entered a relatively small foyer lit only by the sunlight streaming in through stained-glass windows. Immediately before them was a large stone staircase that went up about a hundred feet to a stone landing, which had two doors, one on the east and one on the west. Kael began climbing. Again, the others followed.

Though it had been nearly forty years, he still remembered the way to the main council chamber. It was not difficult, a linear path straight up the stairs to the apex of the tower. Kael's robe flew behind him in the breeze caused by the anticipation of his quickened steps. Galin and the others found themselves laboring to keep up.

Stopping at the first landing to catch his bearings, Kael looked about, examining another set of doors, again on the east and west. While waiting for the others, he looked up to see hundreds of stairs with nearly ten more landings of an identical design. In happier times, the lower levels of the tower housed the Initiates, those who were studying the ways of the Druids. However, they seemed vacant and barren of activity for some time.

As Galin and the others arrived on the second landing, Kael turned to them. "Galin, Druid of Alluviam, please escort our honored guests from Arcadia. I have no more time to waste, forgive me." He bowed his head to Ellis and Misty and suddenly twirled around in a green flash of light, emerging as a brown falcon. He extended his great wings, startling Misty, and flew straight like an arrow toward the top of the tower.

Galin motioned to them. "Minister, Underminister, after you." *Druid of Alluviam*, Galin thought to himself. Kael had never referred to him in such a manner.

Misty smiled in awe as she watched the falcon disappear in the upper ramparts of the tower. She looked at Galin, still smiling, "It must be wonderful to be a Druid."

Galin grinned and started walking up behind them. There was a time when he thought so as well, though at this moment he could no longer be sure.

Kael soared up through the narrowing tower and circled about the top of the spire before locating the main entry door to the Druid Council chamber. It was a rounded oak door with a protruding likeness of the beautiful tree, Yardrasil, etched into the wood. It was a work of master craftsmanship showing no signs of age. Golden sconces hung on each side of the door, dancing in the breeze of the draft that found its way through unseen cracks and crevices, rising with impunity throughout the length of the tower. Kael landed on the cold stone floor and appeared, through a flash of green fire, in his human form only a few feet before the door.

It had been so long ago, and yet there was much that seemed so familiar. The smell of the wood and stone enchanted his senses, triggering memories of a fonder time. He looked straight at the door, the carving of the tree, contemplating his next move. He *was* the Grand Druid, he reminded himself. Now he just had to believe it.

Taking a deep breath, he took a step closer to the door and put his hand out. Slowly his hand glowed and a bright red light shot forth from it, wrapping around the door. The wooden door turned red for a moment, illuminating the dark corridor for an instant before it creaked open, letting the rays of sunlight penetrate from the room ahead to the place where he stood. So powerful was the light shining into his eyes, it briefly blinded him. He stepped forward into the room carefully and slowly.

The sunlit room was large and triangular. Its windows, which completely encircled the room, were clear glass, not stained, as was the rest of the tower. It gave the room the impression of being outside, not encased within a stone structure. Magnificent crystalline chandeliers studded with precious stones hung all throughout the chamber. The rays of the sun danced through them, filtering out all the elements of light, emitting many colors on the council table and the floor of the chamber. Beams of multicolored light struck the stone floor like the sun's rays skipping across a calm lake.

Compared to many council chambers he had visited in the last few months, this room was somewhat smaller than most others. The slate stone floor was polished; he could feel his sandals slip just a bit as he moved across it. A large, oval table of mahogany was before him, comprising the heart of the chamber. The beautiful details of trees, animals, plants, and the many fruits of nature's bounty were exquisitely carved into an exterior band outlining the table. Despite the beauty of the chamber itself, he found his vision pulled ahead to the breathtaking view of the Altmonte Sea, which could be seen panoramically from anywhere in the room.

Equally as stunning was the view of Yardrasil, the Great Tree, which was hidden from their sight earlier as they approached the tower. The base of the tree had a circumference of nearly fifteen feet, which had its beginnings in massive roots that went into the ground deeper than any tree he had seen in some time. Its leaves were vibrant green, sparkling with life. In height, it measured to nearly a quarter of the tower, but its crown boasted dozens of enormous branches with tributaries of smaller ones spreading out from each, ending in teams of emerald leaves. It was the perfect symbol of life. It was the perfect symbol of the Druids . . . as they should have been.

He only just now became aware of the robed men and women sitting in silence at the table where most of the chairs, save two, were filled. The largest chair, which sat in the middle of the table, was more like a throne composed of chestnut. A familiar figure was sitting in the large chair. It was the Druid Talic, who he had defeated months earlier to become the leader of the Druid Council. Several other men and women sat, their faces expressionless for the most part, save Talic who had a slight grin forming on his mouth.

Kael scanned their faces as he walked toward the table. His sandals slapping against the floor were the only noise that could be heard.

At the far end of the table, he saw two thin, blond-haired Elves with sapphire blue eyes staring at him. Next, there was a tall human with short black hair and very dark skin and. to his left, an attractive female with light brown hair covering part of her face. As he followed them closer to the front of the table, he saw another female with long red hair and flowing white robe and next to her a very young man, barely twenty, who Kael thought was too young to be a Druid. Kael reached the largest chair before he could review the rest of the Druids.

The room was quiet as he turned to Talic.

Talic's deep-set, penetrating brown eyes had been assessing Kael since he had entered the chamber. Talic was a bald man with a coal-black beard. A black robe with gold trim covered his frame while an ash black staff rested against the arm of the high chair, meant for the Grand Druid, in which he sat. About his neck and hanging over his chest was a circular, gold medallion with a representation of Yardrasil in small diamonds and emeralds.

"Well, well, well," said Talic, staring in Kael's eyes with a nasally tone. "The prodigal Druid comes home at last." Talic's teeth disappeared behind his lips as he looked Kael up and down. "And to what do we owe this visit from the famous Kael Dracksmere?" Talic asked, unmoving in the chair.

Kael looked around the table at the faces of the others and then turned back to Talic. "I come to address the Order and see what counsel you have regarding the poisoning of the lands."

"Ah, I see you are on official business then. Which land do you represent?" Talic raised his right hand, grasping his chin between forefinger and thumb as if pondering.

Kael stared back for a moment, his eyes and face solemn in their demeanor. "I do not represent any one land. I represent *ALL* the lands, in the name of this council."

Talic slowly leaned forward, interlocking his fingers on the table. "The council has certain etiquette that must be followed, my dear Kael. We cannot just allow anyone to walk into this chamber inquiring on the workings of this body."

Kael took a step closer to the chair. Quietly but firmly, he replied, "Since when does the Grand Druid need permission to address the council?" Kael's words caused grumbling among the others.

Talic stood up, pointing his finger at Kael. He raised his voice. "You dare to enter these hallowed halls to claim your position in which you have refused to participate for months? You, who have turned your back on our Mother Nature for over forty years, playing the part of the adventuring, rogue Druid. Did you know he was even arrogant enough to accept the title of Baron of Wrenford at one time?" Talic directed the comment toward those seated. "So what? Now that your country is no more, you change your allegiance back to us." Talic's face was bright red; a vein bulged from his forehead.

Spit formed at the corners of his mouth as he continued, "You know nothing about the laws and history of our sacred sect. You have no ambitions or goals for this council. You walk through these doors and expect to take control of this council with some pathetic excuse that the lands are poisoned? You, who spent your life traveling the lands with common people, more interested in them than in nature. You are as worthless as you are unworthy of such a post as that of Grand Druid."

Kael waited a moment to let Talic regain control of his breath and wipe the droplets of sweat on his brow. Then he spoke calmly: "It has not been given to you to decide whether I am worthy of such a post, nor any other here: *I* am the Grand Druid."

Kael watched as Talic shook with rage. He could tell the man wanted to strike out at him but fought the impulse. He saw Talic looking to the faces of the other Druids, desperation coming over him that he had been unable to provoke Kael, as he had hoped, before the council.

"There is no Druid on this council who agrees that you should have this chair. There is none that will follow you!" Talic snapped.

"Yes, there is!" It was a commanding voice from the back of the chamber. All eyes turned to see Galin, taking a seat near the two Elves, brushing his snow-white hair from his eyes. For the first time since entering the council chamber, Kael smiled.

Talic looked at Galin for a moment, clearly surprised by his appearance, but his look indicated that he was not surprised by his statement. "Well, the puppet of the Elves has returned as well. He is the perfect disciple for you, Kael, another whose loyalties have long been in question." Talic turned his eyes back to Kael. "Understand this and understand it well, we will not follow you and any Druid who does will be considered a traitor and removed from this council."

Kael's expression became that of flame. Just before he could respond, a new voice came from the back of the chamber. All eyes now fixed upon one of the golden-haired male Elves, clad in red robes. He spoke in a beautiful melodic even tone. "Although I do not know Kael Dracksmere, I have heard of his adventures on behalf of common folk, the good of mankind, and Mother Nature. The Woodland Elves who he helped save many years ago are now all but gone from the world and this council has done nothing to investigate the matter. I am D'oriel, Druid and protector over the lands of Mystaria. I have not seen those lands for many months locked away in this tower, save for one night to witness the challenge of combat between you both. Yet I sensed the poisoning you speak of long ago and attempted to bring it before this council, only to have it fall on deaf ears." He looked down for a moment as if in shame. "Sadly, I am part of the reason for the lack of action. I and others among us accepted things and allowed fear of reprisal from Talic and those who serve him to dictate our inaction. I can no longer bear this shame. I stand with the Grand Druid." D'oriel walked over and stood next to Kael, nodding affirmatively to him.

Talic looked at the Elf with daggers in his eyes and before he could say anything, the female Elf rose from her spot. Kael watched her in her long flowing forest green robe, moving elegantly toward him. Her long hair hung beautifully about her shoulders.

"I am Shalimar, Druid of the lands from the Freeholds of Galandor north." She bowed her head, standing before Kael. "I too stand with the Grand Druid."

With disgust in his tone, Talic addressed the rest of them. "Is there any more who wish to join these simple-minded fools?"

From the other end of the table stood a very tall, nearly white-skinned human in brown robes. He stood taller than even Kael and Talic, though he was so lean as if to appear malnourished. He too moved to stand before Kael. His face displayed just enough wrinkles and cracks to indicate that he was probably the oldest man in the room. Stopping, he bowed his head. "I am Magnus Merrell, Druid of the lands from Averon south to the ocean, and I stand with the Grand Druid."

The rest did not move, save the boy who was clearly the youngest. Kael could see there was a great internal struggle taking place behind his eyes, but he was suddenly distracted by the entrance of two other Druids from the rear of the chamber. One seemed to be supporting the others weight for a moment but quickly let him go upon entering.

"So, Kael, you have succeeded in dividing the council. Was this your grand plan?" Talic asked, his voice dripping with sarcastic venom.

Kael stepped forward, still eyeing the two figures in the back of the room.

"My plan, Talic, was not to divide the council. My plan is to dissolve the council," he stated calmly.

Jaws dropped within the chamber as all eyes turned to Kael in shock and disbelief. Even Galin was struck dumbfounded by Kael's news.

"You, you what?" Talic stuttered.

"Forgive me. Perhaps I was not clear. Among other things, I came here to dissolve the Druid council, removing it from all political affiliations and ties with the countries of the known world," Kael said, never taking his eyes off the two figures that stayed toward the rear of the chamber. The Druids seated grumbled under their breath, and Talic turned many shades of red.

"You *cannot* dissolve the council, fool. You have no authority—" Talic started.

"On the contrary," Galin interrupted. "According to the historic annals of Anagansit, the Grand Druid can make any changes he or she deems necessary for the good of Mother Nature, including dissolution the council itself, though it has never been done," Galin said, his concern evident.

Kael walked toward the rear of the chamber where the two Druids, dressed in gray robes, had just joined them. One of them covered the side of his face with his hand as soon as he made eye contact with Kael and had not removed it since. Both were relatively young men; each was tall with shoulder length hair. Both had dark brown hair with one a shade darker than the other.

Kael walked directly to the man who had been covering the side of his face. The man turned to the side as if he did not see Kael. Kael hesitated and then grabbed him by the wrist with an iron grip and threw him back into the wall.

As the man braced himself against the wall, he revealed a fresh wound on the side of his head, which he had been hiding. Kael quickly turned to look at the other man who was holding his side as if his ribs were injured.

Kael marched across the chamber toward Talic, seeming as if he would walk right over him but stopped inches from his face. His expression was ice. "Druids fighting Druids, is this the ambitions and goals you have for the council?" Kael demanded.

"I don't know what you are—" Talic began.

"Be silent!" Kael shouted, throwing his arms wide. "You will speak no more in my presence!" Kael commanded in the most menacing tone Galin had ever heard him use. "You have spoken enough, not another word will you utter. You see, Talic, I believe that you are more than you appear. I believe you are *not* working for the betterment of this earth and our most beloved Mother Nature. Instead, you are working against the people and creatures of this earth. Your concerns are not of this world. You are a self-centered, power-hungry man whose ideas go against all that the Druids stand for. I hereby and from this moment forward expurgate you and all your misguided followers from this council. May the forgiveness of Mother Nature heal your hearts and make them whole again one day."

Talic's face twisted into a grimace fraught with rage. He lunged for his ash black staff. Suddenly, green fire exploded from Kael's staff, striking Talic in the chest, and causing his feet to fly up in the air. He landed on his back with the wind knocked from his chest. As he looked up at Kael, straining to gain his breath, he saw the medallion of Yardrasil that had been around his neck was now in Kael's free hand.

"Be gone from this place! All of you, *now!*" Kael commanded.

Six of the Druids, including the young boy and the two gray robed men, exited the chamber, leaving only Talic behind. Talic scrambled to his feet, disbelief on his face. "You will rue the day you broke this council. Nature is as harsh as she is forgiving," Talic said, looking at them all. He snatched his staff from the chair and stormed from the chamber.

Chapter 9

The poison had entrenched itself within his arm like a parasite. Ranier stopped for a moment and held it tightly with his hand as if that action might somehow impart a degree of comfort. The potion he had ingested slowed its movement and effect for the time being, but its mere presence within his body weakened him. The toxic nature of it disrupted his blood's ability to coagulate, forcing him to make a tourniquet on his arm to slow the bleeding. Every few minutes, he had to loosen it so as not to completely lose circulation.

He had been walking for days now in the lands south of Mystaria. Each day was becoming longer, and he found himself growing weaker each hour.

Obtaining the key would be extremely difficult under perfect conditions. With the poison draining his strength and will, it would be quite dangerous, even life threatening, to attempt. Yet there was no other who could do it. It would be too risky to go to Cordilleran and attempt to come back for it. The enemy's forces could already be searching for him. His only fortune was that they would have a general idea where he may be but no clue where he would be headed.

He could feel the lands suffering. It had changed much in the centuries since he had last seen it. There had been no sun in the sky, only clouds that seemed to darken more each day. The green of the trees and grass was fading. Birds were scarce and living creatures were few. The earth was slowly dying. Suffering from poison himself, he felt a strange kinship to the lands he had never known. Only updated maps which came to him through the years in his limited contact with the outside world kept him abreast of the geographical changes. He knew precisely what was causing the lands to languish and it would be his unhappy duty to deliver that knowledge to those who had fought so hard against it, to those who still had hope. He himself was not sure if anything could be done to reverse the effect, but there were always possibilities.

He was east of Bazadoom, traveling southeast from Mystaria. He was seeking a geographical sign that had not changed much over the ages, except in name. He sought the mouth of the mighty Steel River. Not far from the source of the great river lay the Cave of Dark Passages. It was a place no other living being knew existed. Even the enemy, for all his vaunted power and vision, did not know of it, nor would he be able to enter if he did.

The wind bit at him. He pulled his hood over his head. The days were becoming colder. Leaning heavily on his staff for support, he continued as fast as his strength would allow.

It was not until midday when he finally heard the sounds of rushing waters, which signaled he was near the mighty river. For the first time in days, a smile crossed his lips. It was somewhat encouraging to hear the river still had some strength to it. He stopped, removed his hood, and looked around. This was a place that had changed significantly since last he laid eyes on it. Ancient trees stood over a hundred feet in the air. He remembered them when they were saplings. It was then his eyes happened upon it. There was an indentation within the side of a large hill. He had found it at last.

As he walked toward the cave, his arm throbbed. The pain came and went more frequently and the periods of relief from it grew shorter. As he approached, he saw that the indentation ran maybe five feet into the hill. This place was nothing more than a speck of earth never detailed on a map, a place where travelers passed by and might shelter themselves from rain or inclement weather, nothing more.

It was ages earlier when the Archmages decided they needed a place to protect the key from the Demon Lord. If this key fell into the wrong hands, the darkness that had almost taken the world from them would summon more demons and beasts from the void between the worlds of space and time.

They had placed the key here within, beyond the reach of mortal men. Their magic had made this place impure and undesirable for men and animals. Passersby would be deterred from remaining too close to it. It had lain untouched by earthly beings for centuries.

The entrance to the cave was covered with webs and signs of decay. It was cold as he stood near the entrance, very cold. Ranier could suddenly see his breath before him. The freezing air gripped his lungs, making it difficult to breathe. It was not the cold air but what was generating it or, rather, those that called this place home.

He sat a moment, removing his bags. He rummaged through one until he came across a vial of purple liquid. He drank the potion quickly. It would make him feel better temporarily. Gathering his thoughts and strength, he stood up facing the cave, leaving his possessions outside. Although the magic bestowed upon him had greatly slowed his aging, the fact was he was still older, his magic was rusty and there was poison within him inching its way toward his heart. The cave, if it did not kill him, would weaken his mind—perhaps even damage it permanently.

A spider ran across the mouth of the cave. Ranier lay his staff on the dry dirt beside the cave. As he took another step toward the opening, a blast of cold air blew his robe and hair back. With the next step, his boots crunched upon the frosty ground. Ice formed around the lip of the dark cave.

Closing his eyes, he entered. Darkness washed over him and sealed the cave shut behind him. He could no longer hear even his own steps. This place was totally devoid of mortal trappings, a place strong with negative-life energy. He stood still, barely breathing, the cold covering over him like snow from a winter blizzard.

Then, as if it sprang from his very person, a small orb of light floated beside his right shoulder, casting a dim ray of illumination toward his next step. He moved forward slowly and silently, the orb shining light one step at a time. The rock walls were frosted over, glittering in the light of the orb. As he walked on, he had the increasing feeling that the cave ceiling was becoming higher, yet there was no proof, not even the echo of his footsteps or deep breathing.

Ice droplets formed on Ranier's brow and nose. Frost built on his shoulders and throughout his hair. His footing became uneven from specks of ice on his boots. Still, he continued to walk on.

Then, within his right ear, he heard something. Not a noise but voices barely audible, more of a subtle cacophony of shrieks that grew louder with each step. Ranier's eyes were closed, the lids covered in frost. He saw the way ahead only with his mind now.

"*Ahh, why, why?*" the low voices spoke into Ranier's right ear. Suddenly, his eardrum ruptured. He cried out and cupped his ear in his hand, cradling it while enduring the intense pain.

"*Why, why?*" the voices cried, only more pronounced.

Ranier kept walking, though he had started mumbling under his breath. He placed all his concentration on every step. Now he started hearing the voices, deep and grave, in his left ear.

"*Ahh, Ranier, whyyyy?*" He was unable to discern the voices; they were unrecognizable, though he knew exactly who they were.

He walked on, the light of the orb following him deeper into the cave. He felt something grab his arm tightly and a hand wrapped around his left shoulder and another around his left arm. They were pulling at him, digging claw-like nails into his skin, tearing at his robe, grabbing his hair, and scratching at his face.

"*Ranierrrrrr!*" They were a multitude of voices speaking as one, "*Ranierrrrr!*" louder and louder they spoke, piercing far into his mind.

Ranier squeezed his eyes harder, ignoring their calls. He tried to pull away from them, his arms and hands still being held tightly, his legs dragging with the weight of their pull, compromising his ability to walk. He chanted to himself, his own voice now louder and louder, trying to drown out their cries and screeches.

"*Whyyyy, Ranierrrrr, whyyyyyy have you commmme baaaack? Whyyyyyy arrrrrre youuuu heeeere? Dieeeeee Ranier, likeeee the ressst of ussss, dieeeee. burrrrrrn, Ranier, like the resssst of ussss, burrrrrrn in everlasssting torrrrrment!*"

Ranier struggled, falling to the floor. He kept his eyes closed and screamed loud the words he'd been repeating under his breath, his mantra, over and over again. Still, he could not escape them, the voices would not let up.

"*Dieeee, Ranier, dieeeee like the ressst of usssss!*" Their continued onslaught filled him with guilt and remorse such as he had never known. They were entitled to their rage and vengeance. He wanted to surrender to them, he wanted to die, as they asked, to make things right.

"*Rippp him apppart, rippp himmm appparrt!*" screamed the voices.

Suddenly, there were hands all over his body, pulling at him, ripping his robe off, tearing at his hair. Ranier fell again and began to crawl forward with what felt like the weight of many men upon his back. He could feel them kicking him in the ribs and about the head as he inched forward. His hands were suddenly stopped by the feeling of iron boot heels stomping on them. The bones of his fingers snapped as the boot heels crushed his hands.

He rolled over on his side, no longer able to move. The screaming was unbearable. It was impossible to concentrate on his own words. He must though, he must concentrate, or he would die. The magic of his words could save him if he could only focus enough to keep speaking them. His hands were useless. He pulled himself up on his forearms and knees and began crawling anew, resisting the torment with all his might.

His face was being clawed by what felt like shards of glass raking into the sides of his head. He howled in pain but continued. Teeth cut through his neck and arms, sinking in so deep that they cut into his bones.

"*Makkke himmmm payyyyy. ripppp himmmm to piecessss. Eattttt himmmm alivvvvvve!*" they continued unmerciful with unearthly resolve.

The voices were screaming, cutting into his ears. His clothes were shredded, and his body was covered in deep gashes and bite marks, blood poured from his wounds. Death was near.

Elenari met High Master Reyblade upon the hill overlooking what had now become the Alliance stronghold. He had already been sitting in his customary position with his eyes closed. His gray robes pulled close about his frail frame, hood drawn over his head.

The morning was bitterly cold, snow flurries were in the air, but it was nothing to enjoy or inspire hope. The morning sky was dark. Not a bird could be seen, even in the furthest reaches of Elven sight. Elenari sat next to Reyblade with her legs crossed and hands loosely resting upon her lap.

"I can feel the evil of this world growing. Its power increases each day. You were right to involve us in this war, child. The darkness that approaches threatens us all and is like nothing the world has ever seen," Reyblade said with his head bent down and eyes closed.

"It is done, master, the disciples and students are safe. They have been taken to the Dwarven sanctuary cave within the Eastern Peaks," Elenari said.

Reyblade raised his head and looked at her. "Excellent, child. They are, at least for a time, safe from the coming conflict. We must take what comfort and rest we can in the coming days, for we will be sorely pressed when the time for battle comes. You have done well Mistress Moonraven."

Elenari bowed and smiled. That was the first time he had ever addressed her in that fashion, acknowledging that she too was a master of the Kenshari way of fighting. It filled her with a pride she had been lacking in days before. She knew he had great affection for her and though she would always be that scruffy little girl that was brought to him, while he still called her "child," it was clear he no longer thought of her as one.

"What did I tell you, lad? I seem to recall it very clearly. I said take some Elves with you, did I not?" Mekko asked.

"Mekko—" Archangel tried to get a word in.

"Yes, I believe that's what I said and then what did you say?" the Dwarf asked, cutting him off. "Perhaps I was speaking in my native tongue, was that it? Perhaps you didn't understand. Then again, maybe I had a little too much to drink and broke out in Elvish like the bloody linguist that I am. Was that it?!"

"General," Archangel tried again.

"No, no, I remember. I was speaking in *Orchish*, that must have been it. They can barely understand each other in that heathen gibberish; however, I do remember what *you* said very clearly. You said, 'Absolutely General, we will, don't worry.' Naturally, I took you at your word."

Finally, Lark stepped forward, "General, forgive me. Archangel and I needed some time alone, as brothers. I cannot condone him lying to you, but my brother did have good intentions nonetheless. We greatly appreciate the fact that you were worried about us."

"Worried about *you*? I could give a flying rat's arse about either of you. I was worried about the head of my scouts and the commander of my siege artillery, two individuals this army cannot afford to lose. You lads need to understand, you're involved in somethin that's bigger than both of you and you need to consider that before you go off on some . . . family picnic," Mekko replied.

"Thank you, General. You are right of course. I can assure you, from *both* of us, it will not happen again," Lark said, grateful that Mekko would entrust him with such responsibility without truly knowing him.

"All right, lads, good enough then. Now tell me again about these scouts you bumped into."

Ranier tried to push himself up but collapsed under the weight upon him. He tried to focus, to concentrate, but each time the screams became more harrowing. The biting continued; he opened his eyes and saw a chunk of skin bitten away on his right hand. Blood poured down his face from scratches on his head, getting in his eyes.

This was his test, his creation, made thousands of years ago to protect the key. Only he could pass through it, but he must clear his mind. It was too difficult; he could feel himself slipping into the iciness of death. Soon he would be a spirit creature, like them. It would be a welcome relief, to fight was so hard, and after all, he did not deserve to live.

He stopped moving and struggling. It was over. He waited with what little spark of life remained for death to take him. One last thought entered his mind through the incessant screaming: This was not about him. There were others at stake. Every free life in the world was dependent upon him, whether or not they knew it. None would have a fighting chance without him.

In a cry of anguish, he threw himself up against the wall and used its leverage to straighten himself to a standing position. He started to think, working through the pain and screams. He remembered what he must do, how he could live. He must believe he was not guilty, that he did not deserve death and could still set things right. He must not give in to despair; he must believe.

He started to speak, "Clear your mind," he repeated as he could feel them peeling the skin off his face below his eyes back in anger and protest. Louder he spoke, "Clear your mind," and still even louder, "CLEAR YOUR MIND," until, before long, he spoke it with such power and faith it even began to drown out the terrifying screams of the creatures that harried him. "CLEAR YOUR MIND!" He could still feel the hands around his neck and legs, but their pull started to weaken.

"Clear your mind," He spoke in a descending tone, calmer and calmer. The arms around him and the teeth that gnawed at him gradually released him. The voices quieted to a whisper and then as if they were never there, blended with the cold silence. His blood-filled eyes, which had been obscuring his vision, finally cleared. He looked at his hands and then putting them to his face with a sigh of relief confirming that he had, in fact, suffered no injuries, save those his mind led him to believe.

The air was still cold, and his breath was still a visible cloud as he slowly opened his eyes. He stood in the center of a large cave covered in sheets of ice, frozen somewhere in time. The orb still floated beside him, shining its light a little brighter. He looked beyond the darkness to find some sign of what he had come for. Still, he knew it was not over yet. All the countless centuries he had waited in the Andarian Mountains, he would hope that he might be spared this day, but, in his heart, he always knew his destiny and despite his hopes to the contrary, he was here to confront it.

His mind was racing now, preparing for what was to come. He was completely exhausted; every step became heavier drawing him away from something rather than toward it. Although he knew what would happen, it did not ease his mind or grant him comfort. He hesitated a moment, then continued a few steps forward. The orb lit his way like a guide. The sheets of ice bounced back a mirror image of him as he passed. His lungs felt heavy as he could feel his airway starting to freeze.

He walked until he came to a dead end. In front of him, a wall of jagged rocks covered in ice barred the way. He turned around and waited.

He had seen this moment in his mind, recalling the amount of time and magic that went into creating this place. He called upon the spirits of the Makers, those, like himself, who agreed to guard the key with their magic, creating this place. He had infused himself with a part of the same magic, a dark magic that would inevitably be his doom. This was the ultimate price they and he would have to pay. It was the only way to protect the world and save its future.

He looked down on the ground through the frost-covered earth until he found a small, round indentation within the ice. He reached up and put his hands around the orb floating beside his shoulder. The light shone upon his hands, a warm pulse shot through his arms, a welcome relief from the bitter cold. Gently, he maneuvered the orb, as if it were a ball of energy, within his hands. He guided it, slowly placing it down upon the indentation on the floor. There was a clicking noise, like a key unlocking a door. The light stretched the length of the floor, revealing not a stone floor but a thick layer of pure ice that served as the ceiling for the crypt below it.

The light continued to brighten all around him, illuminating the chamber under him, which he could see now through the transparent ice. He could see clearly now; there were ten stone coffins in the middle of the solemn chamber.

He walked slowly across the ice ceiling above the crypt and put his hands in the air as he spoke, "My brothers of the past, Archmages of the world that was, I call upon your spirits to be released from your tombs. Come forth!"

Ranier lowered his arms and looked down. It was quiet for a moment and then suddenly the ice began to shake. Pieces began falling into the chamber. A ray of warm light came down from above him and shone upon the ice ceiling. Steam drifted up through the cave as the heat and ice met. Chunks of ice flew into the air as the ray of light cut through, causing the entire cave to tremble. Ranier held on to the wall to keep from slipping.

Then, the cave was quiet. Ranier waited as the steam dissipated, revealing a set of ice stairs before him, leading into the crypt. Pulling his robes close about him, he descended the stairs.

He did not think it possible, but the crypt was much colder than above. Ranier walked to the center of the chamber to the front of the stone tombs and stood motionless. He remembered when last he had stood here. It was many lifetimes ago when he lay his brethren here to rest in this magic crypt, hidden from the mortal world. He waited, staring at each tomb, remembering what they were like in life ages ago. To his amazement, he could picture each one clearly.

Then the wait was over. Nine of the stone lids to the coffins began to move slowly, scrapping against the stone tombs. One after the other, they let out a stream of smoke and debris built up from the time they were sealed. Only his coffin, the tenth, did not move.

Ranier felt his breathing becoming heavy again as his clouded breath nearly concealed his vision. The room became colder still as each lid was now pushed aside.

"Spirits of my brothers, come forth!" Ranier summoned with his hands in the air.

Though there was no connection to the outside world in this place, a cold wind picked up and shot through him, throwing his robes and hair from side to side.

From each coffin rose a transparent figure, outlined in a green haze. More than a shadow but less than an apparition. They had a vague semblance to their human forms. Their faces were drawn and free of expression. They were clad in robes of smoke that danced in the wind. Still with raised hands, Ranier stared into the eyes of the ghosts of the Archmages of the ancient world.

"You have come back, Ranier," the spirits spoke together, voices echoing loudly throughout the crypt.

"Yes, my brothers, as we agreed. It is time," Ranier replied.

"It is time to undo the errors for which we alone must bear the terrible burden." They spoke in pained voices, like the screeching of rusted metal.

"Yes," Ranier said. "The time has come to put an end to the tragedy we created, at last we have a chance for a reckoning that will set all to right."

"He has returned, then, he who controls the demons from the dark dimension of the Nethertime?" they asked, shifting their movements, gliding closer to Ranier.

"Abadon has returned, and he is aware of my presence. I have little time to confront him. I need all of you once again," Ranier replied, pale and remorseful.

"Ranier," spoke the spirits, *"you have come back for us. We shall grant you that which was predetermined ages ago."*

"It is as we thought it would be, my brothers. It is necessary. If we do not take these steps, Abadon's rule will know no end, even until the end of the universe. This is our time, our one and only chance to stop him. I fear he will be more powerful than when last he walked the earth," Ranier cautioned, stepping closer to them, breathing heavier still as the cold air tightened in his throat.

The voices grew louder and harsher. *"Remember your promise to us, it shall be yours in return for taking us with you!"*

"I have not forgotten, brothers; it will be as promised," Ranier affirmed.

The spirits nodded and then floated in all different directions throughout the chamber. The winds increased in the wake of the spirits' movement. Ranier moved to the center of the chamber as they flew about him. This was the moment he had been waiting for and now it was finally here. This would be the pinnacle of his existence. This would be the beginning of his end.

"Archmages of the past, unite now, enter the temple of the living and join with me!" Ranier shouted as the spirits became flashes of white light zooming throughout the cave, bouncing off the walls and ceiling of ice.

Ranier closed his eyes and calmly placed his arms out at his sides. The spirits slowed, then, one by one, appeared before him and shot through his chest, disappearing, leaving only a small puff of white smoke behind. Ranier's body jolted as each spirit slammed into his chest. He grimaced and cried out as his eyes burned with white fire. He screamed louder each time one of them disappeared into his body until, when the last spirit had entered him, he crashed to his knees on the cold stone floor.

Suddenly, the orb of light appeared before him. There was a strange metal shape within the heart of it. With the last of his strength and what remained of his will, he reached for it. A moment later, the orb was gone, and he grasped a large rectangular piece of metal in his fist. The key was his. He collapsed face down and passed out.

Chapter 10

Prince Ceceran roamed the corridors of Castle Iberian, sliding his hand across the stone walls as he went. It was all his, though he had not been crowned king yet. A short time ago, that had seemed impossible, but he was now the sole master of Bastlandia. He would soon be the people's one true king. He had prodigious plans for his kingdom, grand ambitions that his weakling father and goodly whore of a sister could have never dreamed of.

Still, nearly two weeks had passed and the bodies of his sister and Captain Krin had not been recovered. While this fact gnawed at the back of his mind—that there had been absolutely no sighting of them whatsoever—was, at the same time, comforting. If they were alive, there would surely be some news by now. The Dark Warrior and his men searched day and night with hounds; they felt confident the bodies had been taken by the river with its tributaries that reached far into the country.

The people were still recovering from shock that one of the High Riders— the elite guards of the castle and royal family—could have murdered the princess and heir apparent to the realm. Ceceran had it rumored that Sergeant Mulcahey was a jealous lover, which spurred this insidious crime of passion. The Court of Bastlandia now saw him as the sole, albeit reluctant, heir to the throne. By not having himself coroneted king right away, he was fast earning points and respect from the people.

Almost without notice, Ceceran began to move the Dark Warrior's men into strategic positions, saturating both the guard and watch with his men while moving the High Riders out and away from the castle. The strange warriors in their gray robes slowly became more numerous and always accompanied Ceceran, except into the familiar chamber he was about to step inside. They stood guard at the door to give the prince privacy. He smiled as he let himself in. It was Marko's.

With the sudden pounding on the door, the prince stumbled out of bed. As he approached the door with anger in his steps, Marko hurried behind him to place a robe over his shoulders.

"Who dares disturb me here?!" Ceceran shouted through the door. "And at this ungodly hour?!" He looked over at Marko, who quietly informed him of the time. "It is well past midnight!"

"Forgive us, your highness," the reply came through the door, "but it is imperative you come to the throne room as quickly as possible."

"Very well, you may wait for me down the corridor," he conceded.

The prince waited at the door until the guards' footfalls started to fade. Then he strode further into the room, waving at Marko to start dressing him. Marko had done this on numerous occasions and made quick work of it.

Ceceran took a seat and held his foot out. "Wait two minutes, and then come to the throne room."

"Yes, my prince," replied Marko, as he knelt to put the prince's boots on.

Ceceran entered the throne room where he saw the Dark Warrior with several of his men. The men were holding two large rolled-up burlap carpets over their shoulders. Unsure what to make of this meeting, Ceceran took his time reaching the foot of the throne. A moment later, Marko entered the chamber and went to the prince's side.

"This one has *not* been summoned." The Dark Warrior's agitation was clear in his disdainful tone.

"I summoned him. He is here at my bidding. He is my prime minister, and his loyalty is without question," Ceceran said with pride.

The Dark Warrior bowed his head in deference. "Very well, your highness, but *you* will answer for any disloyalty. My master has been patient too long to allow for any mistakes now."

"So be it," Ceceran said, clearing his throat.

At a gesture, the carpets were unrolled, and two bodies spilled out at Ceceran's feet, one male, one female. Both were severely waterlogged, emitting a dank smell. A gleeful smile overcame Ceceran's face, even as he held his nose. Like a giddy child, he stepped forward and used his boot to move the hair off the female's face. "Ah, you've never looked better my sister," he said, but then suddenly became unsettled. He moved her face from side to side with his boot. "Who is this? This is *not* a face I recognize."

"Calm yourself, Prince Ceceran. The bodies have been under the water for weeks. They were pulled under in a rapid current and held beneath the water against a great rock many miles from the castle. We were lucky to find them. Water can do strange things to the skin. Look at the clothes and the injuries. My men have checked them. Fear not, *this* is the princess and the captain," the hooded warrior reassured him.

"Excellent." The prince turned and looked down at the man's body. Hesitating only a moment, he kicked the face with all his might. So waterlogged it was, the skin broke from the force, and brackish flesh and bone burst out onto the prince's boot and all over floor.

Forcing back a gag, the prince smiled. "So, *this* is the mighty Krin." He stepped nonchalantly away from the oozing goo he had freed.

Marko knelt and wiped the prince's boot, tossing the rag away from him. Then he took Ceceran's hand and kissed it, his lips lingering just a tad too long in public. "My Prince, you are *truly* the King now."

"Not quite yet," Ceceran replied. "First, my beloved sister must have a grand funeral so that all Bastlandians can properly mourn, and I shall grieve at the foot of her casket before I am crowned."

Marko was sickened by the thought of the prince grieving over his sister. When he stood, he spat on the bodies.

The prince approached his throne much more swiftly than he had entered the room. "Ah, come now, Marko," he said over his shoulder, "for you too will kneel and pay respect to my sister. We shall weep for her, but few will know we shed tears of joy." As the prince made himself comfortable on the throne, he peered down at the grotesque bodies, gloating. Then, with the wave of a hand, he commanded, "Remove this filth!"

"You now have the rule of Bastlandia as you requested by the grace of my master," said the Dark Warrior. "He demands your absolute loyalty and support should he call upon you."

"Assure your master he shall have anything he asks. Bastlandia is at his service," Ceceran responded.

"Very well," the warrior replied, holding out rolled-up parchments. "These contain my master's instructions. You are to follow them to the letter"—the prince reached for them but the warrior held them back—"Is that clear?"

"Yes, yes," Ceceran replied, practically snatching the documents away. Once they were in his possession, he quickly unrolled the parchments and scanned through them. As smile came to his lips.

"Your master reads my very thoughts."

"The Druid Council is no more," Galin said, looking out over Yardrasil, the Great Tree from the council chamber of Anagansit.

"Only for the time being—until such time as men and women can come together for the benefit of all races under leadership free of corruption and evil influence," Kael said, placing a hand on Galin's shoulder. "More than half the council was tainted."

At that moment, the other Druids present knelt before Kael. Magnus spoke for them. "We bow before you, Kael Dracksmere, you who freed us and lifted the veil of evil from the council." Magnus and the others bowed their heads.

Kael cringed noticeably, and he rushed forward and lifted them to their feet. "No, my friends, no one will kneel before the Grand Druid ever again. We look each other in the face, eye to eye, as equals committed to a common purpose. I hold the symbol of the Grand Druid in trust for a time when we are worthy to call ourselves a council again. I go now to commune with the Great Tree. May its ancient wisdom help guide us in this difficult time." With that, Kael left the chamber.

As he descended the long staircase down through the tower, Kael reflected upon what he had done. Did he really do what was in the best interest of the Druids or was it a dark self-serving desire to do away with the council that forced his actions? He had always despised the formal

Order of Druids, and now that he had the power, he used it to dissolve them. No, despite all that had happened, he would not second guess himself. If there was any doubt in his mind, he felt confident Yardrasil, the Great Tree, would see the truth and reveal it to him.

As he walked outside the tower, a cool breeze washed over him, even in the backdrop of the warm sun. The splendor of Yardrasil was suddenly upon him. The Great Tree was the ultimate symbol of life and the commitment of the Druids to that life. Like all the trees in this part of the world, it appeared to be thriving and full of life. Its massive network of roots ran deep, and its rich-green leaves sparkled. Still, Kael hesitated. It was the duty of the Initiates, the Druids in training, to care and tend to the Great Tree, and Talic had seen to it that there were no more Initiates nor had *any* of them spoken to Yardrasil in some time. He was not sure what to expect. Approaching slowly, he gently placed his fingers against the cool bark, feeling his way along the base of the trunk. With reverence, he knelt among the roots, bowed his head, and concentrated.

Yardrasil was pleased with him, speaking with words that carried no voice. The Great Tree approved of his actions, which felt reassuring, but it had more to share, dark truths that, once revealed, confirmed the Grand Druid's worst fears.

"Galin, you look different from when last you visited Anagansit." It was Shalimar who addressed him, seemingly fascinated by his snow-white hair.

"Much has happened both to me, and to the world, outside this tower since then," Galin responded, still gazing into the distance.

"And we have been dormant instead of doing something about it," offered Magnus, lowering his eyes.

"What type of man is Kael? Do you know him well?" D'oriel asked Galin.

"I have known him for many years. I can think of no finer, nobler man to head the council," Galin replied with a hint of frustration.

"You did not expect him to dissolve the council, though, did you?" Shalimar asked quietly.

Galin hesitated before answering, "No, but now I think it is for the best. Regardless of what we may think, council or no, Kael is the head of our Order, and I stand by his decision."

"Do you trust him?" Magnus asked.

"Implicitly, with my life and with yours," Galin replied immediately and firmly.

"That is good enough for me," Magnus said, and the others readily nodded.

Kael knelt before the Great Tree, letting his hands come down to rest upon its massive roots that dug deep into the earth below him. The bark was smooth. Though this creature was said to be of the old world, in the early days of men, its physical form lived in timeless beauty, seemingly unaffected by the age's past.

He allowed his mind to clear. Speaking with Yardrasil was different from conversing with any tree or plant life he had ever known. Other plant forms were merely regional expressions of Mother Nature herself. The Great Tree, however, was an entity unto itself—separate, but still one with nature. It spoke in images and words, and addressed him by name. *Kael.*

The Druid legends told of the first Grand Druid: A man called Arkhan, who singlehandedly taught the magics of Mother Nature to a group of followers he called Druids. They were priests of nature, men and women wholeheartedly devoted to the preservation of the earth and all its natural life forms. He wrote down and transcribed the secret, nameless language spoken by Druids that no outsider may know. It would be the one infallible method whereby one Druid could identify another. And more important, it would be the means to keep the secrets of Mother Nature hidden from those who might pervert her awesome power.

Then, to prove his great devotion to their faith, it was said Arkhan offered himself to Mother Nature and asked that she accept his sacrifice so he could be made into a permanent symbol of that faith, a covenant of trust between the Druids and the earth. So, it was that Arkhan stood upon this very spot and was remade into Yardrasil. Kael had heard the legend, as had all Druids, but he had never truly believed it—until now.

The tree spoke in wild, rapid images, letting a torrent of thoughts and feelings out at once. While Kael could feel Yardrasil's pleasure with him, he could equally feel its overwhelming anger at Talic and the council. A plethora of images flowed into his mind, mixed with strange words, mostly foreign to him. Some of the images were dark and too terrible to fully comprehend. There were images of ancient wars and battles with creatures he had never seen nor heard of, but their leader was something altogether different. Most forms of evil described to Kael in his lifetime were based on hate, weakness, fear, resentment, and rage. But the evil the tree described to him now conveyed none of that. This was pure evil, calculating, patient, and emotionless, driven by motives beyond Kael's understanding.

Then Yardrasil spoke of the poison that infected the lands. It had been so the last time this evil walked the earth. What this evil was or where it was from was difficult to discern from the images. Even the tree itself did not seem to know entirely. All Kael could be sure of was that it had been here in the past and would be coming again. Only this time, it was more powerful.

Kael asked Yardrasil what the Druids could do to heal the land and fight such evil. The images came flooding through him, occasional words thrown in the mix. The tree did not have all the answers, and Kael could not understand much of what it did say; however, it spoke of a cure for the poison. It was possible, but the manner and deliverance of such a cure came in a haze to him. There was one detail that did come through clearly—what would occur when the cure was delivered. He wished he had not understood it.

When Yardrasil finally finished speaking, he had learned more than he wished to, but at the same time, he found the knowledge woefully inadequate. Worse still, he knew he could not reveal all of it to the others. He wished he had listened to Elenari when she spoke about Algernon's tome. He knew now the book quite probably had some of the answers the tree had lacked.

He walked back to the Tower of Anagansit agonizingly slow, as if he could put off indefinitely what he had to tell them if he didn't hurry to get there.

When Galin saw Kael enter the council chamber, there was a momentary look of remorse upon his face, which he quickly replaced with an assuring smile.

"Yardrasil has imparted much of its great wisdom to me, my friends. While I did not entirely understand much of it, some of what the tree shared was unmistakably clear. It is as we have feared for a long time. The poison that is killing our lands is a byproduct of a monstrous evil that is not of our world but whose coming is close at hand. As I suspected, this evil is *not* related to the Shadow Prince or his minions, but the Great Tree does not know who or what this entity is. It did, however, communicate to me that this entity walked the earth ages ago. Its mode of communication was not entirely clear, but I gather it is a Demon Lord of unrivaled malevolence. What *is* certain is that the closer it gets to our world, the weaker our powers will be . . ." Kael hesitated.

"What must we do? Did the tree offer any words of hope for us?" D'oriel asked hopefully.

Kael looked back at the Elf thoughtfully and then at the rest of them in turn until his gaze settled upon Galin. He nodded affirmatively. "It gave me instructions, such as they were. It may be difficult for you to hear, and you will have many questions. I have very few answers for you. You must be prepared to accept some of what I tell you on faith."

They all looked at him expectantly. He had their attention.

"D'oriel, you, Shalimar, and Magnus must travel north across the ocean to the war-torn country of Cordilleran. There, in the citadel close to the shore, the Alliance army prepares for the war against the Shadow Prince. Find General Mekko, the Alliance Commander. Mention us and you will be welcome there. You must make use of the time before the fighting begins to create what the Great Tree described as a *potion of restoration*. To succeed, this potion must be delivered to the one place where life began upon our world ages ago. Yardrasil no longer can convey where that location is, but I believe there is someone in the citadel who may be able to help us find this location . . ." Kael hesitated again.

"I can't believe what I'm hearing!" D'oriel protested. "Kael, you know we have no place in the wars of men. Are we to fight with this *alliance* as well? Who is this Shadow Prince and what does he have to do with us? Why can we not work on this potion here in Anagansit?"

"And what of this potion?" Shalimar joined. "How are we to begin, what components are we to use?"

"We have no place in the wars of men?" Galin mimicked with sarcasm. "How decadent you have become, locked away in this tower. Every war ever fought in the history of this world has in some fashion damaged our sacred Mother Earth. I have fought with Kael for the last few months in this war against the Shadow Prince. Who is he, you ask? In life, he was a power-hungry man. Now he exists as a lord of the undead, systematically destroying all free life in his path. If he defeats the Alliance forces, the ocean will be the only thing between this tower and the Shadow Prince. To say nothing of this other monstrous evil, this Demon Lord, of which Yardrasil speaks."

"You can no longer afford to turn a blind eye to the affairs of men," Kael began. "It is that type of narrow thinking that has allowed our world to deteriorate so much, and for Talic to remain in power for so long. We must offer whatever aid we can to those in need. I ask you to go to Cordilleran because it is the safest place for you, and I offer your healing services on behalf of the races to the Alliance." Kael left no room for debate.

"Even if we could create such a potion, of which I'm doubtful, who is this person who may know the location it is to be delivered?" D'oriel asked.

"My daughter, Elenari, will find the location," Kael answered.

"How do we know that? How can we be sure of anything you've told us?" Shalimar asked.

No longer able to restrain himself, Magnus stepped forward and raised his hands between D'oriel and Shalimar. "Silence! I have heard enough. The Grand Druid has spoken. It is not for us to question, but to follow. I, for one, have sat complacent long enough. We serve Yardrasil, we serve the Grand Druid, and we serve sacred Mother Nature. More than that, we serve the lands we represent. If this is how we can be of service, then so be it. We must have faith that Mother Nature will show us the path." Magnus bowed to Kael. "You said the three of us were to go north, what of you and Galin?"

"Galin and I must go to the kingdom of Bastlandia, where we must try to stop a war and solicit what aid we can to fight a different war. We will take the emissaries form Arcadia to help us sue for peace as we promised." *Stop a war so that we can fight a war. That might almost be amusing if it were not the truth,* Kael chuckled to himself.

Kael continued, "As I have said, my status as Grand Druid has not bestowed upon me the answer to all things. In fact, I have more questions now than ever before in my life. However, I know beyond question that this is my true path. I ask you to walk it with me. All of us, for one reason or another, became Druids to be of service to life and living things. We have it within our power to make our dreams a reality. May the blessings of Yardrasil be with us all. Good luck to you my friends." Kael bowed his head to them.

"May nature's blessings keep and protect you both on your journey," Magnus said as he bowed in return.

A moment later, both D'oriel and Shalimar bowed and offered their blessing to Kael and Galin.

The next moment, the chamber erupted in a flash of green fire as the three Druids began their transformation. Their clothes and skin seemed to melt away, replaced by the resplendent bronze feathers of sleek falcons. In an instant, they were high away, traveling in the northern sky.

After just a moment's pause, Kael turned to Galin. "Would you be good enough to show our guests from Arcadia in here?" he asked.

"Certainly," Galin responded with a nod and exited the chamber.

"Ambassador Piedmont." Ceceran descended his thrown and approached Piedmont, who knelt before him, clothes ragged and torn. His face was covered in dirt, and his hair was matted and wiry. He was breathing heavily.

"My lord, please accept my most heartfelt condolences upon your . . . recent losses," Piedmont expressed, his exhaustion apparent.

"My lord, a fishing boat picked up the ambassador adrift off the coast," the guard beside him added.

"A survivor of the treacherous attack upon the *Emerald Sea*. You return to us as a hero. Bastlandia is blessed this day by your return. Your many years of friendship and confidence have not been forgotten, my dear friend. Where is your wife? Surely she made it with you?" Ceceran asked as he bade Piedmont to rise, placing an arm around his shoulder.

"Regrettably, my lord, she fell victim to the cowardly sneak attack." Piedmont sobbed for the full effect.

"Easy, my friend. You've come home at an opportune time. Bastlandia has desperate need of someone with your steadfast loyalty." Ceceran whispered in his ear now, "All we always talked and dreamed about has come to pass. Now Bastlandia will be the sublime power you and I always knew it should be."

Piedmont's eyes seemed glued to Marko, who had a goblet of wine lifted to his lips.

"A drink! In the name of all the gods, a drink," Piedmont said as he collapsed into the prince's arms.

"Quickly, take the ambassador to my personal healer. Prepare quarters for him here in the castle. When he is ready, have all the food and drink he can handle brought to him," Ceceran ordered.

The guards quickly led Piedmont away, leaving Ceceran in the throne room with Marko. Ceceran sat upon his throne again with Marko standing beside him.

"What do you think of Piedmont?" Ceceran asked.

"A clever man, masking his loyalties over the years but a slave to money and power. Although some take him for a fool, I think he is smarter than he lets on. He would sell his family for the right price and a little more power. Not to mention, he's a coward," Marko added.

"Yes, useful qualities if properly stimulated." Ceceran smiled. "He's precisely the sort of man we need."

All of Bastlandia filled the city limits the next day to bear witness to the funeral procession of King Zarian's eldest daughter, Princess Angelique, the rightful heir. It was the second such procession in all of two weeks proclaiming the death of a member of the royal family—the first being the king's funeral.

As was custom, the procession started far in the country, traveling through the outlining villages and would culminate at the gates of Castle Iberian where the heir apparent, Prince Ceceran, waited.

The procession amassed a huge following from one end of the great island kingdom to the other. Children dropped rose pedals before the horse-drawn carriage that bore the body of the princess. An honorary guard of gray-robed warriors sat atop huge white Meridians.

Awaiting the procession within the courtyard of Castle Iberian was Prince Ceceran in full dress with his prince's crown and red robe. He surrounded himself with increased security consisting of a dozen gray-robed warriors.

Unexpectedly, the Dark Warrior appeared in the courtyard and approached the prince. "I must speak with you alone," the warrior said from within the recess of his cowl.

"Not now, the funeral procession will be here shortly," Ceceran answered curtly.

The intimidating form stepped within inches from Ceceran's face. "*Now.*" Then he turned on his heals toward shadowy corridors leading from the courtyard.

Ceceran followed him to a passage where they were assured a modicum of privacy.

"You will soon be visited by two Druids, as foreseen by my master—" the warrior started.

"What is their purpose?" Ceceran asked.

"Their purpose is meaningless!" the warrior said forcefully. "My master instructs you to hear them out and tell them you will think upon their proposal."

"Then what am I to do?" Ceceran asked.

"Nothing . . . You may go back to your funeral ceremony now, my lord." The warrior bowed his head then swiftly became one of the shadows in the corridors.

Ceceran returned to his former position. When the funeral procession arrived within the crowded castle courtyard, six warriors raised the princess's casket from the wagon and carried it to the middle of the square. They placed it in front of the prince. The mourning onlookers crowded in close to see and hear.

The prince moved forward and placed both his hands on the casket, then looked out over the people. "People of Bastlandia, thank you for joining me and standing at my side as we say farewell to last remnants of my house and family name, my sister, dearest Angelique. Her life was ended before her time by one of our own, one of our most trusted High Riders. This treachery is a sign that all things must inevitably change. With regret, I am forced to announce that as of today, the High Riders have been disbanded and are no longer in the service of the crown. This tragedy is one of many recent incidents meant to weaken our mighty kingdom. Still, we will prevail against our enemies who wish to see us fall. In the light of the destruction of the *Emerald Sea*, the mysterious death of my father, and now the death of our heir, my sister, we will arise even stronger. We will send a message to our enemies that we will not be forced into submission. We live under threat of invasion from Arcadia. This morning, I sent a proclamation announcing that Bastlandia will be seceding from the Trade Federation. War is on the horizon and to prepare I must ask your patience and resiliency as I am forced to raise taxes to build up our fleets and army so that we will emerge victorious!" He raised his arms high in the air.

Many paid spectators in the crowd began leading cheers for his speech, and while sparse at first, the cheers caught on and all assembled were calling for victory and hailing Ceceran as their new king. As the cheers increased, Ceceran knelt and kissed his sister's casket solemnly. After praying for a moment, he bade his warriors to carry it within the castle to the tombs below.

He then waved out to his admiring people, who were now calling for him to be coroneted king. He smiled and nodded. The rule of Bastlandia was undisputedly his now.

The two sleek Averics glided over the Anglian Sea, approaching the rocky coast of Bastlandia. Misty looked out over Galin's cloak to the crystal sky mirrored in the deep waters below. She smiled as the wind blew through her hair. It felt wonderful to be so far above the land. She was able to appreciate its beauty more fully, and it resonated within her, stirring feelings she thought long suppressed.

The brief trips she had taken in the past were all over small patches of Arcadia. Though she loved her homeland, it was exhilarating to be outside those borders out in the free world. As she looked down at the coast, it seemed very different from the lush beaches of Arcadia. Here, the coastline was harsh, wrought with cliffs that acted as natural barriers against the waves.

They had crossed an ocean to get here. What would have been a two-week voyage aboard a ship had taken two days astride the winged Averics. To Misty, it was like exploring a new world. Still, she tried as best as she could to remain focused. As Minister Freefire had said, there were troubling events happening between these two lands, and they would no doubt not be received well here.

It had taken Kael and Galin some time to convince Minister Freefire that his personal presence in negotiating with Bastlandia would be imperative to their success. The disbanding of the Druid Council did not inspire confidence, and Freefire felt it to be a bad omen of what was to come. The minister felt their presence, if anything, would intensify the matter and not for the better. That is why Arcadia preferred to negotiate through the Druids as their arbiters. However, after much debate, the two Druids finally convinced him this was the best course of action.

As they continued inland, they saw a stone rustic fortress on the high cliffs towering above a large city and several outlying villages. The fortress, though ancient in appearance, seemed well maintained. The walls were huge, triangular on all sides, pointing inward toward the great keep. Each wall was supported by three towers, two at the ends and one in the middle, for a total of twelve. Such a design would force any attacking army in close to the walls where they would be extremely vulnerable to missile fire and siege devices. They had never seen such a design. There was one road upon a winding hill that led up to the castle's main gates from the city below. Within the gates, a massive courtyard acted as a foyer before the castle proper. The inner keep loomed above the courtyard, attached to a long barracks and several smaller structures.

Attached to the eastern part of the keep was a large, circular appendage surrounded by wooden walls. Within they saw hundreds of the largest horses they had ever laid their eyes on. The horses were unnaturally tall and massively built and looked as if they could accommodate Ogres or Giants.

"Meridians, the great steeds of Bastlandia. They are the horses of the High Riders, the elite guards of the royal family," Misty told Galin as they circled.

Galin nodded, clearly amazed by the size of the horses, which were in all other respects similar to any other horse.

They circled high above the austere fortress and noticed even the courtyard, composed of stone walkways in between manicured lawns, had only a single marble fountain to alleviate its demeanor of cool indifference. It was an imposing structure from every vantage point.

"Castle Iberian, home of King Zarian, ruler of Bastlandia," Freefire said into Kael's ear through the wind.

Kael slowed the Averics to a calm glide over the courtyard, bringing them to a landing just inside the main gates near the marble fountain. They could see many soldiers scrambling below and on the walls. Many weapons were now pointed in their direction. They landed softly and did not move a muscle. Armored horsemen with crossbows quickly approached, while foot soldiers with pikes approached from behind.

The lead horseman, dressed in gray robes and plate mail armor addressed them. "Identify yourselves immediately. Only Arcadians ride those creatures. If you are from Arcadia, make peace with your gods for you haven't long to live. Consider yourselves fortunate we didn't shoot you from the air."

"Hold," Kael said raising his empty hands. "I am Kael Dracksmere, Grand Druid, and Baron of Wrenford. I come here seeking an audience with your king on the behalf of many lands. I beseech you, in the name of good and free people everywhere, grant us this audience. Your lives and the lives of your countrymen are at stake."

Chapter 11

"You will be the sword and sword shall be you."

The calm, even voice of High Master Reyblade came from nowhere as Elenari, wearing a blindfold, moved her feet, shifting her weight on dirt and dried leaves, listening to the light breeze bouncing off objects, creating distinctive echoes that allowed her, in essence, to see.

"Each place has its own unique sound. What you must listen for is the sound which does not fit," his eloquent voice faded off somewhere in the distance as he seemed to be constantly moving.

It was an exercise they had not done for years past, but Reyblade had been engaging all the Kenshari in advanced training basics the last few days. He employed the woods close to the encampment as their training grounds. He insisted that if they were to fight in this war, they must be at the height of their skills, and when the time came, it must be they who turn the tide of battle.

"When you have become one with your environment, it will be as if there were no blindfold and your sight will be clear."

She focused, her breathing steady, *Eros-Arthas* held in her left hand with its tip just above the earth. She was homing in on his location, but it was extremely difficult, for he moved like a ghost.

"When my attack comes, it should be effortless to stop me." His words no longer held meaning, serving only as a point of reference to her for the exercise.

The attack finally came in the form of a whirling, two-stroked attack, which she parried and shunted and switched hands, mid attack, extending the sword in her straightened right arm. With her arm fully extended, everything stopped. She could hear her heart beating faster and feel the rhythmic inhalations as her shoulders went up and down, responding to her excited respiration.

"Take your blindfold off, Elenari," Reyblade instructed.

Slowly, she did as she was instructed. She focused her vision to see Reyblade's sword knocked aside and her own blade touching his throat in her extended arm.

He was staring at her, smiling. "You have done well, child, very well indeed."

Reyblade nodded, and they each took a step back and bowed.

Mekko watched from his command platform as the perimeter walls had been completed. They were wooden, but well-crafted by the engineering corps and would be much stronger than they appeared when the time came. The defensive towers, however, were not yet complete, nor the secret weapons they would house. However, they had established heavily manned gates at the north and west walls, guarded by scouting patrols that extended out for five to ten miles in both directions.

Much of the siege equipment rescued from the castle had been walked down from the sanctuary cave over the past several days. The Paladin, Lark Royale, had overseen the placement of the huge catapults and ballistae, mounting them at different heights to maximize their range and damage. He had a defensive mind not unlike a Dwarf, Mekko mused.

Two tents were occupied by blacksmiths working day and night to produce weapons and ammunition, mainly arrows, as they would need a huge supply. Mya had set up a large medical tent to the southeast of the camp.

As Mekko looked over the progress, he let his thoughts drift to Kael and Galin. They had risked so much to aid their cause. He prayed for their swift and safe return. He did not wish to start any battle without the aid of their magic, which had saved them so many times in the past. Having his friend Galin close by also offered a strange comfort. He felt a profound sense of loss without him in the camp. His best friend had been King Crylar since he was a youth, and with him gone, Galin had somehow filled that void. The world was indeed a strange place.

He looked at Prince Crichton and the soldiers of Mystaria. For as long as he could remember, they had been his enemies. Now, they worked as hard as any. Never a grievance or complaint passed their lips. Stories of Crichton, for the most part, spoke of a solitary eccentric man, but all told him to be a powerful warrior and wizard. The old Sage, Algernon, foresaw in his omnipotent wisdom that they would one day become allies. How he longed for a soothing word from the wise old man who had led the small band that had rescued him.

All were working together as one, bound by a common goal and enemy. What would happen though, Mekko pondered, in the future? If, by the grace of all that was holy, they somehow defeated their enemy, would they still all work together in friendship and cooperation as they did now? He thought about it for only a moment and reconciled that he would happily cross that bridge should he survive to see it.

A moment later, he noticed General Valin had joined him on the platform.

"Any word?" Mekko asked.

"No word. Our scouting parties report no activity in any direction," Valin answered. "How long until whoever sent those nomad scouts the Royale brothers encountered begins to notice they have not returned?"

"They would not send scouts ahead if they were near enough to see for themselves. I'd say we still have several days before the Shadow Prince's army makes its way back here," Mekko said confidently. "They may know where we are now, but I'm bettin' they won't dare attack until they are good'n ready. He can't afford another big defeat. He'll take his time and attack when all his forces have gathered."

"And if the Druids are unable to bring back any help from the south? How can we stand against the evil that may be coming?" Valin asked.

"Well, my old friend, we've made it this far with what you see before you. We will stand with faith, heart, steel, and courage." Mekko nodded as he turned and looked to the south at the ocean.

Later that afternoon, Mekko walked toward the tent of Prince Crichton, which was considerably distant from where his men had been quartered. As he approached, he heard faint moans that seemed to escalate as he grew nearby. Rendek and Toran, his now faithful bodyguards, threw themselves in front of him, drawing their weapons.

"Easy now, lads," Mekko said as he eased between the two younger Dwarves and walked ahead of them again.

As they were almost upon the solitary tent, the moans sounded more like the cries of a grief-stricken animal than sounds of fear.

Cautiously, Mekko peeled the flap of the tent back and revealed Crichton on the floor of the tent, atop an ornate collection of furs completely covering the tent's earthen floor. Looking in the tent was like seeing inside a small palace. There were satin pillows on chairs, trays of fruit and bread, and a large bed with sheets and blankets. The opulence disgusted Mekko, as many Dwarves slept four and five in one tent. It was a cry of profound sorrow that turned his gaze back to the Mystarian prince. He was turning from side to side and then upon his back, anguish painted on his face. Tears fell from the corners of his eyes as he reached his hands out in front of him, as if to hold on to something he was losing.

"You lads go back to my tent now; I'll be fine here. That's an order," Mekko said to his guards, blocking their view with his body.

Looking at each other quizzically, they responded, "Yes sir," and obeyed.

Mekko waited until they had walked away and looked again to see Crichton still in the middle of some horrible dream, or more likely a memory, as he seemed to be literally sobbing in his sleep. The pain etched on his face was beyond any physical measure Mekko had ever seen or wished to imagine.

Mekko decided to close the flap and, after clearing his throat in an exaggerated manner, in a booming voice called, "Prince Crichton!" He then lifted the flap to see Crichton already sitting up with a stern countenance on his face, his hair and chest still wet with perspiration.

"You come here uninvited, Dwarf," Crichton snarled. He was breathing heavily, trying to calm himself.

Mekko's eyes widened as he stormed further into the tent. "I think you'll be wantin' to put that another way," he said in an icy tone.

Mekko watched as Crichton's face straightened, and he took a deep breath and reached for a goblet on the floor.

Taking a deep breath, Crichton responded, "You're right, General. What do you want and why are in my tent without my permission?" The anger had left his voice, but the familiar tone of arrogance had replaced it.

"In this land, I ask permission of no one, and I come and go by no one's leave except mine, *Gideon*." Mekko spat out his name.

"Oh yes, I must have forgotten," Crichton said before he took a drink of wine.

"I came to ask you a question, but it can wait," Mekko said, turning to leave.

"No, please, General, by all means stay and ask your question. Where have my manners gone. Please have some wine as well." Crichton poured an amber-colored liquid into another goblet and handed it to the Dwarf.

Sarcasm resonated in the Mystarian's tone, but Mekko accepted the goblet silently and held it up in a mock gesture of toast. After quickly downing the contents, he walked over to the wineskin and poured himself another.

Crichton stared at him, unable to conceal a slight grin at the Dwarf's utter gall.

"I came to ask if all the stories about you are true. Are you the great warrior and wizard I've heard so much about? Because if you're not, I don't want to find out on the battlefield," Mekko said, pouring himself a third cup.

Crichton stood up. He was wearing a pair of loose-fitting leather pants. Mekko could see his chest and arms. He was massively built, though he maintained a lean waist.

"Stories, General, are told by those whose names will never be remembered. Their only hope is that people might remember their stories. And what of the stories about you? Are you the great soldier, general, and strategist they say you are?" Crichton asked as sarcastically as his words would allow.

Mekko smiled wide as he downed yet his fourth glass, which had emptied Crichton's wineskin. After swishing it around in his mouth, he spat the wine on the ground. "Is this what they drink in Mystaria? Tastes like Ogre piss." With that, Mekko turned and left.

As night fell on the camp and the changing of the guard took place all along the perimeter, most of the inhabitants retired for sleep.

Lark was alone in his tent, kneeling in prayer to the gods, in whom his deep faith granted him holy powers to always enforce the ways of goodness and righteousness wherever he could. His eyes were closed, his clasped hands pointed skyward. When he finally opened them, he saw Mya standing at the entrance to the tent, her long flowing white hair resting upon a lavender colored robe. She stood silently, breathtakingly beautiful, staring at him.

Unsure how to act for a moment, he scrambled to his feet and bowed his head. "My lady, please, would you like to sit?" Lark fumbled about his words. "You must excuse me, my lady. I live according to a code that does not allow for some of the creature comforts I fear you may be accustomed to. I cannot offer you much, save my company," Lark said, attempting eloquence, referring to the emptiness of his tent. He had only a lantern, some blankets, some clothes, and his armor and sword.

She smiled as she raised a hand to her lips. "You would be quite surprised, my lord Lark, what my people could become accustomed to, I think. Forgive me for intruding. I did not mean to disturb your prayers. Perhaps I should go."

"No, my lady, not at all, come in and sit if it pleases you, and please do not refer to me as a lord." Lark opened his hand in invitation.

"Thank you, but I understand that you are a Baron of Wrenford, are you not?" she replied as she sat with her legs crossed on the blanket-covered floor.

Lark laughed. "A title conveyed upon both Kael and me by the late King Thargelion. However, there is no room in a Paladin's or a Grand Druid's life, I would expect, for such things."

"Well, Lark, since you are Kael's best friend, I thought it time we get to know one another. I am Mya Almentir." Mya extended her hand to him.

Lark scrambled forward from a sitting position to take her hand in his and instinctively put her hand to his lips. A moment later, he looked her in the eye, realizing what he had done and still holding her hand, suddenly felt awkward and uncomfortable. "Lark Royale, my lady," he replied, releasing her hand and moving quickly away back to a sitting position.

Mya smiled at his discomfort in her presence, though it was not her intention. "So, you and Kael traveled together for many years? I would like to hear something of those times and of your first encounter with the Shadow Prince. What was Kael like back in those days?" she asked.

"Oh, my lady, he was quite different. He was adventurous, bold, and devoted to his beloved Mother Nature. However, I think we both set out to change the world in those days. We wanted to rid the lands of evil and help those who were persecuted and in need."

"I think he is still bold to a certain degree, but *adventurous* is not a term that would first come to mind," Mya said thoughtfully.

"Well, I think he has quite a bit more on his mind these days my lady," Lark said with a poignant look. "Back then, he had very little to lose and his life was much different. True he had Elenari, but he knew she was safe at the Kenshari temple. Not to mention, it was many years ago, and we were both much younger. While boldness sometimes wanes as we leave youth behind, our wisdom strengthens with age. Did you know, my lady, that Kael once fought and defeated a dragon single-handedly?" He looked at her, noticing that he had clearly piqued her interest.

"A dragon? Please, do tell," she implored.

Lark found himself relaxing. "Well, Kael and I had pursued the Prince Wolfgar Stranexx, the Shadow Prince, deep into his homeland within the Pytharian Empire when—" Lark was interrupted by the alarm bells. Without hesitation, he reached for his two-handed sword with one hand, grabbing Mya by the arm with his other, lifting her to a standing position.

"Please remain here, my lady, until it is safe." With that, Lark ran out of the tent without even reaching for his armor.

Lark knew the bells were coming from the west gate. He also knew they were completely unprepared for a night attack. Still, he raced toward the west gate, already seeing a flurry of activity gathered there. As he got closer, he could see many of the Elves already had their bows aimed at someone who was somehow inside the closed gate. There were Dwarves and some mounted cavalry from Averon present all with their swords drawn. Elenari and Archangel arrived just as he did.

Lark looked to see the focus of all the attention was a solitary figure dressed in black robes. He was hooded and carried a large, gnarled walking stick. He was standing still and not moving. They all seemed to be waiting for Mekko to arrive.

Elenari inched closer, sword in hand, to get a glimpse of the mysterious stranger. For a moment, Algernon stood there as if a living image projected from her mind's eye. Had he come to visit them as some sort of apparition? She inched ever closer until she stood nearly directly in front of him. It was then she saw his face clearly in the half-light of many torches. She gasped. "It cannot be . . ." she sighed in disbelief as the soldiers about her prepared to fire.

In the throne room of Bastlandia, Kael, Galin, Ellis, and Misty were brought before King Ceceran, with many guards in gray armor surrounding them throughout the chamber. Marko stood at Ceceran's right hand, dressed in a gaudy, rich, green robe with a golden sash. He looked disdainfully at the party before the throne.

"You will kneel before King Ceceran," Marko commanded.

Kael turned and nodded to everyone and led them to their knees. The old Druid lowered his head for a moment. Then while still kneeling, he looked up and spoke. "My Lord Zarian, allow me to introduce ourselves—" Kael began.

"You have not been given permission to speak yet," Marko interrupted.

Kael arched an eyebrow.

"Know that you address King *Ceceran*, son of the late King Zarian. Now you may identify yourselves but remain on your knees," Marko said with an indignant smirk.

"King Ceceran, my name is Kael Dracksmere, and this is Galin Calindir. We are Druids of Anagansit. Allow me to present Minister Ellis Freefire of Arcadia and Underminister Misty Treehill."

At the mention of Arcadia, weapons were drawn, and guards came to stand by Ellis and Misty.

"How dare you bring Arcadians here! What treachery is this?" Marko asked.

At last, Ceceran spoke. "Allow me to introduce my Prime Minister, Lord Marko," he said, pointing to Marko and smiling. "Take the Arcadians to the dungeon."

As the guards moved to place their hands on Misty, green fire erupted and flashed and where Galin had knelt a moment before, an enormous growling brown bear reared up on its hind legs. The guards reeled backward. Instantly, crossbows were aimed at the bear.

Marko cowered behind the throne.

Kael stood up and threw his arms out wide. "Hold, my lord! I ask that you hear my plea and that you allow Minister Freefire to speak as a senior member of the Arcadian government. I ask only that you hear us out. We are obviously at your mercy," Kael said, looking at the bear.

A moment later, in another flash of green fire, Galin had reverted to his human form.

Misty looked at him, unable to hide her amazement. She had heard that Druids were shapeshifters, but it was quite something else to see it up close. She found herself blushing that Galin had acted so quickly to defend her.

"So, you are Druids," Ceceran commented. "Very well. The Arcadians may remain for now."

"Thank you, my lord. If I may, we have come on behalf of the northern realms and specifically in the name of General Mekko, who currently leads the war-ravaged land of Cordilleran. I have here within these parchments a formal written request by the general for aid from Bastlandia." Without expression, Kael watched Marko slowly come out from behind the throne and resume his place.

"What wars are occurring in the northern realms? We know of no such conflict," Ceceran said calmly.

"My lord, surely even this far south, you have heard that a dark army is conquering the lands of the north, one by one. They have already conquered Wrenford, the Wood Elves, Mystaria, outlying villages around Alluviam, Averon, and Cordilleran. For all we know, Averon and Alluviam have been overrun at this point. An evil being known as the Shadow Prince has united the creatures of Bazadoom with the men of Koromundar and Jarathadar. His armies are systematically destroying all free life in their path. The last bastion of hope and free will in the north is a hand-built citadel with wooden walls and tents upon the muddy earth that was once the Dwarven Kingdom of Cordilleran. Their king, Crylar, is dead and their castle and capital city is destroyed. However, within this camp, Elves, Dwarves, and Men are united in their common fight against the evil of the Shadow Prince. General Mekko fears a menacing army will soon be sent against them. Without aid from the kingdoms of the south, Bastlandia and Arcadia, they cannot stand." Kael saw that his mention of Arcadia had caused the Bastlandian monarch to contort in his throne.

"Arcadia! Treacherous warmongering scum! How dare you mention them in the same breath as our sovereign nation. Perhaps you are unaware, Grand Druid, that the *great* nation of Arcadia recently destroyed one of our naval convoys. One of our fleets sent to their wretched jungle island to celebrate one hundred years of peace. It was a sneak attack, Druid, and it destroyed the flagship of our entire fleet as well countless lives." Ceceran pointed indignantly at Freefire.

"You are a black liar! Why on this earth would we want war with Bastlandia after one hundred years of peace? What could we possibly gain?"

Freefire rose from the kneeling position and took two steps forward. A dozen guards stepped forward, their weapons aimed at the minister, causing him to freeze his position.

"Of course, you have something to gain, you Arcadian dog. You have made your intentions clear. Your country wishes to gain the exclusive shipping rights to the Great Southern Trade Route with Averon. Do you think us fools?" It was Marko yelling and insulting the minister.

"No! We seek joint shipping rights. The Great Southern Trade Route represents a consolidation of the forces of the Trade Federation that will forever solidify our alliance and guaranty peace. It is a whole new era of profit for all nations involved," Freefire responded evenly.

"Eloquently stated, Minister, but imagine the profits if there was only one nation, such as Arcadia, responsible for shipping and security. Your children and their children's children will all be rich for generations to come. Will they not?" Ceceran said, smiling.

"They'll be no exclusive rights during a war. Have you heard nothing the Grand Druid has said? While we wage war against each other, it's likely this Shadow Prince will attack us and the other nations of the Federation while we fight amongst ourselves. Your father would have understood." Freefire said.

"Silence dog! Not another word will you utter on pain of death!" Marko yelled down at him.

Kael stepped forward. "My lord, it is clear your two kingdoms have their problems like anywhere else. But I was in the council chamber of Arcadia, and I can assure you they are fearful at the prospect of war and wish to avoid it at all costs."

"Of course, Druid. I believe you. Of course, they are fearful. They are afraid they will lose, and they will." Ceceran smiled.

"My lord, what of General Mekko's request for aid?" Kael asked, changing the subject.

"Ahh, of course we would like to offer aid to another struggling nation who, in turn, we may call upon for aid in the future against an aggressor; however, as you can see, we have our own war to fight. We must give the matter further thought before we draft a final answer to the general's plea. You may take these people to the city below the castle. There you will find suitable lodgings. Two of my guards will escort you to an inn. We will send for you when we have an answer. You may take *these* people with you since they are under your protection, and we have no quarrel with the Druids," Ceceran responded.

Kael dropped to one knee. "We thank you for your consideration, my lord. We ask that you please keep in mind every moment that passes could be precious to the life of Cordilleran."

"We shall endeavor to draft an expeditious reply, Grand Druid. Farewell."

Two guards, garbed in gray robes and plate mail armor, led the foursome through stone corridors to the castle foyer and out to the courtyard.

As they walked, Misty addressed one of the guards, "What of our Averics? Where are they?"

"They have been taken to the royal stables. They will be looked after until you wish to leave," the guard answered politely but curtly.

Galin noticed, as did the others, that they were not being led down the main road from the castle but instead were traveling east on a lesser-trod path leading into the forest.

"Pardon me, gentlemen, would it not be more direct to take the main road down to the city?" Galin asked as he touched Kael's arm, communicating that the situation made him uneasy.

The more senior of the two guards responded, "Indeed, master Druid, it would, but the king does not think it safe for too many to see the Arcadians with you. We cannot be responsible for how our people may react. After all, many no doubt saw those foul-looking birds you flew in on. It is well known that only Arcadians use such steeds. So, for your own safety, we will take the long way down."

A plausible reason, Galin thought, but something still did not feel quite right. He placed a reassuring hand on *Livinolos*, his sacred mace, hoping, in vain, the weapon may alert him of any hidden evil.

They continued deeper into the forest for several long minutes. Sometimes they turned as if to descend to the city and just as swiftly would change direction, away, deeper into the forest. The lightly traveled path they began on had completely eroded, and they had nothing to rely on except their escorts.

When Kael's patience had finally ended, he stopped them. "I think you've taken us quite far out of the way. I believe it is safe to enter the city now. These people are tired. We've had a long journey."

"As you wish, Druid," the senior guard replied.

When both guards turned suddenly and drew their swords, Galin drew his mace in one hand and scimitar in the other, and Kael took a two-handed grip on his wooden staff.

"Drop your weapons now!" a steady and commanding voice ordered from beyond their sight. It was then Kael and Galin saw at least a dozen forms surrounding them. Some were up in the trees; the rest were on foot. They were the gray-robed knights of Bastlandia, and they all pointed crossbows at them.

Freefire placed himself in front of Misty, who clutched his robe in fear. Kael and Galin reluctantly dropped their weapons and watched as a black-robed figure emerged from the forest cover. He was relatively tall and slender, and his face was shrouded in his cowl. He was armed with a longsword sheathed in a jeweled scabbard and held a crossbow in a one-handed grip.

"Hear me. I am Ellis Freefire, Minister, and senior member of the Chamber of Representatives of Arcadia. Whatever it is you have planned, it does not have to be this way. We are here to find a peaceful solution to our common problems—" Freefire never spoke another word as several crossbows fired, leaving four bolts in a circular pattern in the middle of his chest.

With a look of utter bewilderment, Freefire fell to his knees, panting. Kael quickly steadied him and was about to employ healing magic with his other hand.

"Release him, Druid, or die with him," the dark figure commanded.

Begrudgingly, Kael took his hands away. The man then stepped forward and with one hand aimed his crossbow at Freefire and fired a killing bolt directly in the middle of his forehead. The Arcadian minister's eyes fell back in his head and his body slumped to the ground.

Misty screamed, uncomprehending the cold-blooded act of sheer cruelty. Her mentor and the only father she had known had just been senselessly murdered while speaking of peace. She collapsed on his body, sobbing, and clutching him.

"I don't think you'll be able to heal him anymore," the dark warrior said, his voice devoid of both emotion and, strangely, sarcasm. It was a mere statement of fact. He turned from them but spoke casually as he walked. "Kill the Druids, do what you wish to the girl, but make sure when you're finished, she does not leave this forest alive."

Beyond belief, the old man had somehow penetrated the west gate without detection. He had passed through their lines of scouts and by the Elves and Dwarves on watch along the west wall. It was not until he stood inside the gate itself as if appearing out of thin air that the men of the watch sounded the alarm.

Now, close to a hundred men stood poised around him, waiting for the order to end his life. His stringy gray hair stuck out beneath his dark hood. He had stood motionless now for several minutes. Elenari moved face to face with him. She was the first to look directly at him and sighed her disbelief. As he returned her stare, Elenari saw, for the briefest moment, his eyes burning with white flame. His face was shrouded in weariness, his lids heavy.

He greeted her in a faint voice. "I . . . never did . . . get . . . your name . . . when . . . last we met. I must now . . . confess . . . that I knew it all along

... Elenari." He strained as he spoke her name, barely completing his sentence before collapsing forward into her arms, sliding to the ground at her feet.

Elenari quickly turned him over, taking his face in her hands. His skin was ice cold, and she could tell from his weather-beaten face and dried lips that he'd been traveling for some time.

"Rex, Rex Abernacle?" she said, again in disbelief.

Galin had been concentrating on a spell but suddenly even his acute concentration was uncharacteristically broken. The ground began to shake. Within seconds, men began to fall from the trees and soon those standing fell dead where they stood with long black arrow shafts buried within their bodies. The shots came from beyond their sight from an unknown direction. Within moments, nearly all the gray-robed warriors had fallen.

Kael watched as the black-robed figure turned and, faster than the eye could follow, drew forth his sword and batted multiple arrows aside with it. He stood his ground for a moment before disappearing back into the forest.

The shaking ground suddenly revealed itself in a dozen enormous horses that had galloped into their location as if from nowhere. They were the Meridians, the giant horses. Atop them were men dressed in varying types of armor from leather to metal; most carried longbows some seven feet in length. Kael and Galin had never lain eyes on such bows. Now instead of crossbow bolts, arrows pointed at Kael and Galin.

A heavily armored man on a massive black horse stopped his steed just before it trampled them. He was the only man among them wearing plate-mail. A large silver helmet with a visor covered all but his fierce dark eyes. "You will come with us or stay here and die. Those are your options, choose now!"

Within moments, the riders picked them up, and they were thundering off into the burgeoning darkness of the coming night.

Chapter 12

They had been riding in the darkness for hours before they finally stopped. However, they paused only long enough to bind the Druid's hands behind their backs and gag their mouths. Both searched frantically for a sign of Misty just before they were blindfolded. Then they felt themselves lifted back up upon the great horses, and they took off again at the gallop. The strangers were taking no chances that the Druids might attempt some spell.

As Kael strained his legs to keep himself balanced, he found his thoughts wandering. He knew they had tied him and most probably Galin to their saddles, but he still felt as if he could fly off the animal at any moment. As unsettling as that feeling was, his mind moved toward his good fortune.

They had escaped yet again, by the narrowest margin, what had seemed like certain death. Their luck would only hold for so long, yet he could not believe that Mother Nature had allowed him to live this long through so many close calls only to die now. It was impossible to tell whether they were in better company now than with the soldiers who served Ceceran, but at least they seemed to want them alive.

He could see Mya. Every exquisite detail of her breathtaking form was visible in his mind's eye. Her hair, white in the light of day, appeared silver in the half-light of the underground where he first saw her. He vowed secretly that once he owed no more to the lands as Grand Druid and his part was finished in the war against the Shadow Prince, he would exist only to serve her and never leave her side again. In addition, he vowed just as solemnly not to die until he knew that Elenari was safe and would always be cared for by someone, if he could not be there. He knew logically that she needed no looking after, but consequently, he knew she yearned for it emotionally.

Galin found himself reflecting upon all they had gone through from the beginning until now. How each of them had changed and grown from who and what they were to who and what they are now. He thought of Hawk and how he longed for an encouraging word from the burly ranger who had cautiously but cheerfully guided them so far from the beginning. Unknown to all the others, save possibly Algernon, Hawk was a noble lord from a nameless country. Hawk had never revealed the name of his homeland, only that it was across the eastern ocean where few from the mainland had ever ventured. Nor did he ever reveal his true name; however, he did learn long ago that he had been champion of the joust in his country. Such games and tournaments had not been held on the mainland for centuries. Though he tried to remain a mystery, Galin always knew exactly who he was without ever having known a single fact about his past. He was his friend, a friend he sorely missed.

Galin thought of Layla and how close they had become in the past few weeks. Strangely, it was much closer than they had been all the time he had lived in Alluviam. He wasn't quite sure why he had never spoken with her at length in the past. It may have been because she was King Aeldorath's daughter, and he had no desire to offend a monarch who had been so gracious and made him feel so at home. After all, he had always found her stunning, and her brash fearlessness would attract any man. But the more he pondered it, the more he seemed to always know the answer. He never truly felt worthy of such a woman. He was beneath her in both station and appearance. However, when he thought about the pure nature of the affection Kael and Mya enjoyed, that seemed poor reasoning indeed. He had no doubt what Hawk would say about the matter if he were there. He could almost hear it in his head. It would be very near the same advice he had offered the ranger about Elenari. He smiled.

Once his images of Mya faded, Kael's mind grappled with thoughts of the Shadow Prince. Though he seemed to be the same entity he and Lark had fought more than twenty years earlier, he apparently had enhanced abilities and powers. Kael concluded that some other evil force was using the Shadow Prince's form for a reason that eluded him. Yet something of the old Wolfgar was still there, beneath the mask of metal mesh. It was a puzzle that had even stumped the legendary Algernon. However, Kael always felt that the Sage had been reluctantly keeping information from them, even though he was confident that even Algernon did not understand it all entirely. It was nothing he could prove, just a feeling that gnawed at him like fear and doubt. Perhaps he was wrong entirely. All he knew for certain is that he would not allow the Shadow Prince to escape their next meeting. The next time, one of them would die. This time no fear would hinder him.

They rode well into the night to the point where sleep took them for short periods, even in the saddle.

They awoke to find themselves seated on the ground, leaning back-to-back with hands bound behind them. Without their blindfolds, the room came into view. They were in a large cellar surrounded by crates and barrels. They heard the voices of many men as they tromped up and down a nearby staircase. There seemed a sense of urgency about this place. Two guards standing over the Druids were the only men not partaking of the bustle of activity in the structure.

"What do you think happened to Misty?" Galin asked softly.

"I do not know, but I pray she is not in harm's way," Kael responded.

"Freefire was a good man. That was no way to die. The girl shouldn't have been there to see it," Galin said with frustration.

"It is better she hardens herself to it now. There is a storm of death coming like nothing we have ever imagined. Better she hardens to it now," Kael said flatly.

They passed the next hour in silence until Kael gave Galin a gentle nudge. "This is becoming tiresome and, for me, a little too familiar," he whispered.

"How can you say that? You met the love of your life during your last captivity. Perhaps it's my turn," Galin whispered back.

Kael smiled despite their situation, but the smile faded as heavy footfalls came down the stairs. The men in the cellar snapped to attention. A moment later, a tall, well-built man revealed himself. He had dark, silvery hair that fell loosely about his shoulders. Leather armor that had to be custom made to fit his broad shoulders and chest covered his form. While difficult to discern his age, his physical prowess was without question evidenced by his enormous forearms and rippling biceps.

For a moment, in the shadows of the cellar, he appeared to Kael like the resurrected apparition of the powerful Captain Garin, commander of the garrison of Wrenford. However, as he came into view of the half-light of the lanterns, it was quite clear he was not. The man looked at each of them in turn, measuring them in his own way and then addressed them. "Ceceran's men were about to kill you. Why? Who are you?" the tall man asked, a brooding countenance upon his brow.

"Where is the girl? If you've harmed her after what she's been through, you—" Galin started in a demanding tone.

"You are hardly in a position to make threats. The girl is fine. She is upstairs resting. No harm will come to her, even though she is Arcadian. You have my word as a soldier and Captain of the High Riders. Now, answer my question," he insisted.

Kael noticed the entire cellar was full of men now, watching from a respectful distance behind this taller man, who was undoubtedly their leader.

"We are Druids of Anagansit. This is Galin, and I am Kael. We are inclined to tell you nothing else until we have proof the girl is unharmed," Kael said.

The man swiftly moved forward, his face inches from Kael's. "Druids you may be, well know this Druid: The word of a High Rider is his bond. No paper, royal edict, or proclamation can carry such weight. You have courage, and though I like a man with courage, I will not show you the girl," he said calmly.

"Why not?" Galin demanded.

"Because I am not in command here," the tall man answered in an equally powerful tone. With that, they suddenly heard someone else coming down the stairs, though these footfalls were much lighter.

As the two Druids strained to look up from their awkward seated position, they were surprised to see what appeared to be a beautiful, dark-haired young woman. She moved with grace and elegance, and she was clad in crimson velour boots beneath flowing purple robes. The moment she appeared from the last step, without hesitation, warriors crammed within the basement fell to their knees. They all appeared to be hardened men, both young and old, but they were completely humble before this seemingly young woman, not much older than Misty by all appearances.

"Rise, men of Bastlandia. Krin, I told you this is unnecessary every time I enter a room." Her voice was gentle yet echoed with a latent tone of command.

One of the older men came forward and knelt again before her. "Forgive me, my lady, but is necessary. It is necessary for us so that we may stay focused on our purpose and who the rightful heir to the throne is and always has been. With submission, your highness, we are yours to command. We cannot forget even for a moment, nor do we wish you to forget."

The young woman looked down at him, a mixture of blush and discomfort upon her face, veiling a deep feeling of appreciation. She stuck her gloved hand out to him.

The warrior took it in his own and kissed it. "Thank you, my lady. We all thank you and ask that you be patient." After conferring briefly with the warrior known as Krin, who had been questioning them, she walked and stood where both Kael and Galin could see her.

"Underminister Treehill is quite safe, please be assured. She is resting in my quarters," she began. Her eyes were intense black pools that exuded integrity.

"We would like to see her," Kael said.

"Of course, however, I must ask you to be patient a little longer, gentlemen. We do have a few questions first," she replied.

"And we have questions of our own. Who are you people and where are we? And who are the High Riders?" Galin asked.

"My name is Angelique," she answered softly. "The High Riders, or what is left of them, is here in this basement, for the most part. The High Riders were the elite guards of the royal family of Bastlandia."

"Then why are they not in Bastlandia?" Galin quizzed.

Angelique smiled, but Galin noticed it was a sad smile, so full of remorse and bad memory. He felt sorry for asking anything that would make so strong and beautiful a woman even mildly unhappy.

"We are still in Bastlandia, gentlemen, albeit the outskirts. The High Riders, like me, have been cast out of Castle Iberian. We are, in fact, lucky to be alive."

"And who are you, lady?" Kael then asked.

"We are asking the questions, not you!" Krin exclaimed.

Angelique raised her hand to him. "I am Angelique, daughter of King Zarian, sister to Ceceran, and rightful heir to the throne of Bastlandia," she answered matter-of-factly.

"Then you are the queen of . . . a basement full of men?" Galin said, intending no malice but instead probing for understanding. However, Krin did not make the distinction and stepped forward with a backhand fist to his face.

"Enough!" Angelique commanded as she stood. "Remove their bonds."

Krin nodded to his men, and they immediately untied the two Druids. They quickly stood in the crowded basement. Angelique motioned to them. "Please, come with me," she said.

She led them back up the stairs, with Krin bringing up the rear. As they moved through what seemed to be a common house, the Druids surmised it to be the home of a farmer or woodsman. Strange accommodations indeed, they thought, for the queen and her elite bodyguard. They were led to a small bedroom where Misty was alone, asleep in the bed.

Galin quickly sat and attended to her, noticing she was unhurt and resting comfortably. Angelique then led them into an adjacent bedroom and closed the door so that only the four of them were inside. Krin continued to observe the two Druids guardedly as he stood near the door.

"Why did you go to see my brother with two representatives from Arcadia?" Angelique asked pointedly.

"We're not entirely prepared to answer questions about our purpose just yet. I hope you understand. Put yourselves in our position for a moment. How are we to know who to trust?" Kael asked.

"You make an excellent point, Kael of Anagansit. In that case, rather than tell you, we shall show you. Please come with us." She motioned for them to follow.

Before long they were outside. It was daytime. Though it had appeared to be a sunny morning, the noon seemed to give way to overcast clouds. They were on a small farm. No other lodgings were within sight, only endless fields of yellow and green. Behind the large cottage from which they had emerged was a vast wooded area that extended beyond their sight and became darker the deeper they attempted to peer within.

Angelique and Krin had grabbed black-hooded robes for themselves and gave one to each Kael and Galin. Only two other men accompanied them, walking behind. They soon found themselves at the end of a walkway in the ground leading from the cottage. There before them, a roughshod wooden carriage pulled by two horses waited.

When they reached the carriage, Krin stood before them with two black pieces of cloth in his hands. As he tied them around each of their eyes, he explained, "I'm sure you understand, gentlemen. For your protection and ours, it is better that you do not know the way back here."

"Of course. Trust is something that must be earned, a concept we are more than familiar with," Kael responded as they were guided within the back of the carriage.

They rode for at least several hours, unable to know precisely how much time had passed. They heard little during their journey; however, they recognized the sounds of night within the speech of crickets and other noises that signaled the transition of the sun to the moon. Somewhere along the way, they drifted off to sleep.

The cacophony of many voices speaking at once awakened them. They opened their eyes to find they were no longer blindfolded. They were alone, still within the back of the wagon, as they looked out a crack in the heavy material covering the vehicle's frame. It was daytime, and they appeared to be within the courtyard of Castle Iberian, only now it was full, with hundreds of spectators. They were positioned well in the back of the courtyard behind countless onlookers. For so many people present, there was an unsettling silence in the air. A moment later, Captain Krin jumped into the back of the wagon.

"Gentlemen, I urge you not to make any sudden noise and to speak softly. We are in the courtyard of Castle Iberian. Look straight ahead and left at the wooden structure. Do you recognize it?" Krin asked. At that moment, a second hooded figure joined them in the wagon. It was Angelique.

"We apologize that the journey was so long, but we feel it necessary for you to see this for yourselves," Angelique said.

"You don't recognize the structure, do you?" Krin asked.

Both Kael and Galin looked out of the hole through the wagon. Each man shook his head in the negative.

"Well, then, perhaps we should apologize again for what you are about to see." She pointed their attention to the table atop the marble dais aside the structure around which a number of gray-garbed guards stood. "There, the fat overdressed fellow is Admiral Piedmont, Minister of Military Security," she spat with a disgust that was unbecoming her natural beauty.

The Druids rested their eyes on a heavyset man wearing a dark robe, an overstated black hat with a single feather in it, and a pompous expression on his round face.

The raised platform was approximately twelve feet above the ground and some twenty-five feet long. A loose rope hung down from the upper framework from ten distinct joints. The Druids still were unsure what purpose the structure served until they saw five black-hooded men rise to the platform from stairs unseen behind it. Their hoods completely concealed their faces save perfectly cut slits for their eyes, nose, and mouths.

"What's going on here? What have you brought us here to witness?" Galin asked with alarm.

"Calm yourself, Druid. This is a necessary evil to show you the state of affairs here and to convince you that you are among friends," Angelique said with iron in her voice and an undertone of regret.

They continued to watch as horns blared, silencing the crowd. Krin directed their gaze upward to an overlooking balcony. There they saw two men, one wearing a crown. It was Ceceran.

"My brother and his Prime Minister, Lord Marko," Angelique said with reserved disdain.

Kael looked closely and saw Marko hand-feed a bunch of grapes to the king.

Once silence had fallen, from behind the platform, ten men were led upstairs to stand upon the structure, facing the crowd. Their wrists were bound behind their backs. The Druids could tell the men were soldiers, officers by the looks of their uniforms. They all wore a look of pride. There were no signs of despair or sorrow upon their faces. The expressions of those in the crowd told a different story. It was as if they had witnessed this ritual before and knew all too well what would occur next. Their eyes carried tears of regret and sorrow.

"Those men are officers within the royal navy. They are patriots and loyal to our former King Zarian. Admiral Piedmont has been charged with finding such men and exposing them as traitors to the crown," Krin said reluctantly.

Marko came to the edge of the balcony, overlooking the prisoners with smug condescension upon his face. "Admiral," he commanded, "read the charges to the people!"

The young servant boy who had been attending Piedmont quickly brought him a large scroll and, taking the napkin, preceded to hand Piedmont the parchment. Piedmont cleared his throat, a process that graduated into an uncontrolled fit of coughing. Rolling his eyes with a sigh, the boy quickly poured him more wine and handed him the goblet. The admiral emptied the cup in one swallow and settled his coughing. He took the scroll in both hands and read the following:

"Be it known to all loyal citizens of Bastlandia, the prisoners before you have been found guilty of treason against the state by a council of their peers under the grace of his majesty, King Ceceran. It is the judgment of the council and the Prime Minister, Lord Marko, that they present a direct threat to the sovereignty and security of the Kingdom of Bastlandia."

With that, Piedmont rolled up the scroll, placed it on the table, and commenced with his meal as if there were no distractions.

Marko then addressed the people gathered in the square, "People of Bastlandia, you have heard both the charges and the verdict. However, it is the wish of his majesty, Ceceran the Just and Noble, that you, not he, decide their fate. What is your pleasure?"

No one moved or spoke for a moment, and then it started. Chants arose from different strategic points in the crowd and were then repeated over and over with increasing strength, "Death, death, death!"

Piedmont with his mouth half full managed to speak, "Do the prisoners have any final words?"

With that, one of the older, senior men of the group stepped forward. He was a captain. Though his hair had been thinning and gray, the broadness of his shoulders knew no such atrophy. With pride on his face, he stepped forward and turned up toward the king's balcony. "I have no desire to spend one more minute in a kingdom ruled by you. Once the kings of Bastlandia were noble, but in you, nobility has turned to poison. How dare you call yourself *just*, surrounded by your scheming slaves and that viper's nest you call a council!"

As the captain continued his harangue, Marko gestured to the black-hooded men. Two of them grabbed the officer and forced him to his knees and put his head on a barrel. One held him down while the other pulled a dagger from his robes and made a swift cutting motion, severing the tongue from his mouth. Blood spurted in several directions, and while the captain was clearly in agony, he did not give them the satisfaction of crying out.

"Empty words from an empty mouth!" Marko exclaimed, clapping his hands. "Let the people see what becomes of such traitors!"

Each prisoner's head was covered with a black hoods and rope loops were tightened around their necks. Within the wagon, Galin could stand no more, and as he attempted to exit the back of the wagon, Kael tried to restrain him. Galin broke free; however, the sudden iron grip of Krin thrust him back. Galin sprang up quickly, but Krin was faster and locked his hands around the Druid's wrists, holding him still like an iron vise.

"How can you watch this and do nothing? They are your people!" Galin cried.

Krin placed his forearm under the Druid's throat to silence him and met his eyes. "Druid, none of these men are strangers, and we have seen this ceremony before, and we stay in the wagon. Do you understand?"

Galin let go of his frustration upon seeing a tear run down Krin's cheek. He saw such furious passion in this man's expression that it touched his very soul. He controlled his rage and unbridled sorrow beneath a mask of duty. He took a deep breath and returned to the hole just in time to observe the order given which removed the platform upon which the prisoners stood.

In one terrible instant, it was over: Ten lives became ten swinging forms. There was no applause or sound of any kind within the square. As if moving in slow motion, the people silently dispersed from the area.

Galin let his head fall forward as Kael placed a comforting hand on the younger man's shoulder. There was nothing he could do or say to ease the pain. Kael looked at Angelique, whose gaze never wavered, not even for an instant, and while there was sorrow in her eyes, a fierce determination overshadowed all else. He had seen such a look before upon the faces of the two women he loved most in the world, Elenari and Mya. That was why he knew, without doubt, a battle would soon follow.

Chapter 13

"My lord, we must find a way to replenish the treasury quickly," Marko advised as he paced before Ceceran, who sat on his throne deep in thought.

The aged royal scribe sat off and to the side, scratching away in his leather-bound tome.

The situation had become dire, and the more they discussed it, the more agitated Ceceran grew. If they could not find a resolution, it could prove to be their undoing. Neither relished the idea of telling the Dark Warrior they would be unable to pay the agreed-upon tribute to his master.

"Bring me the royal treasurer!" Ceceran commanded. The guards shuffled in the background to obey him. "What about the nobles?"

"My lord?" Marko asked.

"The barons and, noble Lord Marko, the aristocracy. Why not tax them? They're the ones with all the money anyway," Ceceran whined.

"My lord," the scribe, who had been scratching away in his tome, started, "the nobles have never been taxed in Bastlandian history. The people would never have it."

Ceceran let a curious frown crease his forehead. He rose from his throne and descended to Marko and the scribe's level. Exhaling, he placed a hand on the scribe's shoulder. "Have they not?" he questioned. Suddenly, he grabbed the old man by the scruff of the collar and struck him with the back of his fist and then slapped him with the palm of his hand. "Thank you for that revelation, old fool! I grew up in Bastlandia as well and am aware of its history! It's time to do away with old traditions and practices. There's a new king and therefore new ways of thinking and doing things! The people would never have it, you say . . . it is the king who rules! The people have had their way for far too long."

At that moment, two guards appeared with a middle-aged man dressed ornately with a nervous manner. "The royal treasurer, my lord," one guard stated as they both bowed their heads.

"Well?!" the king demanded.

"Well what, sire?" the man responded uneasily.

"The treasury is empty, idiot, what do you have to say for yourself?" Ceceran demanded.

"My lord, a combination of events has led to this. The answer is not a simple one," he replied, not knowing if he had perhaps said too much.

"Educate me!" Ceceran exclaimed.

"Well, my lord, it started when we seceded from the Trade Federation. We lost our monthly royalties, which is most likely the primary reason the treasury is depleted. Then there were the multiple royal edicts by your majesty, increasing the taxes until the point where half the population could no longer pay. Not to mention, sire, the exorbitant salary of your new . . . royal guard, and the huge monthly sum that is being sent north overseas to parties unknown." He hoped he had not been too blunt.

"Yes, yes, that's a very fascinating analysis of the situation. Now, what do you propose to do about it?" Ceceran asked.

The treasurer looked at him unsure what he meant. "Sire?"

With that, the king grabbed hold of the large leather-bound tome the scribe had been writing in and struck the treasurer across the face three times, causing blood to gush from his nose and the third, knocking him to the ground.

"Guards, seize this imbecile!" Ceceran commanded, throwing the scribe's tome to the stone floor.

The guards picked up the treasurer and faced him toward the king.

"Take him to the dungeon, cut out his intestines, wrap them around his neck, and strangle him with them! Maybe then he'll figure out what I'm talking about! Now get out of here, all of you! I'm surrounded by fools!" He walked back up to his throne and watched them leave as he sat.

"May I have leave to remain, my lord, and help remove these burdens from your mind, if only for a brief time?" Marko dropped to his knees before the king, removed his sash, and reached within his robes.

"Ah, yes, you may, my dear Marko. You are the only intelligent man in my kingdom." He let his hands rest on top of Marko's head, grabbing handfuls of his hair.

Nearly two hours had passed, and still they had no new ideas. Ceceran sat in his throne while Marko sat at his feet until he suddenly sprang up with a fresh idea.

"My lord, perhaps we could do something for the nobles to solicit the money from them," Marko began.

"I will not increase land or title for any of them; they'll think they can hold the throne hostage whenever they want something!" Ceceran retorted.

"No, my lord, I was thinking more of holding a grand banquet in their honor. No, not a banquet, a ball! A masquerade ball, sire. We shall advertise it as an event of such magnificent splendor that they would all be embarrassed not to attend, even if we attached a modest admission price to attend such an event."

He could see that the king was considering his proposal. "A most extraordinary idea. However, would such an event not have considerable cost in its own right?"

"I think not, my king. It has been some time since the castle held such a feast. We have more than enough food and the servants get so very excited at the opportunity to plan such festivities. The cost will be minimal at best," Marko concluded.

"Indeed. Well then, we must make it worth the price. Have that old fool who calls himself a scribe begin drafting the most ornate invitations his old hands can produce. Be sure no one is left out. All the nobles must be in attendance. Summon the royal seamstress and tailors; there are costumes to be made. You may wish to use your own considerable skills as well. See to the preparations immediately!"

"At once my king." Marko bowed low and then quickly exited the throne room.

When Kael and Galin emerged from the wagon, after an inordinately long journey, they found themselves within a deep forest amidst a whirl of activity. There were several men within the woods, far more than they had seen in the cellar. There were fletchers making bows and blacksmiths hammering out swords. They had to quickly step aside as men rode past on huge, muscular horses. Others lined up, shooting arrows at man-made targets, with bows far larger than any they had ever seen.

"The Meridians, the great horses of Bastlandia," Angelique began. "What you see before you, gentlemen, are the last of the High Riders, the elite royal guard loyal to the true sovereign of this land. Those who escaped my brother's tyranny with their lives, as well as some loyal friends, have come to this place to train and prepare."

"Train and prepare for what?" Kael asked.

"The retaking of Castle Iberian, of course, and the overthrow of my brother, the illegitimate king," she responded.

Galin turned to Kael. "Of course. Why do I feel like we've found ourselves on the verge of another siege?"

"So it would seem," Kael said. "Your majesty, may we have a word in private?"

"Of course, follow me, please." She beckoned for Krin to join them as well.

Angelique and Krin led the Druids past dozens of men training in sword fighting and horse-mounted archery to a large tent.

"When are you planning your revolution? Why have you done nothing until now?" Kael asked as soon as they were inside.

Krin took a step forward, restraining himself. "There are other considerations which must be weighed," he said with a strange look at Angelique.

It was only then that both Kael and Galin noticed something about Angelique they had not noticed earlier, a slight shape about her stomach; she was pregnant.

"*I* can never be king, however, my child—our child—be it boy or girl will one day rule Bastlandia. Do you understand now? There is much to risk," Krin said.

"There is always much to risk when those who are free stand up to evil and the forces of oppression. Can you live with the alternative. How soon can you attempt an attack upon your brother?" Kael asked.

"That is the question," responded Krin. "They far outnumber us, and as you have seen, we cannot afford to lose. All would be lost and more even than that," he said as he looked at Angelique, who was rubbing her curved belly.

"We came here to solicit aid from Arcadia and Bastlandia. Many nations north across the oceans have allied against a monstrous evil that has systematically attacked our lands and driven the last of us who would be free south, very nearly to the ocean itself. A loose alliance of Elves, Men, and Dwarves is all that stands between this evil and the ocean that separates your lands. We went to Arcadia first, with a formal request from General Mekko, commander of the Alliance army and leader of the Dwarves. However, upon our arrival, we learned of the recent breakout of hostilities between their country and yours after nearly one hundred years of peace."

"How were you received by the Arcadians?" Angelique asked.

"It was difficult at first, but we came to an accord," Kael responded.

"So, they agreed to help you. To send men to aid you across the ocean. It's much to risk for a cause that is not their own," Krin said. "What did you agree to provide them with?"

"We agreed to use all of our powers to try to reconcile your two nations, in point of fact," Kael answered.

Both Angelique and Krin stared at them incredulously.

"Because," Galin added, "we believe the Shadow Prince's influence has already reached down here and is the driving force between the recent outbreak of hostilities between your two kingdoms. It is his nature to thrive on age-old animosities and exploit our fears and doubts so that people will not only begin to distrust each other but also hunger for war. All the while he sits back and attacks after both sides have been sufficiently weakened. He used the same strategy on the Republic of Averon and Elves of Alluviam, only we were able to intercede and expose his treachery before they destroyed each other. We would not see the same thing happen to Bastlandia and Arcadia, two kingdoms that have worked and prospered together for nearly a century. The unprovoked attack upon the

Emerald Sea is precisely the type of maneuver the Shadow Prince would employ to such an end."

Angelique and Krin exchanged glances as if reckoning the truth of Galin's statement.

"What is it?" Galin asked.

Krin began in hushed tones, "It is said a dark-clad warrior had been meeting secretly with Ceceran when he was still prince. No one ever got a good look at him, but the High Riders determined this warrior had been able to penetrate the castle, almost at will, without being detected. Shortly after his appearance followed the tragedy of the *Emerald Sea*, the death of King Zarian, and the attempted assassination of the queen. It is said this dark warrior is so swift that he can catch arrows in his bare hand and bat them away with his sword. Could he be this Shadow Prince of whom you speak?" Krin asked.

Kael furled his brow. "I fear this dark warrior is more dangerous than mere rumor. I would advise your men not to confront him alone, only in force."

"I do not think this warrior is the Shadow Prince, more likely one of his agents. I think there can no longer be any doubt that his influence has grown far indeed," Galin responded with a concerned look at Kael.

With a look of steel determination, Kael faced the others. "The Shadow Prince has immense power that he uses with evil intent. He has returned from death to exact his revenge on the world. He leads an all but invincible army that has already destroyed several lands and now masses on the borders of Cordilleran, the homeland of the Dwarves. The Alliance has constructed a citadel of wooden walls and towers to defend against what may well be our end. Without reinforcements, we cannot stand against the darkness that threatens to claim us. The time for pleasantries is over. Without our assistance, there will be war between Arcadia and Bastlandia. We can help make the peace between your two kingdoms. In addition, we offer our services as Druids in the upcoming battle against your brother. In return, we ask that you accept and agree to help with General Mekko's formal request for military aid."

"I think you overestimate your bargaining position, Druid," Angelique said.

Krin stepped forward. "How do you suppose your assistance is the only thing saving us from war with Arcadia? How exactly can *you* help us with our current situation? You say you are Druids, but I've seen no proof that you are any more than robed meddlers with your own ends above all concerns."

Kael raised his voice ever so slightly. "It was no vessel of Arcadian design that sank the *Emerald Sea* and her escorts. It was a dark fleet of metal-encased ships that are mounted with devastating weaponry far more powerful than either your kingdom or theirs could conceive."

"How could you possibly know that?" Angelique asked with a mix of amazement and doubt.

"Because we saw this dark fleet on our flight across the ocean from the north," Galin answered.

"You mean when you were riding atop those ridiculous pink birds the Arcadians use to fly about their islands?" Krin scoffed.

"No, we arrived from the north by other means, but that's right . . . you've seen no proof we are Druids, as you say." Kael looked at Galin and nodded.

Green fire exploded within the tent. The sheer suddenness of it caused Krin to protectively pull Angelique toward him. When they took their hands away from their faces, they looked with disbelief. Where Kael had stood was a magnificent brown eagle with a crown of white, and where Galin had stood was a huge black bear on its hind legs, taller than Krin.

With another flash, the two Druids again stood facing them.

"Was that sufficient proof, Captain?" Kael asked.

"Indeed, ah, yes. I think Druids could be most useful in what is to come. Don't you, your highness?" Krin asked with a stammer.

"Second, we, along with Underminister Treehill, are witnesses to the tragic death of Minister Freefire, which was not committed by the legitimate government of Bastlandia. I think such accounting will go far in forging the peace between you," Kael said.

"You should have been a politician, Kael of the Druids." Angelique said, smiling.

Kael and Galin exchanged a satisfied smirk.

"In point of fact, my lady, I am one . . . but that is a story for another time. What is your plan to retake the castle?" Kael asked.

"It is not so much a matter of our plan as when to execute it. Timing is critical. They have most our horses, the Meridians, secured in the royal barracks. Our spies indicate that the king's guard is ever vigilant, and their number seems to be increasing," Krin responded.

"Well, we aren't exactly strangers to storming a castle," Galin said with slight sarcasm.

"Is this true?" Angelique asked Kael.

"It is. There are many ways we could assist you. Regrettably, we've taken part in castle siege before with some success," Kael responded.

"Druids are more formidable than I would have ever guessed. We need something to distract their forces. We need surprise. If they know the castle and its defenses, our attack will be short lived . . . Druids or not," Krin said.

At that moment, several of the men from the camp barged within the tent and fell to their knees. "Your highness, please forgive us, but we've received urgent news." Three men waited for leave to speak.

"Rise, all of you. Please, tell us what news you've heard," Angelique urged.

"Your highness," began one of the young men garbed in green forest cloths, "there is word that Ceceran is planning to have a grand ball at the castle. Preparations have already begun for a huge feast to be given in honor of the nobles. There is even word of festivities, music, entertainment, and costumes."

"That does not at all sound like my brother. He would not just throw a feast in honor of the nobles," Angelique said, looking to Krin.

"No indeed, your highness, word is your brother has squandered all the money in the Royal Treasury. He has even executed the royal treasurer. Truly, the nobles will have to pay a tribute to attend this feast," the young ranger continued.

"The nobles will never agree to that. They'll see that snake starve before they divvy out any money to him," Krin said.

"No, sir, all will attend. The Prime Minister has made it clear, in no uncertain terms, that any who does not attend will be dealt with severely. Fear of the king's royal guard will force them to attend."

"You were looking for the right time, Captain," Galin said. "I can think of no better opportunity."

Kael nodded and continued, "Since it is a costume ball, we can get most of your men inside, right through the main gate. With our help, we can free your horses and open the gates to the waiting force outside the castle."

"This is just what we have been waiting for your highness," Krin said to Angelique, taking her hand and holding it gently.

"Come with me," Angelique said, leaving the tent. She went to a small clearing and called the men to her near a small fire.

"High Riders, rangers, scouts, friends, and all those who would live free in Bastlandia, come close. Make your final preparation, for the hour of our reckoning has come at last! The time has come to relieve this usurping upstart of an imposter and his wicked slave of a prime minister from the throne. For too long have they murdered and wrought suffering upon us and our people. Too long have they spread treacherous warmongering about our neighbors and former allies, the Arcadians. I say these people are *not* our enemies. With proof provided by our Druid friends, we will heal the wounds caused to our two nations and be the better and stronger for it. For the people, for Bastlandia, and for freedom we will fight!" She raised her sword high in the air, and her subjects went wild with cheers and roars of approval.

"For the queen!" they roared.

Galin whispered in Kael's ear, "It is just as Algernon said when he first spoke to us in the halls of King Thargelion: *For one man defending his home is greater than ten of the strongest mercenaries.*"

"He was right," Kael responded. "His wisdom and foresight went further than even the enemy's dreaded reach."

That night, they returned to the small cottage. When Misty laid eyes on the Druids, she ran to embrace them. They greeted her warmly before taking her to a private room to inform her of all that had taken place.

When they were done, she stood. "Of course I will join this fight to avenge my mentor," she insisted.

"You cannot be a part of what is to come here," Galin said solemnly, quieting her protest with an upraised hand.

"Don't you understand?" Kael said. "Someone must go to Arcadia to tell what has occurred here. We cannot risk all of us in the battle to come. If we do and we are lost, there is no guarantee that even victory here will be enough to heal the troubles between Bastlandia and Arcadia. There are many more lives in the balance than just those here. Galin and I have tens of thousands depending on us to the north in Cordilleran."

"Do not be so sudden to take up the mantle of vengeance, for there will be consequences to such actions that you dare not guess," Galin added. "Not the least of which is living with your actions afterward. I do not think Minister Freefire would have wanted you to pursue vengeance, even for his death. Do you?"

Misty cast her eyes downward, and tears trickled along her cheeks. "No, he would not have wanted it," she whispered but then her voice rose with frustration. "But once all is said and done, I intend to train to become a Druid. I don't want this life in politics, I never did."

"The time is coming where we will need new Druids," Kael assured her, "and while none will be denied the opportunity, you must be willing to serve Mother Nature for the right reasons. Do you understand?" Kael reached out and wiped away her tears. "If one comes before her with self-serving ends, it is she who will reject you, not any Druid."

"Yes, I understand. I will become a Druid for the right reasons," she said confidently.

"I look forward to that day, Misty," Kael said.

"As do I," Galin added.

"Let's get you up and away from this place. Come with us," said Kael as they led Misty outside. Galin waited with her as Kael moved off from them and raised his hands to the sky in deep concentration.

"What is he doing?" Misty asked Galin.

"He is communing with nature in order that an Averic might be sent to come and pick you up."

Misty looked at him hopefully.

"It is a difficult summoning, beyond most Druids," Galin added.

"I can only imagine what it would be like to possess such ability," she said with awe, then asked, "Galin, when the day comes that I attempt to enter the order, will you speak on my behalf?"

Galin put his arm around her shoulder. "I will . . . as long as you keep your course true and your motives pure." He glanced over at the Grand Druid.

With closed eyes, Kael stretched out with his feelings as he made his request. He could sense Nature's life force, her reassuring presence. Still, he sensed uneasiness. While the poisoning of the land did not seem to be evident here in the south, Mother Nature warned that it was just a matter of time before the deterioration spread. But, despite all, she bent her thought to hear the will of one of her great servants. After an hour had turned on the clock, he bent his head and dropped his hands to his sides.

Wiping the perspiration from his brow, he rejoined Galin and Misty. "Remain here, Misty. An Averic will arrive shortly to bear you hence to Arcadia. You must report what you have witnessed and all that may yet come to pass if we are successful," Kael said, placing a trusting hand on her shoulder.

"I will, Kael. Good luck to both of you. May . . . may Mother Nature protect you," she said, touching his hand.

Kael stepped back, and the Druids bowed their heads.

"And you, Misty Treehill, until the end of your journey," said Kael, and Galin echoed his sentiments.

In the days leading up to the masquerade ball, all the towns and villages throughout the Bastlandian countryside buzzed with activity. The people had been invited to the inner courtyard to behold the splendor of their king and nobles at banquet, dressed in the most finely woven costumes. There was even rumor of additional festivities to entertain all present. It was the first time in many years such an event had been held in Bastlandia, and it was high time.

Dissent among the people had been growing. The multiple edicts from the king restricting freedoms and raising taxes were swelling the rage of the population to near rebellion. Never in the collective history of the country had any king dared what Ceceran had: public executions and restructuring the government and military. Most were outraged. Still, there was fear of the king's new royal guard and the mysterious dark warrior who led them. Fear of them seemed to be the only thing holding back those who would otherwise not be silent.

Meanwhile, deep in the Borderland Forest, the remnants of the High Riders, rangers, and free folk of Bastlandia prepared for the night ahead of them. They gathered, for one final time, to face their queen. Angelique emerged radiant before them, but to their dismay, she wore chain mail armor beneath her crimson cape. Her hair fell like shadow upon her shoulders. There was a fierce sparkle within her eyes and iron determination upon her face.

"Until this moment, you have kept my existence a secret to the rest of our people. Krin, we've sent word to all the nobles to be ready to have our people join with theirs as they enter the castle," She watched as her lover nodded his approval. "Tonight, we will reveal to all that not only is the rightful heir to the throne still alive but also so is the true people's guard to the royal house, the High Riders!" Angelique exclaimed.

This was met with many cheers, but several of the older men stepped forward and knelt before her. The oldest among them, Corporal Rogent, spoke for them. "My lady, you are with child. You cannot join this fight. Your survival and the survival of your child, our heir, are paramount among our concerns. It is our sacred duty to protect you and well . . ." His words trailed off, unsure of where they were to end.

"What Corporal Rogent means, your highness, is they will not be able to fight their best against your brother's men if they must also be concerned for your well-being. And I find myself in agreement," said Krin, bowing his head.

"I appreciate and understand your concern, and I thank you for it," Angelique said calmly. "However, I will not put any of you in harm's way where I would not stand with you before any and all such danger. No, I will hear no protests. I will be queen, and our child will be an heir this night, or my family line will end. There will be no half ground. Know that I am honored to fight alongside such noble men as served my father and his father before him. I will see your glory restored, and I would see our people free and happy again." With that, she pulled her crimson hood over her head and unsheathed her sword, raising it high. "For Bastlandia!"

By tradition, all gathered responded, first, "For the Queen!" and second, "For Bastlandia!"

The night of the grand masquerade ball had finally arrived, and Castle Iberian knew a festive warmth that had not been seen in many years. However, to the good people of Bastlandia, it was a facade; this night was the product of political maneuver.

Noble lords and ladies from all across the island made their way to this event, where the price for their attendance was described as "a modest one thousand gold pieces" on the gaudy invitations. Prime Minister Marko had sent communication through more discrete means to ensure they understood the dire consequences of not attending.

All manner of lights and decorations adorned the archway to the main courtyard. Balloons wavered over every post as well as the main gates, while wreathes of white roses outlined the battlements of the towers. Red, blue, and green lanterns had been placed within the fountains to create a shimmering spray of color. Every manner of mime, jester, and traveling magicians had been called upon to keep the people amused as they crowded within the main courtyard, waiting patiently to see the king, lords, and ladies adorned in the finest costumes.

A regular procession of nobles and their retinue entered the castle on a winding pathway that allowed spectators to see; however, all were heavily garbed in dark robes, concealing most of their costumes, which would be displayed later at the proper time. It was an amusing pastime for commoners to try to guess which lord or lady was entering the castle.

The royal guard, clad in gray and plate mail armor, was out in large force, as was to be expected. The watch patrolling the upper levels of the perimeter wall and keep had been doubled, as well as the guard at the main gate and courtyard. In addition, several crossbowmen took positions on the perimeter wall around the courtyard to ensure the crowd knew the limits of what behavior would be tolerated.

Kael moved through the crowd easily as one of the magicians, using small Druid magic to astound children and adults alike; Galin worked another side of the crowd, performing entertaining feats with small animals and birds.

Outside the castle, far in the darkness beyond the sight of the sentries, dwelt the High Riders on their huge steeds, each armed with their oversized longbows. There was one for each sentry patrolling the castle walls, save for those sentries within the castle courtyard. They would have to be dealt with by different means. There they sat, unmoving in the darkness, silently waiting for the signal. The remainder of their forces lay in wait just beyond the patrol sight of the main gates.

Within the courtyard, Galin worked his way toward a well-lit entrance to the castle. In fact, it was the entrance that the nobles would most probably exit from to briefly show the crowd their costumes and then retreat back inside. As such, it was heavily guarded with six members of the royal guard: Two armed with pole arms, two with crossbows, and two with broadswords. However, if all went to plan, none of that would matter much.

Toward the center of the courtyard was a troupe of little people led by Malachi, formerly chief court jester to King Zarian. He was not only an entertainer for the king but also his friend of nearly fifteen years. The king treated him and those like him with respect and paid them an honest wage. Ceceran, being who he was, had no use for the little people and summarily had them dismissed from the castle. Malachi had his people doing all manner of juggling, card tricks, comedic plays, and he himself was a master storyteller and was telling many who had gathered the story of how the High Riders had first come into being, all the while keeping his eyes on Kael and waiting.

Kael took a handful of acorns from his belt and threw them up in the air. They ignited into small balls of flame, exploding in every direction, causing the crowd and surrounding guards to duck. At that moment, Malachi gave the signal. His people suddenly went berserk, starting fights not only with one another but with those in the crowd. Even the disciplined soldiers of the royal guard found humor in people throwing and kicking the little people about, until their commander appeared, tall and hooded. Immediately, three guards left the nearest entrance to deal with the rabble makers. All fighting quickly ceased, and the Malachi's people disappeared deep in the crowd.

Kael's pyrotechnic display had also ended, and all normal activity resumed; only one thing went unnoticed. Somewhere in the confusion, Galin had knelt down in the crowd while others covered him in a dark robe, and within seconds, the robe fell flat to the ground and Galin was gone. He had entered the castle, unseen, as a mouse, easily and stealthy maneuvering around the guards and their dark-clad leader.

The first part of their plan had been a success.

Some hours had passed now, and several hundred Bastlandians filled the courtyard. Anticipation had been building, for it was near the time when each of the nobles would be announced in turn and would come out alone in their costume on a raised platform within the center of the courtyard, likely to rousing ovations from the crowd. The king would show last, in what would surely be the most magnificent costume.

Finally, several colorfully dressed trumpeters emerged from the castle, signaling the commencement of the gala spectacle. All other activity ceased as the people pushed in close to see the small circle from which the nobles would emerge.

A herald appeared first wearing a white-plumed hat and a rich, dark velour cape covering him from head to foot. He spoke in a commanding voice with the usual overtures and pleasantries until his loquacious narrative ended in the words, "And without further ado, let the pageant begin."

Cheers erupted. When they finally died down, the Herald announcing the provincial nobles, those who hailed from faraway parts of the island and were the least influential and wealthy. Yet their costumes were wondrous, tailored in silver and gold bases with the appearance of shimmering gems outlining the tunics and dresses alike. They shined brilliantly off the torchlight, causing the crowds to both gasp and hush at their beauty.

Kael slowly backed himself out of the crowd and worked his way toward the stone perimeter wall until he felt his back against it, and he found himself between the south and west walls with several guards standing on the battlements above him.

Galin had worked his way through the castle outside a window on the east side until he reached the stables and the huge pen that housed the Meridians. It, too, was guarded by two crossbowman and two swordsmen clad in plate mail covered by the gray robes of the royal guard. He waited in the grass, contemplating his next move.

The nobles continued to emerge, each more resplendent than the last, and each to increasing degrees of applause. Following the king's appearance, the costumed nobles would all retire to the main audience chamber to dance, and the common people would go home, their entertainment ending after the pageant. The plan devised by Angelique and Krin with refinements from Kael and Galin had been carefully timed, but, above all, it required the presence of the people to succeed.

As the last of the lords and ladies were introduced, the applause continually increased in volume as did the grandeur and opulence of the costumes on display. It was nearing the point for the prime minister and the king to be announced.

Marko emerged, clad in a magnificent silver-sequined vestment with gauntlets and greaves to match. A radiant silver-plated helm with multicolored jewels and a square top, with sides that covered his head, reaching out in front of his face much like the knights of old would have worn. Though his costume was beyond compare, there was a definite decline in enthusiasm at the sight of the prime minister.

At that moment, as Ceceran waited momentarily for his introduction, a powerful voice bellowed from within the crowd: "And finally, behold Queen Angelique of the House of Zarian, the rightful sovereign of the Kingdom of Bastlandia! All hail the queen!"

Suddenly all applause and activity within the courtyard stopped. In silence, the crowd looked around as if expecting to see a ghost. Ceceran's jaw dropped in utter astonishment, which quickly morphed into a snarling rage. In shining armor and a crimson cape, he clumsily raced along the narrow platform onto the circular platform. "Marko! Marko! What is the meaning of this? Who dare utter such blasphemy?" he cried.

Marko quickly exchanged words with the nearby guards and then ran to the king's side.

Ceceran's face contorted in anger, and he turned his fury to the crowd. "Which of you sniveling vermin shouted such treason? Does not one of you have the guts to admit to it? Seal the courtyard! I'll have every one of you whipped until the lowly coward reveals himself!"

Marko grabbed the king by the arm and violently pushed him off, balancing him, forcing him to step back. "My Lord!" he began strongly and then uttered in a calmer tone, "Get ahold of yourself. It was nothing but some upstart malcontent. The guards will deal with it; it is nothing to concern yourself with."

For a moment, Ceceran's rage had consumed him so thoroughly that he seemed confused and shaken. The people looked on, aware of the presence of the foreboding royal guard but also disgusted and disdainful of the man who was their king. He saw the displeasure and hatred in their faces and still cared not. He was absolute master of Bastlandia. They were nothing, and what they thought was meaningless. "They should be on their knees thanking me for this night, Marko. When in their miserable lives have they had the privilege of a night like this?" Ceceran whispered.

"True enough, my lord, however, the people do have their uses. Not the least of which is their tax dollars," Marko said encouragingly to quell Ceceran's fire. "We must at least give the appearance of benevolence, sire. While *we* control the castle, much of the military comes from the people and a revolt is something we dare not allow. We do not have the resources to combat such an event."

Ceceran scowled, "They should all be crushed, but very well, Prime Minister." With that, he turned toward the crowd, who was just starting to turn toward the main gate and bowed humbly. "My loyal subjects, I hope you enjoyed this night, which I labored to arrange for your entertainment and amusement. It is my wish when you go to your beds this night, you do so proud to be Bastlandians. A good night to you and your families."

There was mild applause at these words, barely audible from such a large gathering, and then without warning there was an answer: "How can anyone possibly be proud to be a Bastlandian with you as king! A man who murdered not only his father but attempted to murder his sister as well!"

The guards reached for their weapons, eyes searching the crowd, but the crowd suddenly parted, leaving a lone figure standing in the middle. He was tall and broad, wearing a brown leather tunic and green cape. Across his back was a huge black-ash longbow, the weapon of a High Rider.

"Captain Krin! Look everyone, it's Captain Krin!" members of the crowd cried out in increasing numbers and strength.

Ceceran froze, and Marko's mouth gaped open. Finally, with an uncharacteristic shake to his voice, Marko called out, "Imposter! Guards, cut him down where he stands!"

Quickly and without warning, green vines sprang up from the ground upon which they stood, twisting, and entangling the guards on the walls and atop and around the courtyard, confining their movements. Meanwhile, within the courtyard and about the gate, the guards fell as black arrows buried themselves within their bodies. Other guards fell from the battlements, victims of a synchronized missile attack from somewhere deep in the woods. Only the bows of the High Riders could penetrate plate armor.

Krin pulled his bowstring back and fired an arrow directly at Marko's head, striking his ornate helmet just above his forehead, knocking it off his person to the ground.

Going impotent with fear, the blood drained from Marko's face.

"That was intentional, worm. If you so much as blink, I'll put the next one through your eye," Krin said mockingly, as he already had another arrow ready.

Ceceran saw the guards all about him either dead or immobilized. In the whirl of activity, he saw the Druid Kael, who stared back at him with confidence. He was alive as was Krin. It was too much to behold. In a flash, he fled into the castle. Like a wild man possessed, he raced through the corridors, balancing himself upon the walls, knocking down the occasional servant and trampling right over them in his haste to escape. Living was all that mattered to him.

The people in the courtyard rallied around Captain Krin quickly, picking up what dropped weapons they could, standing guard for him at the main gates, allowing a host of other High Riders to enter both on foot and on horse.

In a flash of green fire, Galin took form in the center of the men guarding the stables. They shrank back from the sudden light. It was more than enough time. With his scimitar in one hand and the mace, *Livenolos*, in the other, he sliced the abdomen of the first man while bludgeoning the second across the face with *Livenolos*. Never stopping, he pushed into the other two, the sheer force of his unexpected attack knocking one to the ground. He placed his foot on the man's neck to hold him still and, using both his weapons, thrust his blade across the back of the last man and then swung his mace into the back of his head. In an instant, he held both of his weapons at the man on the ground beneath him. He saw the man had accepted that he was about to die.

Galin released him and stepped back. "You will be spared. Go back north and tell your master, the Shadow Prince, that he no longer holds sway over these lands and the hour of his defeat is hastening to meet him."

The man stood up and nodded with a deep breath of relief; He quickly made for the woods. Galin stood guard at the coral, awaiting the High Riders.

Ceceran was still running wildly through the corridors, desperately trying to get to the king's private chapel. It was a room that received no use from him as king but became the most important chamber he could think of at the moment. It had a window from which he could escape around the far side of the castle. Few knew of its existence. He only knew because his father had showed it to him when he was a small boy. There was a bit of a drop from the window but it would not be life-threatening. Once he made it there, outside the castle, his chances of escape would increase dramatically.

Krin, Kael, and a handful of High Riders ran through the corridors dispatching any of the royal guard they saw until finally, within the throne room, they saw the dark leader sitting upon the throne as if it were his very own. With fighting still in the halls behind them, only Krin, Kael, and one of Krin's men had made it this far. The Dark Warrior was clad in all black, with a hood obscuring his face. It was unclear what type of armor he wore beneath his robes, but the jeweled scabbard of a sword could be seen. Enough of his chin could be seen in the shadow to discern he was no creature.

He addressed them calmly. "So, Captain, you survived our first meeting, and you as well Druid. You truly have no idea how lucky you are to be alive, do you? I also suspect you have no idea with whom you are dealing. The king, what a pathetic fool. Once he was out of the way, these were to be my lands to rule. Well, it seems that must wait a little longer, but it is of no consequence. The two of you, however, will not live to see that glorious day." He slowly rose from the throne.

Krin's man did not hesitate. He drew an arrow back on his black bow and fired. In one fluid motion, the Dark Warrior both unsheathed his weapon and blocked the feathered shaft. Jumping and spinning in the air, he landed while throwing a killing dagger right between the bowman's eyes. The man fell slowly to his knees and then collapsed to his death, leaving Krin and Kael to face the unknown stranger.

"Is that all the Shadow Prince promised you, a kingship? You may as well have the title slave, for that is all you are to him," Kael said as he held his staff guardingly before him. Krin drew his two-handed sword and, taking the hilt in both hands, took a defensive stance.

"Who are you?" Krin demanded.

"A much greater warrior than you, fool, as you are about to see. Patience Druid . . . your death will come a moment after the captain's."

In that instant, nearly a dozen High Riders flooded into the room, aiming their great ash bows at the mysterious dark warrior.

"Fortune continues to smile upon you, though I wonder for how long." With those words, the Dark Warrior leapt straight up in the air, higher and longer than any normal being would be able and, with his blade, sliced through a massive tapestry that covered the ceiling above them. As the artwork fell like a blanket, it was more than enough of a distraction for the warrior to take his leave.

"Captain, the Druid Galin has secured the Meridians. They are ours again," one of the sergeants saluted as he spoke.

"Excellent, send men to relieve him. Search the castle in groups of six. No one is safe until one so dangerous is found. Take no chances. If any of you find him, call out for help," Krin ordered as the men sprang into action.

Kael stared into the darkness of the corridors that led from the throne room and wondered.

Ceceran finally burst through the door of his private chapel, slamming it behind him, feeling the slightest bit safer than he did a few moments earlier. He spun around to face the window only to see a small form in front of it as if on guard.

"Can I be of service, my lord?" It was Malachi.

Malachi had been present when King Zarian had shown his children this window and told them, if the castle was ever attacked, this was the only way to flee an attacking force unseen.

Ceceran froze momentarily and then snickered.

Malachi put his hands on his hips. "You, you murdering snake, are not fit to wear your father's crown. What a disgrace you've grown up to be," he said regretfully.

Ceceran took a step forward. "Treacherous imp, I should have had you killed along the rest of your deformed, wretched people," he said with a slow approach. He stopped momentarily as if in thought and then resumed his approach. "Actually, there is a way you can assist me, chief of the king's jesters."

Ceceran made a sudden swift movement and was upon Malachi without warning. Ceceran spat in his face and lifted Malachi with both hands, smashing his body through and out the window. As he lifted one leg up to the window frame, he found himself being pulled backward by several High Riders, who had spilled into the room.

As they dragged him away, he shouted, "Unhand me! I am the king! I am the king." His claim trailed behind as the High Riders led him away.

Within the castle's grand ballroom, all the nobles as well as any commoners who could fit crammed together in anticipation of what would happen next. Their eyes followed the long red carpet that extended through the length of the room all the way to a small set of stairs, leading to three chairs on a raised dais.

A figure in crimson appeared. She wore dark clothes concealed in a crimson cape. She removed her hood, revealing a second hood of silver chain mail. At her waist hung the black scabbard of a long sword. Nearly knee-high velour boots covered her legs as she stood before them with her face still somewhat hidden by the chain mail hood. As she pulled back the chain mail and shook her head from side to side, raven locks let fly and lay to rest past her shoulders. The crowd was aghast.

"It's Princess Angelique!" many cried.

"Nay, it is *Queen* Angelique," Krin said, joining her on the dais. "All hail Queen Angelique, rightful ruler of Bastlandia." The captain fell to his knees. Though the crowd was astonished, they in turn knelt in silence. Then as they raised their heads and confirmed what their eyes were telling them, they suddenly rose and began cheering louder and louder as if a dreary darkness had been lifted from their lives. People began hugging each other, noble and commoner alike.

When the cheers finally died down, Krin announced, "Bring in the prisoners!"

From the end of the chamber, nearly a dozen High Riders appeared with two men in tow: Marko and Ceceran. They had been stripped of their shining costumes and ceremonial armor and wore only tunics and cloaks. They were marched up the length of the red carpet in silence as the crowd viewed them with looks of shame and disgust. They were brought to the bottom of the small staircase, where they were stopped. Angelique and Krin looked down at them. Ceceran still wore a smug look of superiority. Marko was fiercely perspiring and his lips quivered.

"Majesty, your brother murdered Malachi before we could stop him," one of the guards said.

Suddenly, Marko lunged forward, dropping to his hands and knees, crawling up the steps and placing his hand on Angelique's boot. "Your highness please, mercy," he begged.

Before he could touch her boots further, Krin gave him a sharp kick to the mouth, knocking him back down the stairs. "You are not worthy to touch her boots, scum," he said, stepping two steps down.

Marko climbed to his feet and stood back next to Ceceran, who looked at him in bewilderment. Then he gave him a backhanded slap to the face.

"Behold the men who stand before you," Queen Angelique began. "King Ceceran and Prime Minister Marko. Two men who single-handedly have murdered or banished all those who opposed them for the sake of money and power. Two men who murdered my father, King Zarian and conspired to murder myself and Captain Krin. Two men who disbanded the loyal and righteous High Riders. Two men who have put a tax stranglehold on the entire country in an effort to appease a foreign master. Yes, they have entered into an unholy alliance with a dark lord who lays waist to the lands of the north and, in preparation for his coming, have sown the seeds of distrust and war with the Arcadians." She whispered now so only Ceceran and Marko could hear, "What do you think would happen, dear brother, if I handed you to your subjects? What mercy would they show two such benevolent rulers as yourselves?"

Ceceran snarled, "You are too weak to do what is necessary. You will run the kingdom into the ground with naivety and this fool at your side giving you advice."

For the first time in some while, Angelique let out a boisterous hearty laugh. "Oh brother, how little you understand me. Even now, after murdering our father and nearly destroying our land, your childlike ego blinds you to the fact that the only fool in this kingdom is decidedly you." She came down the steps and stood with her face only inches from him, waiting for him to return her stare. The moment he did, she struck him in the face with a wicked open hand slap. Then she smiled at him. "That, brother, is the smallest taste of what it feels like to be helpless," she said with a triumphant look as she turned and joined Krin atop the dais.

She then addressed them all. "Yes, these men have sinned greatly against both you and me, however unlike them, I am inclined to show mercy." She then whispered to Ceceran again for a moment, "But know, brother, I show you mercy with my eyes wide open." Again, she addressed the crowd. "From this moment forward, the false king and his mockery of a prime minister will be banished from the kingdom of Bastlandia, never to return except upon pain of death. Furthermore, they will be stripped and led in chains from town to town out of the country so that all may see and know them should they ever return."

Ceceran went wild. The men had to restrain him and, at Krin's order, gag him.

Marko fell to his knees, "Thank you, your highness."

Angelique looked at him with contempt. "Get out of my sight, both of you." As they were dragged away to sudden cheers from the crowd, Angelique turned to Krin. "Where is Piedmont?"

"He has not been found, your highness, it is possible that he has escaped," the captain responded.

With that, Angelique and Krin stepped off the dais to address Kael and Galin, who had been looking on from behind them. "We thank you, Druids of Aanagansit. Know that we will immediately send peace envoys to Arcadia. In addition to our gratitude, we will send what aid we can to your General Mekko . . . as soon as the country is stable and secure." She smiled.

Captain Krin extended his hand to both of them. "I was honored to fight alongside you. I have come to have a new respect for Druids."

The Druids bowed their heads.

Kael stepped forward to address them. "May the blessing of Mother Nature be upon you both and your child in the days ahead as you reclaim your Kingdom. May you rule long and wisely. Goodbye, your highness. Farewell, Captain."

Kael and Galin then faded into the crowd as a grateful people welcomed their new queen to their bosom.

Chapter 14

It was near midday when the Druids arrived back in the Alliance Citadel. The air was cold and damp with dark gray clouds covering the land, seeming to soak up all the warm color that once was. The Citadel looked much different as they had been gone for some weeks. All the walls and towers were completed and manned with heavy guards and watches. Thousands of tents of varying sizes had been erected. Siege artillery had been set up in rows of ascending height. As they landed near the south part of the camp and changed back into their human forms, they looked at each other.

"I think we have left the battle only to arrive in time for the war," Kael said.

"When it is finally ended, what will our lives be like?" Galin wondered aloud.

"At least we know what we are fighting for," said Kael as he pointed toward those who were fast approaching.

Elenari and Mya flew into Kael's arms, unable to contain their joy. Galin looked down, a grin upon his lips. A moment later, to his surprise, they greeted him just as warmly. Galin was so busy thanking them for their kind greeting that he did not see Layla standing there at first.

"My Lord Calindir," Layla said, bowing her head.

"My lady," Galin replied, returning her bow.

When they looked up and caught each other's gaze once again, Galin could see the genuine pleasure in her face.

After a slightly awkward moment, Layla stepped forward and embraced him. She whispered, "It is good to see you back safe, Galin."

The scent of her intoxicated him. He found his arms coming to lightly rest around her waist as he closed his eyes, breathing in her hair. "And it is good to be seen by you, Layla." As they separated, Galin asked, "Your father is well?"

"He is," she replied, a slight blush upon her cheeks. "He has often mentioned his concern for you. Was your journey successful?"

"As successful as it could have been under the circumstances," he replied, "but we will speak more of it first to Mekko, if you will forgive me." He bowed, and then went to catch up to Kael and the others, though he could feel her eyes still on him. He stopped suddenly and turned back toward her. He reached his hand out toward her, "Come on, don't you want to hear about our journey?" Galin asked.

Layla smiled warmly and walked toward Galin, taking his hand in hers.

As they walked through the camp, Elenari and Mya caught the Druids up on the arrival of the individual they had previously known as Rex Abernacle.

Kael remembered Rex from when they had passed through the Andarian Ranges. He was just an old, lonely alchemist. *What is he doing here?* the Druid wondered.

Mya explained that he had come to them mysteriously, suffering from a poison, the likes of which she had never seen, coursing through his system and leaving him near death. Though the poison was unknown to her, it had similar properties to the extremely potent venoms and toxins found in the deadly creatures beneath the earth's surface. With a careful mixing of potions and exotic ingredients, she'd found a way to render the poison inert, at least temporarily.

Elenari explained that during the old man's convalescence, he has spoken very little except to reveal that Rex Abernackle was not his true name.

"Mekko asked Crichton do a spell to detect evil, and he emitted no such aura, nor did Lark detect any hint of evil from him, which seems to clear him of being in league with the enemy beyond all doubt," Mya said.

"Indeed," Elenari added, "your arrival is timely, for . . . *Ranier*, he calls himself . . . wishes to have a council tonight and has requested that we all be present."

"There will be much to tell at this meeting beyond what this stranger wishes to say, I sense," Kael said uneasily.

"That will be for tonight. For now, you need to eat and drink . . . and rest," Mya said, pulling Kael away from the others and making it clear that they needed to be alone.

Later that night, they gathered in Mekko's tent. Upon seeing Galin enter, the Dwarf shook his hand and pulled him into an embrace, nearly lifting him off the ground. "Great to see you again, laddie! I bet you missed me somethin' fierce out on the road. Tell me, did you do any singin'?"

Galin smiled as he rested his hands on the Dwarf's shoulders. "I only sing when I travel with Dwarven generals."

When Kael walked in, Mekko grabbed both his wrists in greeting. "I feel better havin' you Druids back safe and sound."

"I assure you, General, we are most glad to be back," Kael responded.

Mekko continued to heartily greet all as they entered, even Crichton. Once all were present, Mekko gave Rendek and Toran specific instruction that no one was to approach the tent.

Mekko took a seat at the large round table, and the others followed suit. He'd had the engineering corps design the table with a large firepit in the center. He'd chosen a circular design so that all those seated could comfortably see one another. General Valin sat to his right, followed by Galin, Kael, Mya, and Elenari, and to his left sat King Aeldorath, followed by Layla, Lark, Archangel, Captain Gaston, and Prince Crichton. Directly opposite Mekko sat Ranier. There were pitchers of water and drinking cups set for all but no wine or ale by design.

Mekko waited until they had all settled in and had fallen silent before he rose to speak. "My friends and allies . . . first, we welcome our Druid friends back from their difficult journey across the oceans. We welcome a stranger, Ranier, who is not a stranger to all but comes to us bearing urgent tidings. All who wish to speak shall be heard this night. Let the Druids tell the first of the tales to be spoken this night."

With that, Mekko sat, and Kael and Galin proceeded to tell all that befell them from the time they left the camp: Their visit with the

Chamber of Representatives in Arcadia and finally their audience with the king of Bastlandia. They continued with the tragic death of Minister Freefire and their adventures with Angelique and the High Riders, until at last, they concluded with their flight over the Anglian Sea and their unsettling news of a black fleet that could prevent all potential aid from the southern countries.

Mekko looked on in deep thought but gave no hint of dismay, even at mention of the fleet. "Once again, you lads have risked your lives for all of us," he said. "Never think that all you have been through and sacrificed will be forgotten. . . . that goes for all seated here." He then turned his attention to the man known as Ranier. "I suppose it's your turn, old man. What tale would you tell us?"

The old man, wizened and pale, folded his hands out before him. His stringy white hair and beard came to rest upon the table as he bent his head. Then suddenly he lifted his head and his eyes burned with a strange power that captivated them. "You must prepare yourselves, for what I must tell you will not only be difficult to comprehend but will doubtless be painful to hear—especially from one who is a stranger to most of you. Much of what I have to tell you will be entrusted upon you to accept on faith alone. But know this, I have come down from my mountain sanctuary after ages of observing what has become of our world for one purpose—to stand with you against the evil that threatens us all."

Ranier made eye contact with each of them in turn, examining their faces. Galin opened his mouth to speak, but Ranier's gaze silenced him.

"Listen closely and avoid the urge to question and interrupt, for now. Expedience demands that you hear all first and that may take some time," he added with mild frustration. "There is no other way to begin than truly at the beginning. By beginning, I mean to tell you of a time shortly after our world began. There were many races in those ancient times, all of which are extinct in the world you know today. These races, such as they were, existed much differently than those of this era. They worked and lived cooperatively with one another, in peace.

"It was a time when the earth was saturated with magical energies and great study was done on the science of what we call magic. Great scholars and men of learning were born and worked together to harness and unlock the secrets of such power. However, power was not coveted in those times; it was shared. What you call *magic* was used for the good of all to advance the means of living day to day life.

"As time went on, these scholars and men of knowledge began to stand out and soon came to represent their respective races. In those ancient times, they came to be known first as the Makers and later as Archmages. They coexisted in a loose council together. They thought of it more as a brotherhood. It soon became realized that they were the most powerful individuals of the times, yet while there were political leaders in those days, it was before the times of emperors and kings, or the concept of one ruler for all.

"So far sighted were they that an agreement was soon made that no *one* Archmage would ever attempt to use their powers to rule in any fashion over the others, and in the event such a thing occurred, the others would agree to join their powers to thwart any such attempt. You see, they recognized that immense power could breed superior ambition, and they took steps to guard against it at all costs. It was a time of far-reaching vision where anything seemed possible, and *nothing* was beyond the reach of society.

"It was then, in their wisdom and vision, that they conceived of the greatest contribution they could ever make to the world. They thought to create a device so vastly powerful, that the very idea of was so profound, the implications of its creation dwarfed any prior inventions that their limitless minds could contemplate. In the spirit of safeguarding the world against those who may one day cause harm, they embarked upon the greatest project in history. . . . The arrogance, the supreme folly." He stared into space as if reliving a memory.

As Ranier spoke, Kael stood and moved to the outer rim of the circle of his companions. He stared at the old man, his eyes fixed and bent upon him as if trying to decipher the truth from his very soul. He looked over at Lark, who was perhaps better at detecting deception than any of them. His eyes met Lark's for a moment, and the expression Lark conveyed seemed to indicate even he wasn't sure whether the man spoke the truth. Kael returned to his seat and poured some water.

As the old man continued, his voice became distant and harder to hear and a dim haze permeated the tent. Seamlessly, they were all present as casual observers in a different place and time.

"Imagine if we could fold space and time as our brother, Abadon, suggests—" posed Mestaphar to the other Archmages.

"Then we could conceivably travel backward in time, perhaps even forward, perhaps even to other planes of existence," Glycas continued, twirling his dark beard.

"Hold, brothers, we must proceed with extreme caution now. We are discussing primordial powers that perhaps were never meant to be disturbed. Think of the cataclysmic effects that could result in meddling with such raw power," Ranier, oldest and wisest of the Archmages, added.

"Why are you opposed to trying, Ranier?" Abadon, the most powerful, asked. "Do you not see the infinite possibilities?"

Ranier saw that Abadon's question had struck a nerve with many at the table of the Council of Archmages. "Indeed, I see the potential, but there is also infinite possibility for danger of epic proportions."

"Yes, there are many of us who agree with Ranier," Glycas said. "We must think carefully and advise extreme caution. The fact that we have grown so powerful as to construct a machine that could enable us to travel through time and dimensions and contact other beings and planes is awe inspiring and must give us pause to consider."

Abadon's face brightened. "Yes, awe inspiring! Consider that with such a device we would be able to right the wrongs of the past. Think of what we could learn from other beings within other dimensions. The possibilities are endless. It is the pride of this council to achieve in the name of all the races. Doesn't prudence demand that we put forth our finest efforts for advancement?"

"Just because we can do a thing does not imply that we should do it. The possibilities for tragedy are equally endless," Ranier cautioned.

Many nodded in approval.

Abadon's expression was one of controlled fury as he took a deep breath and steadied himself before speaking. "It is true there are many dangers, but imagine for a moment the danger there would be if one of us decided to build this device in secret without the approval of the council. What I am proposing is that we attempt to build the device together under the supervision of us all. We may even find that it is not feasible. It may well be beyond us to construct such a device, and the attempt may be abandoned. However, the good of our people, in my opinion, outweighs all risk and danger, and in the end, nothing matters more than our people. Brothers, even if we build this thing and it works, we can render it powerless and put it under guard until a time arrives where we may need it. What do you say?" He could see his arguments had won many over.

"I submit there is little to be gained from further debate," Mestaphar said.

"I agree, it is time to call the question," said Glycas. "Very well, brothers. Let us vote on whether to construct the device that will enable travel through time itself, unlocking different planes and beings that we may learn from and communicate with. Let all those who are for the construction now indicate such by standing."

Abadon rose first. Ranier watched as the others followed suit. Slowly at first, but then more and more continued to rise until he soon found that he alone was the only one still seated. He thought for a moment; perhaps his mind refused to comprehend and accept such wonders as the machine could bring them. Perhaps he could not leap beyond what was basic and mundane to what could bring great benefits to their world. Perhaps Abadon was right. Reluctantly, he too stood with those he called brother.

Abadon smiled. He had won them over. How perfectly predictable they all were.

Over the next several months, every disciple, apprentice, acolyte, and helper of the Archmages collaborated in the building of they came to call the Chronos Device. Naturally, the project had been kept secret from those who were not Archmages or their trusted companions and would remain so.

Archmage Kastigir traveled to the various lands of the age and met with the battle lords of each great army. The most elite fighters were chosen from each army to be trained to guard the Chronos Device, keeping it both safe and secret.

As seamlessly as before, the group felt themselves present within the surroundings of Mekko's tent.

Ranier pulled his tattered robe closer to his thin frame, briefly grabbing his arm where the Rasilisk had scratched him. He stared into the fire in the middle of the circle. He seemed to see many places and people through the flames from times long since passed. He wondered if this group believed anything that he had told them thus far, if that had believed the vision they had all shared.

He turned back from the fire and looked over at Mekko, who returned his glance with an iron countenance, searching intently for some sign of hope within his words.

"It was decided that the machine had to be constructed underground. In fact, it rests below our very feet," Ranier said.

With that, Mekko stood up sharply. "Impossible! There are few who know the caverns below better than I and at the very least the Dwarven engineers would have found it when they carved the tunnel complexes centuries ago."

Ranier forced a smile to his lips. "True enough, my dear general; however, they would have to know what it is they were looking for and the magic concealing it is powerful enough that your engineers would not have seen it, even if they happened upon it. I assure you the machine is there *for we can sense its power even in its dormant state.*" Something strange had happened to Ranier's voice with those last words. It sounded like many voices meshed into one.

"*We?* Who are we addressing, or more to the point, how many of you are there?" Kael asked.

"*We are all present in this vessel. All of us who were once called Archmages reside within the corporeal from of Ranier. To ease your minds, we shall speak through his one voice again.*"

Shock stamped the faces of all those assembled; the soldiers present instinctively moved their chairs away from the table.

Then, Ranier spoke with only the singular voice again, the same voice he had begun speaking with. "I am one."

"You mean to say the spirits of the Archmages you speak of, from ages ago, reside within you, and that you, yourself, are the same Ranier from ancient times?" Prince Crichton asked with disbelief.

"That is exactly what I mean," said Ranier.

"Most fascinating." Crichton smiled and leaned back in his chair. Then, with a carefree wave of his hand, he said, "Please, continue."

"The device exists here, now, in the tunnels beneath Cordilleran. It is concealed with a powerful magic. But, for our immediate purposes, it is enough to know that it does exist here in the present. The device was constructed over a period of years. It was not only an unprecedented collaboration of the Archmages, but also with men of great knowledge and wisdom who possessed no magic whatsoever. As the device was built, the Archmages imparted some of their arcane powers into the machine to operate it. In addition, they drew forth from the earth magical energies and transferred this power, such as it was, into the machine. The science and magic combined to create this thing were more powerful than anything ever conceived of since. If anything, the world has regressed since those ancient times, becoming less advanced and civilization has sadly followed suit," said Ranier.

"We will try not to take that as an insult," Galin said, grinning, turning to Kael for some kind of agreement.

"I assure you, Galin Calindir, no insult was meant. I would never insult those who have fought and sacrificed so much. You must understand, I am from a much different time. It has been centuries since I have spoken to anyone. You must forgive my lack of social etiquette. I am from an age where we were much more direct with one another, for good or ill."

"Indeed," said Crichton. "Many prefer it more honest, more open."

Ranier sensed some frustration within the group. He could almost hear their individual thoughts and frustrations and yes, even disbelief.

Continue Ranier, the voices called to him from within his mind. *We must make them understand. Do not stop.* Ranier massaged his temples and looked toward the younger Druid. "Now I must ask you, humbly, if you wish, not to interrupt me further for there is still much to tell and not the least of it will be easy for you to hear." He waited until he saw signs of consent.

"So, it was in the fullness of time that the device was finally completed . . ." Ranier's voice faded again. He recounted in detail what had transpired the day they tested the device, including his trepidation at first and his utter shame afterward.

"When Abadon returned, a beam of light preceded him. Within this light we saw thousands of creatures, nay, demons from another plane of existence. They were creatures that would prove to be more fierce and powerful than anything your minds could conceive of in this age. And they were evil, so terribly wicked beyond mortal experience. You see, on their plane they were immortal, but upon entering this dimension they became as mortal as the rest of us. However, many of them possessed great arcane powers in addition to their teeth, claws, and hatred borne of an innate killer instinct.

"The demons had been transported to an unknown location, but Abadon appeared before us on the spot where he had left. Physically he was different, yet very much the same. However, it was clear that he was no longer the man we knew. His skin had become crimson and dry, almost leathery. His hands and feet ended in claws. His hair became dark and coarse and his eyes . . . his eyes conveyed the root of all that we know as evil. There is no comparison or description I can tell you without seeing it for yourselves.

"A battle ensued, and we attempted to destroy him. Digging deep within our inner cores, harnessing great and powerful magic that would have destroyed almost any creature in existence merely knocked him off his feet, slowing him temporarily."

Ranier raised his hands to the heavens as if he was picking up a great boulder, reliving such a terrible moment. He then brought them down slowly to his side. Catching Elenari's eyes in his, he said, "May the gods save you from such a day."

For the first time, Elenari saw both pain and fear within the old man's eyes.

"Needless to say, we failed. And every life that has been forfeit since has been our responsibility." Ranier looked down in defeat for a moment and then lifted his brow as if suddenly renewed. "However, we did succeed in sealing away and hiding the Chronos Device for all time. . . . Abadon joined his demons and thus the Demon Wars began," Ranier said as if each syllable pained him to speak.

"The Demon Wars—I thought they were only legends," said Mekko in disbelief.

Ranier continued despite the interruption, "To all at this table they would be long-forgotten legends indeed. The Demon Wars raged across the lands for centuries, slowly taking from the world some of the mightiest battle lords who have faded out of memory and timeless legend. But great and terrible were the deeds of ancient times, in battles fought for much more than land and power. And, one by one, the Archmages fell throughout the centuries. He hunted us down systematically despite our best efforts. Only I eluded him in the end. But Abadon's demon armies died as well, faster than he could breed them.

"We paid for each victory and defeat with many precious lives. It was not until the time of the Elves when a genius named Thargelion came along, and the last army of demons was defeated. Yes, I believe you all recognize that name. It was Thargelion's army that defeated the last of the demons in this world, and it was Thargelion himself who defeated Abadon."

Ranier watched as they looked at him in widespread disbelief.

"Where were you when Thargelion was doing this?" Kael asked suddenly.

Ranier smiled at the hint of skepticism in Kael's voice. "A fair question, Grand Druid. At that time, I was already last of the Archmages. Suffice for you to know I was in a dark place preparing a secret power for the future defense of our world. To be honest, I had no hopes that Thargelion or anyone else could defeat Abadon's forces without my help. In fact, I was sure of it. History, however, has proven me incorrect but only from a certain point of view." The old man smiled.

"We have listened keenly to what you have said, old man. I grant you, it is an excellent tale and well told, but you will find those gathered here have little patience for talk in riddles," Prince Crichton said.

"My Mystarian ally speaks the truth, Ranier. Get on with it. How did Thargelion defeat this greatest of evils?" Mekko asked sharply.

Ranier closed his eyes, searching the cellar of his soul for patience and strength. *Complete the story, Ranier,* spoke the voices of the Archmages within his mind, *and tell them all they need to know. They will accept your words as fact. They are our only hope.*

Ranier opened his eyes again to see that Mekko was staring him down. The old man smiled thinly and continued, "Thargelion and his army defeated Abadon's demons to the last creature through innovative battlefield strategy and forging treaties with unlikely allies. As a military commander, he was much akin to you in that regard. As far as Abadon himself, Thargelion enlisted the aid of the Elven wizards of old. They used their magic to forge a mystical gemstone, the Emerald Star. Truly, this is a different history of the Emerald Star than either Thargelion or Algernon would tell you, but much like myself, they had their own reasons for what knowledge they have shared."

At the mention of the Emerald Star, everyone present became uneasy. This was a history they clearly were not expecting. Mekko reached into his tunic and held the metallic box that contained the Emerald Star, given to him by Kael to watch over.

The Elven king, who had been quietly taking in all up until this point spoke quietly to himself, "The Emerald Star of my ancestors."

"Indeed, King Aeldorath, it was the Elven race and not the all-knowing and powerful Archmages who conceived the one item that could contain the demon lord."

Before they had a chance to interrupt or react, Ranier continued, "Thargelion put some special touches of his own magic within the gemstone. Again, a genius, who realized that sometimes the simplest magic is the most potent. There were multiple enchantments, the first being a spell of negative power absorption. When Thargelion finally confronted Abadon, the Emerald Star literally absorbed his negative life force, completely trapping his essence within the emerald itself. Then, in the best tradition of Elven magic, Abadon's vaunted dark power became the energy source that powered the Emerald Star. The more he used his vast dark power to escape, the more powerful good magic the Emerald Star became capable of using.

"However, as you may have guessed, there were limitations and restrictions to its use. Only Thargelion, or those completely pure of heart from his bloodline, had the ability to wield it and, of course, Algernon. From that moment on, any army that possessed the gemstone was invincible and any land that housed it became impervious to invasion. In addition, it had the ability to make the surrounding land fertile and the woods and streams team with life. Indeed, good living became a byproduct of its nearby vicinity. But you've no need to hear any more of its history as Kael and Lark could tell that tale far better than I, but unfortunately, we don't have the time.

"Now we come to it at last, that which will be hardest for you to hear and accept. Thargelion's life force is tied to the power of the Emerald Star. For the spells that imprison Abadon are largely of Thargelion's design. Since his death, the ability of the Emerald Star to contain him is waning. In fact, so powerful has he become, that part of his lifeforce has already escaped and found another kindred evil spirit to resurrect so that he exists both within the confines of the Emerald Star and within the shared being of the one he has chosen to bring back with a fraction of his life essence."

"The Shadow Prince," whispered Kael in utter horror.

"Correct, Kael Dracksmere," Ranier said nodding.

At that, Lark stood up suddenly taking a step back. "What do you mean the Shadow Prince? You mean this Abadon is the force behind the Shadow Prince?"

"Calm yourself, Lark Royale," Ranier said as if addressing a child. "Abadon seduced the wayward, formless spirit of Wolfgar Stranexx in much the way his own was seduced and, in so doing, restored him to life. Only this time, Abadon's intelligence and power have greatly augmented your old adversary."

"If any of this is true, Thargelion and Algernon knew this all along, didn't they? They knew and never told us, did they?" Galin demanded.

General Mekko stood quickly, his face beat red under his beard, and turned to the Eleven king. "Leave it up to the Elves to create such a crazy thing as this Emerald Star. You pointy-eared jack rabbits always think you have the answers to the world's problems. But it's always the Dwarves who end up cleaning up your messes. And the price is always the same: Dwarven lives. Because of you blond-haired fairies, this Abadon is commin' to destroy my land." Mekko pushed his chair halfway across the room and stood right in front of the king.

King Aeldorath rose quickly, looking down his nose at Mekko. "I will not be insulted or threatened by this Dwarven jackal."

"Your very borders are being kept safe at this moment through the sacrifice of my entire race. Our fortress, our city, our king—all lost and for what?" Mekko demanded.

Layla stepped to the side of Mekko, placing a restraining hand on her father's chest, while Galin stood and laid his hands on Mekko's shoulders. "Easy old friend," the young druid spoke calmly. "You cannot hold a man responsible for the debts of his fathers."

Mekko let loose a growl and put his fist near the king's face. "Bein' that his relatives are all dead, I ain't got a choice but to take it out on him." The Dwarf watched as the Elven king looked down on him with growing anger.

"Yes, you do have a choice!" Ranier stood with great fire in his voice. "You can blame me. For none of you can hold a candle to me on the subject of blame. It is I—*we* alone who are responsible for this tragic menace that has fed on the lives of this world for ages before any of you were born."

"You see, Dwarf, have a care where you point your misshapen finger," King Aeldorath said disdainfully.

Ranier's tone was bitterly cold. "Indeed, Elven King, the situation is not unlike that of the Elves and White Elves. There is not an Elf alive today who existed in the time when the first White Elf was imprisoned in the darkness below the surface, and yet to this day, there is blame and malice on both sides. Yes, all of you make sure you dare not cast the shadow of blame upon others lest you cast it first upon yourselves, and when the sun stops shining, there will only be one shadow still, long and deep upon the ground, and it shall be my form that casts it. So do not talk any more of blame in my presence."

Kael put himself in the middle of the king and the Dwarf. "There are no enemies in this room," spoke the Grand Druid with a commanding but soothing voice. "We are brothers united for one cause, to save the known world from annihilation. We have joined together of our own volition to sacrifice all for those who would live free from fear, tyranny, and the despair of evil. We have all been through far too much together to turn on one another now."

Aeldorath and Mekko stepped back from each other in thoughtful contemplation. Kael moved toward Elenari and smiled at her. He reached down to touch her face and whispered, "It will be all right."

No one spoke, and time stood still. Finally, after an interminable silence, Elenari asked, "What does this mean, Ranier? Will Abadon escape from the Emerald Star and, if he does, what will happen?"

Ranier rose. The questions he'd hoped to avoid had arrived at last. He bent his head, carefully weighing his next words. The voices in his mind were now talking at the same time; their words meshing into one drone. Ranier's inner voice quieted them down until there was silence in his mind once again. "We are in unexplored territory regarding the Emerald Star. None can predict what or when anything will happen. The gemstone may still have power to save us, in the right hands"—he stared at Lark—"And Abadon may break free of it at any time. Then we will have two dark lords to deal with, but know the Shadow Prince is nothing compared to Abadon's power. Lark is the only one here who could attempt to use the Emerald Star and any such attempt carries great risk with it. It may still be our only hope, or it may be our doom. General Mekko, open the box containing the Emerald Star, if you please," Ranier requested.

"Very well," Mekko said, opening the box.

They looked in fear and wonder at the gemstone.

"It's lost much of its former luster, it no longer glows," said Kael with thoughtful concern.

Elenari peered over her father's shoulder to look at the magical gem. The others came closer to see the legendary talisman.

"It grows weaker, and he grows stronger. That is the great and terrible secret of the Emerald Star; the secret Thargelion and Algernon have bet all your lives upon," Ranier added.

Elenari pulled back quickly from the center of the group. She pushed her long blonde hair from her eyes and stared at Ranier; thoughts of Hawk filled her mind. A vision of his death by the hands of the lava creature made her clench her fists in rage. "They had no right. Why, why did they not tell us everything?! Why not tell us the whole truth?!" she asked, outraged. "Perhaps if we had known some of this, so much could have been different. Preparations could have been made. Perhaps some would not have had to—"

"Die?" Ranier interrupted, looking deep into Elenari's raging eyes. "There are limits as to how much hopelessness can be thrust upon us. Without the added knowledge of Abadon, you were already being asked to face impossible odds, overwhelming enemies, and what little hope you were offered was constantly unraveling, like a string about to snap. How then would you have received the knowledge that your real enemy was not the Shadow Prince but something infinitely more powerful and that the time of his release was upon you? Tell me, how would you have weathered such information?"

"That is not the point, Ranier!" Elanari cried. "To choose to involve us in their struggle and not trust us enough to reveal all is nothing short of betrayal!"

Mya moved over to Elanari and rested her hand on her shoulders. Elenari's sleek frame and chiseled face seemed poised to lunge at Ranier. The old man knew as he looked at her. He could feel her pain. Truly he empathized. He sensed the conflict of the warrior within her, always competing against herself, and the other part of her, a beautiful young woman with grace and sensitivity. She was only afraid of one thing, loneliness.

"Your anger is understandable. And yet, the situation is what it is." Ranier turned away from her.

"Who or *what* is Abadon truly?" Prince Crichton asked.

"He is the Lord of Demons. Prior to entering our plane, I would have described him as that force that speaks to us from afar, to your mind, taunting you to pursue paths you knew to be evil. He is the opposite of hope: Evil in its purest form and his power is beyond all of you." Ranier said this in such a fashion as to leave no room for argument.

"Well, in that case, perhaps we should all surrender to the enemy now and not bother about putting up a defense," said Crichton.

"While sarcasm does become you, Prince Crichton, hopelessness surely does not," Rainier said. "Indeed, much will depend on your courage in the coming days. Despite your words to the contrary, I sense you eagerly await challenging Abadon. I shall save you the trouble of worry. This foe is far beyond even you." His eyes flashed with power, and there was finality in his words.

"Have a care, *Archmage*," said Crichton, "for while you would have us accept this fanciful tale, this sprawling woven yarn on naught but your word alone, know that I give you my word that you have no idea who I am and my own counsel I will keep on what foes are beyond me." His words hung in the air as the fire suddenly crackled, releasing a wisp of floating embers.

Ranier stared at him, his expression unchanged. "General Mekko and the rest of you must contend with the vast dark forces that will soon assail us. *We* shall be present, standing with you should Abadon appear, for he is not beyond *our* power, though I must now warn you: *We* must harness all our power for the gathering darkness. Our strength must be complete for us to contend with Abadon. There will be little else we can use our power to aid you with, though I will be standing with you, giving what council I can through it all." Ranier's voice wavered throughout his speech, becoming many and then back to one.

Kael rose to his feet. "That's it then? We just fight and carry on, hoping Abadon will not appear, but if he does, you'll take up the fight with him? Should the rest of us stop fighting his vast army and just watch? Tell me, what is Lark to do? Should he, the only one left who can use the Emerald Star, attempt to wield it when the enemy arrives and try to destroy them or not? Should he wait until thousands die before he tries? What if he waits until we've lost and all hope is gone and then in a last effort to save us, he releases this Demon Lord to destroy the last of us? What wise council do you have for him?!" Kael slammed the table with his fist.

As if on cue, Lark stood, patting the air with his hand. "Enough, my friend. I appreciate your frustration on my behalf, but it pales compared to mine. Be seated. Ranier, I have thought more about this than most assembled here know. A Paladin, by his very nature, knows not fear of evil and yet . . . I confess to all a lingering trepidation concerning my role with the Emerald Star. Is there nothing you can tell me about its powers and how I might tap into them without releasing this greatest of evils?"

Ranier sighed and looked down thoughtfully before meeting his gaze. "Truly, I say to you, there are none living who have the answers you seek. I would only say, trust to your faith and your inherent goodness." He looked away from Lark and swept his gaze around the table. "To the rest of you, I would only say this, before you leave this tent tonight to revel in your self-doubt and recriminations of Thargelion and Algernon, know this. While they did not know the entirety of what I have revealed this night, it is true they knew much and what they did not know they suspected, but before you demonize them, ask yourselves this: What would you have done? What information would you have revealed? Remember always, if not for their vigilance, *all* would be lost by now. If not for their superior judge of character in choosing many of you to shape the fight against this coming darkness, most sitting here would be dead by now. Consider these things well as you lie in thought and reflection this night. If you have questions, I will not answer them until the morrow. I've grown weary of my own voice and feel fatigued and need to retire. I wish you all a good night." With that the old man exited the tent without a moments delay. His words resonated within the air.

After an uncomfortable silence, Elenari turned to her father. "How do we know anything he has told us is true?"

Archangel spoke up, "Indeed, a tale of convenient fiction. Nor will I believe King Thargelion lied to us, a more noble sovereign I have never known." He sat down and placed his hand over his mouth in a thoughtful posture.

"He had no reason to make any of it up. Although I am as distraught as you, old friend, my heart tells me he told us the first complete truth we have heard in some time," Galin said with a brief smile to Lark as he felt Layla take hold of his hand.

"If he has told us is the truth, what do we now?" Archangel asked.

Crichton looked across to the head of the table where Mekko sat. "General?"

Mekko hesitated and then said, "We continue with our preparations. Nothing of what was shared in this tent is to ever be repeated among the Men, Elves, or Dwarves. There will be no talk of an invincible demon lord or hopelessness or despair. Once we leave this tent, we leave with the mindset that we go to prepare the way for our victory over the enemy. Anything short of that is too dangerous to comprehend," Mekko said and got up himself to leave. Much to his surprise, all those present, even Crichton, stood up in a gesture of respect.

"By withholding all that we've heard tonight, how are we different than what the rest of you are all so upset about?" Captain Gaston offered calmly, silencing them all into thoughtful contemplation.

Chapter 15

Cordilleran braced for the bitter-cold dawn that announced itself with a light snowfall. With the falling snow came an eerie quietness, which, despite its tranquil nature, left a feeling of uneasiness in the wake of a sleepless night. In the middle of the night, Elven scouts rode frantically into the citadel and announced they had spotted the approaching enemy army and estimated they would arrive shortly after daybreak.

It was the distant sound of marching that snapped the Alliance forces to a heightened state of battle readiness. Within the citadel, troops ran into formation and scurried to their posts. Horns blew from the towers, alerting all within that the enemy army had finally arrived.

Mekko climbed the stairs of his elevated command platform at the south end of the camp, allowing him to view everything from on high, in all directions. Trailing behind him was General Valin, along with Rendek and Toran, followed by Ranier.

As they gazed to the north and west for the first time, Mekko's stalwart confidence inwardly wavered as they beheld the enemy procession. No horns were necessary to announce their presence as their forms blocked out both land and sky. It spread further than the eye could see, in all directions, with a vastness and volume that defied their most dreaded nightmares. It was worse than any scouting report could ever describe. Thousands upon thousands of dark creatures of all shapes and sizes marched, blotting out the landscape as far as the horizon, it seemed. Black banners displaying the red multiheaded Hydra, the symbol of the Shadow Prince, could be seen by the hundreds. This was no mindless mass of creatures with spears and clubs needlessly throwing themselves into harm's way. They marched in tight ranks, heavily armored, brandishing their weapons.

The forward ranks consisted of Goblins, at least a dozen lines of a thousand, with the last row consisting of archers. They were small, gangly, green savages with hatred burning in their dark eyes. Beyond them was a virtual sea of Orcs, fifty thousand strong if there was one. Pig-faced and yellow-eyed, they were heavily armed. Their skin was dark, almost black, as they had come from deep within the bowels of Bazadoom. Along the edges of the lines of infantry were Orc-mounted archers on Chalderons, salamander-like lizards with thick bodies and long tales.

In the rear ranks of their force, Mekko could make out larger creatures, such as Ogres and fearsome others he did not recognize, grouped in massive battalions.

Even the skies became blotted out by what looked to be a swarm of locusts in the distance but became larger as they grew closer to the far rear of the enemy forces. Mekko looked to Ranier, who leaned heavily on his staff.

"*Rakkins*, larger and fiercer than the Averics of Arcadia," he explained. "Indeed, our enemy has searched the four corners of the world, both above and below ground, through mountains and beyond, to amass these creatures before us. I sense we are still far from seeing all his forces."

A queer fog hung to the east and west of the northern wall. It was thick, only a few feet off the ground, but had not yet dispersed from the early morning. Its presence was also deep within the mountain-like rocks that once connected to the Barrick Cropaal. Now, they served as a natural barrier, starting where the north and east walls of the citadel met. Mekko looked down at the infantry below. He knew they could not all see the enemy procession, but they could hear the awful marching, and they could see the walls tremble. He looked next to the artillery division, dug into their trenches save for one shining silver figure on horseback, the Paladin Lark. He looked atop the battlements of the northern wall, and standing courageously alone above the main gates were Kael and Galin, there to offer what magic they could to defend those within as if they could bear the brunt of the enemy attacks themselves.

Just within the main gates were two mounted figures: Prince Crichton astride his white steed, Stryker, and Captain Gaston. Both men were outfitted in full suits of armor. Next came the pike division, one line of a thousand men with two lines of five hundred behind them. Then there came the infantry, nearly fifteen thousand strong, the bulk of their force, lined in columns of a thousand, each man more concerned about the one next to him than himself. It was in that one respect, Mekko thought, that perhaps they had an advantage over their numerically superior enemy.

He took a final look at their citadel. The north wall was nearly seventy-five yards long. The wall itself was twelve feet high, save for the main gates, which were closer to twenty. Four towers nearly thirty feet high were on the north wall, two at the ends and two in the center. Within the heart of the towers was a large, round opening facing north, and something covered with a black tarp lay within each of them. The wall to the west was over one hundred yards long, also with four watch towers and one main gate. The east wall went only a few yards until it met the rock mountains, which extended to the base of the Eastern Peaks above the buried entrance of the underground city of Cordilleran, effectively cutting off the east side of the citadel. They were still vulnerable along the south wall but only via the west side. Any force that came directly toward them from the south would come from the sea. Mekko prayed reinforcements were on the way from Arcadia and Bastlandia. Looking down, Mekko saw the fear and uncertainty on the faces of his people and the other races as well. He stepped forward and grabbed the railing of the platform with both hands. "Dwarves of Cordilleran, know the spirit of Crylar looks down upon you this day! His spirit fights within us all! Will we not make him proud?!" Mekko roared.

Cheers rose from the Dwarves who raised their weapons high.

"Look all of you into the eyes of the man to your right and left, in front and behind you. Be he Dwarf, Elf, or Man, no bond is more solemn, no oath more sacred, than the one you make now to each other. We fight for one another! We fight for freedom!" Again, Mekko roared, raising his fist.

Rousing cheers of approval answered him from the three races below, drowning out even the marching feet of the enemy. Mekko watched with a smile as Lark drew his sword and rode up and down the trenches, waving it in a circular motion in the air, stirring the troops of the siege artillery on to cries of righteousness.

At that moment, Mekko allowed himself to look up and the smile quickly left his face. The enemy army came to a sudden halt a little over a hundred yards from them; however, dark forms as far back as he could see were making way for the massive structure, moving slowly forward through their ranks. The dark forms scurried, pushing each other on for fear of being crushed. It was a huge pyramid of stone, nearly one hundred feet high at the tip. The tip was an ornate, oversized throne of gold on which a dark figure sat—the Shadow Prince. At his feet were four round objects Mekko could not yet make out. Four enormous beasts pulled the pyramid, chained to it by thick bonds of iron around their necks and wrists. They were huge, muscular giants, standing nearly fifteen feet in height. Their skin was dark, almost black, and to Mekko's amazement, they had no eyes. Their eyes had not been removed; they seemed to naturally have been spawned without eyes and, as a result, their ears and pig noses were disproportionately large for their rounded hairless heads.

"Do not let their apparent blindness fool you. They are Morrangs, from deep beneath the surface, and their senses are more acute than bats you would see in a cave. They can be very deadly at night," Ranier cautioned.

Kael watched from the battlements with mixed feelings as his old adversary approached. He had believed him to be their one true enemy; now they were expecting the Demon Lord, Abadon, more powerful and cunning then anything they had ever faced. Whatever this *Abadon* was, it had manifested terrible power and intelligence through Wolfgar Stranexx, enhancing his appetite for death, destruction, and revenge.

"Sacred Mother Nature, protect your servants and guide us in this battle so that we may serve you best," Kael said as a small blessing.

Galin closed his eyes and bowed his head for a moment, then looked at Kael, "May Nature's power guide and protect you, Kael."

"And you, my dear friend," Kael replied, looking at Galin, smiling, taking comfort in the presence of his most loyal Druid and companion. He turned to look behind him, and as he expected, Lark was looking toward him. A final nod between them conveyed what otherwise would have been spoken.

As the pyramid of stone drew closer, Mekko recognized the four objects that lay at the feet of the Shadow Prince. They were severed heads—two Men, one Dwarf, and one Elf.

"A Mystarian, Averonian, Elf, and Dwarf. He is sending us a message. If we oppose him, that will be the fate which awaits us all," Ranier said.

"We may yet send *him* a message before the day is done," whispered Mekko.

The Shadow Prince was clad all in black. A leather vestment covered his chest, while a chain mail robe cloaked him, in addition to a layer of black ring mail beneath his vestment. Long leather gloves covered his hands and a golden helmet with metal mesh covered his face with dark openings only where his eyes would be.

A second figure could now be seen standing next to the throne, it was a huge broad-shouldered Orc with a great ebony metal helmet shaped in the form of huge snapping jaws with four fangs. Though the mark of the red Hydra was on its chest, a small flag was set into the back of his armor depicting a crimson stone.

"The Blood Rock Clan, the fiercest and most disciplined of Orc warriors," Mekko said, mostly to himself.

As the great pyramid came to a halt, the Orc turned. Facing the Shadow Prince, he fell to his hands and knees, bending his head until it touched the base of the throne. He then rose and began descending the many stairs from the throne down to the ground. At the base of the pyramid, a single Chalderon-drawn chariot awaited, with two Orcs armed with pole arms. Mekko watched, keen with interest, as one of them fastened what appeared to be a white flag to the top of his weapon.

When the tall Orc finally made his way to the base of the pyramid, he climbed aboard the chariot with the other two and came forward through the ranks of Goblins until they approached the main gates of the north wall alone.

"Well, this should provide some much-needed entertainment at least," said Mekko as he turned to descend the platform.

"No, General, you cannot go to meet him. It's a trap," cried Rendek with Toran fast to agree.

"Well then, I guess you lads better come with me then, hadn't you?" Mekko asked, but it was more of an order.

Ranier grabbed Mekko's shoulder suddenly before he could move again. "General, I advise caution. I do not know what there is to say between us. Your bodyguards may be right."

"Aye, true enough, but fear is something we dare not show. Come on, lads, down we go," Mekko said.

As Mekko, followed by Rendek and Toran, moved from the back of the citadel forward, cheers rose up from the men as they saw him pass by each division of the army until finally, he reached the main gates. "Open the gates!" Mekko ordered.

A moment later, the gates slowly swung open and outward, revealing the chariot had stopped some twenty-five yards away. Mekko hesitated a moment and then walked out to meet it.

Prince Crichton and Captain Gaston trotted along behind Rendek and Toran.

"No one invited you boys, go back inside the gates," Mekko ordered.

"Forgive us, General, but you would not deprive us of a chance to have a closer look at the enemy, would you?" Crichton asked mockingly.

Mekko chuckled as he continued observing. The enemy line was still a considerable distance, and there were only three Orcs in the chariot, so while he did not expect a trap, it never hurt to be prepared.

As Mekko approached, he saw the Orc leader clearly now. Standing over six feet, he wore plated armor that covered his chest, shoulders, and legs. The fangs of his helmet were painted red. He carried a bastard sword sheathed in a scabbard. His grayish-green skin was thick and muscular, losing its firmness only around the stomach, which leaked out of his chest plate. He had several ridges atop his great pig snout and the lids of his yellow eyes were painted red. His two guards stood by the chariot as he walked right up to Mekko, stopping only inches from him.

As he only came up to the Orc's sternum, Mekko looked up at the Orc, but his powerful frame was evident even beneath the bulky chain mail he'd become used to. Rendek and Toran raised their shields to conceal that their free hands gripped their sword hilts. Mekko's expression was one of impatient disinterest.

The Orc let out a hanging guttural growl before he spoke. "I am Red Fang, Chieftain of the Blood Rock Clan, and General of the Shadow Prince's armies. Lord Abadon, your master, and lord of the earth commands you through his Chancellor, the Shadow Prince, the following: If the leaders of the races within your walls come out, kneel before him, and swear fealty to him, your lives will be spared. All within will be disarmed and—"

Before Red Fang could continue, Mekko inhaled, deeply sighing as if he was growing impatient, but suddenly he exhaled, spitting fully and directly up into the Orc's face.

Instinctively Red Fang reached for his sword, but the other two Orcs rushed forward, restraining him.

"Begone from here, fool! Crawl back to your master and tell him I do not treat with filthy animals or is there Orc dung in your ears as well as in your mouth?" Mekko retorted.

Prince Crichton grinned wickedly as Mekko turned and walked slowly away.

Red Fang struggled furiously against his guards. "Kill them, kill them all!" The Orc howled.

Hundreds of Goblins charged at the order, screaming vitriol.

Rendek and Toran started to run for the main gates, but Mekko put his arms out, stopping them. "Walk. We walk to the gates."

"General, we must run, there is no—" Rendek started in a panic.

"We walk slowly!" Mekko ordered.

The young Dwarves did as they were ordered but constantly looked back at the charging Goblins, who were swiftly closing the distance.

"General, I'd like to think that there was some higher purpose in all of this other than us getting trampled by Goblins. It would certainly reflect well on you," Captain Gaston said, nervously looking back at the Goblin horde.

"I told you to stay put, but you men of Averon, damn stubborn breed," Mekko said, maintaining a slow pace never once looking back.

"General, I'm starting to like you more and more," Prince Crichton said.

"Sorry to disappoint you, Gideon, but I dislike you as much now as I did when you first entered the camp," Mekko replied.

The Goblins would be on them easily in a few seconds, long before they would make it to the gates. Calmly, still in mid-stride, Mekko put his fingers to his mouth and whistled loudly.

That moment, atop the battlements of the north wall, hundreds of White Elves armed with longbows rose where only Kael and Galin stood a moment earlier. They fired in unison. The arrows sung through the air past the Dwarves and the two riders, catching the first wave of attacking Goblins, dropping those closest. The unexpected attack caused the remainder of the charging Goblins to hesitate.

"Captain," Crichton said to Gaston, who nodded to him.

The two riders stopped just outside the gates and did not enter with the Dwarves. Instead, they turned toward the Goblins, and Captain Gaston grabbed his horn and blew for all he was worth, marking the first signal.

With that, the misty fog in the west and east started shifting until it evaporated to reveal the cavalries of both Mystaria and Averon; the magic mist had been Ranier's doing. Five thousand horses charged forth. Crichton and Gaston took the lead of their men, swords drawn and shouting a rousing charge to their forces.

The cavalry thundered toward the Goblins, who had been caught wrong footed on the field by the deadly missile fire of the White Elves. Fear overtook the creatures as they frantically turned and tried to escape in vain.

As soon as Mekko entered and the gates closed, cheers rose from all within. They raised their weapons in salute as Mekko ran past with Rendek and Toran toward his command platform.

The cavalry closed like a vise on the Goblin horde, tearing into them, slashing and hacking at them. The middle ranks of the Goblins began to flee back toward the main body of the enemy army.

Mekko glided up the stairs to join Ranier and Valin in time to see that the cavalry had advanced nearly halfway through the Goblin force. He could see Prince Crichton in his grand red cape and golden armor skillfully swinging his great sword, cleaving heads as he went. However, he could also see the last row of a thousand Goblin archers taking aim, preparing to fire on the cavalry.

"Quickly Valin, signal the Elves!" Mekko roared.

General Valin grabbed an emerald banner and waved it frantically.

Behind the mist, within the jagged rocks of the small mountains connected to the citadel, King Aeldorath waited with Layla and Elenari beside him. In addition, five thousand Elves of Alluviam awaited the king's command to fire their bows.

"Your majesty, the signal has been given," Elenari said as she took a high aim with her longbow for a far-arcing shot.

"Elves of Alluviam, may all our shafts fly straight and true, and may they find our enemies," King Aeldorath said as he nodded to Layla.

The magical mist dispersed, and they adjusted their aim at the Goblin archers.

"Loose!" Layla ordered, and they fired as one. The sky filled with five thousand feathered arrows, raining them down into the rear ranks of the Goblins and front ranks of Orcs behind them.

Nearly the entire line of Goblin archers fell, as well as hundreds of others around them. A second volley of Elven arrows blotted out the sky with deadly shafts of wood, driving the entire enemy army into retreat.

"Order the cavalry back within the walls immediately! They have done enough for now. Have the White Elf archers on the north wall cover them as they withdraw!" Mekko ordered, looking keenly on as the enemy withdrew.

"A decisive victory for the first engagement, sir," Rendek offered happily.

"This was no victory. The Shadow Prince used the Goblins to probe our defenses and see how we would deploy our forces," Mekko said disgusted. "By makin' us show our cards early as it were and wastin' a good defensive plan on their weakest forces. You follow, lads?"

"Indeed, there is no limit to the life he will waste, be it creatures or men. He will send wave after wave by the thousands until he feels he has weakened us sufficiently to bring forth his more powerful minions," Ranier added.

"General Valin, I want the watch doubled tonight. If the enemy decides to attack during the night, I want our men to have expected it," Mekko said to the old Dwarf.

"Yes, sir," Valin replied as he descended the stairs.

"Valin," Mekko said before he got too far away. "Let the men celebrate it as a victory, but I want them sharp at their posts. The real battle has yet to begin. Meet me in my tent afterward; I'll be there for the remainder of the day if anyone needs me. We'll have a meeting of the war council there after dinner."

Valin saluted.

"Lads, I wonder if you'd give us a minute. I'll meet you in my tent," Mekko said to Rendek and Toran.

"Of course, sir," said the two young Dwarves, leaving Mekko alone with Ranier.

Together, they looked out at the seemingly endless numbers of enemies as they moved off, regrouping. Even the great stone pyramid had been moved back, though the Shadow Prince never moved from his golden throne.

"We cannot last without reinforcements from Bastlandia and Arcadia, can we?" Mekko whispered the question.

"No," Ranier answered simply and concisely as he watched Mekko grab the railing, leaning his head downward.

"Can the Emerald Star save us?" Mekko asked.

"Prior to Thargelion's death, I would have said yes; however, the answer is beyond my vision. As Abadon grows more powerful, the Emerald Star becomes weaker. Whether Lark can tap into its power, I do not know," Ranier replied. "But you must make them believe they can win, General. Look at them. Right now, they believe that you can do anything."

Mekko looked down at their forces, cheering and celebrating as the cavalry came riding through the gates to a victorious welcome. Many looked up to him, shouting and raising their weapons. He could barely hear them.

Ranier placed a hand on Mekko's shoulder. "For their sacrifices to have meaning, they must believe in you, and you must believe in them, until the very end."

Mekko masked the hopeless frustration that gnawed at him with a smile and waved down to the men.

The remainder of the afternoon passed with little activity from the enemy army. As night approached, the temperature dropped, further chilling the already harsh, frigid air. Numerous fires were visible in both camps. Just before the skies darkened, the Shadow Prince had been reported as disappearing within the stone pyramid.

Mekko waited alone in his tent, pacing back and forth. His mind was irrevocably lost in thought. He waited, wondering if this was what it was like for King Crylar as he defended Cordilleran with only five thousand men, knowing that both his death and theirs was certain. Mekko did not believe in certainties, however, no matter what the Archmage had told him. He was responsible for all their lives. The burden was his, the planning and final decisions were his, agreed upon by all of them. He prayed he would prove worthy of their faith and trust.

"General, he is here." It was Toran who pulled the flap back to inform him.

"Show him in quickly, lad," Mekko replied.

A moment later a dark-hooded form entered his tent. Mekko turned to face him as he removed his hood. It was an Orc. Pig faced and yellow eyed, it stood before him. The Orc's huge snout and fangs were moist with drool. Its greasy knotted hair fell long and loose about its brownish skin down to its neck.

Mekko felt his fingertips instinctively curl about the shaft handle of his axe. With his other hand, he covered his nose. "Hell, you even have the same stink they do," Mekko said.

With that, the figure reached up and pulled off the dark leathery material that comprised his face, leaving much makeup and adhesive material around his eyes, head, and mouth. It was Archangel. "Lady Mya knows the art of disguise well indeed, but you were correct, General. I had to stay on the outskirts and in the shadows mostly. These Orcs are highly disciplined and had I made myself any more visible, we would not be having this conversation," Archangel replied.

"Aye, Mya told me on many occasions her people needed to conceal themselves as subterranean creatures to pass safely through certain areas below the surface. She said she'd have no problem makin' you look like an Orc . . . and smell like one. Now tell me, lad, what are we up against?" Mekko asked.

Archangel's face took on a grim countenance as he looked down to the ground, still pulling bits of his disguise off.

"Come on, lad, out with it!" Mekko raised his voice.

Archangel locked eyes with him. "Even now, forces from the north, east, and west are coming, bolstering their forces. Men from the east,

Orcs from the west, creatures from the mountains to the north—their numbers are more than I could count. I stopped counting at one hundred thousand. There's something else. The Orcs are disciplined, but they did speak about something *in* the pyramid. There is something in that structure beside the Shadow Prince that they fear, even worship. The Goblins as well greatly fear, with reverence, something within the pyramid. I could not find out what, though. I was lucky to escape their camp unseen when I did."

"Aye, lad, thank you. Get some wine in you, and some dinner. Warm yourself against this night air," said Mekko.

Just then, the warning bells of the citadel rang out in all directions. They drew their weapons and ran out of the tent. Upon emerging through the flap, they found themselves immersed in the sheer chaos of the moment.

Everyone was running, and screams came from all directions. Mekko heard something from above roaring through the air. At the last moment, Rendek and Toran threw him to the ground as something large swooped down. Archangel stood his ground and, with an arching stroke of his sword, tore into the belly of the flying beast, but the blow was not without consequence. The talons of the beast raked across his chest, sending him flying through the air and landing nearly a dozen feet away on one of the tents. The creature tumbled out of control, smashing into a group of men and tents.

Mekko jumped to his feet and noticed the flying creatures Ranier called Rakkins were all throughout the camp by the hundreds. They dove in at high speeds, destroying tents and killing with their deadly talons.

Suddenly General Valin appeared with a small group of Dwarves, who quickly made a circle around Mekko.

"Why are King Aeldorath's Elves not shooting these creatures out of the sky?" Mekko demanded.

"They are under attack from those sightless giants. There are dozens of them outside the walls hurling huge boulders into the rocks, pinning them down. The White Elves along the walls are firing at them, but there are too many. They flew to a great altitude and dove down on us in the very center of the camp. We did not see or hear them until it was too late!" Valin had to yell to be heard over the chaos around them.

Mekko watched dumbstruck as huge flying creatures with mud-green feathers and gnarly humanoid bodies with claws for hands and talons for feet snatched the White Elves from the battlements. They impaled them with their talons and dropped them to their deaths. Soon they converged on the siege artillery, smashing the catapults to splinters with their powerful bodies.

"Quickly, defend the artillery!" Mekko screamed, coming to his senses.

Suddenly, from the ground came jets of red flame, filling the air and igniting the birds in mid-flight, sending them spinning out of control into the ground, crashing into tents and men. It was Kael and Galin shooting flames from their hands, but there were far too many.

Prince Crichton also commanded the elemental magic of fire as he could suddenly be seen atop Stryker, racing toward the artillery. Raising his hands, huge balls of flame formed from his palms, and he hurled fireballs into the evil creatures, either knocking them from the sky or sending them flying off screeching. Still there were too many. Mekko looked around frantically until suddenly Ranier was there up on the command platform alone.

"Come with me, lads. They'll kill him up there, we must get him down!" Mekko ordered as they raced toward the platform. Suddenly, Mekko stopped in his tracks. All eyes were trained on the old man.

Raising his staff high, he cried out, "Enough, be gone from here!"

A small circular band of fire encircled the top of his staff. Then the band of fire grew outward, larger and wider, increasing in scope and volume. The fire spun in a circular motion outward from his staff into the skies above the citadel until soon it outlined the perimeter of the entire structure. The raging flames and intense heat drove the creatures away as they flew north, back toward the enemy camp. Within moments, all the Rakkins were gone, and the raging band of fire died down until it too was gone.

Mekko ran up the stairs and joined Ranier on the platform as they looked to the north. The giant Morrangs could be seen withdrawing as well, pulling their huge carts of great boulders away with them. The Elves began firing arrows at them, filling their huge bodies like pin cushions, until many went down, but they moved swiftly for such huge creatures, escaping to a safe distance before long.

"See to the wounded. They will not attack again before daybreak," Ranier said.

"They surprised me tonight. It will not happen a second time," Mekko replied.

"See to the wounded, take them to the medical tent. Take the most serious cases to Lady Mya and the Druids immediately. General Valin, I want reinforcements to the battlements immediately!" Mekko ordered, as he raced down the steps when he saw them carrying Archangel.

"How is he?" Mekko asked as Lark suddenly barged through the men to see his brother.

"Not good, sir. He lives, but his wounds are deep," Rendek replied.

Mekko saw the deep gashes across Archangel's chest. "Take him to the Druids!" he ordered.

"That will not be necessary, General," Lark said as he pushed forward. Closing his eyes and bowing his head, he placed both hands on Archangel's chest as the Dwarves held his body off the ground.

They watched. Their eyes widened as white energy flowed from Lark, washing over his brother's chest and through the wounds, slowly closing the huge cuts and repairing the flesh. A moment later, the white glow subsided.

"*Now* you may take him," Lark ordered, and they quickly carried him to the wounded tent. Lark fell to his knees, giving thanks in prayer.

"Say a prayer for us all, lad," Mekko said, placing a hand on Lark's shoulder.

Chapter 16

The bitter cold of night carried on well into the next morning. There were no snow flurries in the air, but the ground was hard and unyielding. The days were growing darker as well as colder. It was as Ranier predicted. Abadon's presence spread, making itself felt deeper in the land around them with the passing of each day.

Ranier was feeling fatigued and had retired soon after the previous night's battle. He explained to Mekko that he had to conserve his power as much as possible in the coming days if he was to be of the greatest service. Mekko had Valin placed twenty guards around the Archmage's tent.

They lost nearly two hundred men in the attack and at least a hundred more were injured. Additionally, three catapults and two ballistae had been destroyed. It was a well-planned attack that showed Mekko they were clearly more vulnerable at night than they originally had thought.

Lark rode out to the field early, riding through the trenches, slowly at first, greeting the artillery crews. Encased in a metal skin of silver, he shone like a light upon the dark field so all could see him. He began galloping faster and faster, rallying his troops until they cheered each time he passed, signaling their readiness.

"This is our time! It will be the only moment we ever have to fight this evil that threatens us. Live every moment with the sincerity you would if it were to be your last on this earth! If you should suddenly find the sun on your face in the heat of battle, then fear not, for you have already passed through the trial of death and have become more powerful than our enemy could ever imagine—for you have taken your first step on the path of life eternal!" Lark raised his sword, rearing up on his horse.

The men responded with roars of approval.

Mekko looked down from the command platform, smiling down at Lark. The Paladin was a natural leader, both charismatic and inspiring. It seemed nothing could dampen his spirits and the prospect of a hopeless battle seemed only to raise them higher. He had chosen his siege artillery commander well. There were three rows of artillery to the west and north with trench lines between each of them. The fist rows consisted of five ballistae, while the second and third rows consisted of five catapults each, in both directions. Each siege device had a crew of five handlers and within the trenches were the men who would defend them.

Suddenly, the sound of beating drums crossed the field, hailing from the deep in the enemy camp. As Ranier joined Mekko and Valin on the platform, they looked to the north. The enemy was moving.

"Damn, they're using turtle formations! Valin, signal our engineers to stand by atop the north wall!" Mekko ordered.

Valin waved the flag with the golden hammer, signaling the engineering corps to mobilize atop the north wall.

"Turtle formations, sir?" Rendek asked.

Mekko pointed to the Orcs who had begun marching in several brigades of a hundred each with large black shields surrounding them on all sides as well as overhead like the shell of a turtle. Rendek understood.

The Dwarves quickly took their places, spreading out across the battlements behind the White Elves. With their huge mallets, they began hitting away at the oversize bolts secured into the structure atop the wall in equidistant spots. After loosening the bolts enough that they could lift them out, they reached in and each grabbed a heavy metal chain from inside. Bracing their feet against the inner battlements, they looked toward the command platform and awaited the next signal.

"Signal the Elves to start firing!" Mekko ordered.

Within the rocks, King Aeldorath saw the signal. "Fire at their ankles and feet or anywhere they were careless and left a hole. Do not waste your shots. If there is no clear shot, do not fire!"

With that, several hundred Elves began firing at the Orc's exposed skin. As some of the Orcs began taking fire to their feet, they lowered their shield formations so none of their extremities were exposed. It did, however, dramatically slow their forward movement.

"Now!" Mekko shouted.

Lark reared up on his horse, drew his sword, and swung it down for all to see. At that moment, every catapult and ballistae fired in both directions. Six-foot bolts and rocks that weighed two to three hundred pounds soared over the walls into the approaching enemy.

Not every shot hit the Orc brigades, but most did, breaking their formations long enough for the Elves to strike with lethal precision, burying arrows in their exposed bodies. The rocks smashed many to the ground, knocking away their protective shields. The bolts landed, piercing through the shields, and throwing Orcs back and to the side. The White Elves on the northern battlements fired their arrows as well, exploiting any opening they could find.

Kael stood atop the north wall, while Galin was on the west wall. Both Druids had been concentrating on a powerful spell. With their arms outstretched, they concentrated on the metal in the armor and shields of the Orcs. They focused on the composition of the metals down to the molecules themselves. With great concentration, they excited the molecules of the metal so much that they began to heat up. It was a slow process, and they could only affect a limited range of the closest few brigades. To the Orcs, it started to feel like an annoying itch but quickly grew to a feeling of unbearable heat.

The affected Orcs cried out, breaking formation and dancing around, trying to free themselves from their armor. Others threw down their shields to free their hands of the burning metal. The Elves struck mercilessly the moment an unprotected body part was exposed.

Though the Druid spells affected only the closest brigades, it was enough to slow the others behind even more, enough so to make the enemy send the next wave. The Rakkins charged through the air, flying directly at the Elves in the rocks.

Elenari and Layla were first to see them speeding toward them.

"Your majesty, look!" Elenari pointed to the legions of evil birds.

"Quickly, as one, cease fire on the Orcs, and fire at the flying creatures!" King Aeldorath shouted.

Instantly, the Elves obeyed. They fired in concert, their arrows blotting out the sky, striking the bird-like creatures and dropping them by the hundreds.

The siege artillery continued firing seamlessly as the machine crews loaded one huge rock after another onto the catapults immediately after the previous one had been fired. Still, the Orcs did not give ground. They continued marching from the north and west with dozens of brigades, many thousands total, creeping forward behind their shields. Their numbers were endless, and while they had slowed, their resolve seemed to have strengthened. The Rakkins had done their job, diverting the Elves attention from the advancing Orcs.

When the first line of Orc brigades was fewer than one hundred feet from the north and west walls, great horns sounded from the west. It was enough to at least momentarily halt the Orcs' approach, but none would expose itself to discover the source of the sound.

Then the ground shook, and the Rakkins were first to see them. Two lines strong, nearly twenty-five hundred in each: It was the cavalries of Averon and Mystaria. They charged from the west toward the unsuspecting flank of the Orcs.

Mekko smiled as he watched the charge. During the night, he had ordered the cavalry out the south wall, and they walked their mounts far to the west and lie in wait for the signal to charge the enemy's flank. It had worked far better than he could have hoped. "How's that feel?" the general muttered.

With Prince Crichton and Captain Gaston leading the charge, they crashed into the Orc brigades, knocking them to the ground to be trampled by the horses that followed. The bewildered Orcs only heard the sounds of thundering hooves that crushed their heads and limbs underfoot, and those that did not fall met their end at the tip of a blade from a mounted rider.

The cavalry swept up behind them, charging through the enemy ranks, hacking down at them, spraying their black Orc blood in many directions. The White Elves on the battlements cheered as the cavalry moved deeper and farther into the enemy ranks, galloping through them, and halting their advance on the citadel.

The Rakkins quickly abandoned their assault on the Elves and swooped down to the west toward the cavalry. Their talons extended, they dove at high speeds, picking riders off their horses, hoisting them high in the air before letting go. Many others were torn apart or impaled by the birds' talons and were dead before they dropped.

Upon seeing the unrelenting attack, Mekko told Valin to signal the towers on the north and west walls. The dark tarps were removed within the towers, revealing one of the special weapons the Dwarven Corps of Engineers had developed at General Mekko's request. Within each tower was a large circular turret with ten crossbow bolts across attached to a main cord. The devices could swivel and had one operator to them, with White Elf archers covering them in the towers as well as on the walls.

The devices were loaded from the bottom from within the tower. With one pull of a trigger, the devices could fire ten armor-piercing bolts at once and were immediately reloaded. There were four towers on the north and west wall, so eight devices total. These special siege crossbows immediately started firing at the Rakkins, taking down two and three of them at a time with one shot. The creatures were suddenly falling faster than they could attack. Their huge bodies occasionally collapsed on an Orc brigade, though they sometimes fell on riders from the cavalry as well, crushing them and their horses. The towers tried their best to avoid firing at creatures above their allies, but it couldn't always be helped. Many riders were skillful enough to avoid the falling creatures but not all were lucky.

Within the Citadel, Lark ordered the siege ballistae brought to higher angles and began firing at the birdlike creatures, impaling them with six-foot-long bolts supporting the towers. The remaining Rakkins, smaller in numbers now, retreated from the field at high speeds; hundreds had fallen dead.

The operators of the tower crossbow devices then concentrated their fire on the Orc brigades, penetrating their shielding and dropping as many as ten at a time with each shot. The attack had been stopped; the Orcs were now in full retreat. They were easy prey for the cavalry, who hacked them to pieces as they attempted to escape. Others fell from arrows in their backs as the Elves fired at the retreating enemy.

Mekko watched from the command platform as another group of enemies formed at the far end of the fields. It was two ranks of Chalderons, the four-legged lizard-like creatures. Each rank seemed to consist of nearly a thousand of the Orc-mounted Chalderons. They were maroon in color, thick skinned with large tails. While slow-moving, they were durable. They could lash out their acid-tipped tongues at great distances.

The Orcs atop them carried shortbows. They took aim at the Elves up in the rocks and along the battlements. They were barely in range to hit them; it was more cover fire to allow their brigades to retreat. The cavalry, however, was well in range. Mekko ordered Valin to signal the cavalry to return to the citadel.

The Orcs began firing high-arching volleys. The Elves in the rocks and battlements of the walls were too well protected. As the arrows cascaded down, they found their marks in some of the unshielded riders of Averon and Mystaria, striking many in the back. Captain Gaston blew his horn, signaling all riders to make all speed toward the west gates. With that, they galloped madly toward the Citadel and safety. Once all the riders had cleared the gates, the arrow fire of the Orcs ceased, and the Chalderons and the Orc infantry retreated far across the field.

"Stand down the engineers on the battlements; it looks like we may not need them today. See to all the wounded immediately. Set the watch and the guard for tonight as soon as possible. Tell them to be especially alert!" Mekko ordered.

"Immediately, sir," responded Valin.

Mekko looked at the field where thousands of enemies lay dead before the citadel, but he could see allies dead as well, far more than he'd hoped. Men from Mystaria and Averon lay mixed with carcasses of Orcs and Rakkins.

Mekko felt the strong hand of Ranier upon his shoulder.

"Fear not for them, General. You must command the living. Your strategies turn death into a fighting chance at life for us all. However, there will come a time soon where no strategy or trick of war will avail us. You must be prepared for that moment," Ranier whispered so the young Dwarf bodyguards could not hear.

"They'll see one hell of a fight before that moment comes. I swear it," Mekko replied and headed down the stairs with Rendek and Toran behind in tow.

Kael made his way to the far southeast end of the citadel to the large tent that served as the infirmary. It was also here where the other Druids, assisted by Ranier, worked tirelessly on the potion they prayed would restore life to the earth and weaken Abadon.

Kael watched as the Druids tended with their magic and potions to the injured. Though their magic could heal severed skin and repair subcutaneous wounds, it could not restore the strength they had lost or traumas they incurred through battle; only time and rest could mend those. He was discouraged to see that the huge tent was almost completely full. Two massive fires burned at opposite ends of the tent to generate heat against the growing cold. Hundreds of blankets had been laid down and room was sparing; however, they were lucky to have such healing magic. Most of the wounded, if tended early enough, could be battle ready the same day or by next morning.

It was then he saw her, ministering over many who were freshly brought in. Even now, her dark dress, white hair and skin, stained with blood, she was the most beautiful thing he had ever seen. When she caught his glance, even her brief smile as she administered a healing salve to a patient was more than enough to make his misery drift away.

Mya asked Shalimar take over for her. She walked over to Kael, embraced him, and kissed him hard on the mouth. "Your friend has been here since the fighting stopped, helping with his healing magic. He has quite an uplifting way about him." Mya pointed to a corner of the tent.

Kael looked and saw Lark tending over some of the inured.

"He holds their hand if necessary, joins them in prayer if they wish, or says an encouraging word, whatever the case may call for. For a warrior, he has the comforting touch of a priest," Mya said.

"He may well be the last of his kind; more than both warrior and priest and still not unlike the common man. His order was destroyed many years ago, though rumor speaks of Paladins still on some of the southern islands, though I have never seen any," Kael replied. He took Mya's hand in his. "Walk with me for a moment."

They left the tent, but as they neared the south wall, Kael grabbed her suddenly and kissed her passionately. A moment later, he looked at her. There was fear and sadness in his eyes.

"What is it, my love?" she asked.

"I know we discussed this all ready, but I want you to leave here. Now, this very minute. If one of us lives, then something of the other does as well."

She put her hand to his lips, silencing him. With a soft smile, she said, "You forget that there are people here, my people, who I convinced to follow me and who have already died. I will not leave them; I will not leave you. If both of us survive, then all of the other does as well."

Kael marveled at her levity. Her smile had the power to remove all his fears. "Forgive me, I can think of no other way to protect you. Forgive my weakness."

"Do not fear. We will meet this darkness together. Whatever may lie ahead, we will face it together, no matter what the cost."

"No matter what the cost," Kael agreed as he held her hands tightly in his.

"Good, because I will be joining you on the battlements tomorrow," Mya said as she walked back toward the infirmary.

"Mya, Mya wait!" Kael trailed after her.

Commander Bainor entered Mekko's tent, unsure what to expect. He saw General Valin there as well. He quickly saluted, placing his right fist over his heart.

"Come in, Commander. Excellent job, lad. You earned your pay for the week. The engineering corps is to be commended. Now where do we stand on the last line of defense?" Mekko asked.

"The weapons are ready as we speak, General," Bainor answered.

"You understand, Commander, they must hold the enemy armies off long enough for us to get our forces into the mountains should we have to withdraw?" Valin asked.

"I understand, General. We will be ready," Bainor replied.

"Very good, Commander. Prepare your men. Tomorrow we will see if your plan for the walls functions to our advantage. An extra ration of wine for you and your men tonight. You are dismissed, lad," Mekko said.

"Thank you, sir." Bainor saluted again before he exited.

As night fell upon the land, the men huddled together throughout the citadel for warmth. Small fires burned wherever groups could gather to benefit from them.

Galin walked out into the jagged rocks that concealed thousands of Elven archers. The wind bit at him as it whipped harshly through the elevated rocks. He carried extra blankets for them, knowing they could not benefit from fires in such terrain.

King Aeldorath met him. "Ahh, you come with blankets for us, my young friend. You forget Elves have a much greater tolerance for climate change than your people; still, we feel the cold even more in these dark days when the earth languishes. It does my heart good to see you. Come sit with us a while."

"I bring more than blankets, my lord," Galin said.

King Aeldorath followed the Druid to a large rock formation. Closing his eyes, Galin placed both his hands upon the stone. As the moments passed, the stone began to take on a reddish hue that expanded and spread throughout the rock, generating heat. The Elves smiled and many gathered around, putting their hands out to feel the warmth.

Galin moved throughout the rocks from the top to the base of the mountainous formation, heating other large stones. When he had finished, he turned to find Layla next to him.

"You are generous with your power. We thank you," she said.

"It is the least I can do for them, stuck out here in these rocks," Galin replied, "How are you holding up, my lady?"

She looked at him quizzically.

"Forgive me, how are you holding up, Captain?" he rephrased.

Still, she looked at him waiting.

Galin smiled. "How are you holding up, *Layla?*" he said finally.

"All things considered, well, and yourself, Galin?" she asked smiling.

"Well, thank you," he replied.

They walked a bit away from the others and sat looking up at the sky. Though darkness obscured the stars, still there was something calming in its vast emptiness.

"Tell me, what are your plans when this war ends?" Galin asked her, noticing how her golden hair shone even in the absence of moon or starlight.

"You presuppose our victory?" she replied, smiling.

"You know what I mean," he stated.

"Perhaps I shall resign my post and join my sister at court," she said mockingly.

"And wear beautiful dresses, meet with heads of state, and be waited on by servants?" Galin asked playfully, his white hair blowing across his face.

Together they enjoyed a laugh at the prospect. When they had stopped laughing, they found themselves smiling at each other in an uncomfortable silence.

"Perhaps I shall think about starting a family," Layla said rather suddenly. "And you?"

Galin looked at her for a long moment and found himself bringing his hand up to her face and brushing her hair aside out of her eyes. "I should go," Galin stammered. "Be careful, stay low when you can."

"And you as well," she said, standing to watch him leave.

When he walked back up to where the king was, he bowed to him. "May blessed Mother Nature protect and watch over you, my lord, you and your people."

"And you, Galin. Our thanks for your kindness this night."

Elenari knelt beside the flap of High Master Reyblade's tent and listened for movement, unsure if he was sleeping.

"You may enter, child, no need to stay out in the cold," Reyblade's voice greeted from within.

Elanari smiled and entered the tent. She sat beside the old Elf, in the same cross-legged position she often found him in as of late.

"Tomorrow, I fear the battle will go heartless. The masters and I intend to join the fight should the opportunity present itself. I spoke to General Mekko earlier this night. I would like you to fight with us when we join the battle. As a cohesive unit we may be far more effective than split apart," Reyblade said.

Elenari bowed her head. "I would be honored to fight alongside you and the other masters."

"Spend this night in meditation, for tomorrow if you can find the quiet voice within you, your battle prowess will be unmatched," Reyblade said, never opening his eyes.

Elenari looked at him closely. By all accounts, he appeared a small frail figure, and though she knew of what he was capable, still she feared for him. "I will master, until tomorrow then," Elenari said.

"Until tomorrow, my dear, good night." He opened his eyes and smiled at her.

"Good night, my master."

Elenari left his tent with mixed emotions. She had never seen him fight, other than when training her or a student. It was difficult to imagine him and the others in actual combat. She had always dreamed about fighting at Reyblade's side, though she never imagined it would be during a war such as this with so much else at stake. She wanted to see Kael before she retired for the night.

As she walked past the many tents, she pulled her cloak tight about her, feeling her shoulders tremble at the night air. She could see her breath passing in front of her. She let her mind drift, thinking back to memories of Hawk.

"My lady?" The greeting had come from the dark.

She turned to see an outlined figure lovingly stroking his horse. She was so startled for a moment she did not realize it was Prince Crichton. Placing one hand over her chest, she said, "Oh, it's you. You and your men fought well today. You should be proud."

"Proud? Pride can be both a sin and a virtue, lady. The fact I am proud of my men does no good for those who died and serves as only a platitude for those still living," Crichton replied.

Elanari took a few steps forward. "What is wrong with you?" she admonished. "I watched your men on the field. They do not fight for this alliance or freedom or any other high idea—they fight for *you*. I sense they would live and die at your command. How someone like you can command such fanatical loyalty is beyond me. I can only assume you do it through fear, but what any of your men wouldn't do for you if you gave them the smallest word of encouragement, the smallest sign you cared for them. They would move mountains for you."

Crichton studied her for a moment before replying, "Your passion is commendable, lady, but such gestures, though not without merit, can be construed as weakness."

"I think your base indifference makes you weak," she said bitterly. "You treat that horse with enough kindness, are the rest of us so unworthy? I feel sorry for you. Good night, Prince Crichton."

Elenari picked up her pace away from him.

Crichton stopped stroking his horse and stared at her, following her as far as his sight would allow.

Captain Etienne Gaston walked through the camp after having visited his wounded men. It had been another exhausting day, and the next day would no doubt be much worse, and though he knew he should get some sleep, a sudden curiosity led him toward the southwest end of the citadel where the Mystarians were quartered.

As he suspected, there was a lone fire burning with one man still up, sitting alone. It was Captain Alizar, his counterpart from the Mystarian Royal Army, still wearing his golden plate armor visible beneath a dark blanket. Though Prince Crichton led the Mystarians in battle, Captain Alizar functioned as the prince's right hand and garnered enormous respect. He appeared to be sipping a hot beverage. Alizar was not an overly imposing man though he did have a full, red beard. The cracked lines of his forehead supported by bushy eyebrows indicated middle age. After seeing him fight, Gaston could only deduce this man had been a professional mercenary most of his life.

"Captain, am I disturbing you?" Gaston asked.

Alizar rose quickly to face him. "Ah, Captain Gaston, not at all. Won't you sit down?" he offered.

"Yes, thank you," Gaston answered.

"Some coffee, Captain?" Alizar asked. "The men made a pot before the last of them went to sleep."

"I would love some, thank you," Gaston said as he slapped his hands together, rubbing them vigorously as if to stave off the freezing cold. "Call me Etienne, please."

"Very well, Etienne, you may call me Nigel—except in front of my men of course."

They both chuckled.

For a long moment they sat in silence, drinking coffee with their clouded breaths visible in the air before them.

"I never thought much of any other country's army before. We were far more disciplined, far better trained, and far better equipped. However, that was before we ever had to fight a war, especially one of this magnitude. Your men fought extremely well, Etienne; you should be proud," Alizan said.

"As did yours, Nigel. I think we can both be very proud of our men. Where is Prince Crichton?" Gaston asked.

"It is his custom to retire in private. He sleeps away from the men," Alizar responded.

"An unusual man. What is he like?" Gaston asked.

"That, my dear Etienne, is a question that cannot be easily answered. I have known him nearly twelve years, longer than most, and still, he is an enigma. He is the last descendant of the ancient Wizard Knights of Mystaria, an unparalleled warrior and powerful wizard. While the other wizards look down their nose and scoff at him, in truth, they all fear him. Though he is committed in his role as commander of the army and defender of Mystaria, what motivates him beyond that, even the wisest do not know. Courage and valor in battle draw his respect and admiration above all things. Beyond that, you know as much about him as I do," Alizar answered.

"Well, I will let you get to sleep, Captain," Gaston said as he stood. "Please know that on behalf of the Sentinels of Averon, we are honored to fight alongside the Royal Soldiers of Mystaria." Gaston put out his hand.

Alizar rose and grasped Gaston's hand in a firm shake. "Good luck tomorrow, Captain."

"To us all," Gaston replied.

Mekko lay awake in his cot, tossing and turning. By all accounts from Kael and Galin, the reinforcements from Bastlandia and Arcadia should be on their way, but there was no guarantee. If the black fleet they saw was numerous enough to secure strategic blockades, help might never arrive. Cordilleran had no formal relationship with either kingdom though they had given their words to the Druids. Much was still uncertain. It disturbed him that the Shadow Prince's influence had clearly reached that far south. It stood to reason that he would have clairvoyance enough to see the approaching fleets.

What occupied his thoughts most, even though he denied thinking about it during the day, was Abadon—another dark lord whose powers dwarfed the Shadow Prince's by Ranier's account, a being not of their world or even their dimension. Ranier foretold that, most likely, Abadon would make his presence known at some point during the battle, and at that time, they must retreat without delay. The idea of defeat was unimaginable, but even more terrifying was the potentiality that evil, darkness, and death of all that was good would forever reign on earth. With each passing moment, the prospect became frighteningly real. Worse yet, he could feel hope slipping away, losing the struggle against his deep despair.

Chapter 17

The third morning brought a light drizzle. Carried by the swirling winds, the rain droplets struck like stinging icicles against uncovered skin. Charcoal gray clouds blanketed the sky. Frozen bodies of Goblins, Orcs, Rakkins, Men, Dwarves, and Elves lay scattered across the ground outside the citadel, their flesh frozen from the night's bitter cold. Death was a lingering but elusive presence, its stench penetrating even through the cold.

The Alliance stood ready at daybreak, yet no attack came as expected. Across the north and west battlements, nearly five hundred White Elves stood with bows ready. Among them was Mya Almentir, wearing a black cloak over dark leather armor. She carried a black longbow with a quiver of arrows.

Kael went to her side. "I would be less nervous if you were attending to the injured in the infirmary," the Druid whispered.

"I stand with the other races; I stand with my people; I stand with you. You, who taught me this was possible. Would you have me abandon it now?" she asked.

He gave her a crooked smile. "Each day I find something new that I love about you. Very well, here it is." He held her hand for a moment then walked away.

The next moment, ten White Elves with shields and swords formed a semicircle around Mya.

"What is this, Sergeant?" Mya demanded.

The leader of the group knelt before her and bowed his head. "My lady, the Grand Druid advised us you intended to be here. Captain Arnir ordered us to be with you always should you insist on being near the fighting. In addition, he ordered me to beg you in his name and the name of our people not to put yourself in harm's way."

Mya gave him a hard stare. "I have my duty to do just as you and your men do, Sergeant." she said and turned to face the battlefield.

The young Elf rose, staring at her in disbelief mixed with pride and blared out, "The High Priestess stands with us in battle this day! Let no evil befall her!"

Cheers rose from the White Elves on the battlements. Never before had a member of the religious caste fought side by side with those of the warrior caste in a conflict of this magnitude. They would die to protect her.

Mekko heard the Elven cheers for their high priestess, as he Ranier, and Valin looked out across the field from the command platform. Large formations of Orcs stood motionless far across the field in front of the stone pyramid that served as the Shadow Prince's throne.

"What are they waiting for?" Mekko asked.

Ranier took a step forward, a strange look in his eye. "I sense something." At that moment, he looked to the skies. The others joined his gaze.

To the east, the heavens darkened over the rocks where the Elven archers took refuge and attacked from. The clouds moved rapidly, giving way to something unnatural, and began changing from dark gray to black above their location.

The Shadow Prince stood from his throne and stretched his arms toward the sky. "It is time," he hissed through the metal mesh of his gold helmet. He began chanting an arcane verse in an ancient tongue. As he chanted, a round hole started to form in the clouds over the Elves in the rocks. The hole was completely black and still.

Standing on the dais with the Shadow Prince, General Red Fang looked down at the thousands of waiting Orcs. He raised his arms and lowered them, signaling the beginning. With that, the Orc infantry, in lines of a thousand, rhythmically and repeatedly smacked their weapons against their shields, a deafening noise to those within the walls of the citadel a hundred yards away.

Layla watched as the massive black void began to form over their position. "My lord, there is devilry afoot in the skies! Something evil prepares to assail us," she said urgently.

The Elf king sensed the evil without time to contemplate the void and shouted, "Take cover! Behind the rocks now!" King Aeldorath shouted.

There was a flurry of activity among the Elves just before the hole in the sky exploded. A swirling vortex of air saturated with large snow crystals poured through, assaulting the rocks with wind, snow, and hail. Dozens of Elves had not been swift enough to take cover and were lifted and slammed against the rocks, tumbling down the jagged rock cliff to a grim and painful death.

"They are trying to take our archers out of the fight and mean to charge and breach the walls. Valin, prepare the Engineers to execute on my command, north and west walls. Tell the pike division to stand by and prepare to repel invaders. Signal Lark, have all artillery prepare to fire."

As Mekko barked out the commands, both Rendek and Toran helped General Valin signal their units with flags and hand signals.

Waiting upon his horse, Lark found himself holding the small metal box which contained the Emerald Star. All night he sat studying the gemstone, trying in vain to reach out to it with some part of him. Something was wrong. He had felt uneasy ever since entering the citadel. A feeling of dread had been welling up within him, growing in intensity. What unnerved him most was he couldn't discern if it were coming from the evil locked within the gemstone or from deep within him. He looked up just in time to see General Valin waving the flag, signaling him to prepare his men. Immediately he placed the metal box beneath the chest plate of his silver armor and drawing his two-handed sword high, began riding down the rows of the artillery, rallying his men, who cheered as he went by. All siege devices were loaded and ready.

Atop the battlements, Dwarven engineers ran to their posts behind the White Elves. They used their heavy mallets to knock the caps off the posts along the fences and pulled the thick metal chains that resided within. They braced themselves against the walls and waited for the signal to pull. This would be the first battle test of their plan with the walls. If anything went wrong, all could be lost. Dwarven engineers also manned the great multi-firing crossbows in the towers, with White Elf archers to defend them. Other engineers loaded the weapons from below to feed the devices a constant supply of ammunition.

The allies held their breaths as the Orc lines broke into a full-out running charge from the north and west. Wave after wave, thousands strong all charged at once.

Mekko looked to the rocks, which were nearly invisible beneath the twisting vortex of snow-driven winds. The nearly five thousand Elven archers they relied so heavily upon were now unable to fire a shot. Mekko looked to the battlements on the north and west walls. They bolstered the towers with additional White Elf archers with approximately five hundred archers atop each wall. They would barely be enough to even slow the thousands charging on the citadel. Mekko knew that if the enemy breached the walls, the battle was over, and they would be massacred before any retreat could be attempted.

"Rendek, get Commander Bainor up here now. Take a horse, lad, go!" Mekko watched as Rendek scurried down the stairs.

The engineering corps had never let the army down before, but everything was riding on their plan with the walls. Bainor was an untried commander, but their only chance of survival was on his word that his men could deliver.

Kael watched from the north wall the supernatural blizzard-like storm. As he had explained to Mekko, each day the power of the Druids became weaker and weaker, especially their ability to influence the land or the weather. Even if he and Galin and the other Druids combined their powers, they would not be able to counter such a focused summoning. With the charging Orcs running closer with each step, they would not have time to even attempt a counter spell. He looked at Galin over on the west wall and knew he felt equally as helpless.

There must be a way they could help protect the walls from the charging beasts—*The walls*, he thought. Still, they could command elemental magics. Kael made several gestures to Galin until the younger Druid nodded his understanding. If they meant to penetrate their defenses, then they would have to earn it, Kael thought as he closed his eyes to concentrate.

Mya saw Kael and knew that he was concentrating on a spell.

The Orcs were nearly halfway to the walls.

"Hold your fire!" she yelled to her kinsman.

"Sir, shall we signal the engineers on the walls?" Valin asked.

"Hold on, the Druids are up to something. Give them a few more moments," Mekko replied.

"Sir, if we don't execute now, there may not be enough room to maneuver," Valin cautioned urgently.

Mekko looked at Galin, his friend who had never let him down yet, then at Kael who had equally come through for both him and his people more than once. "A few more moments, General Valin."

Just then, both Druids extended their fingers and red fire burst forth, shattering through the drizzling rain. Jets of flame poured from them, arching down, striking the ground only a few feet from the first line of charging Orcs in both directions. The fire tore into the ground, blowing hardened dirt and mud into the air. The flames grew in height and expanded rapidly in length, developing into a fire wall between the citadel and the charging Orcs. Some Orcs dove headfirst through the fires, their armor melting into their skin. Those that did not die came through the other side shrieking, their bodies writhing in flames as they rolled about the hard ground in an attempt to extinguish the stubborn magical flames.

Within moments, both fire walls extended until they met and joined together as one. The flaming wall was only about seven feet high, but its height and the intensity of its flames fluctuated. Both Kael and Galin perspired despite the cold; their force of will alone would not be enough to sustain the fire. They could maintain it at that size only for a few moments more. Nevertheless, the Orc charge was brought to a momentary halt.

Mya called out to the White Elves, "Aim your bows skyward for arching fire. Release arrows!"

A thousand arrows soared to the sky, arching over the fire wall and raining down into the Orcs. Some blocked the arrows with their shields, others were caught unaware as the wooden shafts buried themselves in the beast's heads, eyes, backs, and unprotected extremities.

As the Orcs crowded against the flames, many got down on all fours side by side so the others could run across their backs and jump over the flames, which had dropped to scarcely five feet.

"Sergeant, you and twenty-five of your men shoot the Orcs jumping over the flames. The rest of you keep firing into the main body!" Mya ordered.

"All units, set for maximum elevation and fire!" Lark Royale yelled to his men as he rode furiously up and down the rows of artillery, swinging his sword through the air as if dueling with an unseen enemy.

With his command, levers were released and both boulders and bolts were launched over the walls into the masses of Orcs they could only hear. The rocks crashed into the Orc lines, landing with such terrific force as to crush several, or their trajectory landed them in a roll, bowling over the creatures and smashing their bodies like twigs.

Bolts the size of logs impaled three and four Orcs at a time with them grouped so close together. Still, thousands had gathered and began beating their weapons against their shields and armor in anticipation of the flames dying. Any moment, they would renew their charge. Nothing would stand before their fury.

Ranier stepped forward on the command platform, raising his black staff with one hand toward the blizzard to the east. "Enough of your foul craft, Stranexx!" Ranier exclaimed.

Mekko watched as the head of Rainer's staff began to glow, outlined in a pale golden light. As he looked to the east, the wind and snow gradually settled into a mild breeze and flurries; the hole in the sky started closing, replaced by slow-moving gray clouds.

"The moment the flames die, Valin, give the signal to the engineers, not a second before!" Mekko ordered. He watched the old Dwarf grab the flag with the golden hammer and stand ready.

Archangel Royal emerged from the infirmary, buckling his sword belt. He still felt weakened but had no doubt the feeling would dissipate once he joined the fighting. Hurriedly glancing about, he found a nearby horse that he mounted in a running jump and dashed toward the center of the camp.

Kael and Galin could no longer maintain the fire wall, their powers unable to match their wills of iron. The flames died down until they were naught but smoking embers. Their arms lowered, and the Druids fell back against the battlements for support.

The Orcs, hatred burning in their yellow eyes, reignited their charge, trampling their fallen comrades on their path to vengeance.

"Now, Valin!" Mekko roared, and Valin waved the flag of the engineering corps.

The Dwarves along the battlements awaiting the signal began pulling the thick iron chains upward as rapidly as possible. As the chains came upward, the very walls themselves released from the ground and extended up and outward from the citadel toward the charging invaders.

The entire length of the north and west walls rose almost as if to invite their unwanted guests in without even a fight. It was such a grand spectacle and so unexpected, even the charging Orcs slowed their pace for a moment.

Horns thundered from the openings. In the next moment, four lines of cavalry, five hundred strong each, charged outward, grinding their heels into their mounts, spurring them on to battle speed.

At the same moment, the Dwarves manning the multi-firing crossbows began firing a hail of armor-piercing bolts into the waves of Orcs, cutting them down by the dozens and causing those running behind them to trip and spill into others alongside them, falling over their dead.

Heavy cavalry thundered out of the citadel beneath the raised walls and met the charging Orcs head on, tearing through them, hacking down at them with their swords. The bewildered Orcs were barely able to get their shields up to guard against the killing blows of the heavily armored horseman.

The colorful figures of Prince Crichton and Captain Gaston led the horse charge as always, with Crichton in his flaming red cape and golden armor atop Stryker, and Gaston with his white tunic visible over silver chain mail. Embroidered in the tunic was the symbol of the Sentinels, the black eagle. His black cape separated him from his men.

Blood splattered as the two armies clashed. The horses had built up just enough speed to drive a wedge into the Orcs, killing as they broke through. Congested as the Orcs were, the armored war horses of Mystaria and Averon breached through them with ferocious strength and speed. The men hacked from atop their mounts from side to side with their weapons, some with swords in both hands, dark blood spraying their faces, its bitter taste lingering on their lips.

Within the citadel, artillery fire had stopped as not to endanger the cavalry. The White Elves on the battlements fired their arrows nonstop at the Orcs who slipped through, attempting to charge the walls. Alongside them, the towers continued to churn out volleys of bolts, fighting off those closest who survived the horse charge.

Once the last of the cavalry cleared the citadel, the Dwarven engineers released their chains and the walls fell back into place a section at a time.

Archangel rode near the artillery toward Lark.

Wearing a worried frown, Lark came alongside him. "Are you sure you're well enough to be up and about?"

"Are you sure you're not our mother instead of my brother?" Archangel replied. "What can I do to help?"

"All we can do is watch the towers and the walls for breaches and do what we can to keep the enemy out. I'll watch the west wall, you take the north," Lark said as he pulled his reins, jerking his horse toward the west wall. "Oh," he said, stopping and looking back. "Take care of yourself, little brother."

"You too, big brother," Archangel replied.

Both men nodded a final time and were off.

Dripping in sweat and his face marred with dirt, Commander Bainor arrived on the command platform with Rendek. "Sir, the walls were a success," he said with a proud smile.

"Aye, Commander. I want you and a small number of your men standing by at our last line of defense," Mekko said, keeping his eyes on the battlefield.

At that order, the commander's face dropped, and an expression of dismay crossed the features of Rendek, Toran, and General Valin.

"Sir, I don't understand," Bainor said.

"The enemy's not finished with us yet. They're waiting for something. We take nothing for granted. Follow your orders, Commander," Mekko said flatly, again without looking.

The young Dwarf saluted. "Aye, sir," he said, though confusion marked his face. He turned on his heels and descended the stairs.

On the battlefield, the cavalry had driven a triangular wedge nearly halfway through the attacking Orcs, effectively turning the tide enough to prevent the charging hordes from penetrating the citadel's defenses. They hacked as they rode forward into the enemy, charging through and over them. They could hear cheers across the fields from the battlements, urging them on.

King Aeldorath and the Elves emerged from the protection of the snow-covered rocks, finally able to view the battlefield. There were still thousands of Orcs charging from far into the enemy lines still some distance from the cavalry.

"We must attack deep into the enemy formation and soften their lines for our cavalry!" he shouted. "Steel yourselves and prepare to fire as far as your skills allow. Too long have we been kept from this fight!" The king drew forth an arrow and prepared his longbow.

Beside him, Layla rang out, "Let us show them how right they were to fear our bows!" She notched an arrow and pulled back on the bowstring as far as her Elven muscles and the weapon would allow.

In an almost simultaneous twang of longbow strings, thousands of arrows were released, sailing great distances, flying ahead of their cavalry and landing deep into the crowded enemy formations. Hundreds of Orcs fell beneath Elven arrows. Never expecting them to shoot such great distances, they were not even looking up. Many fell dead to the hard earth with expressions of pure astonishment.

The cavalry rode deep, penetrating into the Orcs and completely halting their attack. Combined with the Elven archers shooting into the rear of their formation, the Orcs turned and ran toward the enemy lines.

Cheers rose up from the Elves on the battlements as the tide had now turned, and it seemed as if the citadel would be safe for another day.

At that moment, the Shadow Prince rose from his golden throne. He slowly pulled his black leather gloves on more snugly. "We have allowed them enough petty victories. Release the beast!" he commanded. "Now, we crush their hope."

At the back of the stone pyramid and unseen by the Alliance, four Morrangs, the eyeless giants, were chained to huge wheel-like gears. At the Shadow Prince's command, several Orcs began whipping the blind giants, signaling them to turn the enormous stone gears embedded within the pyramid.

Suddenly, an unprecedented rumble shook the fields and those standing upon it. A dreadful sound of churning metal erupted from the pyramid so loud that all activity on the battlefield ceased.

Crichton and Gaston halted the cavalry, allowing the remainder of the Orcs to escape. The Elven archers ceased firing in the resonating wake of noise, protecting their ears from its high metallic pitch with their hands. All eyes watched as the massive stone pyramid slowly separated. As the two halves slid apart, their stone bases dragged along the hard ground, tearing up chunks of earth and forming a cloud of debris that obscured the opening.

For a moment, there was silence. Then, from within, emerged an ear-shattering roar so deafening it caused nearly all to cover their ears. Two steps, and the very earth beneath them shook. In that moment, *it* emerged from the gaping nothingness—a monstrosity such as human eyes had never beheld emerged through the cloud of debris. The enormous creature was nearly forty feet high, despite its hunched-over gait. It took two more earth-shattering steps and came into full sight. Mottled pale-white skin covered the whole of it, connecting to its exoskeletal spine. The raised bones protruded from the back of its neck down to its spiked tail. Within its concave face in a disproportionately small head was a protruding snout that oozed thick fluid over its gaping maw. Its long neck appeared to be composed of thick layers of overlapping skin, and many rows of razor-sharp teeth were visible even from the distance.

The cavalry and those in the citadel beyond could see that the creature's huge chest was protected by interlocking plates of crocodile-like scales. Bristles of spiky, black hair dotted its round head and coated the length of its body. Its legs were massive and muscular though slightly bent. Bags of skin conglomerated at the joints. Black pools of death formed its eyes, large and expressionless set far within the pale gray hide of its head. Layers of skin bunched beneath the eyes as if to indicate ancient age to the creature, but its dense muscle structure shattered all hopes that age was in any way a handicap to a beast such as this.

The Orcs around the pyramid fell to their knees with their hands out before them and foreheads to the ground in abject worship.

Shock and horror were the only expressions the faces of the cavalry could convey to those who were not as close to the beast. They watched as the creature slowly, as if for the first time in eons, extended its fingers. Its claws jutted out through the skin, extending to lengths of nearly three feet before retracting back into the fingertips. Its arms hung loosely at its sides, giving no indication of their speed or dexterity.

In the rocks, and atop the battlements, Elves were horrified by the creature's unparalleled grotesqueness. They were dumbfounded that such a being could exist.

Those within the walls of the citadel who could see the beast looked to the command platform for some sign of hope from Mekko. But Mekko could only watch in gut-wrenching fear. Ranier, a look of despair upon his brow, stumbled forward and grabbed on to the railing.

"What in the hell is that thing?" Mekko begged to know, looking to Ranier for any sign of hope.

The ancient mage leaned heavily on his staff with both hands. He spoke slowly, "Sadly it appears our world is not without its own demons. That, is the Creeg Mor. In the tongues of Goblins and Orcs, it means *Great One*. They worship such creatures as deities. I did not think such a creature could still exist. They must have woken it from dormancy from deep within the earth."

"It's not one of the demons from the Nethertime you described?" Mekko asked.

"It hails from a time before the civilized races inhabited the world."

They all watched as its black-hoofed feet moved it closer in their direction, causing the ground to tremble, as though the earth itself knew to fear it.

"Call them back, the cavalry!" Ranier turned suddenly to Valin. "Sound the retreat now!"

In the time it took Valin to look to Mekko for the order, the creature let out with another ear-shattering roar. They watched the extra layers of skin about its neck puff up, forming a hood around its head, and with unbelievable swiftness, the beast lurched forward, launching itself through the air and landing at the front ranks of the cavalry.

Before anyone could move, the creature bent over them, its arms extending in length as if made from rubber. In long, sweeping motions, they raked at the cavalry, spilling dozens of riders and horses. Then, the claws extended and impaled both horses and riders through their chests, lifting them up and hurling them in all directions.

The citadel horns rang out the retreat call as loudly as possible.

The creature spun around with merciless speed, snapping its huge tail into the forward ranks, smashing through hundreds of horsemen, dropping them like a line of dominoes and leaving them dead from the impact.

From high in the rocks, King Aeldorath and Layla rallied the Elves.

"Take aim at the beast's head. We must bring it down. Fire!" the king yelled as they drew their bowstrings and released a hail of arrows at the creature.

Disbelief paralyzed the Elves as they watched their shafts bounce off the creature's hood. Their arrows were mere gnats flying about its head. Now, the Creeg Mor spun around with inordinate momentum, snapping its tail again and killing dozens more, the screams and shouts short-lived. Some it reached down for, impaling horse and rider on its claws and delivering them to a ghastly death in a bed of razor-sharp teeth. Fountains of blood gushed out onto the broken bodies at its feet as the creature sloppily chomped its food.

Madly, the cavalries of Mystaria and Averon rode for the citadel. Some screamed to rally their mounts that much faster. One lone form had maneuvered to the back of the procession but held his position as others fled past him. It was Prince Crichton. He sat unmoving on Stryker as the others fled. The other horses fled with their mounts in terror, yet Stryker held his ground.

Again, the Creeg Mor leaned forward, its terrifying claws fully extended, spearing both riders and mounts like huge forks. More blood spurted through its teeth as it chewed through bone, staining its face and chest. Its appetite was like that of a starving bear feasting on spawning salmon.

Those in the battlements watched in horror, taken prisoner by their own helplessness. The creature was fast approaching the main gates, but they did not flee. Whether held captive by their fear or camaraderie, none could be entirely certain.

From the command platform, General Valin noticed something unusual. "Sir, look to the field. It's the Mystarian prince. He's holding his position," Valin said in disbelief.

"What the bloody hell is that crazy wizard up to?" Mekko whispered, watching in awe.

On the battlements, Kael and Galin exchanged signals and pointed to the command platform. Kael looked toward Mya, who met his glance. In the next moment, Kael raised his arms, dropped his head, and in a flash of green fire, he reappeared as a bronze-colored falcon. Galin had also changed form and both Druids flew toward the command platform.

Moments later, they stood in their human form with Mekko and Ranier.

"What is it?" Kael barked at Ranier.

"A creature of the ancient world," Ranier answered.

"How can we stop it?" Galin asked.

"It cannot be stopped. When its rage is incited, its strength will only increase. Its body produces massive amounts of adrenaline, giving it more strength than any creature in existence. They would have all killed each other in time until a massive earthquake reshaped the face of our world and destroyed all such great beasts. This one must have found a way to survive underground."

"Is there no magic you can use? We can't just stand here and watch while it kills our men. By the gods!" Mekko implored.

Ranier looked away from Mekko out to the field as the creature whipped its tail from side to side, killing dozens of fleeing riders like flies. With disgust upon his face, Ranier looked back at Mekko. He felt the Dwarven general's fear and frustration. "I must save my power until the appointed time," he said, shaking his head.

They all looked to the field as the last of the cavalry finally reached the citadel. Prince Crichton faced the beast, alone and unmoving.

"Has Crichton lost his mind?" Kael blurted.

"Of all things, I wouldn't have figured him to give up his life so uselessly," Galin added.

"I do not think that is his intention." Ranier said softly.

The Creeg Mor took four steps forward, albeit warily, bringing it only a few feet from Crichton, who bent down low in his saddle, resting his chin on Stryker's white mane, and patting the horse softly on the neck.

After a quick assessment of the situation, the creature lunged for him with both arms. Nudging Stryker forward and to the side, horse and rider swiftly evaded the attacks and rode through the creatures' legs and coming up behind it.

Spinning its tail like a lethal whip low to the ground, it lashed out at the white stallion. In an incredible display of agility, Stryker leapt over the tail, evading the lethal strike by only inches. The Creeg Mor roared its displeasure.

Cheers rose from the battlements and from the Elves within the rocks. The Dwarves in the towers immediately aimed their multi-firing crossbows and fired their bolts. Though some stuck in the beast's hide, they did no damage.

"He's giving us time to stop it," Mekko said, turning to Ranier.

"Tell us *anything* you know about the creature," Galin begged. "How does it produce such incredible amounts of adrenaline?"

"The Creeg Mor has a symbiotic relationship with parasites called Megleons. They are long soft-bodied parasites that bite into the Creeg Mor's back muscles and spine. They feed off adrenaline, and as the Creeg Mor secretes more adrenaline, the Megleons bite harder, exacerbating the creature's rage," Ranier quickly explained.

"These, parasites—if we could remove them, could we kill the best then?" Galin asked.

"Their teeth grow into the bone and muscle of the host animal, becoming part of it," Ranier answered. "They cannot be removed."

They all looked outward again as Crichton tried to lure the creature away from the citadel; he raced into attacking range, only then to barely dodge another clawed lunge. The beast, however, did not turn away from the citadel or even flinch.

"If we can't remove the parasites, maybe we can kill them," Galin said as he moved to Kael's side and spoke briefly. In a green flash, the Druids transformed into eagles and flew toward the battlefield.

Careful not to hit the eagles, the Elves and the towers continued to launch projectiles by the thousands, doing little more than annoying the Creeg Mor. The beast seemed to be losing interest in Crichton and started toward the northern gates, the ground trembling with its every step.

Crichton reached back and drew forth his two-handed sword. Wielding it with one hand, he struck a blow at the tail as he swiftly passed. The magic blade made a gash. Though negligible, damage was done, it was the first blow to draw blood.

Kael took human form directly in front of the main gates to the north wall, standing in the Creeg Mor's path. Raising his hands to the sky, he closed his eyes and concentrated.

Galin transformed into himself several feet behind the creature. Extending his fingers, water flowed freely from his hands at the beast's feet, forming a pool in which it stood.

As Mya saw Kael only a few dozen feet from the hulking monstrosity, she passionately cried to her warriors to fire their bows. "At its face, blind it!" Mya screamed. As she fired her own weapon, she could feel tears forming in the corners of her eyes. It was real fear she felt, just as she had on the eve of the attack on Alluviam. She knew she was only a moment away from throwing herself over the battlements down to stand with Kael, even if it meant dying with him.

Kael's intense concentration did not allow him to think of anything but the task before him. Fortunately, with the weather so poor and the clouds so full of precipitation, it was magic that was well within the Druid's power. The elements were still accessible. He lowered his left hand while leaving his right one high above his head. Opening his eyes, he looked up to see the clouds, already dark, responding to his wishes.

The Creeg Mor twisted its body and swung its tail with such speed and force that it smashed into the tower that connected the north and west wall, obliterating the entire structure and killing all within the tower and destroying one of the massive crossbows. The White Elves along the battlements wailed as their defenseless kin fell to the ground in the wreckage.

At that moment, a forked bolt of lightning came from the clouds to Kael's raised hand. He redirected it toward the Creeg Mor. The bolt struck the creature, charging and lighting up the exposed bones of its spine, causing its whole body to convulse; the shock had been doubled because of the water in which it stood. As the charge subsided, the beast answered the attack in a roar of rage, but a second attack followed. Galin now directed a bolt from the sky at the creature, paralyzing the beast.

"Sometimes the simplest magic is indeed the most effective," Ranier whispered as he raised his staff and lightning exploded from its crown. It joined Galin's bolt, striking the creature and further electrifying it.

Prince Crichton pulled Stryker's reins, halting his swift steed. Sheathing his sword, he bent his arms inward and snapped them out, releasing lightning from his fingertips at the beast, which was now writhing in pain at the mercy of the electrifying charges. Over and over both Druids and

Wizards struck, firing lightning bolts into the Creeg Mor, until finally, beyond all belief, the massive beat fell with a smashing thud that nearly knocked them off their feet.

The Creeg Mor still lived, breathing heavily and moving slowly like a turtle on is back trying to right itself.

Crichton dismounted, pulling his sword once again. Coming up behind the beast's head, the prince removed his red cape and carefully threw it over the creature's eyes. Without hesitation, he sprang up onto its head, and raising his sword high with both hands, he turned the blade downward and came crashing down with all his weight through the middle of the Creeg Mor's forehead, burying the blade to the hilt.

The beast's arms and tail extended and shivered for several moments until they collapsed unmoving. After a moment of complete silence, Crichton reached down and with an upward wrenching motion, he ripped his sword free. Turning to the citadel, he raised it high for all to see. The Alliance forces cheered their loudest, and Elves hugged one another along the battlements.

Crichton turned and still standing on the face of the Creeg Mor, he looked in the distance at the Shadow Prince and slowly, mockingly, raised his sword again in victory.

Kael looked up to the battlements and found Mya and nodded to her. He then looked to Galin, who smiled broadly. General Mekko released the breath he'd been holding and took a gulp of air. Then, with a heavy sigh, the Dwarf grabbed Ranier's arm and shook it in sheer joy.

"Hope appears in the strangest places, even in the face of despair," Ranier whispered.

The Shadow Prince stood, unmoving, his mood and expression hidden behind the metal mesh of his mask. His gloved hands slowly curled into fists. Suddenly, he raised his shaking arms, pointed at the citadel, and screamed in the unholiest of voices, "All attack! Destroy them all! Do not cease until all lives are taken! Retreat, and you will suffer horribly! My gift to them is their death! ATTACK!"

Chapter 18

It was midday, and the air was only growing colder; no sun had warmed its aching womb for weeks. Trees along the edge of the fields were twisted stick figures, starving for the leaves that once decorated them. The birds had long since left, taking their exodus south toward warmer skies. Land animals that could not endure the unnatural cold either fled or died. Everything seemed to be ending, and a terrible new horizon loomed.

The Orcs raged with fury and bloodlust, no longer able to distinguish thought or fear. They charged, knowing only that they would kill or be killed. In their simple minds, death from the enemy was far preferable than death by the hands of the Shadow Prince.

Mekko watched from on high as countless thousands of the Blood Rock Clan approached with who knows what evil forces coming up behind them. He looked to the tower and parts of the wall that the Creeg Mor had destroyed, leaving a gaping hole, an invitation to the enemy. They would breach the walls; there were too many, and they could never drive them back. Mekko looked south in the distance where Commander Bainor stood with their last line of defense, awaiting his command. He looked about, unsure of his next command, barely aware of the orders being shouted below him. Was retreat the only option?

Below, inside the walls, Captain Gaston called out orders to all able-bodied horsemen. "All riders, dismount and report to the rear!" Gaston shouted and heard Crichton repeating the order to his men.

The riders quickly did as instructed and led their horses to the rear, moving past and through the ranks of pikemen and infantry, who moved up close to the gates.

Lark rode furiously through the siege devices, barking orders in their remaining moments. "Into the trenches! Grab your crossbows, you know your positions. Rank one, rank two, and rank three, stand ready." Lark watched as they hurriedly obeyed him.

The Orcs were nearly halfway across the fields, and the Elves in the rocks began firing.

Layla went to her father. She waited for him to fire and then grabbed his shoulder.

"My Lord, many are nearly out of arrows. We may not have enough to last the day," she said regretfully.

"Then we shall throw rocks down at them, for even a child may topple a giant with a well-cast stone. Order any who run out of arrows to gather at the foot of the rocks, and when enough have formed, order them to charge the field," Aeldorath commanded.

As she turned to convey his orders, he grabbed her suddenly. "You are not to charge the field, Layla. I need you with me."

"My Lord, with submission, I will not give any order that I myself would not obey. When I deplete my arrows, I will lead the charge on the field." She ran from him before he could reply.

King Aeldorath knew, in a strange way, that his daughter was right. His pride in her was only surmounted by his love and concern for her well-being. Something he also knew he should share with his daughter far more often than he did.

"Sir, what are your orders? The Orcs are closing." Valin whispered to Mekko.

Rendek and Toran looked on nervously, watching as Mekko continued to look about, finally locking eyes with Ranier. The old mage looked at him and could see indecision had finally caught hold of him. Just as he was about to accept despair, Mekko heard singing from below. The Dwarves in the pike division and infantry division were singing the *Contorq Khant*, the Dwarven song of victory. They sang it loud and in the common tongue for all to hear and comprehend:

We have faced battles great.
In our hour of need our arms remain strong.
Courage is not a word but our way.
Honor is not taught but who we are.
Love is for those we have lost.
Hope is for all who remain.
We will live free and die proud.
Our home is forever Cordilleran.

Here, in their darkest hour, his troops sang joyfully of victory. Before a tear could fall down his face, axe in hand, he was moving toward the steps. "Draw your swords, lads. Come with me, now," he ordered Valin, Rendek, and Toran as he flew by them.

Suddenly, he was down and among them, pushing his way from the rear of their ranks straight up through the middle. Some removed their helmets and yet others raised their weapons in salute mixed with cheer as he passed.

On the battlements, Mya saw the Orcs were nearing firing range. She looked for Kael and found him only a few feet away from her, staring back as she expected him to be. They passed strength to each other in the joining of their eyes.

"Fear no darkness now, for we have lived in darker places than these foul beasts have ever known, and we have risen above it to the light. Let us show them true darkness as we take the light from their eyes. Fire!" Mya cried as the White Elves across the battlements fired their bows, complemented by the repeating crossbows of the towers.

Mekko made it to the front of the formation within the walls and turned to face his men, Dwarves, Elves, and Men alike. "This will not be our final hour. No, instead I believe this will be our *finest* hour. Do you believe me?" Without giving them the chance to reply, Mekko roared, "Do you believe me?!"

"YES!" they thundered back in one voice.

Mekko raised his axe and cried, "Then to war, to victory!"

He watched them cheer and raise their weapons high before turning toward the north wall. "Open the gates and may our enemies tremble before our wrath!" Mekko ran toward the open gates, leading them, with Valin, Rendek, and Toran struggling to keep up; the whole of the Alliance ground forces behind them.

The pike-wielding Dwarves spilled out of the gates, and instead of bracing for the attack, they raced with their long spears to meet it head-on. Screaming with the rage of the freeborn, they poured out of the north and west gate to meet their attackers.

"Wedge formations!" Mekko bellowed across the field, and somehow, even while running, the troops managed to form huge triangular formations designed to break into enemy charges and split them apart.

Above upon the ridges of the rock wall, King Aeldorath paused from firing to observe the Dwarven charge. He watched as they raced from the citadel to meet a force that outnumbered them at least ten to one. It was a breathtaking display of courage, which made him think of all the years the Elves wasted hidden away from such noble friends and allies as they had made here. Despite his love of nature and life, a part of him longed to lead the Elves down to the field to join the others.

"Concentrate your fire toward the rear of the enemy. Our brothers-in-arms have taken to the field. Be wary of your targets. Cut the enemy down! We fire until the last arrow be spent!" Aeldorath yelled.

Upon the field below, the two opposing forces collided. Swords clashed, Dwarves and Orcs screamed battle cries and death throes in the exchange of blood-splattering blows. Tangled bodies of man and beast lay strewn across the battlefield everywhere underfoot, hindering the movements of both armies.

Dwarven pikes impaled Orcs, driving them backward and knocking down troops behind them. The Dwarves then drew their swords and pressed on to the next rank of the enemies, and while their formations did break the Orc charge apart, many hundreds of the enemy bypassed the Dwarves and ran for the citadel walls, some carrying torches.

On the battlements, both Druids and White Elves braced for the approaching enemies. White Elf archers fired incessantly at all those who went around the pikemen. Multi-firing crossbows from the towers took down entire groups of Orcs at once as they launched projectiles without mercy.

The Orcs charged, hungry for blood, trampling over the dead and even up and over the huge sprawling corpse of the monstrous Creeg Mor like ants upon the carcass of a dead animal. There were too many for the archers and even the towers.

Kael stepped forward. Raising his hands high and extending his fingers, he let loose searing jets of flame down upon the corpse of the Creeg Mor, igniting the body in a burst of magical flames, creating a small explosion that consumed dozens of Orcs and threw many more to the ground.

On the west wall, Galin took handfuls of acorns from a basket. He hurled them up into the air and uttered, *"Tempas Tal."* The acorns ignited and one by one shot down into the Orcs faster than if they had been shot from a bow, piercing the Orc bodies like stone bullets. Through their heads, throats, and chests they tore, each killing one Orc, and many times two or three behind the first that fell.

It was not enough; the enemy numbers were too great. Still, they approached, wave after wave, undaunted. Just as it seemed the Orcs would reach the walls, a horn blew, and with it came the Dwarven infantry. Raging through the gates, shields on their backs and swords in hand, they emerged by the hundreds to meet the Orcs who had made it to the walls.

The Elves from the rock wall filled the air with enough arrows to block out what little light there was from the sky. With every flight, hundreds of Orcs fell.

Aeldorath noticed the Elf next to him slump over, an arrow in his chest. He looked down and around and could see no cause for it and then suddenly arrows were striking his Elves all over. They seemed to be coming from the foot of the rock wall, but there was nothing there but empty ground. Nearly a hundred Elves had gathered at the foot of the mountainous rock wall. Before they could take a step forward to investigate, they were cut down by arrow fire.

"Take cover, we are under attack. Get down, all of you!" Aeldorath ordered.

Many more Elves fell dead, the bewildered victims to the strange, unseen attack.

From the command platform, Ranier stood alone with the ghosts of the Archmages raging within him. He stepped forward and noticed the unnatural assault upon the Elves. Fumbling about his waist for a moment, he produced a small, amethyst crystal. He held it at eye level, cupping it with his hands. He then dropped it, but the crystal did not fall. Instead, it floated in the air before him. He placed his hands around it as if shielding it and blew on it. The crystal spun faster and faster. Dropping his hands, Ranier then inhaled and took a mighty breath and blew on the crystal in the direction of the rock wall.

The crystal flew to the area of the fields just below the rock wall near the dead Elves at its base. In a flash of light, the crystal burst in mid-air, raining purple powder over a large area. Within moments, it revealed the cause of the strange attack as several creatures seemed to materialize at the foot of the rock wall. They were the reptile-like Chalderons, four-legged creatures with fiery red skin and tails. Sitting upon them were hundreds of Orc archers.

"My lord, our attackers have been revealed!" Layla screamed out.

Aeldorath looked out over the rocks, quickly drawing an arrow. "Drive these foul beasts back to the pits that spawned them!"

As the Orcs started taking fire, they dismounted and screamed in a foul tongue at the beasts that bore them. With that, the Chalderons started climbing the rock wall. The Orcs knelt, holding their positions, and continued firing up at the Elves.

Despite their thick bodies, the Chalderons made excellent climbers due to their muscular legs. Upon reaching the Elven archers, they attacked with their forked tongues, whipping their tongues out several feet and knocking the bows from the hands of the Elves. Their bodies took arrow fire with little consequence.

Layla fired between the eyes of a Chalderon and watched with relief as the creature immediately keeled over and tumbled down the rock face, taking some others down with it.

"Aim for the area between their eyes on the forehead!" she yelled to her troops. "One shot can kill them!"

Upon the fields, the fighting was furious. Mekko wielded his double-bladed battle-axe in an array of powerful spinning moves, cleaving Orc flesh and limbs as he went; his chain mail bathed in the blood of those he had killed. Valin, Rendek, and Toran formed a semicircle around him, attacking the Orcs with equal rage but never straying from Mekko's side.

Blood sprayed through the air, both red and black—death did not distinguish. A layer of mud had formed in the midst of the fighting and began to melt from the heat of death and bodies massed together. The frozen ground had no choice but to yield. With each death, be it Dwarf or Orc, mud splattered up on the living while blood splashed down upon the dying.

The Dwarves rallied around Mekko, spurred on by each blow his axe struck. They fought with a rage rivaling the Orcs' bloodlust. Standing their ground against overwhelming numbers, they fought the creatures to a standstill on the field.

The Dwarven infantry defended the walls in an unbroken line, supported from above by missile fire and magic, allowing none to get past they barred the way as Orc dead piled at their feet.

With the Elves no longer firing into the Orcs, their onslaught continued unchecked. Their last lines could finally be seen far in the distance but closing in fast. The whole of their strength would soon bypass the pikemen fighting in the middle of the field and bear down upon the citadel.

Ranier now looked far across the field as a new enemy force formed before the stone pyramid. They were huge creatures, larger than the

Morrangs, pulling some sort of devices behind them. He noticed that a group of much smaller creatures led them. Small, hooded creatures, barely four feet tall, guided them on long chains that connected to leather muzzles on the larger creatures. They were giants, fifteen feet tall; some were larger. While they walked on two legs, they moved slowly.

It took a moment for him to notice, but then Ranier saw their legs were secured by massive shackles. It was then he knew what the beasts were. The giants were an old race of creatures said to dwell beneath the Morval Mountains known as the Morgrave Orgatu, mindless beasts as dumb as they were excitable. However, they were incredibly dangerous, capable of eating anything in sight, including their masters. Strangely enough, it was the smaller creatures who controlled them, the Paudellos. The sniveling, wretched little creatures used steel-tipped whips to herd the giants along. They considered the Morgraves as slaves or pets, at best. Communication occurred through a telepathic link from one species to the other; however, the muzzles soon became a necessity. The Paudellos found that if they lost concentration for a moment, the giants would grab them and eat them. They dominated through pain and fear.

The perfect allies for the enemy, Ranier thought bleakly.

He looked closer and saw they were dragging catapults. It was the well planned and calculated attack he would have expected from Abadon. They were not the immediate problem at hand, however, as he looked down and saw the vast numbers of approaching Orcs. Still, they had fighting forces of their own to reveal as his gaze looked down toward the northern gates.

Again, the main gates of the citadel opened, this time releasing a force of only twenty. Elenari was among them. It was the Kenshari Masters. They were Elves, strangely dressed, and most wore leather armor padding and vestment. Metal armor would only slow them down. They were led by High Master Quentil Reyblade, an ancient wiry Elf by all appearances, his face was strangely wrinkled for a sylvan creature. He was clad in no armor whatsoever, merely a brown robe of simple fabric. He appeared to carry one weapon, a long sword with a thick blade and hilt gleaming gold on one side of the blade and silver on the other.

Though sword masters all, the others had fashioned and designed their own weaponry to complement the sword-fighting techniques they had developed over centuries of combat. Master Quenya, a tall, lean Elf clad in a green hooded cloak over brown leather armor wielded a long staff with curved blades on each end. Master Sylaire, an Elf of smaller stature, wielded two short, jagged blades; it was a strange-looking short sword he favored, known as a Kris.

Elenari wore dark leather armor over the brown and green forest clothes of a ranger. This was the fight she had waited her entire life for. She walked calmly at Reyblade's side. She carried her curved silver short sword, *Eros-Arthas*. Like all the weapons of the Kenshari, it had been forged by the anonymous ancient Kenshari blacksmith, who had found a way to make weapons that were virtually invincible and could cut through stone and steel alike. Legend said that only High Master Reyblade knew who and where the blacksmith was.

The Kenshari Masters walked in front of the Dwarven Infantry, making a line, and preparing to receive the charging onslaught of Orcs. The Dwarves looked at them incredulously—a small group of Elves with no heavy armor led by an old man in a cloak.

Reyblade grabbed the hilt of his weapon with both hands and brought it up to his forehead as if saluting the approaching enemy. He could see the charging Orcs laughing at them as they raised their weapons for the kill. Suddenly, in a flash of movement, he was holding two weapons, a golden long sword and a silver short sword, *Hunir* and *Munir*. He moved in slow motion as he sliced through the first three Orcs, or they moved in slow motion; it was difficult for an onlooker to discern which. Reyblade's moves were subtle, balanced, and perfect. He parried and struck faster than Dwarven eyes could follow.

Elenari joined the battle with relish, her blade cutting through Orc armor and flesh with equal ease. Master Quenya spun his bladed staff above his head, tearing through the throats of a group of unwary Orcs who had surrounded him. The other masters spread out into the charging enemy, killing multiple targets with spectacular attack sequences.

The Kenshari killed them as fast as they came, spreading into the sea of enemies like a wildfire blazing out of control. Rousing cheers came from the Dwarven infantry and from the Elves above on the battlements. Still, there were so many Orcs that large groups managed to circumvent the Kenshari and headed toward the walls.

With a crunching impact of metal on metal, the Orcs slammed into the Dwarven defenders. Through sheer amassing numbers, they pushed them back and were suddenly flooding through the gaping hole the Creeg Mor had made. The Orcs flooded through the wall like roaches, some with torches, looking for anything to light aflame while the rest ran ahead, looking for anything to kill. Quickly they homed in on the man in the shinning silver plate mail who seemed to be alone in their path. As he started turning toward him, they heard him shout, "Rank one, fire!"

Suddenly dozens of Dwarves and Elves popped up out of a long trench in the ground with crossbows and bows and fired into the nearest Orcs.

"Rank two, fire!" Again, at Lark's command several figures popped up from the second trench and fired into the Orcs, who fell forward, tripping the ones behind them.

"Rank three, fire!"

As the third rank fired, nearly all the Orcs who had penetrated the walls had fallen dead. Still, those Orcs who hadn't fallen continued wreaking havoc, throwing torches into wagons and tents near the inside of the main walls. Others ran for the stairs leading to the battlements, where the White Elves were. But Archangel was there on horseback, and removing the knives from his wrist gauntlets, he took aim and struck one Orc in the throat and a second in the back. They fell back into the others, clearing the steps and collapsing in a heap. Some of the White Elves turned to fire into the fallen Orcs.

Then, without warning, four Orcs surrounded Archangel and his horse. He pulled back on the reins for his horse to kick them away, but they held the animal down by the bridle and pulled Archangel to the ground. As he fell, he rolled onto his back and launched himself away, but those four Orcs plus six more rushed at him. And that's when he heard the battle cry, "Osprey Falls!"

Lark charged full gallop and smashed into the Orcs with his horse, knocking them apart. In moments, he was off his saddle and cutting through the Orcs with great sweeping strokes of his huge sword. Again on his feet, Archangel joined his brother, swinging savagely, fighting back the beasts of Bazadoom. A dozen more Orcs charged, and soon the brothers were surrounded. Arrows and bolts continued flying, but no one wanted to chance striking an ally.

The Kenshari Masters attacked with such speed and ferocity, it seemed to the Orcs as if they were invulnerable. Their skill was such that no enemy weapon touched them, though many had thick black Orc blood on their clothes and armor.

Elenari was in perfect sync with her weapon and body. Every parry became a strike, every strike of her blade formed the next parry. She took their limbs as if they were hers alone for the taking and moved on to strike the next enemy before heads and arms hit the ground. From the corner of her eye, she caught Reyblade, who seemed more like he was dancing than fighting. Every stroke from either of his two swords dealt a death blow. Bodies piled around them to such a degree that they found themselves standing on the dead to battle the living.

Captain Gaston led what was left of the cavalry of Averon to the hole in the walls where the Orcs rushed in. He rallied them as they charged the enemy from the rear of the camp. "Remember Fort Renault, my brothers, may those who died live again now through us!" He cried as his men drew their swords and charged the walls.

Archangel, bloodied and injured, faced two Orcs with a sword in each hand. They were slashing at him with all their hate and might. The young ranger managed to block each swing from the beasts. To his left, he could see Lark, his once-gleaming plate mail armor splattered in blood and his shoulder plates hanging on by a thread. Lark was swinging his two-handed sword with such fury he had just killed two Orcs with a single blow.

Quickly Archangel ducked, dodging an attack from one Orc and thrust one of his swords deep into the stomach of the other. The wounded Orc fell back, taking the blade with it. The other Orc was hastening its swings, pressing its attack. Archangel's remaining sword vibrated with each hit as he was being driven further back by the strength of the blows. All around him, men and beasts struggled for control, allies falling as quickly as Orcs.

"Live free and never surrender!" Archangel heard Lark cry out as he rallied some of the artillery crews to his side. Again, he could see his brother behind the attacking Orc, swinging his sword in a wide arc, splitting an Orc nearly in half.

Now Archangel found himself face to face with the beast, its disgusting breath forced heavily upon him as they struggled to disarm each other.

"Iiss will eat you alives humon," hissed the Orc from his rotting pig-like snout.

Turning his head in disgust, the ranger pushed the beast away with his right leg and forced them apart. However, the thrust made Archangel stumble and trip over a broken, burning wagon. He dropped his remaining sword in the middle of the burning wreckage. Unable to reach in the fire, the Orc took advantage of the situation and charged him.

Archangel fell to the ground and scurried backward as he watched the beast raise the sword, ready to strike the killing blow. Instinctively, he reached into his boots with both hands and drew his daggers and launched them together in a quick throw, burying them in the Orc's forehead. The beast stood momentarily over Archangel with its blade poised over its head as blood rushed down its face. Archangel waited. Finally, the Orc came forward two steps, then turned and fell onto its back.

Mud covered Archangel's body and face. He pushed himself up and walked to the fallen body. Stepping on the Orc's face, he pulled the daggers from its forehead and replaced them in his boots. He then took the sword from the creature's hand and ran toward Lark, who was mid-battle with three angry Orcs.

Mekko sent Valin to lead the other pike brigade. Between them, they had managed to drive a large wedge between the attacking forces, but still too many were able to go around the fighting and make a charge on the citadel.

Mekko roared at the top of his lungs, "Line formation, two ranks, one behind the other! Spread out as wide as possible! Hold the line at all costs! Fight for Cordilleran, fight for all our lives!"

Somehow, during the chaos, the two divisions were able to form two lines, with the second line supporting any breaches of the first. Amazingly, they held the charge back to such a degree that hundreds of Orcs got held up in the middle of the field, bunched up before the Dwarven pikemen who were now all fighting with swords.

This was the event Ranier had been waiting for, hoping against hope that Mekko could pull it off. He should have known better than to doubt, he thought with a thin smile. Taking the emerald-green flag, he waved it high back and forth from atop the command platform.

Strange horns attempted to penetrate the sounds of metal clashing and the screams of those dying. Some Orcs bunched up behind their brethren and heard them coming from behind from the far edges of the fields back into the trees.

It was then the Orcs saw them, charging the field from the enemy's flank was the Emerald Watch of the Elves. Half their force had been put on the rock wall adjacent to the citadel; the other half, Mekko sent out to lie in wait for a chance to charge the enemy's flank. Their emerald-green robes flying in the wind, they charged with long, curved swords.

Orcs were now on the battlements of the north and west walls, fighting the White Elves. On the north wall, they rallied around Mya as they fought them back, many times knocking them clear off the walls.

Unexpectedly, a great inhuman roar sounded and, standing on two feet, an enormous brown bear stood, swatting the cringing Orcs off the wall like flies with its great claws—It was Kael.

Galin leapt off the west wall toward the battlefield as if he were diving into a pool of water. In a flash of green fire just before he struck the ground, his body changed. He became larger and longer until he landed on all fours in the form a long and lean striped tiger. Racing a few steps, he leapt, claws extended into a band of attacking Orcs, tearing into them.

The Elves of the Emerald Watch, nearly five thousand strong, met the flank of the Orc army who turned to meet them, now held between a gauntlet of Dwarves and Elves. The Orcs still outnumbered both forces and fought savagely, selling their lives dearly. Back to back, locked in tight formation, the beasts' rage fueled them; driven by fear and hate, they fought until their last breath.

Mekko rallied them all on against overwhelming numbers. Each time the lines broke, it seemed as though he was somehow there, Rendek and Toran, at his side urging them not to falter. Through sheer force of his will, they managed to hold the enemy at bay.

Valin, the oldest Dwarf upon the field, felt the strength of his sword arm return, such as it was in his younger days. He knew in his mind the spirit of King Crylar was with him and throwing caution into the wind, allowed the rage of righteousness to drive him as he slapped enemy weapons away with his gloved hand and dealt killing thrusts and slashes with his other.

The Morgraves began loading huge balls of flaming pitch into the firing line of black catapults, preparing to fire into the heart of the fighting, no matter they would hit their own troops. They aimed toward where the Dwarves and Elves had pinned the Orcs between them.

Meanwhile, the last Orc within the walls had been killed. A cheer arose from all the defenders as Lark raised his blood-stained sword. He ran beside Archangel, and they took the steps to the battlements to stand with Mya, Kael, and the White Elves. From there, brief moments of joy turned to horror as they saw what the Morgraves had planned.

"They would slaughter their own forces?" Archangel asked in disbelief.

"I have been within the Shadow Prince's council. He would kill a hundred of his own if it meant killing one of ours," Mya spat out disdainfully.

From the command platform, Ranier quickly yelled down into the camp. "Crichton! Crichton! The Morgraves are going to fire catapults at our men; they must be warned!"

Crichton reared back on Stryker. "Horseman of Mystaria and Averon, ride with me now to the armory. Every man grab a lance as fast as you can."

Every man still able to ride quickly followed Crichton as they rode toward the large tent on the east part of the camp. As they approached, Crichton saw a small circle of Elven and Dwarven smiths gathered and cried out to them. "We ride to save your fellows! Pass a lance up to each rider as he passes and pray we are not too late!"

The Dwarven blacksmiths quickly heeded his commands by passing long, black lances up to the riders as they galloped past.

Crichton led them to the far east side of the battlefield along the base of the rock wall where King Aeldorath's Elves were still fighting the Orc archers and Chalderons. The middle of the field was saturated with dead bodies making it impossible to ride through. Even as Crichton led them on the field, he knew they were too late.

He saw great balls of flame soaring through the air, landing within the heart of the fighting. Screams filled the air as Elves, Orcs, and Dwarves alike were set aflame by a bombardment from nearly two dozen catapults.

The moment Mekko saw what was happening, he quickly called for all the Alliance troops to fall back to the citadel, disgusted that they would fire into their own troops but expecting nothing less. He saw that it was the Elves of the Emerald Watch who were taking the brunt of the attack. Swinging his axe with everything he had, he hacked away at the Orcs, trying to get to them, to help them, somehow. There were far too many Orcs between them.

Suddenly, General Valin was at his shoulder. "Mekko we must fall back, there is nothing more we can do." Valin grabbed him by the arm and shook him for a moment. "We must fall back now," he said softly. Nothing but the reluctant truth showed in the old Dwarf's eyes, even as they heard the screams of the Elves as another round of flaming pitch struck.

Mekko took one last look at their Elven allies, their saviors, as he gave the order to fall back. As he pulled the men of the pike division back, he saw Crichton atop his white stallion, leading a lancer charge toward the giant beasts. His heart rejoiced as he and his men struck the Orcs, blocking their path back to the citadel with renewed strength. Before long, they had killed every Orc between them and the Kenshari Masters, who had themselves killed countless Orcs, even causing some to flee from their battle prowess. Both Dwarf and Elf turned to watch a cavalry of men race to save their allies.

As Crichton raced ahead of the rest, he transferred his lance to his right hand and raised his left hand high with an open palm toward the center of the field. There was a blue glow visible from his gloved palm, just as another wave of flaming balls was launched. Just as the projectiles became airborne, their flames were smothered in ice. As they fell and struck the battling forces, they splintered into many fragments, harming no one. Cheers rose up from the Alliance forces both on the field and from the citadel.

"Ride now, ride forth and skewer these beasts!" Crichton yelled to the horsemen as he led them right at the great lumbering beasts. Holding his lance tight against his body, he targeted the nearest Morgrave, nearly fifteen feet high, and he ducked as it attempted to swat him with a lethargic swing of its arm and buried his lance within its upper chest.

The beast wailed loudly but still lived, clinging on the lance that impaled him, trying to pull it free from its body. Crichton turned and watched as the other riders met with little success. Some were unfortunate enough to be struck by the giants, sending the riders far through the air, landing dead upon the unforgiving ground. He found himself looking at the smaller creatures that held them under sway by long chains. Turning Stryker about, he grabbed his black crossbow from his saddle bag and took careful aim at the Paudello that held the Morgrave he had attacked with the lance. He struck the sniveling creature between the eyes with a bolt. The instant it fell dead, the Morgrave attached to it went mad. It pulled its chains apart and even demolished the catapult it was chained to. Tearing its leather muzzle off, it quickly picked up its former master and bit the small creature's head off. As terribly wounded as it was, it seemed desperate to eat the creature it had been slave to.

"Kill the little hooded creatures! Ride them down if you must—they are the key!" He yelled to the others, who were already following his example, using the lances to impale the Paudellos or trampling them under their hooves.

The moment they killed the smaller creatures, the Morgraves attacked one another, completely losing any ability to think or act. Wild and out of control, they fed off the corpses of their former masters.

Without sign or warning, enemy horns began blowing from beyond the stone pyramid and, as if awakening from a bad dream, the enemy who still greatly outnumbered them began to fall back and retreat.

Mekko hesitated as he watched the enemy's retreating forces. He then raised his battle-axe and screamed, "Victory!"

All the Alliance forces from the Elves in the rocks to the forces behind the walls and those upon the field joined in the celebrating hails of victory. All, save Ranier.

The Shadow Prince slowly rose from his golden throne. Red Fang had sounded the retreat as he had been ordered to only moments ago. He looked to the Shadow Prince and waited, unsure why he had ordered a retreat. It was then he heard the icy whispers through the metal mesh of his helmet.

"The time has come. The Grand Master Abadon is prepared to join us, his loyal subjects," the Shadow Prince hissed.

Red Fang fell to his knees, his forehead pressed to the stone.

The sky darkened, though the battle raged throughout the day and into the afternoon, it was not so late to lose so much light. The air became colder despite the strange lack of wind.

The cheers of the Alliance died down as everyone became painfully aware there was something dark stirring in the air on the verge of revealing itself.

Ranier felt the change in temperature but that was not all. Something was terribly amiss within the walls. There was a strong presence of evil very close. He looked all around, unsure what it was he would see, yet he knew something was very wrong, something he had not expected. It was then as he looked down below him that he saw the smiling face of Lark Royale. However, the smile was not Lark's. His eyes were glazed over, filled with a gray haze. In his hand, he held the Emerald Star.

Before anyone could react, Ranier watched the smile on the Paladin's face turn to an expression of hate-filled rage. He turned and pointed toward the rock wall adjacent to the citadel. and with malice burning in his dead words he screamed, *"Death to them, by the power of the Emerald Star."*

After he uttered the last word, lightning crackled in the skies directly overhead. Black clouds raced in from the north, obscuring nearly all light. Blight seemed to color the land a dull gray as the very ground became tainted with evil and a touch of death. A torrent of rain was released upon them, pouring through the thunderclaps and wind, which suddenly raged with the fury of a blizzard.

The Emerald Star glowed green for a split second and then took on a black hue until a thick bolt of black energy exploded forth from it with an inhuman roar trailing only moments behind the light like thunder. The energy struck the rock wall with such force, there was an explosion, bringing nearly everyone within the citadel and on the battlefield to the ground.

As Mekko lifted his head from the mud and looked up through wind and rain, to his disbelief and horror, the mountainous wall of rocks that held thousands of Elves along with King Aeldorath was no longer there. It had been totally blown apart into thousands of stone fragments, cascading through the air, carried by wind and rain in all four directions. All near and within the citadel looked on in sheer amazement, paralyzed by shock and fear.

The Elves fell to their knees, tears streaming down their faces, unable to comprehend the slaughter that had just occurred, harried by a loss they could not entirely comprehend. Mya held her stomach, feeling as though she would vomit. Her men had to hold her to keep her from falling with grief.

Ranier sank to his knees, the rain assaulting him, blowing his beard and hair across his face. He held on to his staff with all his strength. Sinking his head between hunched shoulders, he wept to himself words no other could hear. "I am a fool. The evil was among us always, and I did not see. Forgive me, forgive me." Through his tears, his head snapped up, and he saw a figure aloft in the air above where the rock wall had been only moments before. It was a figure all in white. It seemed to be floating upon the very currents of the air. Hunched together, it straightened itself into the form of a man, looking at its limbs as if to account for them all.

Archangel watched in disbelief as Lark suddenly became himself again, the gray haze had left his eyes, and he seemed in control of his actions. He watched Lark drop to his knees, tears streaming down his face.

Kael was forced to turn back to his human form feeling suddenly weak, unable to summon his magic. Standing on the battlements, he looked down at Lark, unsure how to feel. They exchanged glances, and Kael felt his pain. It was both sincere and immense. So impassioned was the loss and utter tragedy, the life seemed to have drained away from him, leaving only remorse and despair. It was as if Lark had become as dark and barren as the land around them. Lark then took his great two-handed sword and placed the tip beneath his throat and closed his eyes.

"NO!" Archangel screamed, knowing he had only seconds as he ran and dove at Lark, spilling into him and knocking him to the ground while batting his sword away. Archangel held him as he wept uncontrollably in his arms.

Ranier watched through the rains as the figure in white straightened himself and seemed to be looking at him, waiting. "Abadon, it is time at last," Ranier said in a voice that echoed many.

Chapter 19

Ranier flew through the air, standing upon twisting wind currents that propelled him through the rain. He landed on the battlefield next to Mekko.

"Now you must listen, General. You have done more than any would have thought possible, but if you stay, you and all who fight with you will die in vain. You must withdraw your forces *now*, this instant. Other armies' approach and will arrive by daybreak. *Now is* our *time to fight.*"

Mekko heard the many voices melded together in Ranier's words.

"We are to just leave you at the hands of this demon?" Mekko asked above the thunder, pointing at the figure in white that floated high above them in the sky.

"*All of you are with us, and we are with you. Go now, General. There is nothing more you can do to help us. Farewell,*" Ranier said as the winds suddenly twisted beneath his feet and made him appear to fly skyward.

"Valin, take half the pike division, half the infantry, whatever is left of the cavalry of Averon, and the Kenshari; make for the pass in the Eastern Peaks. Take all the wounded with you who can travel and whatever Elves that are left and our reserves. Leave me the other half of pikemen and infantry, and Crichton and his men.

"General, you heard what Ranier said. There is no point to staying, you'll die." Valin grabbed his arm as he spoke.

"I've no intention of dying, old friend. Look on the field—there are thousands of our men wounded. I will stay the night with them, and we will heal however many we can. We will be gone by morning. Now go and do as I command," Mekko said.

Valin shook his head, and as he turned, Mekko placed his hand on his shoulder and turned him around to face him. "You fought better than twenty Stygian Knights today, you old warhorse," he said with a grim smile.

Valin saluted, holding his right fist over his heart, and then held Mekko in a firm embrace. "Good luck, my friend."

In the skies above, amid the lightning and rain, the two ancient adversaries—good and evil—faced each other like titans. Neither had looked upon the other in ages: Ranier, clothed in dark robes and holding his wooden staff with a gnarly tip, looked much as he had when Abadon had last seen him. His stringy hair and beard were matted to his face from the wind-driven rain. Abadon wore a simple white robe that accentuated the crimson hue of his skin. Coarse black hair fell around his head and shoulders and along his cheeks in thick sideburns. The hair also covered the backs of his hands and tops of his feet. His unusually long fingers and toes ended in sharp claws. His eyes were pools of burning red evil, and his sinister smile reflected ivory-white teeth with pointed incisors. Hi coarse skin appeared smooth in the darkness.

An unnatural guttural laugh resonated within him. His voice was had an amplified, otherworldly quality to it. Even through the storm's fury, it seemed to strike many eerie tones. *"Is that you, brother? How did you ever manage to live so long—not that I am disappointed, mind you, no. I relish the fact that you have the honor to die at my hand. Yours is a death that I longed for during my imprisonment."*

Ranier responded in many voices, "We are all here, Abadon, just as we were when we first sent you foolishly into the device, unaware of your true nature and consumed by an arrogant thirst for forbidden knowledge. Today is our day of reckoning."

Abadon squinted as a strange expression overcame his face for a moment but ultimately culminated in a wide smile and then a deep laugh from an empty well in his chest. *"So that is how you have survived. All of our brethren dwell within you. I could not in my deepest longings have wished for anything better."* Abadon looked down upon the battlefield and watched as the Alliance forces retreated. *"I see your choice of pawns to use against me* suffers. Your warriors have grown weak through the centuries, pale shadows of the great battle lords who vanquished my kindred so long ago."

"You see through tainted eyes, demon, and that which matters most evades your vision. Their strength and courage are a testament to all life through the ages," Ranier responded.

Abadon looked at him, his smile slow and mocking. "I make you the same offer I made you when last we were together. Kneel before me now. Take my hand and vow your undying loyalty to me, and I shall allow you the privilege of watching your precious world die before I grant you the end you will beg me for. Fear not, I will keep enough alive to worship and adore me. They will live and die for my every whim and pleasure. Their every breath will be in my service, and they will endure pain everlasting for me, fighting one another for the privilege to suffer for my amusement. That will be my testament to life in the ages to come."

Ranier met his smile and suddenly his free hand shot forth from his robes and his fingers extended, white fire exploding from them, striking Abadon in the chest and enveloping his form, burning his flesh. The demon cried out in pain from the suddenness of the attack.

Without hesitating, Ranier flew on the air with the speed of the winds at Abadon and, with a two-handed stroke, smashed the demon's face with the end of his staff with such a blow it sounded as if in tune with the thunder. The force sent Abadon flying down through the air, smashing into trees, and breaking their brittle limbs.

Ranier watched through the storm as the Shadow Prince reached for his black staff. Spinning quickly, the Archmage extended his staff, and from its head, white fire burst forth and like a missile, struck the Shadow Prince near his golden throne, impacting like a fireball. The explosion knocked the staff away, and the fire formed a cage around the dark lord, driving him to his knees and trapping him.

Ranier smiled as he watched the Orc general cringe in fear. "You will keep your place, lackey. I will tolerate no more interference from you."

Abadon slowly levitated up toward Ranier, brushing himself off. "Powerful you have become, my brothers. Still, as hot and holy as your fire burns, you cannot stop me. Thanks to all of you, I am eternal in this place."

Again, Ranier struck. He threw a small orange ball that expanded and grew, exploding in a mass of fire as it struck Abadon. But the demon held his place this time, clawing through the flames, dispelling them with his very anger. Now, Ranier raised his arms, bringing his hands together along the shaft of his staff and caught a bolt of lightning from the dark heavens. His form shook as the staff glowed white and blue, and he swung it downward. The bolt erupted from it, striking Abadon with such concussive force that it sent the demon hurtling through the air and into the stone pyramid like a stone. His body slammed halfway up the pyramid and collapsed in a heap on the ground.

The Orcs around the pyramid ran away in fear, and in the next instant, Ranier landed on the ground with the struggling body of Abadon at his feet. With his free hand, he covered the demon in white fire, causing his body to writhe and contort from pain. Again and again, he struck with white fire, causing Abadon to cry out louder and louder.

Ranier then grabbed his staff with both hands and struck the demon with overhead, drilling blows to his body, cracking against his ribs and back. Screaming in fury, he struck blows that would break a mortal body into a heap of ruined bones, over and over. Though Abadon cried out in pain, he continued scrambling on the ground until he was able to spring up and catch Ranier's staff in mid-air with both hands. He rose, and suddenly they faced each other, struggling fiercely for the upper hand.

Ranier could see the hatred and fury in Abadon's lifeless, red eyes and smell death on his fiery breath. "What's wrong, demon, you're not smiling or laughing. Are you no longer amused? I hope I didn't hurt you too badly," Ranier asked with a crooked smile.

To Rainer's surprise, Abadon turned the staff to the side and, with a show of strength, tossed Ranier like a sack nearly fifty feet, smashing him into the base of a tree. The old mage struck with amazing force and cried out. He was conscious but had difficulty getting to his feet.

Abadon walked toward him, lifting his arms out to the sides of his body. The demon curled his fingers, and black flames appeared within his hands, suddenly taking shape and expanding in thin lines until he was holding two long whips of dark flames. "*Hurt, did you say? I come from a place where pain and torment are concepts your feeble brain could never comprehend, but perhaps I can relate it to you in ways you can.*" With that he snapped both whips, striking Ranier and tearing through his clothing and flesh, causing a scream of unapparelled pain.

From the battlements Mekko and Crichton watched the battle as their forces retreated and they gathered the wounded.

"We must help him!" Mekko said, turning toward the stairs, only to be stopped by Crichton.

"We risk all the lives here if we do!" the prince yelled.

"Will you watch him die and do nothing?" Mekko demanded.

Crichton hesitated, and then said, "Come with me, General."

The two ran down the stairs toward the main gates. Crichton put his fingers to his mouth and released a queer lingering whistle. As if from nowhere, Stryker appeared behind them. Crichton mounted him and pulled Mekko aboard, and in a moment, they were off through the gates.

They didn't get more than a few feet before a huge wall of flames arose on the field before them so close it caused Stryker to rear back, throwing both riders to the ground. The flames moved toward them. In an instant, Crichton pulled Mekko back on the horse, and they just beat the flames through the main gates where the flames stopped.

"It appears we cannot help him after all," Crichton said.

"*Those fools care for you, but you are more like me than you could imagine. You would sacrifice them all to stop me, wouldn't you? Wouldn't you?!*" Abadon whipped him across his face and chest, leaving welts of blood.

Ranier came to his knees, and Abadon snapped one of the fiery whips around his throat, dragging him through the dirt to where he stood. Ranier wailed as the flames burned his throat. He was helpless, on his knees, looking up at Abadon's twisted smile. "*You fool. I have manipulated you from the start to this moment I foresaw. You, on your knees before me, as you deserve to be. Do you have any final words of bravado, my slave, before I end your pathetic existence?*" With the one whip of flame still coiled about Ranier's throat, the other whip fashioned itself into a long dagger of black flame, poised above the old mage for the kill.

"Abadon . . . is there nothing of the good man we once knew, within, to fight this demon that has possessed your soul?" Ranier gasped as he secretly tightened his grip around his staff in the dirt.

A sinister laugh escaped from the demon. "*Fools, I welcomed the ecstasy and power of evil with open arms!*" Abadon closed his eyes in a moment of bliss.

It was then Ranier struck. In a cry of rage, he drove his staff into Abadon's side just above his waist, piercing his body and coming out through his back. Abadon's eyes burst wide and his jaw dropped. His weapons of flame dissolved as he staggered back.

Ranier rose, grabbed the staff, and looked Abadon in the eyes as he forced it further into the demon's body. "Can your mind comprehend *this* pain?"

The demon roared in agony.

Then, holding the staff, Ranier generated white fire along the length of the it, causing Abadon to howl as the fire singed the inside of his body.

Despite his great pain, Abadon locked eyes with Ranier. "*I smell something familiar within you, old fool.*" He reached his clawed hand out and grabbed Ranier by the wrist. Lines of dark magic entered Ranier's arm like parasites. Suddenly, Ranier released his grip on the staff and convulsed, bending over and holding his stomach.

Abadon pulled the staff forward out of his body, crying out once he was free of it. He snapped the staff over his knee, creating a discharge of energy that knocked him to the ground. Abadon was on his back, barely moving, but he motioned with a clawed finger.

Suddenly hordes of Orcs could be heard in the rain, approaching their location, wailing their battle cries through the thunder.

Ranier fell to his knees. He recognized the pain instantly—it was the demon poison from the Ravager. Abadon had reactivated it from its state of dormancy. He was sweating and weakening. Still, he managed the strength to raise his hands and launch white fire into the Orcs, singing their bodies and burning them to death on contact. The others hesitated out of fear, but more were coming.

Then Mekko was there. The Dwarf tossed Ranier over his back and threw him up on Stryker's back. Crichton reached down and pulled the Dwarf up in front of him, holding Ranier's inert form behind him.

"On, Stryker, let no mere storm impair your swiftness!" Crichton yelled and they were off toward the citadel.

"Fool"—Abadon laughed and coughed—"*All you managed to do with all your toil is make your death long and extremely painful. I could not be more satisfied.*" His laugh came from some deep, dark place where the concept of joy was a rich perversion.

The Orcs backed away, kneeling and scraping on the ground as Abadon limped toward the pyramid of stone, holding his side.

Night descended swiftly. The thunder and lightning had faded, but the rain was steady. A dank smell of decay pervaded everything. It became so routine none seemed to notice it any longer. They had gathered all the wounded still breathing within the walls and lined them up outside the infirmary. Thousands lay on the ground waiting.

The other Druids took time away from their critical work on the potion that would restore life to the land to lend what aid they could. Kael and Mya were loosely in charge. They had long since exhausted the last of their healing potions. Since Abadon's arrival, the Druids had lost even their healing magic; the negative life force exuding from the demon lord had rendered them impotent. Thousands lay shivering and moaning, huddled under soaking blankets, wondering if they might get tended to before death called for them in the night's blackness.

As Stryker raced in through north gate, Kael and Mya rushed to him, ready to treat Ranier's wounds and provide water.

Mekko lowered him from the mighty steed, and Ranier fell to the ground at first, trying to stand on his own strength.

"Ranier!" Mya cried. She dug into her pouches and pulled out a handful of herbs, which she quickly doused in water to make a healing paste for Ranier's deep facial wounds.

"Steady, Priestess," Ranier assured her in a calm voice. "We are fine." Ranier pulled himself to his feet. Black smoke billowed from the back of his singed robe as he leaned upon Mya. The battle with Abadon had been furious and draining. And while he was a tattered mess, his face showed little sign of fatigue or, in fact, any emotion.

Kael was amazed to see Ranier in such good form after such an intense battle.

"By Delgados's beard!" Mekko yelled, looking around as if waiting for the enemy to burst through the gates. "Ranier, yer lucky to have gotten outta that battle with the scratches you did and still in one piece."

"*In point of fact, General, we were not lucky,*" Ranier said in the voices of many. "We have prepared for this battle since before your race was born. Although Abadon is weak at the moment, having only just escaped the confines of the Emerald Star, his powers are vast. Soon his full strength will be restored and then nothing, I fear, will be able to stop him. I was foolish to think that perhaps we could defeat this evil. It was the same foolish arrogance that allowed the demon to enter our world initially."

Neither Kael nor the others knew how to respond to such a dire statement. Kael chose to follow up with more bad news. "My druid powers are gone. I no longer can commune with Mother Nature, nor can the others."

"Of course, Grand Druid," Ranier said matter-of-factly. "Once the Paladin unwittingly released Abadon, Mother Nature as you know her ceased to exist. He draws his strength from the living; he feeds off of it, leaving death behind. In time, all life will fall to the darkness of death. Existence will no longer be a gift but a curse."

"Ranier, what are you telling us?" Mya whispered. "Are you saying it's over?"

Ranier raked his gaze over the hundreds of dying or severely injured men. Then his eyes focused, as if searching for something.

Kael stood in front of him. "What do you search for?"

Ranier did not answer; he seemed to be staring through him. Then, the Archmage sidestepped Kael and strode purposefully toward the center of the encampment, despite the limp and the pain that flooded his body. It was then that the angry voices of Elves could be heard in the distance. Ranier and the others moved toward the commotion.

Another evil had begun to manifest outside of Lark Royale's tent, where several hundred Elves had gathered, demanding justice for their fallen kin. Shouts and taunts called for Lark's death.

Wearing a scowl, Archangel emerged from the tent. "My brother is chained to a post within at his own request. This is his sword," Archangel said as he drew a great two-handed sword with a frost white diamond etched in the hilt. "Any of you who wish to harm him will get to know this blade faster than you wish."

"You make a brave noise," a tall Elf officer said. "Brother or no, it was not *your* king he murdered. It was not thousands of your brothers. He released a monstrosity that will be the doom of us all. No, human, he will be judged by the Elves for his crimes. Stand aside lest you cast your fate with his." The officer drew his sword, and others reached for their weapons.

Before Archangel could react, several Elves came alongside him, men of Lark's artillery division. One held his hands high. "Brothers, stop this madness! I saw how Lark Royale led and fought the enemy, and I will *not* believe any such man knowingly caused the death of our people."

But there were too few supporters, and as the angry Elves closed in on the tent, Stryker came barreling in between the two sides. A moment later, Dwarven soldiers arrived. Crichton and Mekko dismounted and stood before the furious Elves, who now lowered their weapons but did not give ground. Rendek and Toran quickly appeared at Mekko's side with their swords drawn.

"Alas, have we finally to come to this, lads? After all that happened, after all we have bled and fought for, is this what we have become?" Mekko asked with melancholy.

"*You* are not our lord or king. Do not presume to tell us how we should feel!" came a taunt from within the riot.

Mekko sighed heavily. "Aye, I'm not your king. But can one of you, just one, tell me what you think your king would have said at this moment? What a proud moment this must be for him lookin' down on us now, eh? In fact, I think if he were here, he'd say 'Let's burn the human at the stake' or better yet, 'Let's give him to his Demon Lord.' No, this was not King Aeldorath's way, and you all know it well." Mekko's admonishing tone increased as he looked at the Elves, many of whom looked down in shame.

"Listen, lad, I understand what yer feelin'. I lost more of my countrymen in the last few months than I care to think—"

"You lost them to the enemy, Dwarf," the Elven officer said, cutting him off. "We lost ours to a traitor!"

These words stoked the Elves' anger once again.

Mekko thought for a moment; he knew the difference well enough. He would never tolerate a traitor, and he would be the first to kill one but despite his mixed feelings, he knew there was more to this than what it appeared. He knew it was not Lark who had killed the Elves and released Abadon. He quickly remembered meeting Lark at Shadowgate Castle, where they were both held prisoners and tortured for days. The images angered him.

"I watched that man lead, inspire, and give everything he had in defense of this citadel. I watched him heal and give courage when it was needed. I'll not believe he's evil." Mekko grabbed his axe. "I'll not believe it! Anyone who tries to harm him better plan on killin' me as well."

Some of the Elves held their swords up, and some from the rear even drew arrows. Prince Crichton stepped away from Stryker and stood directly behind Mekko with a menacing grimace upon his face. Not wishing to challenge the Mystarian prince, most of the Elves lowered their weapons and took a step back. However, they did not turn away, and more were gathering amidst angry shouts.

Having arrived on the scene, Kael and Mya came to either side of Crichton, and Ranier laid a hand on Mekko's shoulder but faced the Elves.

Rainer addressed the mob in a calm voice: "The evil you wish to exact your revenge upon is not within these walls. The man in there is a puppet, the victim of a malevolence that existed long before your people graced this world. I dare say there is *nothing* any of you could do to make Lark Royale suffer more than he does now. No weapon can pierce his heart on this or any day. For when a man of godly presence is turned against those he was meant to protect, his heart is broken beyond repair. Yes, evil always exists in the dark recesses of our minds, but we have a choice to listen or not. Not in this case. It is such an immense evil that the man had not the strength or the ability to fight it off. Truly, he never had a chance—or a choice."

With relief, Ranier saw the Elves' desire for revenge against Lark deflate, but when he noticed that they all now stared past his shoulder, he turned and was filled with even more sorrow.

Shoulders slumped, Galin carried Layla's lifeless, battered body in his arms, moving slowly toward the group. The Elves fell to their knees, tears streaming down their faces. Galin walked slowly as all parted to make way for him. He stopped; his face was dead, with tears long dried on his cheeks. "She is only one of many. *She* would have forgiven Lark. Can you do any less?" Galin asked softly.

But the sorrow at seeing their princess dead fueled the Elves' anger, renewing their desire for revenge. The Elven officer, the ringleader, shouted, "Do not speak for the princess, Druid! How can there be forgiveness? There *must* be a reckoning!"

Several lifted their weapons up, clamoring for violence. Rainer shook his head and walked away.

"No!" an unknown voice cried out. "There must be no vengeance for this by anyone!"

A sudden silence befell the group as all heads turned to see an Elven scout with the remnants of the mountain still fresh on his clothes, hair, and face.

"Lorin, Wood Elf scout is that you?!" the officer roared. "You have no voice here; you are not of Alluviam! You are *not* one of us!"

Lorin stepped forward, shoving others aside. "No, I am not a High Elf of Alluviam, but I am your full-blooded kin, and I *will* be heard. I joined you after my people were needlessly butchered. I watched monsters ravage our women and murder our children. I joined you with the intention of bringing vengeance to those who wronged me and mine. But for this magnificent lady—your captain and princess—explained that it takes courage *not* to not seek revenge. She said that our Alliance was forged in hope, not hate, and that our greatest power lies in our mutual respect. I pledged myself to follow her wisdom from that moment on. The rest of you can do as you will, but know you betray all she was and everything she believed if you raise a weapon against this victim."

Lorin then knelt before Galin and took Layla's hand in his and kissed it. "Forgive me, my Captain, but now you are a princess, and I beg the privilege to kneel before you as testament to your courage."

One by one, the Elves knelt, and Galin resumed his earlier path. When Mekko touched his arm, Galin looked over, pausing but a moment. "I'll help you bury her, lad," the general offered.

Galin shook his head. "This task I do alone." He gave Mekko an appreciative nod and, cradling Layla closer, he walked away.

Mekko addressed the crowd. "I'll take personal responsibility for Lark Royale from this point on. He'll remain in my custody, unarmed and bound until he can get help. We will not discard him to the wolves, as our enemy would do to their own. Many need our help tonight. If you are able-bodied, see what you can do. And get some rest when you can. We make for the sanctuary cave beyond the pass in the Eastern Peaks before daybreak."

Mekko watched the crowd disperse. Archangel gazed at Mekko for a moment, a look of doubt in his eyes before he went inside to his brother. Crichton raised his eyebrow at Mekko, wondering about the nature of Archangel's look, and then quickly caught up with Mekko as he began navigating his way through the wounded huddled outside the infirmary.

"Look what I've done this day. Look what I've accomplished," Mekko whispered.

"You did what you had to do, General. You gave them hope. No matter how many die, that is more than any of us could have accomplished," Crichton said, looking over his shoulder at Mya and Kael.

The couple joined Mekko on either side, and Crichton called for his horse.

With the crowd temporarily appeased, Ranier came from behind Lark's tent and went inside. A single candle provided light. Chained to the pole in the center of the tent was Lark, stripped of his armor and head hanging. He was shivering but not from the cold.

Seeing Archangel with his sword at the ready, Ranier said, "Be still, Ranger."

"I tried to put down some hay for comfort, but he pushed it away," Archangel said. "It was not him, Wizard. In my father's name, I tell you, the Shadow Prince was controlling him, just as he had done in Dragontree."

"Indeed, he was." Ranier lowered himself to his knees and lifted Lark's dirty and tear-stained face up with a crooked finger under his chin. Lark's eyes were glassy, unseeing. Darkness and despair had displaced the Paladin's glow of confidence. "We knew Abadon and his demons would find a way to release him from the confines of the Emerald Star," he said. "However, the shadows of malevolence clouded our ability to see deep into the future. This burden is seared no deeper into your brother than into us," Ranier said, speaking for all the Archmages.

Archangel fell to his knees, dropping his sword. "What will happen to him?"

Ranier touched Lark's forehead and spoke flatly, "Lark Royale, Paladin and holy knight, finds himself within the prison of his mind. Tormented at every moment by acts he was forced to carry out. He will live within the impenetrable walls of his mind, reliving the moment he released Abadon. He will hear the cries of the five thousand Elves who fell to their deaths. He will feel the pain of those left behind to pick up the pieces. He will believe himself to be void of goodness. He will exist in a shadowy place between life and death. And he will come to believe his worst fear—that there is no hope."

Archangel fell, his face collapsing into his hands. Ranier rose and exited.

Three human females clung to each other as well as they could with their wrists bound behind their backs. The Orcs led them by leashes around their necks into the dark stone chamber where Abadon sat upon a metal throne. The Shadow Prince stood behind and to the right of him.

The Orcs forced the women to their knees a few feet before the throne. Abadan watched them prostrate, licking his lips with delicious anticipation.

"As you requested, master, three human females," the Shadow Prince said with a bow and started to leave.

"Remain a moment, my servant, and observe," Abadon said deliberately. "Humans are such exquisite creatures. Aesthetically, they are no more appealing than any other race, but their magnificent capacity for betrayal knows no worldly bounds. Observe the dark-haired one on the right. She has committed no appreciable sin, yet she would gladly murder the other two if I assured her she would not be harmed."

Abadon made a long guttural noise of approval. The Shadow Prince stood silent, unimpressed. "Grand Master, what does it matter what any of these foul animals would do to each other? With respect, shouldn't we be attacking the enemy . . . destroying them once and for all?"

"Patience, slave, you must learn the virtues of patience. Now, the blond in the middle would gladly defile and abase herself in such foul ways as to defy the most vivid imagination. If I guaranteed that no harm would come to her, she would crawl on her belly through the foulest-smelling dung to lick every inch of this dirt floor."

Abadon's chuckle was sinister. The Shadow Prince failed to see the humor and wondered why Abadon hadn't ordered him to just have them killed. Why bring them here?

"Finally, the red head. She is not unlike our friends within the Citadel. Though she fears death the same as the other two, she will do nothing to demean herself. She would make a brave noise before I snapped her neck. All for this senseless sickness called freedom. And yet, how much longer the other two would survive and how much more they would potentially accomplish by simply sacrificing their pride and the illusion of freedom. Fools. Do they not see? Their way can end only in a quick or lingering death. None are more deserving, and I yearn to deliver it to them. Leave us."

The three women shivered with fear as they tried to inch away from the throne. Their sobs gradually grew louder and more intense. The Shadow Prince looked down at them. Despite Abadon's philosophical monologue, they should simply be caged to serve as livestock. He left the chamber feeling disgust, but when he heard their blood-curdling shrieks, he smiled with satisfaction.

Within the enemy camp, hundreds of Ogres beat upon drums, loud and furious, for hours, as if they would continue through the night. The drums were close, and their noise made it hard to think. Prince Crichton visited his wounded men. He stopped to talk with one of the youngest. An impressionable young man named Marten, only come of fighting age a few years back. Captain Alizar sat beside him.

When the boy saw Crichton, he attempted to lean up. "My lord, forgive me. I cannot stand," the boy said.

"No, Marten, stay where you are. You must rest now. You fought well today," Crichton said as he looked at the boy's wound, a sword thrust through his chest. His eyes locked with Alizar's.

"Thank you, my lord. Forgive me for getting wounded. I did not—"

"Shh, think of nothing else but getting better. The Captain and I need you, so sleep now," Crichton said, running his hand over the young man's head.

Alizar took Crichton aside. "There's nothing more that can be done for him," Alizar said regretfully.

"And the rest of our wounded?" Crichton asked, looking around at the many shivering men. Some struggled, trying to cover their ears.

"Most will die before morning." the captain replied.

A hard countenance crossed Crichton's face. "Die they may, but not as victims to their fear and not in the wake of enemy drums." With that, he stormed off.

Moments later, Alizar saw the prince return, carrying his violin. He stood within the middle of the wounded and began to play. The rain began to fall softly at first but soon was pouring straight down. It was a wondrous melody that transcended not only the rain but also the horrible pounding of the drums. Soon it echoed throughout the camp.

Even within the infirmary amid the feverish attempt to save lives, Elenari poked her head out of the tent and saw Crichton playing. It was an impassioned tune of joy and hope that allowed the wounded to drift into a relaxed sleep. Though many would never waken, they drifted to sleep in comfort, most with smiles upon their faces. The music was magical, transporting them to different times and places when life had been at its best and happiest for each of them. Elenari closed her eyes and saw Hawk.

No one knew for how long he played, nor did anyone care. They only knew his music drowned out the evil drums and, for even the briefest of moments, brought joy and hope to every soul within the walls of the citadel.

When he finally stopped playing, Crichton met with his captain again and placed a hand on Alizar's shoulder. "Watch over them. The violin's magic should keep them from hearing the drums and allow those whose time has come to die with some small measure of peace." With a nod, he headed away, stopping when he heard someone calling his name. He turned and saw Elenari running toward him.

"My lady," he said, expressionless, not even meeting her eyes.

She looked at him for the first time in a different light. There was softness in her eyes and voice. "I apologize, Prince Crichton. I was wrong about you. Your music . . ." her voice trailed off; she was sincerely at a loss for words.

He looked at her with a mocking grin. "No, you weren't. This was merely a gift from someone special long ago," he said, holding up the violin, "nothing more."

He walked away into the night, leaving Elenari confused and frustrated.

Throughout the remainder of the night, they evacuated their wounded who were able to travel up the mountain pass as silently and secretly as possible. Still, the enemy drums beat loudly in the heart of night's darkness, offering no solace.

Ranier was first to be evacuated, still languishing from the poison deep within him. Mya had given instructions to move as little as possible.

Morning had become a time of the day when there was only less darkness than at night. Mekko walked amid the bodies sprawled outside the infirmary, as he had throughout the night, with guilt and a sense of failure weighing heavily upon him. He looked down at them, both the dead and dying alike and knew no matter what this day brought, he would secretly never forgive himself for living when so many others didn't.

He strode hurriedly within the tent to see Mya, the Druids, and Elenari still trying to save as many as they could. Their faces were flushed, fatigue and lack of sleep shown upon them all, but despite all, their efforts were relentless.

Mekko pulled Kael aside. "There is no more time. The rest of you must leave now. My men will keep them occupied to cover your escape. Take as many as can move or be moved. The White Elves will escort you," Mekko whispered.

"General, we have no magic left to aid you with—" Kael said.

"But we will fight at your side all the same," Galin said, coming upon behind Mekko, a trail of bitterness in his voice. He held the hilt of his scimitar.

"No, lad, not this time. I appreciate all you've done, but I'm askin' now that you let me do my job, which is to get you and the rest of these people out of here safely," Mekko said.

"General—" Galin started, but Mekko grabbed his arm with an iron grip.

"I ask this, please, lad. I don't think I can take too many more deaths on my conscience. You go help 'em figure out that potion. It will give us a fightin' chance. That's where you're needed most right now. That's where you can make a difference. I'm needed out on that battlefield, that's where *I* can make a difference."

Mekko looked at the Druids intently until he saw reluctant acceptance in their eyes.

"Dear friend," said Kael as he clasped arms with Mekko, "*Sinestran-un-fros-males-embracen*, may Nature's Blessings guide and protect you and your men. Farewell, General, and thank you."

Kael went back to tending the wounded with Mya, leaving Galin and Mekko alone.

"Well, we've had our share of good times haven't we, laddie?" Mekko said as his smile fought back against his sadness.

Though hard like stone, Galin's countenance allowed for tears to form in the corners of his eyes. He nodded and put out his hand.

What began as a somewhat cold handshake ended in the warm embrace of two close friends.

"I'll never forget our friendship," Galin whispered and quickly went to help the others.

Mekko left them to join his troops and face his destiny.

Commander Bainor and a dozen of the engineering corps stayed behind with Mekko's troop division. Throughout the night, they moved the last of the special weapons forward so that they were just inside the north and west walls. It would be their last surprise.

The remainder of the Dwarven pike division went to the armory throughout the night arming themselves with fresh equipment and weapons, preparing for what they knew would be their last stand. Survival was not their objective in this fight. They knew every moment they held the enemy off bought precious escape time for last of the wounded.

Prince Crichton remained with nearly three hundred mounted cavalry from Mystaria. What they lacked in numbers, Mekko knew they would make up for with their superior armor and weapons, and in the courage of the who that led them.

Mekko strode out upon the battlements of the north wall to view the battlefield in the wake of morning's half-light. Death and carnage visited upon both sides littered the field, but even the buzzards and crows were nowhere to be seen for such a feast. The foul presence of Abadon made itself felt in the air and on the ground. His heart sank further as he looked across the way to observe the enemy formations.

As Ranier had promised, fresh armies had arrived to reinforce the enemy. He could see at least a few thousand new troops. The great stone pyramid had apparently been pulled back to the rear sometime in the night. It did not seem Abadon would be leading this fight, but when he saw the size of the enemy force, he knew it made little difference. There was an army of Ogres, still beating on their drums, perhaps two thousand strong. Another two thousand Chalderons with Orc archers and alongside them was a new force consisting of several hundred Berbaks, white ape-like beasts with orange faces. They were incredibly fast and strong, capable of running on all fours. They would beat their chests before an attack,

Mekko knew they could only be found in the south islands, which meant the enemy forces had already made their presence felt to the lands beyond the sea, bringing their worst fears to the surface. Bastlandia and Arcadia, he thought, had been most probably already overrun. He took a deep breath as he watched the final army, a large force of mounted Stygian Knights. In their black armor and tunics, they appeared as black riders of death.

Mekko looked down and wondered what would become of those who were retreating to the sanctuary cave up in the Eastern Peaks, those they were sacrificing themselves for? What would become of them? How would they meet their seemingly inevitable end? He thought of his friends and that alone made him smile despite everything. With that, he turned and faced his remaining troops. He looked down upon them, his brow furled, but he spoke with clarity.

"Lads, I once heard a wise man say, the true measure of an individual is in how that person meets with failure, disappointment, loss, and ultimately, how they meet their own end. So I ask you, how then do we want our friends, allies, and countrymen to speak of how we met our end this day. Will they say we met it with fear?"

His answer was thunderous "NO!"

"On *their* day, when they stand in final victory over this scourge that plagues this good earth and mother to Dwarf, Man, and Elf alike, will they say we met *our* day with despair?"

Again, his troops responded.

"Or will they say we met ours with love, honor, and courage? I think they will say that their victory came about because of what *we* did, here and now, this very minute! We fight now, and we will never surrender!"

The cheers from the men were contagious and rousing beyond any camaraderie they had ever known.

Prince Crichton watched in wonder as his own men rallied, raising their weapons high and cheering in salute of the words of a Dwarf, their one-time sworn enemy. He too, without realizing it, had drawn his sword and, hesitating a moment, thrust it high in the air with a cry of righteous rage, affirming the sentiment of all gathered.

Even across the battlefield and over the drums, the cheers of the Alliance could be heard by Red Fang. He showed his disdain in an exhale of black spit. Riding slowly on his blue Chalderon, he moved toward the commander of the Stygian Knights. The salamander-like forked tongue of his mount licking the air, anticipating what was to come.

Facing the commander in his dark plate mail and black helmet, he spoke in a snarl from the side of his mouth, "You will lead the charge through the hole in their walls. Ride them down, give them something to scream about. I want their heads on spikes all along those walls. I want the decapitated bodies lined up on their knees with their empty necks spilling blood in the dirt to greet our master when he enters there. All except the Dwarf general, him I want brought to me alive. Now, attack!"

With that, the commander used his sword to knock the visor down of his dark helmet and signaled the cavalry charge with the other armies following behind.

Mekko watched as they approached. He turned and quickly went halfway down the stairs of the battlements and waved Crichton over.

"Yes, General," the prince said as he rode forward.

"Gideon, I want you and your men to take up the rear of the last of our people escapin' into the mountains. If the enemy figures out what were doin', I'd sure feel better if I knew you were protectin' their flank."

The Dwarf measured the Mystarian as he returned his glare unmoving.

"Please, Gideon, I've never really asked anything of you and your men until now," Mekko said sincerely.

"Is it an order, General?" the prince asked coldly.

"Aye, I suppose it is," Mekko answered.

"Very well. Since you are the commander, I am duty bound to obey it." Crichton watched the Dwarf nod and turn to go back up the stairs. "General," Crichton said in a much softer voice.

Mekko looked back at the Mystarian prince to see him remove his armored glove and extend his hand out toward him. Mekko looked at him for a moment and then reached down to grab his hand and meet the firm grip with his own.

"It has been both an honor and a privilege, sir," Crichton said.

"Aye, and to my surprise, for me as well," Mekko replied.

Crichton smiled sincerely for a moment, then released the Dwarf's hand and was gone.

Mekko ran up to the battlements and quickly yelled down to his troops, "Here they come lads, pikes at the ready!" He heard the command repeated below and could see the men were ready. "Commander Bainor, stand by at my command now, lad. Watch me closely," Mekko said as he raised his hand.

"Engineers, stand by to execute," Bainor said as he watched the Engineers scramble on the battlements with their mallets, preparing to hoist the chains to lift the walls.

Mekko watched as the Stygian Knights charged well ahead of the others. He knew they would start to mass together toward the hole from the collapsed tower. He could feel the wind on his hand coming from the south behind him. That was good, he thought; they were riding against the cold wind, which could obscure their vision somewhat. He watched eagerly as they closed the distance. He waited until they were approximately twenty yards away.

"Raise the walls!" Mekko yelled to Bainor, who repeated the order to the Engineers, who hoisted the walls up as they did before, almost as if to invite the enemy within.

The first ranks of charging knights brought their mounts to a sudden halt, unsure of what to expect from within. When their vision cleared, they heard Mekko's command: *"Fire!"*

It was at that moment they saw the opening walls revealed huge metal cylinders, more than twenty, some twenty feet long, each with large, rounded openings facing them. Each exploded so suddenly, the knights never saw what killed them. Nearly a hundred hot, metal balls shot from each device, filling the air with searing-hot metal, tearing through armor and flesh as if through butter, with a blast radius great enough to bring down hundreds of the enemy knights in one fell swoop.

Mekko then slung his axe on his back, grabbed a pike, and headed down to join his men, with Rendek and Toran close behind him.

"For Cordilleran, for freedom!" Mekko roared as he led them past the cannon-like weapons with their pikes. They ran beneath the propped open walls, spilling onto the battlefield and meeting the enemy armies head on.

From a ridge above, still at the foot of the mountains, Captain Alizar looked on at the one-sided battle below as their courageous Dwarven allies bought them precious escape time. He knew they would be routed to the last man.

"My lord, the Dwarven General, he's cut off from the main force, surrounded and heavily outnumbered." Captain Alizar handed his spyglass to Prince Crichton.

Crichton quickly took the glass. He saw General Mekko with only a handful of Dwarves at his side, savagely battling Orcs and mounted Stygian Knights, who closed around them, cutting them off from aide. As Crichton surveyed the area, he spotted a large contingent of Orc-mounted Chalderons and charging Berbaks closing on Mekko's position. He watched as Mekko swung his axe, carving through and almost single-handedly driving back their mounting attackers, even as his defenders fell all around him.

"Magnificent valor," Crichton whispered to himself.

"Stryker, to me!" Crichton cried out behind him. In a moment, his shining white steed ran to his side. Without hesitation, Crichton put on his golden helmet. Grabbing his black crossbow, he quickly mounted Stryker. The fearless horse reared back on its hind legs as the prince pulled on the reins.

"My lord, you cannot help them, they are too far away and there are too many—even for you!" Alizar said, rushing to Stryker's side.

"You will aide in the retreat. Do all that you can to get these people to safely up to the mountain pass. Do you understand me, Captain?" Crichton ordered in a tone that left no room for discussion.

"Yes, my lord, it will be done as you command," Alizar answered reluctantly. He quickly turned and ran toward the procession of wounded.

With that, Crichton took off like the wind across the Fields of Aramoor. Stryker raced like a white arrow fired toward the dark gauntlet of Stygian Knights barring his way. As he closed the distance, the prince grasped his great black crossbow and took aim at the largest man he could see, while spurring Stryker on with his heels.

Nearly twenty of the dark clad knights had formed ranks of two lines as they saw the approaching rider on the white horse.

Crichton urged Stryker on even faster, so much so he could barely maintain his aim. He found his target and aimed just above his eyes in the center of his forehead.

The dark knights stared in disbelief as the rider increased his speed, charging directly toward them. He would never get past. They braced for impact, swords at the ready.

Crichton fired, hitting one of the men in the center of the front line, striking him right between the eyes with a bolt from his crossbow. He guided Stryker immediately toward that man's horse as he watched him fall haplessly to the ground. He drew his huge sword with his left hand and, still holding the crossbow in his right, dug his armored heels in Stryker's hind quarter, forcing his mighty steed into a running jump directly over the fallen man's horse. In mid-air, he struck the knight to his right with the crossbow while simultaneously swinging his sword, decapitating the knight to the left, a look of shock and astonishment still upon his severed head.

Crashing into the second line, two knights and their horses fell, driven to the ground from Stryker's sheer power and momentum.

Barely losing a step, Crichton urged Stryker on. Suddenly before him, a horde of Orcs attempted to bar his way. Stryker slammed into them, bowling them over and crushing them beneath his hooves. Any that stood in his way were knocked aside.

Crichton kept his eyes on the approaching Chalderons and Berbaks. They clearly saw him now and a pack of them headed to cut off any potential escape while the rest continued closing on Mekko's location. Crichton bent down so low that his face was nearly in Stryker's mane; he galloped even faster. The fearless steed had endless endurance and a great reservoir of strength, making him seem tireless.

In a few moments he would be at Mekko's location. He could see the last Dwarf had nearly fallen and Mekko stood alone, with only Rendek and Toran, against many foes. Crichton sat up and raised his right hand in which a ball of growing orange flames appeared. In the next instant, he hurled the ball of flame into the heart of the attacking Orcs. It exploded with such force that, for a moment, it created a clearing, driving them all back.

Mekko bled from many wounds and could barely stand. He suddenly realized Rendek and Toran had stopped moving at his sides. To his horror, he saw that they had been pierced by the swords of four Orcs who had escaped the fiery blast.

"No!" Mekko raged as he swung his axe in a circular motion over his head, backing them up. He spun into them one at a time, striking chests and taking their heads. He turned and looked at his two young fallen bodyguards, returning his gaze with death's vacant stare. He dropped his axe and fell to his knees, the fight suddenly taken out of him. To his astonishment, he looked up and saw Crichton on his horse leaning down with an outstretched arm. Instinctively, he took it.

In one motion, Crichton hoisted Mekko atop Stryker and changed the horse's direction, heading back the way he came. He held Mekko with one hand and the reins with his other. A huge force now had gathered to close the gap left by Stryker. The Orcs on the Chalderons had pikes and bows and were lined up, blocking them in. Berbaks ran on all fours, beating their chest in war challenges, awaiting them. In addition, nearly a hundred Orcs had gathered where the others had fallen in his path. There was no escape in any direction.

Without hesitating, Crichton started back the way he came, charging directly at the pike wielding Orcs who were hungry for his approach.

Mekko, barely conscious, mumbled, "You'll never make it."

Crichton did not seem to be listening as he continued straight at the eager enemy. They were twenty yards away; Stryker would be impaled, perhaps both of them as well in only seconds.

"*Matar Pegasai!*" Crichton yelled unexpectedly.

Just before Mekko lost consciousness, he saw behind Stryker's shoulder blades large, white wings suddenly extended outward from his body, and at the last second, they were airborne, safely above the deadly blockade of enemies. Crichton took one look back, ensuring no flying creatures had pursued them. He then turned to the southeast, riding the wind upon Stryker's back.

Crichton patted Stryker's neck, rubbing his mane. "To the Eastern Peaks, my friend! Well done indeed. It may someday amuse the general to know he owes his life to a horse."

Chapter 20

Deep within the Dwarven sanctuary cave somewhere in the Eastern Peaks, Elenari looked with wonder upon Stryker, his great wings folded close to his body. Slowly, she approached, having never believed such a creature could exist. Gently, she put her hand out, and just as she was about to touch his wing, a soft voice from behind startled her.

"Nothing is more magical," Prince Crichton said in a low voice.

Elenari quickly withdrew her hand and turned to face him, her cheeks flushed from embarrassment. "Why did you not tell us you had a flying mount?" Elenari demanded.

"For two reasons, my lady, not the least of which was to protect him. Sadly he, like myself, is the last of his kind. No other horse shall ever fly again in this world. Oh, he can mate with other horses, and they will inherit his blood, strength, and speed, but none shall ever take to the skies again. If the enemy knew about him, it would make him an early target. Once, long ago in another time, there were many Pegasi. They were the magical steeds of the Wizard Knights of Mystaria and in ancient times . . . they were like the birds of the sky."

The prince walked forward to pet Stryker firmly, encouraging Elenari to touch his wings.

She smiled as she glided her hand across his wing. "They're so soft."

He looked at her, captivated by her smile, having not seen it in so very long. He found himself following the paths of her blond curls. He could not even remember the last time he felt anything while looking at a woman. "May I ask you a question, my lady?" Crichton asked softly.

"Of course," Elenari replied with her attention still fixed on Stryker.

"Why did you let Hawk face me during the hunt when you were clearly the more skilled warrior?"

The smile left her face but she continued stroking the horse. "I don't know, precisely. There was a strength in his personality that I had never seen in another man, but I do not wish to speak about him with you or anyone else. What was your second reason for not telling us about Stryker?"

Crichton chuckled. "Because quite simply, it was none of your business or anyone else's." With that, the prince walked away.

Elenari thought to respond but fell silent. When she saw her father, she was thankful for the distraction.

"A magnificent creature, one of nature's true miracles. It is difficult to believe such a creature serves a man like Crichton," Kael said, as he too could not help but stroke the great horse.

"There is more to Crichton than he would wish us to know, Father. In any event, he has proven to be a powerful ally."

"True enough, my dear, and he saved Mekko's life—one of many lives he has saved since this war started."

"I have come to bring you to Ranier. He has asked for many of us to join him. He wishes to speak to us about what is to come," Kael said, placing his arm around Elenari's shoulder.

"How is he?" she asked.

"Not well. He puts on a brave front, but the demon poison courses through his body. I do not think he has long to live," Kael replied.

"What will happen, Father? What will happen to us all?" Elenari asked as they looked on in the distance of the inner cave and saw thousands of Dwarven civilians sitting in the darkness, waiting in fear and helplessness for whatever fate was to befall them.

"I do not know, my child. I only know that I love you, and we must do the best we can not to lose hope, even now. There are many, whom we don't know and will never meet, who depend upon us," Kael said as father and daughter embraced.

Crichton watched Mekko as he tossed and turned, shivering from a deep fever. The Dwarf was moaning, plagued by dark dreams. There was a younger Dwarf dressed in purple robes tending to him, wiping his brow.

"How is the general?" Crichton asked, startling the young Dwarf.

"You are the Mystarian wizard Crichton?" the young Dwarf asked, though not sounding as a question.

Crichton nodded affirmatively.

"I don't like wizards, and I like your country even less. However, I thank you for saving his life. My name is Cormayer. I am a member of the Dwarven High Council, by the grace of the late King Crylar." Cormayer turned and continued to tend to Mekko.

Crichton instinctively liked the young Dwarf; his face conveyed a rare frankness. "I am honored."

"Don't be. I'm the youngest and probably least respected member of the council; however, I serve out of respect to my former king. The White Elf priestess was just here. She said the general will be sick for several days and the next few hours would be critical. If his fever breaks, he should recover. If not—"

"I see. Do not worry, my young friend. I do not think any mere fever could defeat such a great warrior," Crichton said.

Two Dwarven guards entered the small chamber at that moment. "Councilor Cormayer, the mage, Ranier, wishes to speak to the Mystarian wizard and has requested your presence as well. You will follow us."

"Have one of your men stay with the general at all times. Post guards outside this chamber," Cormayer ordered.

Crichton nodded to Cormayer and accompanied the two guards, following behind them.

Crichton entered a rounded chamber where several others had already gathered. Ranier was in the center of the chamber, lying propped up on many pillows and blankets with Mya close to him. He looked pale and perspired about the forehead despite the chilling coolness throughout the cave. He looked about the chamber and saw Kael, Elenari, Galin, Archangel, Captain Gaston, the Druids of Anagansit, General Valin, and High Master Reyblade.

Once they were all seated and guards were posted outside, Ranier began, "There is much to tell, and time continues to be against us. Since our encounter with Abadon, we have been deep in thought. However, all is not lost. Know that there is hope, even now in our darkest hour. The Druids, with our assistance, have completed the mystic potion that will restore life to the earth and will weaken Abadon, considerably draining his power. The fact that we have such a remedy has not yet reached his knowing. The potion *must* be delivered to the place where life first began on our world. The tome of Algernon describes such a place as the *Cradle of Life*, and while its exact location is unknown, we have pinpointed it to a region far beneath the surface of the Darkstone Sierras."

The Archmage was suddenly overtaken by an uncontrollable coughing fit. Mya helped him sit up a little straighter until the coughing stopped. He settled back down and took a few deep breaths.

"Ranier, the Darkstone Sierras is the vastest mountain range in the world, in addition to the fact that it's virtually been unexplored. No one has ever traveled through its treacherous passes and slopes," Elenari said quietly.

"True, but as the Druids draw nearer to the origin, their powers will grow stronger and there will come a point where they will be able to guide you. However, until such time, they will need to be guided and protected. That is why *you* will go, Elenari. From the Druids, Magnus and Shalimar will accompany you. Captain Gaston, you will help Elenari protect the Druids. Once you begin traveling beneath the surface, you will need advice from someone who has lived there. Lady Mya, your skills may be most valuable to this group." Ranier took a few more deep breaths.

At mention of Mya going, Kael shot a concerned look in her direction.

"Make no mistake, this journey will be perilous every step of the way. But it must be undertaken and completed successfully."

"Why are Galin and I not to go where the Druids are needed?" Kael asked suddenly.

"Because you are both needed elsewhere. At this moment, Abadon plots to find the Chronos Device. He is no longer concerned with us for the moment as he knows we do not have the strength to stand against him; however, he knows his victory is not yet complete. He will task the Shadow Prince to use all their resources to find the device so that he can fulfill his ultimate goal to bring more of his demon brethren across to this world as he promised them ages ago. He knows then his victory will be secured. Unfortunately for us, he has considerable patience and time is on his side. We must therefore bring time over to our side." With that, the old man produced a gold key from his robes.

"Kael, you and Archangel will go to the device. You must reach it before Abadon does. You will use this key to activate it and then destroy it the moment after you use it. You will both go backward in time to a point before Abadon was first trapped in the Emerald Star. You will take the empty Emerald Star of our time back with you and you must then convince Prince Thargelion to allow the Elven wizards of old to impart a fraction of their magical life force to reenergize the gemstone. Once you have done this, you will use the device of that era to return to this time. You will then bring the Emerald Star to me. We will use our powers as the final ingredient necessary to imprison Abadon—this time never to escape. You will be traveling to an age when demons of strange and terrible powers roamed the land and Abadon walked freely upon the earth." He hesitated to rest a few moments and then set his eyes upon Galin.

"Galin, you and the Kenshari Masters I charge with stopping the naval blockade that has prevented military aid from Bastlandia and Arcadia. We still have allies in this fight, but our enemy's arm reaches far, even into the south where an evil fleet prevents the alliances you and Kael forged from aiding us as promised. You will go to Arcadia where you will find a captain and ship to aid you. From there, you must find a way to get the reinforcements here before Abadon's armies find these caves."

"Prince Crichton, in General Mekko's absence, you must work with General Valin to protect us here in these caves and keep us alive." He coughed, spitting up into a towel that Mya held out for him.

"Councilor Cormayer, the Dwarven High Council's faith will waver. You must keep them together. There will be fear, dissension, despair, even talk of surrender—*you* must remain the voice of reason for the people."

The young Dwarf nodded in acknowledgment.

Ranier sat back and looked at the faces staring back at him, incredulous at the outrageous and all but impossible tasks he just set before them. Disbelief and shock overshadowed the hope he had seen in them before he began speaking.

"You must all forgive us. We foolishly thought we could defeat Abadon, and none of this would have been necessary. Our mistakes have had dreadful consequences for the world and for each of you. We are sorry, more than you will ever know."

He hesitated a moment before continuing: "Three quests, three groups, each as vital to our survival as to each other. If any one group fails, then all will fail to the ruin of us all. Do not give in to fear, but do not be confident in the secrecy of our plans. The demon lord is ever watchful. If he learns of what we intend, he will do his worst to stop us. Hope and courage remain our two greatest weapons; let us wield them powerfully in the days to come."

Here Ends Book II

Join the heroes in the final book, *Knights & Demons*, where the Quest groups attempt to complete their impossible tasks and the heroes come face to face with their destiny in the struggle against evil while the fate of their world hangs in the balance.

Printed in Dunstable, United Kingdom